UP TO THE CHALLENGE

MARIA V. SNYDER

MARIA V. SNYDER

PRAISE FOR MARIA V. SNYDER

"Maria V. Snyder is always up to the challenge when it comes to deliver intriguing characters, worlds, and stories." *New York Times* bestselling author Jennifer Estep on *Up to the Challenge.*

"Maria V. Snyder is more than up to the challenge of crafting fascinating stories in every conceivable genre. Brilliant, insightful, weird, heartbreaking, and way too much fun!" Jonathan Maberry, *New York Times* bestselling author of V-Wars and Kagen the Damned on *Up to the Challenge.*

"An enriching mix of fantasy, adventure, suspense with a touch of romance filled with witty dialogue that made it very easy for me to grasp the new world and terminology...The fast-paced plot made it almost impossible to put down." The Nerd Daily on *The Eyes of Tamburah.*

"Oh. My. Stars! I just raced through Maria V. Snyder's *Navigating the Stars* and *Chasing the Shadows*, and I'm blown away! ...The plot is fantastic, the pacing spectacular, the intricacies, the snark, the banter...oh my! Go, go, go. You'll love this!" Amanda Bouchet, *USA Today* bestselling author on The Sentinels of the Galaxy series.

"What do you get when you throw some space travel, network hacking, ancient archaeology, and page-turning danger into a fantastic genre-blender and switch it on high? The Sentinels of the Galaxy series of course!" Checked.in.ya on Instagram.

Also by Maria V. Snyder

Healer Series

TOUCH OF POWER

SCENT OF MAGIC

TASTE OF DARKNESS

Insider Series

INSIDE OUT

OUTSIDE IN

Discover more titles at MariaVSnyder.com

Up to the Challenge / Maria V. Snyder

Cover design by Joy Kenney

Published by Maria V. Snyder

Print ISBN 9781946381125

Digital ISBN 9781946381132

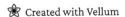 Created with Vellum

In memory of my Aunt Vickie. A strong, independent woman who raised her children single-handedly. A kind, loving woman, who always put her family first. A role model for a budding novelist and god-daughter, who loved to share and discuss books. I'm lucky that she was a part of my life. She will be missed.

Dear Reader,

Welcome to my first short story collection! Within these pages, you'll find sixteen fantasy and science fiction stories. These stories were written over the last fourteen years. While I was tempted to update them...cough...flip phones...cough...I resisted the urge to do more than light edits. These are "time capsules" of my writing and I wanted to keep true to their original versions.

When I first started writing, I mistakenly thought that a short story would be easier to write than a novel (it isn't). My first attempt was a cheesy science fiction story about a boy who runs away from home and stows away on a spaceship. The stories I wrote after that were only slightly better. So I joined a critique group to help me improve. Further attempts to write short stories resulted in the same response from my group, "This is the beginning of a novel." Sigh. Seemed writing short stories wasn't in my wheelhouse. I switched to writing novels. My first novel, *Poison Study* topped out at ninety-five thousand words. Hmmm.

Poison Study was published by Harlequin's Luna Books imprint in 2005, launching my career as a novelist. I happily continued working on my Study series. Then in 2008, I was asked to submit a short story for a themed anthology about vampires. Honored to be invited, I wasn't sure I could write within the word count limit (a max of seven thousand!). Managing time and meeting deadlines was a constant battle. Plus vampires? Seriously?

However, I thought writing something outside my comfort zone would give me a break from my fantasy world, and would flex my creative muscles. I viewed it as an opportunity to try something new, and I wrote *Sword Point*. After that, I received more anthology invites, and I embraced the challenge offered to me. I experimented with third person point of view, and with writing in present tense. I wrote about ghosts, were-wolves, vampires, and even dug deep into my scariest child-hood memory to write a horror story.

All but two of these stories have been published in different anthologies over the years. Pulling them together into one collection was an interesting experience. I discovered quite a few things about myself. One, I have a "type." He has black hair and blue eyes. He wears jeans and tight-fitting T-shirts. Good thing my husband has dark hair and blue eyes!

I also really like names starting with the letter J. Lots of J names in these pages, including Jayden (a name used in my Archives of the Invisible Sword series—imagine my surprise!). And clearly, I like to use men's first names as last names. You'll get to meet Lexa Thomas, Evelyn Mitchell, Matt James, Ava Vaughn, Josh Martin, Sophia Daniels, and Eunice Daniels. No, they're not related. Nor are they related to Lyra Daniels from my Sentinels of the Galaxy series. Guess I really liked the name Daniels!

There was another commonality in this collection that struck me. In all sixteen stories, the main characters are persis-tent and brave. They rise to the challenge, overcoming their fears and doubts. They fight hard for what is right until the very end.

That common thread also applies to the writing of this collection. Doubts, fears, deadlines, and the endless "to-do" list all presented obstacles. Was I up to the challenge? I think the title of this book says it all.

Happy Reading!

Love, Maria

MONGREL

Werewolves? What did I know about werewolves? Practically nothing. But I'd agreed to submit a short story about them for the anthology, Running with the Pack. *This challenge was two-fold—I had no story ideas. None. And I had no time. I'd procrastinated. Big time. Before I knew it, I only had two weeks to write the story. Desperate, I thought of a situation where someone finds an injured "dog" that isn't quite what he seems. I've no clue where Mongrel's story came from, but as I started writing, her voice came through loud and clear. The style was so different from my other stories at that point in time, that I thought the anthology editor would reject the story. She didn't and, in the end,* Mongrel *turned out to be my favorite short story.*

MONGREL

They call me Mongrel. I don't mind. It's true. My blood is mixed like vegetables in a soup. I've lived in so many different places and I've never belonged to any of them. But the other homeless people don't know that when they tease me. Say I waste food on my mutts. That I reek of dog.

So what? I like the smell of dog. Better than people. Better than the ones I hang with. Not that I enjoy their company, but they're useful at times. Warned me about the police raid a few months back, let me know when the soup kitchen opened and the women's shelter—not that I would live there without my pups, but a hot shower is a hot shower.

As long as no one messes with my stuff, I don't care what they say. It's mid-January and I need everything I've scrounged to survive. My spot is near perfect. I sleep under the railroad bridge and share my blanket with five dogs. The term hot dog has a whole new meaning for me.

The others huddle around a campfire on the broken

concrete slabs of the abandoned parking lot. We're all trespassing on railroad property, but the owners only send the police about once a year to chase us away. So far, never in the winter. Nice of them. (Yeah, I'm being sarcastic).

Late in the night, snarls and growls wake me. Animals are up on the bridge fighting. My lot is awake with their tails tucked under and their bodies hunched low. A yelp stabs me in the chest and I'm running toward the sound. Something rolls down the side of the bridge, crashes into the underbrush, and lays still. Something large.

A wounded animal can be dangerous, but I'm next to him before my brain can catch up with my body. It's the biggest dog I've ever seen. He lifts his head, but the fight is gone. He's panting and bleeding from lots of cuts. I yank off my gloves and run my hands along his legs, searching for broken bones.

He's all black except for the tips of his fur. It shines with silver like he's been brushed with liquid moonlight. No broken bones, but a knife is buried in his shoulder. Up to the hilt.

I spin around and scan the bridge. Sure enough a figure is standing there, looking down at me. My pups catch the stranger's scent and start barking and baying. I don't hush them, and soon the person leaves.

The noise brings the others. They tsk over the injured dog, but will only help me drag him to my spot after I give them cigarettes and booze as payment. They laugh and lay odds on how long the dog will live. People disgust me.

When the others go back to the fire, I open up the good stuff—eighty proof vodka. By now the big brute is shaking and I grab the handle of the knife. He's either going to live or die quicker without it in him. I tug it out, scraping bone. The dog shudders once, then stills as blood pours.

Staunching the blood, I use the eighty proof to clean the

wound before stitching him up. He doesn't make a sound as the needle pierces his skin. I count them as I tie the string. Fifteen stitches in all. When I'm done, I lay beside him with the pups nestled around us and cover us all with the blanket.

He's still alive in the morning so I make my daily rounds, searching for food, checking dumpsters, and my usual haunts. Wearing layers of grimy clothes, I'm practically invisible to everyone. Slush covers the city's sidewalks and cars zip by, spraying water without care.

A couple businesses are aware of me, and once in a while, they'll add a few extra leftovers to their trash cans. I chuckle as I score a dozen hamburgers still wrapped up like presents in the dumpster behind Vinny's Burger Joint.

Vinny doesn't like me, wouldn't help me if I was starving to death on his sidewalk, but he's got a soft spot for dogs. People are funny like that.

I don't linger long—Vinny doesn't like that, but I spy a small terrier crouched next to the dumpster. Almost missed the little rat. She is trembling and wet. Dirt stains her white coat gray. I lure her with a bit of burger and have her in my arms in no time.

Back at my spot, I'm greeted with wagging tails and excited mutts that are all happy to see me. Can't get that from people. Not for long. Eventually they ignore you or abuse you, then leave you.

I spilt the burgers among my pups, counting heads. I've got to be careful not to keep too many pups and the ones I do keep are the littles who have no homes. The big brute eats half a burger—a good sign. I think he's one of those Irish Wolfhounds or Scottish Deerhounds I've read about.

The new pup isn't sure what to make of the pack. Doesn't matter. She's wearing a collar and won't be here long. I inspect my bags, arranged just so. Funny that foster kids use garbage bags to carry their stuff, too. I don't have much—a few clothes, some toiletries, a propane stove that's a life saver, and cigarettes and booze for paying for favors. Nothing's missing.

Most of the others won't leave anything behind, pushing their belongings around in stolen shopping carts instead. We're not a trustworthy bunch. But no one's stolen from me since I've been sharing my spot with the mutts. I just smile whenever I see one of the others limping around with bite marks on their ankles. Serves them right.

However, if the hound recovers, I'm gonna need more food than I can scrounge. So I grab my nicest clothes and head to the women's shelter for a shower.

The lady who answers the door is nervous. She keeps the chain on and looks at me like she wants to call the police.

I hold up the white dog. "Found your dog, Ma'am."

And there it is. The woman's face changes as if a button is pressed inside her head. Joy beams from her and I soak in it.

She flings the door wide and presses the pup to her chest, kissing and hugging the little squirming rat. "Thank you so much! We've been so worried. My kids will be thrilled."

She goes on, but I don't listen. It's always the same. What's not the same is what happens next. I'm polite and not demanding as I ask about the reward money. Just a gentle reminder. "Your flyer at the grocery store offered fifty bucks?"

The joy dies and she eyes my best clothes with scorn and suspicion. I smooth my pink sweater and tuck a strand of long brown hair behind an ear.

"Where did you find Sugar?" she asks.

"Behind Vinny's on Sixth Street."

"That's over two miles away. Sugar would never go that far. You took her from our back yard, hoping for reward money. That's why the gate was still locked."

"No, Ma'am. I—"

She slams the door in my face. No surprise just disappointment. Sometimes I get the money. Not often.

I hurry away before the cops arrive. Since I wore my best clothes, the library staff won't bother me. Ducking a few sharp glances as I enter the building, I head for non-fiction and pull my favorite book, *The Complete Dog Encyclopedia* from the library shelf, I flip through the pages until I reach the hounds. The big brute is thick in the body and tall legged like the Irish Wolfhound, but his long face doesn't match. I scan the various breeds. The Siberian Husky has similar eyes and muzzle, but not quite. I guess he's a mongrel like me.

On my way home, I do a sweep of the flyers hanging in the vet's waiting rooms, grocery stores, and churches. Looking at the pictures of lost dogs, I think they're easier to find than missing children.

Halfway home, I remember the knife and rush to get it. The dogs press near me, hoping for supper. I shoo them away, explaining about the ungrateful woman. Yes, I know they don't understand me. I'm not stupid nor am I crazy. It's just nice to talk sometimes. And the big Wolfhound (better than calling him a brute) peers at me with his intelligent gray eyes as if he does understand. He's sitting up—another good sign he'll be on his feet soon.

I find the knife, clean the blood off and hurry to the pawn shop before it closes.

"Stolen?" Max asks, examining the weapon. The silver blade gleams in the fluorescent light. The pawn shop smells of engine oil and mold.

"Found it," I say.

"Uh huh." Max sucks his teeth while he thinks, making slurping sounds that crawl over my skin like lice. "Cheap metal, imitation leather handle...I'll give you ten for it."

Never accept the first offer. It's crap.

"It does have a nice design...how about fifteen," Max says.

"That blade's got silver in it. A hundred bucks at least."

He gasps and pretends to be horrified. It's all an act and all I want is to go back to my pups. In the end, Max gives me sixty dollars. Enough for a fifty pound bag of Science Diet and a couple packs of ground beef. I carry the bag of dog food over my shoulder. It's getting dark and I'm almost home when I figure I'm being followed.

A quick check confirms a man is trailing me, but I keep going. Not that the others will help me. They'll disappear as fast as the ground beef in my bag. Not like this hasn't happened before. I'm invisible to most people, but despite the smell of dog and layers of grim, the strays of society still find me. At eighteen, I'm young for a street person, and high school boys, college boys, and even foster fathers can't resist. My scent attracts them just like a female dog in heat.

The curse of developing early and curvy. My foster father called me beautiful. He named the dog Beauty, but never bothered her the way he did me. Lucky dog.

I reach my spot and my pups. Too bad the big Wolfhound is too weak to stand. Dropping the bag, I grab the metal baseball bat a kid left at the park and wait for the stranger. As long as the guy isn't armed, me and my lot'll do just fine.

Wearing khaki pants, brown loafers and a long wool coat, the guy resembles a lost professor. As he nears, the Wolfhound pokes his head out from under the blanket and growls deep in his chest.

The man takes his hands from his pockets. "Hello?" he calls all friendly like.

But my pups' hackles are up.

"I was hoping you could help me," he says, stepping closer. "I'm looking for my dog. Someone reported seeing him in this area."

Bull. I wait as his gaze scans the mutts and lingers on the baseball bat in my hands.

He tries a smile. "He's quite large."

"Haven't seen him," I say. "Go away."

"Are you sure?" He keeps coming.

I raise the bat. "Yep." By now all the dogs are growling.

He is unconcerned. "Settle your dogs."

"No."

He is close enough to see the Wolfhound. They exchange a glance and it reminds me of two competitors acting nice until the game starts.

"Settle them or I will." His right hand dips into a pocket and pulls out a gun. He aims it at me.

A bone chilling cold seizes my heart. "Quiet," I order. They're familiar with this command. It's the first thing I teach a new pup. They sit down on all fours and wait without making a sound.

"Drop the bat," he says.

I let it clang to the ground.

The man tries to comfort me. "I'm just here for my dog."

Yet the Wolfhound doesn't seem happy to see him. Go figure. Now the guy is under the bridge and the hound lurches to his feet. The dog's massive jaws are level with my chest. The blanket remains on his back like a superhero's cloak.

The man shakes his head as if he's amazed. "How many

near misses, Logan? Four? Five? Only you would find some homeless person to nurse you back to health. Too bad I found you first."

And people call *me* the crazy dog lady.

He turns to me and says, "His injuries are too extensive, I'll have to put him down." He aims the gun at the Wolfhound.

The urge to protect one of mine is instant and hot. "Wait," I say. "Can you take the blanket off him? It's my only one and I don't want it full of holes and blood."

The man laughs. "I see your charm with the ladies remains the same," he says to the Wolfhound. He's careful to keep the gun out of the dog's reach as he pulls the cover off.

My pups are well trained. And while being quiet is important, I've taught them protecting my stuff is essential. They hop to their feet and attack the man's ankles and calves with their pointy little teeth. He yells. I scoop up my bat and slam it down on his arms. The gun fires, but there are no yelps of pain so I swing again and again until he drops the gun. Until he rolls on the ground, shielding his body from my bat.

I taste the desire to pound him into a pile of broken bones and bloody meat. Coming here and thinking he can just take what he wants. Just like my foster father sneaking into my bedroom. But this stranger isn't him, so I pull myself together and call my dogs off.

"Go away," I say to the man.

He staggers to his feet, but his gaze is on the Wolfhound. Odd, considering *I'm* the one holding the bat.

"Next time I won't come alone," he says to the Wolfhound before limping away.

That's bad. I look at the Wolfhound. "Does he mean it?"

I swear the dog nods a yes. Okay so maybe I am the crazy dog lady. I pick up the gun and unload it as I think. If I hock it,

I'd have money, but no weapon. The bullets are shiny silver. Living on the street, I've seen my fair share of guns and bullets, but these are special. Expensive, too.

We could move before he comes back. But that rankles. Nobody's gonna run me off my spot.

"How many will come with him?" I ask the hound. "Two?"

A shake—no.

"Three?...Four?...Five?"

Five. Crap. "When? Tomorrow morning? Afternoon? Night?" Yes to the night. I've a day to plan, but the Wolfhound gives me a decisive nod (yep, this confirms the crazy), and he takes off. Well, he tries. Poor boy stumbles after two strides. The knife damaged his muscles and he's still weak. And he's ripped his stitches.

Half carrying him, I help him back and fix him.

"Look," I say. "I didn't spend all that time and energy on you to see you throw it away, trying to be noble. You're part of mine now and I protect mine."

A day isn't much time so I'm at the Humane Shelter's door as soon as it opens.

"Hey, Mongrel." Lily greets me with a smile. "Find another pup?"

She's filling bowls with generic dog food (such a shame!). I help her feed her charges. Excited barks and yips ring through the metal cages. Lily's the only person I talk to on a regular basis.

"Not today."

"Take a look at the flyers. There's a black lab missing. Owner's offering a hundred dollar reward."

Lily sees my face. "I can be your go between and make sure you get the money," she says.

"How did you know?"

"Police came yesterday asking questions about you. They thought you have a dog napping scheme going on."

So much for earning money that way. "What did you tell them?"

"The truth. You're better at finding lost dogs than anybody in town. That you're providing a service to this city and should be paid."

Lily is good people. "Thanks. Now I really hate to ask you for a favor."

She straightens and looks at me as if I just told her the sky is orange. "In the two years I've known you, you've never asked for anything. If I can, I will. Ask away."

I blink at her a moment. Didn't she want anything in exchange? She insists not, and I make an unusual request which she grants. Did I tell you Lily's good people? Well she is.

After a stop at the pawn shop, I take my littles to Pennypack Park—a tiny snake of green in the middle of the city. I find a nice safe place for them, ordering them to stay quiet. They're handy against one intruder, but against five, one of them is bound to get hurt.

I return to the Wolfhound about an hour after sunset. He's alert with his nose sniffing the cold breeze. Somehow, I know the professor and his goons aren't going to arrive with the wind, so I sit close to Logan and keep watch downwind. The others are nowhere in sight. Their sixth sense accurate once again.

As I wait, my heart is chasing its tail, running fast and going nowhere. It's not too long before five black shapes break from the shadows and approach. They're easy to see in the bright moonlight.

My insides turn gooey, but I draw in a breath. Nobody messes with mine. Not anymore. I stand as they slink toward me. No, I'm not being dramatic. Slink is the perfect word. Five big brutes just like Logan. Massive jaws and shaggy hair. The professor isn't in sight, but a tawny wolfhound leads the group (give him two pairs of loafer's and he'd fit the part of the professor).

Now, you're gonna tell me something like this just doesn't happen, and I'd agree with you every other night. But not tonight.

The pack fans out, and I've seen enough street fights to know if they surround me I'm dead. I raise the gun, aim, and fire. I'm a pretty good shot. Thanks in part to my foster father. Unlike all the others before him, he'd taught me a few life skills and I'd loved him until...well, you know.

The tranquilizer dart hits the shoulder of the far left hound. (If you thought I'd shoot them with bullets, then you haven't been paying attention).

I squeeze off a couple more darts, picking off two more wide receivers before the remaining two catch on and rush me. Dropping the gun, I palm a dart in one hand and pull the silver knife I reclaimed from the pawn shop. I exchanged it for the professor's gun.

Then it's all hair, claws, and teeth. The wolfhounds are fast and it's like fighting a giant yet silent dust devil. I jab the dart into dog flesh and strike, stab, and slash at anything I can reach with the knife. The tawny grabs my wrist with his teeth when his last goon is overcome by the tranquilizer.

Tawny bites through my skin like it's paper. I yell and drop the weapon. He pushes me over and stands on my chest. Breathing with his weight on me is an effort, and my heart lodges in my throat. He stares at me for a second with regret in his gaze, giving me just enough time to thrust my arm between his sharp teeth and my exposed neck.

A bit of surprise flashes in his black eyes as he latches on. I'd coated my sleeves and pants with Tabasco sauce. Useful for keeping pups from chewing things. In this case, not so smart as the burn makes Tawny angrier. The pressure increases in my forearm and I'm convinced my bone's about to snap in two when the brute is knocked off.

Logan and Tawny roll together. And the fight's no longer silent as they growl and snarl. I worry about Logan's shoulder as I dive for the tranquilizer gun. Lily showed me how to wrap up his leg to support his weight, but it's not much.

I'm outta darts. With Logan injured, the fight isn't fair. Most things aren't. And I guess that's the only way Tawny can win.

I spot a glint just when Tawny pins Logan. Sweeping up the knife, I lunge toward Tawny and bury the blade in his hindquarters. Up to the hilt.

He yelps and bucks. Logan presses his advantage and regains his feet. In a blur, Logan strikes and silences Tawny. Logan's muzzle is dripping with blood. I meet his gaze and can tell by his expression that he's sickened and sad. He's not a killer, but Tawny forced him to be one. Why couldn't he just leave Logan alone?

I'd asked my foster father the same thing. He said I was too irresistible so I ran away when I turned sixteen, removing the temptation. I'd thought I was smart, but no one knows about his inability to resist. It's been two years. What if he has a new foster child? Staring at Tawny's ripped throat, I realize a person has to stay and fight until there's a clear winner and loser or else your problems don't ever go away.

The burning pain in my arm snaps me back to my current problems. I inspect the damage. Ragged, bleeding flesh too mangled for eighty-proof vodka and Band Aids, but I don't have another option. Once Logan's cleaned up—his stitches have ripped again—and hidden under the blanket, I hurry to the Humane Shelter.

Lily's working late and I suspect she's there for me. She sends a couple volunteers to pick up the sleeping wolfhounds. I return the tranquilizer gun.

"A pack of wild dogs that are all the same breed is so unusual," she says. "Usually they're a bunch of mongrels." She slaps her hand over her mouth. "I didn't mean—"

I smile. "I know. Nothing wrong with mongrels."

Lily sees my arm and insists I go to the emergency room. I almost laugh. Invisible on the streets, I'm nonexistent in an ER. No money. No insurance. They'd fix a cockroach's broken leg before attending to me. I lie and say I'll go, but she sees right through me. Despite my protests, she escorts me to the ER and stays until I'm seen. The ER doctor gives me thirty-two stitches. Funny how the number of stitches is always reported like it's a source of pride.

By the next day, my life returns to; well, not normal, but back to the same—taking care of the pups. Logan is healing faster than me and eating like a horse. I feed him my share most days. Don't matter to me, my stomach's upset anyways. Tomorrow—one week after I found Logan—I'm gonna tell the authorities about my foster father.

I'd rather face a pack of wild dogs, but I'm determined to

grab the man by the throat and not let go, finally doing what I should have done two years ago.

~

Five days later, Logan takes off and doesn't return. The hurt cuts deep and reminds me of how I'd felt moving from one foster home to another. Crazy lady that I am, I'd been talking to him about the police and the lawyers and the questions. No one is quick to believe me, and I don't have much proof so it's been rougher than I thought. Somehow telling my problems to Logan made the whole ordeal bearable.

But he's gone, and my resolve to go after my foster father wavers. But there is also a tiny bit of relief inside me. Keeping the Wolfhound fed was hard. And with one of life's little twists of fate and timing, I find the missing black lab after Logan left. Lily handles the reward money. Without Logan to feed, there's plenty of money to keep feeding my pups Science Diet.

Three—maybe four weeks after the night I helped Logan, a stranger enters the parking lot. Wearing blue jeans and a leather motorcycle jacket, he doesn't hesitate, heading right for my bridge. His black hair hangs in layers to his shoulders, and his stride is familiar.

I'm searching my memories to place him when my pups race toward him. Good. Except they don't bite him. They dance around, tails wagging and yipping in excitement. He crouches down and pets them! I grab my bat.

He glances up as I swing and dodges the bat with ease. Strike one. I pull back for another.

"Mongrel, stop," he says. "It's me."

I freeze and study him. He's a few years older than I am, about six feet tall and lean. Good looking enough to attract the girls. His gray eyes don't belong in the face of a man though.

He opens his jacket, and pulls his collar down, showing me an almost healed scar on his right shoulder. "Fifteen stitches."

I lower the bat. "Logan."

"Yep."

He moves closer and I back up. Logan pauses. "You weren't afraid of five werewolves, but you're scared of me?"

Werewolves. Saying the word out loud makes it real. Before I could explain them away as really smart mixed breeds.

"Guess I'm better at trusting...werewolves than men," I say.

"One man dooms the whole species?"

"What about the guy...wolf after you?"

"He wanted to be in charge."

"And that's my point. Dogs...or wolves'll fight it out. One dominates and the other slinks away. The human side of him tried to cheat. Right?"

Logan says nothing.

"He used a knife and then returned with a gun. Very un-wolf like behavior."

"Let me prove to you we're not all bad."

"Why?"

"You saved my life three times."

I tap the bat against my leg. "So buy me a couple bags of Science Diet and we'll call it even."

"No. I owe you much more than that."

He's serious and I suspect stubborn as well. "Go away, Logan. You don't belong here," I say.

"Neither do you."

I huff and squash the sudden desire to take another swing at his head. He must think my silence is an agreement 'cause he's now standing a foot away. And my heart's acting like it's scared. I expect him to crinkle his nose at the smell of dog on my clothes or for him to try to hide his disgust at my unkempt appearance.

Instead he takes my hand in his and pushes my right sleeve up with his other one, exposing the jagged purple scars on my wrist and forearm. I didn't heal as fast nor as well as he did. Logan traces them with a finger.

A strange teeter totter of emotions fill me. My first impulse is to flinch away from his touch, but his familiar scent triggers fond memories of the big Wolfhound I cared for.

Logan taps his thumb on my arm. "You've been bitten by a werewolf deep enough for his saliva to mix with your blood."

"So?"

He quirks a smile. "You accepted our existence with ease, yet you don't know the legends."

I gesture to his shoulder. "I believe what I see."

"You've been infected, but one bite isn't enough to change you into a werewolf." All humor is gone as he stares at me with a sharp intensity. "For you to become one of us, a bite from two different werewolves within a month is required."

He turns my arm over, revealing the light underside. His canines elongate. "I've never offered this to anyone, and it's a hell of a way to repay your kindness, but it seems...right. Interested?"

My mind races. He's giving me a choice. "What about my pups?"

Another smile. "Only you would think of them first. They can stay with you."

"Here?"

"No. My pack has a network of places. We try and keep a low profile, but we'll support you in going after your foster father."

"Why?"

"Because you'll be part of mine and I protect mine."

I grin at the familiar words.

Logan adds, "It's not an easy life, and there is no cure. No going back. We don't belong to the human world or the wolf world."

"So you're a bunch of mongrels?"

"Yep."

"Then I'll fit right in." I raise my arm to his mouth, and he sinks his teeth into my flesh.

CAPTURING IMAGES

Aside from being an avid fan of the reality TV show, Project Runway, *I don't have a fashionable bone in my body. So when I was asked to submit a fantasy short story set in the world of fashion for* Bloody Fabulous, *I almost declined. I can't tell one designer from another and I think spending more than fifty bucks on uncomfortable shoes is outrageous. However, I do enjoy photography and the fashion world hires many talented photographers. Feeling more in my comfort zone, I began my story with a confident professional photographer who is challenged to take an impossible photo.*

CAPTURING IMAGES

MONDAY
     Evelyn's brain cells had declared war inside her skull. The right side of her brain attacked the left with mortars and heavy artillery, while the left responded with bombs and gunfire. Why did she order that *third* Long Island Ice Tea? Because she had already drunk two and logic and reason had left her to photocopy their asses.

Memories of last night's party pulsed. Had she really bragged to the publisher of *Vackra* magazine that she could transform anyone from ugly to beautiful? And then make a bet with the woman? God, she hoped not.

And who was the idiot who had scheduled a party on a Sunday night? She rested her forehead on her desk as more brain cells died. The doorbell to her studio dinged. Without checking the security camera, she buzzed the door open. Evelyn rolled her head to the side and watched Vincenza, her make-up artist, through a curtain of blond hair. The tall Italian woman sported the latest European fashions. Even her nickname—Vee was trendy.

Vee spotted her. "What happened?"

"Too much alcohol, not enough sense."

"I knew I should have stayed last night." She tsked. "Not to worry. I'll make you a tonic." Vincenza bustled off making way too much noise with her heels.

Another painful ding sounded and Evelyn's assistant—a bundle of energy contained in human form—arrived. The girl was too young and too inexperienced, but she was whip smart.

"What stinks?" Olivia asked.

"Vodka, gin, tequila, rum, and triple sec fumes, courtesy of our boss lady," Vee called.

"Oh." She crinkled her nose. "Do you want me to cancel your appointments?"

"No. We're doing the cover for *Glam More*." It had taken Evelyn two months to find an open date with the model and the magazine's deadline loomed.

Another time limit popped unbidden into her mind. *Produce a beautiful photo of the model I send to you in one week. If you cannot, then you are mine.* Camilla D. Quinton's liquid voice sounded in her head. Maybe Camilla would forget all about the bet. She snorted. Not Camilla, otherwise known as the Demon Queen. She had not only earned that reputation, but embraced it.

The only reason Evelyn had gone to that party was to meet her. One of Camilla's rare public appearances, and Evelyn had hoped to impress the woman and be offered a cover shoot for *Vackra*. But Camilla's notorious resistance to using freelancers remained, preferring to do everything in house.

Evelyn raised her head, causing another brain cell salvo. "I'll need my Nikon with the fifty millimeter lens, the white backdrop, and two strobes," she said to Olivia.

As the girl hurried to set up the equipment, Vee pressed a

hot mug of... "What the hell is this? It smells like rancid cottage cheese."

"Drink it, you'll feel better."

She cringed at the taste, but kept sipping until Vee appeared satisfied. The model for the photo shoot arrived in a fit of tears over her blotchy skin. Vee whisked the girl back to the dressing room. It didn't matter how horrible the model's skin tone, hair, or shape was, with Vee and Evelyn's expertise, her photo would show a gorgeous young woman.

Evelyn admitted to a certain amount of confidence. After all, she had the best reputation in the business, and it hadn't occurred overnight. She committed years, sacrificed her social life, and worked hard. Seven years later, she owned a studio and loft in the heart of Manhattan. Still, she shouldn't have made that boast. Yet a part of her felt equal to the challenge.

Vee returned with a now radiant model. Feeling steadier, Evelyn picked up her camera. The familiar weight of the Nikon in her hand was like a caffeine fix. Dismissing her worries about the party, Evelyn concentrated on her work.

After her last Monday client left, Evelyn uploaded the day's photos to her computer. Taking pictures was only the first half of the job. She scanned the shots and didn't look up when Olivia chirped a good bye or when Vee admonished her not to work too late before leaving.

Pulling up the *Glam More* job, Evelyn picked the best pose and clicked on the photo's histogram. Then she proceeded to turn the pretty model into a goddess.

When a low cough sounded, she jumped from her seat. Her heart banged in her chest as she stifled a scream.

"Pardon me," a man said. "I didn't mean to startle you." He stood near the door.

How the hell did he get in? Evelyn's New Yorker instincts kicked in, and she assessed him to determine the level of threat. Well dressed, well groomed, clean shoes. Not a vagrant. No jacket and short sleeves despite the chilly October air. No obvious weapons. Designer clothes.

She met his amused gaze and was stunned. His features were perfectly proportioned, eyes a deep sapphire blue, pale skin without a single flaw, and thick black hair that reached the base of his neck. The best looking guy she has seen before make-up and Photoshop. The best looking guy *ever*.

Evelyn raked a hand through her messy hair. "If you want a portfolio, you need to make an appointment."

"Camilla sent me." He gave her a wry smile. "I'm your...test subject."

A rollercoaster of emotions rolled through her. Relief—he was gorgeous. Suspicion—what game was the Demon Queen playing? She had expected Camilla to send a hag. Surprise—that Camilla would act so soon.

Evelyn shrugged. This would be easy. "Call my assistant tomorrow and we'll set up a time."

"It has to be tonight," he said.

"I can't, I've a deadline."

"Should I tell her you concede?"

That word sent a rush of memories. Concede meant closing her studio and working solely for the Demon Queen. Fear shot through her. "She said I had a week."

He nodded. "Yes. A week to produce a photo or to get your affairs in order."

That made it sound as if she had a terminal disease. He had an odd formal way of speaking as if he'd be more comfortable wearing a fedora and suit than the gray slacks and black polo shirt. However, with his athletic build, he'd look good in a T-shirt and off the rack jeans.

"All right. Give me a minute." She considered calling Olivia and Vee, but the man didn't need make-up. She'd adjust for his pale skin, and shoot in black and white.

As she set up her equipment, she watched him from the corner of her eye. Unlike most models, he didn't check his appearance in the mirrors.

Instead, he studied her framed photos. Not the ones filled with magazine covers, but the ones from Iraq. The stark images of war that she had taken on her last "vacation" had been tucked out of way. All the major magazines had rejected the photos, claiming the images were too disturbing.

Yet he didn't flinch from them. Perhaps he had more depth than the other male models she'd photographed. He was a little older than them—closer to her age of thirty. Maybe they'd have something in common. Oh, who was she kidding? He probably dated gorgeous women barely out of high school.

"I'm ready, Mr...?"

He extended a hand. "Grayson Windsor. But everyone calls me Gray."

She shook his hand. His cold fingers grasped hers a little longer than proper. But he let go and stood before the white background.

"Stand on the X and face me," she instructed.

He smirked when she aimed her camera at him. Her opinion of him dropped a few notches. Oh well. Camilla wanted beautiful, and even smirking Gray met that require-ment. Evelyn snapped a few shots to test the lighting, aperture, and shutter speed, then brought up the pictures to view.

Odd. His clothes and shoes showed up, but not his face and arms. She frowned, tried a few more shots, netting the same results. To the camera, it appeared as if he were invisible.

Aiming at her desk, she took another set. The pictures were fine. Evelyn tried her Canon and then her Olympus. Same thing.

"Are you ready to admit defeat?" Gray asked from right behind her.

She yelped. "There must be something wrong."

"There's nothing wrong with your equipment. Please, allow me to show you." He gestured to the mirrors.

Curious she followed him. He stood in front of them. His reflection matched her pictures of him. Just his clothes. To prove his point he removed his shirt. Gaping, she glanced between the pants and shoes in the mirror to his muscular torso. Impossible. She could *see* him.

Now he gave her a full smile, revealing straight teeth and fangs. She stepped back as fear coiled around her heart.

He stayed close, grabbing her upper arm. "Nothing can take a picture of us. Our souls have already been taken. You will not win the bet with our queen."

That was way too much for Evelyn's sputtering brain. She focused on one thing. "Us? You mean there are more of you?"

"Many more. A whole nest of nasties."

Her heart rate jumped.

"Don't worry." He stroked her throat with his free hand. His icy fingers sent tremors through her muscles. "I'm not allowed to drink from this lovely neck. My queen wishes for you to be healthy. She desires only your photographic genius."

"Your queen? Camilla?" Her voice squeaked.

"Yes. Her nickname is more accurate than anyone can imagine."

"Or believe."

"There is that. But pictures don't lie, Miss Mitchell. You know that."

"Actually, pictures lie all the time."

"No they don't. *You* change them with your computer. Except, I suspect your war photos haven't been altered."

"That wouldn't be right."

"I agree. Now according to the terms of your bet, you're to pack up your studio, fire your staff, put your business up for sale, and be available for our queen next week. She will provide everything else. And don't bother the police. That will just anger us. You really don't want to do that."

His words felt like a death sentence. Evelyn had worked so hard to be independent.

Gray released her. "I'll return each evening to check on your progress." He headed toward the door.

"Wait. Can I try to take your picture again?"

"How you decide to spend your last week is up to you. However in one week's time you *will* be the queens property regardless." He left.

Evelyn sank to the floor as the whole encounter with Gray replayed in her mind. Disbelief warred with panic. She debated calling her lawyer, her mother, or calling the police despite his threat. *Would any of them believe her?* Anger at Camilla flipped with fear that she'd send more of her...vampires to harm her if she didn't comply. God, she was so screwed. Or was she?

Snapping out of her shock, Evelyn jumped to her feet. She checked the pictures—still the same, but she wrote a list of techniques she could try in order to capture Gray's image. After all, she could see him. It was just a matter of finding the right combination of lighting and equipment.

TUESDAY

When Olivia arrived the next morning, Evelyn told her to cancel all her appointments for the week.

"What should I tell them?" the girl asked her.

"Tell them I'm sick."

Too new to question her boss, Olivia nodded and rushed to her desk. Vee, however, had been working with her for the last six years. She peered at Evelyn through thick mascara-laden eyelashes when Evelyn gave her the rest of the week off.

"What's going on?" Vee waved a hand at the mess of cameras heaped on the table. "This isn't you." She picked up an old camera, and gasped in mock horror. "This has *four* megapixels."

Evelyn decided not to tell her friend about the bet. "It's a... special retro project. A real challenge and...very important for my career." *And my life.*

Vee arched a slender eyebrow. "You're not photographing cadavers again?"

She stifled a cough. Were vampires cadavers? "I haven't done that since grad school." Back when she had needed money she'd worked for a funeral home, photographing the deceased for grieving family members. She'd also photographed birthday parties, worked in a one-hour photo lab, and tutored freshmen.

Vee gestured to her war photos. "Then what do you call those?"

The conversation with Gray replayed in Evelyn's mind. "The truth."

"This isn't about some man is it?"

She stared at Vee. "Why would you think that? I haven't had a date in over a year."

"Exactly. Desperate people do desperate things."

"I'm not desperate. I just haven't found a kindred soul yet."

"Hard to find one when you don't leave your studio," Vee said.

"I went out on Sunday night and look what happened."

"A hangover isn't the end of the world." But after another uncomfortable scrutiny, Vee agreed to take the week off. "Call me if you need me for *any* reason. Okay?"

"Okay." She relaxed.

Evelyn spent the remainder of the day prepping for Gray. Olivia broke her concentration when she announced that she had finally rescheduled all of Evelyn's appointments.

"Do you need me tomorrow?" Olivia asked.

Just in case tonight's efforts failed, Evelyn told her to come back in the morning. Disappointed, Olivia schlepped out without saying good-bye.

Unaffected by the dramatics, Evelyn returned to her work, skipping supper in order to be ready.

Once again Gray arrived without warning or sound. Surprise mixed with instant fear. She only had his word he wouldn't kill her. This time he wore tight black jeans, cowboy boots with silver buckles, and a white T-shirt with a design of black wings spread across his chest.

Proud that her voice didn't warble, she asked, "Something wrong with the door bell?"

Smirking, he glanced at the security video screen. "I'm camera shy."

She considered. "It must be difficult to avoid them. They're all over the place, and everyone has a camera on their cell phone." Another connection popped into her mind. "Is that why Camilla avoids the public?" And probably why the light had been so dim at the party.

His smirk faded. "It helps that we are creatures of the night, but it does limit our...social life."

An image of him hunting a hapless person to feed on popped into her head.

"It's not what you think," he said as if he could read her mind. "We have volunteers who donate blood. It just would be nice to go out without worrying. To be able to attend a Broadway musical instead of lurking in the shadows."

"A musical? Really?"

"Did you think all we do is read *Dracula* and watch episodes of *True Blood*?" Amusement sparked.

"Since I didn't know you existed until yesterday, I haven't had the time to imagine what your...social life is like."

"It's better than yours," he said.

Not about to dignify his comment with a response, she gestured to the area she had prepped. "Please stand—"

He was there before she finished her sentence. And the smirk was back. *Wonderful.*

Evelyn tried a number of different cameras, backgrounds, and techniques. Then she mounted her camera on a tripod and instructed him to keep still, hoping a long exposure would work. She set it for one minute, then five, then ten. Nothing.

Next test involved covering Gray's bare skin with make-up. He agreed and sat still as she spread the liquid foundation on him. Although his skin felt cold, it was...normal.

Feeling awkward with his proximity, she asked, "Why do you think your social life is better than mine?"

"Our queen has been interested in you for a year. We've been watching you to make sure your withdrawal from regular society wouldn't make waves."

Unease rolled in her stomach. "Withdrawal?"

"We are a close-knit group. We limit contact with outsiders to a bare minimum. Discovery of our...existence wouldn't be well received."

She huffed. "Are you sure? There's a reason books and shows like *True Blood* are popular."

"We're more concerned about the military."

"Oh." She considered. "My friends and family would be alarmed if I disappeared."

"Friends? Your only friend, Vincenza Salvatori has success-fully interviewed with *Good Morning America* to be their executive make-up artist. According to our sources, she has accepted the job and is scheduled to start next month. At a considerable higher salary than what you pay her, by the way."

Her hands stilled as his words sunk in like acid sizzling through her heart. *Why didn't she tell me? I would have been happy for her. Or would I?*

To avoid the hurtful truth, she said, "My mother will tear this town apart looking for me."

"When's the last time you talked to your mother?" he asked.

"Last week...I think."

"You don't know?"

"Do you know *exactly* when you last talked to yours?" she countered.

"No."

"See?"

Gray gave her a flat look. "My mother's been dead over a hundred years. What's your excuse?"

"I'm very busy. Which your vampire spies should be well aware of." She snapped.

"We are. And we also know that you haven't called your mother in over a month." He leaned back, looking smug. "So we have at least a month before your mother even realizes you're gone."

Evelyn clamped her mouth shut. Gray's blatant attempt to distract her wouldn't work. She finished covering him and snapped a few photos. When she pulled them up on screen, the make-up appeared as tan blobs.

"Give up?" Gray asked, peering over her shoulder.

"No. I've more things to try."

He swept her hair to the side and brushed his lips over her

neck. A strange tingle shot through her, igniting fear and, she'd like to say revulsion, but to be honest it was more akin to desire.

"It's two hours until dawn. And unless you have a bottle of A positive in your fridge, I'd better go before I rip into this lovely throat. Until tomorrow..." He kissed her neck and was gone.

She groped for the chair and collapsed into it, suddenly exhausted. Nothing she tried tonight had worked. At least she could rule out capturing a digital image. The next logical step would be to try her old film cameras. And that would require a number of items she no longer owned.

~

WEDNESDAY

The studio door dinged, waking Evelyn. She had fallen asleep at her desk. Buzzing Olivia in, Evelyn handed her a list of supplies along with her company's—E. Mitchell Studios—credit card. She had been so proud when her company's name had been painted on the glass doors to her studio. It was simple and genderless and hers.

Renewed determination not to lose her business pulsed through her body. After Olivia left to go shopping, Evelyn sucked down an extra-large cup of coffee and dug through old boxes until she found her thirty-five millimeter cameras.

When Olivia returned with the supplies, her assistant helped Evelyn clean out one of her walk-in closets.

"What are you using this for?" Olivia asked as she dragged out a dusty container of old photos.

"I'm converting it into a darkroom."

The girl paused and wiped her hands on her tattered jeans. "Darkroom? What's that?"

Now it was her turn to pause. "Didn't they teach you how to develop film in art school?"

"Not in my classes. I majored in new digital media and experimental photography. Not ancient history."

Evelyn suppressed a sigh. Despite her own troubles, she wouldn't be remiss in her mentor duties. "Tomorrow I'll show you how to make pictures the old fashioned way."

Olivia wasn't quick enough to hide her frown, but she continued to lug boxes and even asked a few token questions about the process. After they had set up the darkroom, she sent Olivia home.

Loading a Nikon with black and white, thirty-five millimeter film, Evelyn lamented the demise of Kodachrome film. She could have hoarded a few rolls, if she had known... well, if she had known, then she would have kept her big mouth shut on Sunday night.

She hardly reacted to Gray's silent arrival. *Funny how you could get used to anything.* Evelyn glanced at her war photos. *Well, almost anything.*

He noticed the boxes littered around the studio. "Are you finally accepting your fate and packing?"

"No. I'm trying a new tactic tonight."

Gray examined the mess, picking through the piles of camera equipment. "Some of these are antiques. I remember when the Nikon L35 was first released. It caused quite a sensation."

When she connected that comment to the one about his mother, Evelyn realized he might have been around during the early years of photography. She asked him a few questions and soon they were discussing the evolution of the camera—a subject that fascinated Evelyn.

With a genuine smile, Gray said, "I don't know why you're so resistant to working for our queen. You'll be among people with similar interests."

It was as if he had thrown ice cold water on her, snapping her to her senses. Once again, he had distracted her.

"If you please..." She swept a hand toward the backdrop.

With a sigh, he posed with his arms crossed. "I don't know whether to admire your determination or point out the fact that you're wasting time."

Ignoring him, she took a few test shots to familiarize herself with the camera. Evelyn then burned through ten rolls of film.

After Gray left, she was too exhausted to do more than crawl up the stairs to her apartment and fall into bed.

~

THURSDAY

"Uh, Evelyn? I think I did something wrong again." Olivia passed her a negative. "I'm not sure 'cause it's hard to see with this red light."

She peered at the image. Shirt, pants and boots on an invisible man. No Gray. They had been developing film all day in the darkroom, and the results were the same. All ten rolls.

Dejected, Evelyn sent Olivia home, glad to be alone. The girl had complained about the smells, the chemicals, the red light, and how labor intensive it all was. Evelyn would have enjoyed returning to her photographic roots in the darkroom if the stakes hadn't been so high.

She slumped in her chair and scanned her studio. Covers for every major fashion magazine in New York, Paris, London and Rome covered her walls. *Vackra* had been the only one who hadn't hired her to shoot a cover. And she just couldn't let that one go. Oh no. She had to chase after it. Now here she stood facing a lion with a butterfly net.

Out of ideas, Evelyn called her mother.

"Evie, it's so good to hear your voice," her mother said without a trace of sarcasm or even a guilt-inducing inflection, which Evelyn fully deserved.

"I was beginning to worry about you, sweetie, but I never know when to call you. I'd hate to disrupt an important shoot."

"I'm sorry I haven't called."

"What are you working on?" her mother asked.

"A very difficult assignment and I'm stuck about what to do next."

"Why don't you ask that professor you liked so much in graduate school? The one who helped invent that bluescreen thingy?"

"Chroma keying," she automatically corrected, but her mind raced. The chroma key technology made things and people invisible on TV and the movies, like Harry Potter's invisibility cloak.

"Didn't you say there was nothing he couldn't do with a camera? Maybe he can help you."

"Professor Duncan passed away last year." Genuine sorrow filled her.

"Aw. Too bad." A pause. "Didn't he write a textbook or something?"

Stunned, Evelyn gripped her phone tighter. "He donated all his research to the School of Visual Arts' library." Equipment, notes, computer. Everything. "Mom, you're a genius!"

Her mother demurred, but Evelyn could tell she was pleased. Evelyn promised to call more often, then hung up.

Grabbing her purse and jacket, she dashed out to hail a taxi before Gray arrived.

The library was open until midnight. As a distinguished alumni, Evelyn had full use of the facilities, and was soon tucked into a quiet corner, searching through Professor Duncan's research for the next several hours.

Taking notes, Evelyn devised a rough plan that used a video camera and reversed the chroma key graphics. Would Gray agree to wear a blue body suit?

"Find anything interesting?" Gray asked.

She jerked. "How did you know I was here?"

He wore a jacket, gloves, hat, scarf and sunglasses. No doubt to hide from the security cameras hanging from the ceiling. "Was your mother happy to hear from you?"

Evelyn rubbed her eyes. "Vampire spies. How could I forget? Did you listen to my conversation?"

"Of course, sweetie."

Surging to her feet, she confronted him. "That's illegal."

He shrugged. "Call the police. Good luck proving it."

"I can prove it right now." She reached for his hat.

But he snagged her wrist, stopping her before her hand came close to his head. "I don't think you fully realize the danger you are in." He tightened his grip.

Pain ringed her arm as panic ringed her chest. Thinking fast, she said, "If you break my wrist, then I'll be unable to take photos and the bet will be put on hold until I'm healed. I'm sure *your queen* will not appreciate *you* causing a delay."

Gray released her even though he was clearly unhappy. "I'll be waiting for you outside."

Score one for the photographer. She returned to her notes. At midnight the library closed and Gray escorted her home. No need to fear being mugged with a vampire bodyguard.

Evelyn spent the rest of the night searching Craigslist for

the video and computer equipment she'd need. Gray left, Olivia arrived, and she sent Olivia to pick up her multiple orders before collapsing.

∾

FRIDAY

"You want me to wear this?" Gray held up the blue garment. "Is this a joke?"

"Think of it as a Halloween costume," she said, gesturing toward the changing room.

He paused. "I always go as Count Dracula for Halloween."

She laughed. Call it exhaustion or sleep deprivation, she couldn't help it.

He grinned and studied her. "So nice to see you smile. That scowl you favor doesn't belong on your beautiful face."

Sobering in an instant, she shooed him into the changing room. She wasn't going to fall for another delaying tactic. Yet she tucked her hair behind her ears. When she had been in college, many of her fellow photography students had asked her to model for them. They'd called her a classic blond beauty. But that was ten years ago, and, although they'd flattered her, she found the experience utterly boring. Far better to be behind the camera.

When he returned clad only in the skintight bodysuit, Evelyn pressed a hand to her mouth to keep a fit of giggles from bubbling out. For the first time, he appeared uncomfortable and that cocky smirk of his was nowhere to be seen.

And she would know since the suit left nothing to the imagination. Nothing. A flush of heat spread to areas of her body that hadn't felt anything in years. Perhaps living with Camilla's nest of nasties wouldn't be so bad.

Focusing on the task at hand, she instructed him to pull the hood over his head. "Cover your face as well, it will only be for a second."

"You don't have to worry. I don't need to breathe."

"Oh." Curious, she asked, "How much is true? You mentioned blood and dawn, what else is right?"

"Are you planning to attack me with garlic and a wooden stake?"

"You're too fast and strong. I wouldn't get near you would I?"

"No. And I'm not telling you our secrets until you're part of the...nest." He gazed at her with a predatory intensity.

"Or is it because you're afraid I might win the bet?"

"I'm not afraid of anything." He yanked the hood down over his face.

Liar. But she wasn't going to waste anymore of her precious time. After she filmed a few minutes of video, she asked him to pull the suit down to his waist, exposing his upper body. He smirked as she recorded another couple minutes. She wondered if his attitude was a defense mechanism to keep people at a distance.

God, she had lost her mind. Who cared about a soulless demon? Once she took his fricking picture, she would never have to see him again.

He stayed as she ran the video through the computer program, hoping to reverse the process. Nothing but blue filled the screen.

She closed her eyes and rested her head on her desk.

Gray put his hand on her shoulder. "You should be commended for effort. I'll ask our queen to allow you to call your mother from time to time. She owes me a favor."

Sympathy from a vampire. Could she go any lower or was that the bottom? No, she wouldn't give up.

Evelyn shrugged off his hand and stood. "I still have two

more days. I'll see you tomorrow." Without waiting for a reply, she headed to bed. A good night's sleep should help clear her head. She hoped.

∾

SATURDAY

With panic simmering in her chest, Evelyn spent the day going over all the techniques she had tried this week, trying to find inspiration. When that failed to work, she surfed the Internet for information about Camilla D. Quinton, Grayson Windsor, and *Vackra* magazine.

No surprise that there were no pictures of Gray, but there were dozens of Camilla all taken prior to 2000. A memory tugged. She recalled a campaign by the magazine to find the most beautiful man and woman in the world to mark the new millennium. The staff traveled all over the world, including some very exotic lands. Perhaps they found more than they could handle. They had eventually featured a stunning couple, but after that, Camilla withdrew from the spotlight.

She searched for more information, but found nothing. Switching to her favorite photography websites, she spent a few hours looking for ideas. Googling "how to photograph a vampire" produced a number of interesting results, but none of them amounted to anything useful.

When she started reading articles written by paranormal investigators on how to capture ghosts on film with a hybrid digital/film camera, she knew she had gone beyond desperation. She scanned her studio and wondered how many boxes she'd need to pack it all up.

Evelyn was slumped at her computer when Gray arrived. He wasn't alone. Standing by his side was the Demon Queen decked out in the latest name brand fashion. She noted the woman's pale skin and how much younger and prettier she looked than her photos from the nineties.

Camilla greeted her with the mock air kisses to her cheeks. "Evelyn, my dear. So nice to see you again." Her gaze swept the messy studio. "Grayson tells me you've been resistant to holding up your end of our little bet."

Little? She glanced at Gray, but he stood behind Camilla and kept his face impassive.

"You took advantage of my inebriated state," she said.

"Oh hush." Camilla waved long fingers at her. "You would have boasted just the same had you been sober. You know I'm right."

Evelyn considered. "Probably." But not now.

"No probably about it my dear. You've been chomping at the bit for an assignment for *Vackra* magazine and I gave you one. One that you couldn't fulfill."

"I still have a day."

Camilla phished at her. "It's impossible. It's the magic and the curse of the transformation."

"Which means the task you set was unfair and renders our bet null and void."

"Nice try, my dear. But you said *anyone.*"

"Yeah. Anyone *living.*"

"Then you should have been specific. Too late now." Camilla circled the room, avoiding the mirrors. "I certainly hope you don't plan to renege on our bet."

"What if I did?" She challenged.

"Grayson," Camilla said.

He crossed the room in a nanosecond, grabbing her. His fangs pricked her neck before she could draw a breath. Then he froze. Her false bravado shattered as her attention focused on his teeth on her skin.

Camilla stepped into her view. "He drinks and you disappear. That's what happens."

"But…"

The Demon Queen waited.

"I still have a day," she said.

"You do. Grayson, release her."

He closed his mouth, sucking on her neck before setting her down. She touched her throat.

Gray's arms remained around her. "It's just a nick. I couldn't resist."

"Grayson," Camilla snapped.

He returned to his position, leaving Evelyn to stand on her unsteady feet. Her world was quickly spinning out of control. She latched onto the one inconsistency.

"Why does he obey you?" she asked. "He's older than you. Why are *you* the Demon Queen?"

Camilla shot Gray an annoyed frown. "I found him and his nest mates living in self-imposed isolation on a tiny island in the middle of the Pacific. The modern world had defeated them more effectively than vampire hunters with wooden stakes. But I had enough money to offer them a life of luxury if they changed me." She preened. "My magazine empire was the perfect hide-out for a bunch of gorgeous people."

"Except for being unable to be photographed," Evelyn said.

"It makes it difficult, but it's a small price to pay for eternal life."

Touching her throat again, she asked, "Are you going to make me one of you?"

"Oh no. Creativity is snuffed out during the transformation, but in exchange we gain heightened senses, beauty, and intelligence to name a few. I need your talent, my dear. You will be well taken care of in my nest."

"Gee, I feel *so much* better now."

"Now, now. Don't be like that. You're the one who agreed to the deal. Tomorrow I will send Grayson to fetch you. Please be ready." Camilla swept out with Gray in tow.

Evelyn remained in place. Camilla's visit was meant to intimidate her, and it worked. Yet, it gave her a renewed determination to prove the Demon Queen wrong. Or was that a new surge of desperation?

Back at her computer, she re-read the ghost articles, jotting down details about the hybrid camera. Yep, that proved it. It was desperation.

~

SUNDAY

Consuming mass quantities of coffee and sugar, Evelyn had searched for information all night. But she couldn't get passed the fact that neither the digital, video, nor the film cameras worked. Therefore, a hybrid wouldn't work either. She needed a different lens or medium. Or a miracle.

What else? She pulled out all her old photography textbooks and flipped through the pages. Listing everyone who had any knowledge of photography, she dug deep into her memory. Old jobs, ex-boyfriends, colleagues.

What else? kept repeating in her mind like a mantra.

Around noon, the answer popped into her head. She dismissed it for a split second as insane. But like Vee had said, desperate people do desperate things. Back at her computer, she looked up information on an old acquaintance, before heading to Best Buy for a new and secure cell phone.

As the phone rang on the other end, Evelyn tried to come up with an explanation that wouldn't make her sound like a lunatic.

"Hello?" a man's voice said.

"Hi, Antonio, it's Evelyn Mitchell. I know it's been ages, we used to work together at—"

"Evelyn! How the hell are you?" he asked.

"Truthfully, not good. Are you still in the business?"

"Yes, why?" His friendly tone had turned cautious.

One knot in her stomach eased. He still had access.

"I've a big problem and I need a huge favor."

Silence, then, "What do you need?"

The request came out in a rush of words. There was a long pause on the other end.

She jumped in before he could say no. "I won't tell a soul, and if you do this for me, I'll take pictures of your kids every year for the rest of their lives. I'll hire them as cover models if they want. It's vital, Antonio."

No response. But he hadn't hung up.

"I'll pay—"

"No money," he said. "If I do this for you, will you photograph my daughter's wedding in exchange?"

If it worked and she was free. "Of course."

He chuckled. "You used to scoff at wedding photographers."

"I've a new perspective on life."

"I see. And this is a onetime request?"

"Oh yes. I won't ask again. I promise."

"Okay. When do you need it?"

"Now."

"Uh. That could be a problem."

She sank to her knees. So close!

"Hold on," Antonio said. "Let me talk to my wife."

SUNDAY NIGHT

After meeting Antonio uptown, Evelyn spent the rest of the day building a hybrid camera of her own. Using her new lens and thirty-five millimeter film, she prayed it would work. She couldn't test it until Gray arrived.

As daylight faded, Evelyn raced around her studio, piling a few boxes and dumping a couple of empty suitcases next to them. At least it would look as if she had packed.

Gray appeared. He glanced at the pile, then at the rest of the studio. "You didn't get much done."

She brandished her new camera. "Very last try. One roll of film."

Suspicion creased his forehead. "How long?"

"Two hours at most. Please."

"And then?" he asked.

"If it doesn't work, I concede defeat and will go...quietly."

He harrumphed. "I doubt the quietly part. All right. Two hours."

Evelyn didn't waste time. She snapped twelve pictures and then grabbed her coat.

"Where are you going?" Gray asked.

"CVS. There's one down the street. I can't develop film and print pictures that fast. But they can. Are you coming?"

"I guess I have to." He frowned as he donned his coat, hat and sunglasses.

When they arrived at the store, Evelyn was fully prepared to bribe the tech to do hers first. But the processing department had been slow and the tech promised to have prints in an hour.

Her hands shook as she dropped the canister into his hand. God, he looked like he was twelve. Her life rested in this single roll. Ironic.

"Now what?" Gray asked.

"We wait."

"Here?"

"Yes. I'm not letting that film out of my sight."

He sighed, but didn't argue. What followed was the longest hour in her entire life. Sweat soaked her bra and her shirt clung to her. When the prints were ready, she paid for them then tore open the package.

Gray snatched it from her. "Wait until we get back to the studio."

She almost ran back. When they were inside, he handed the envelope to her. Wiping sweaty palms on her jeans, she pulled out the stack of photos.

A joy like no other spread through her. She felt as if she'd just been told she'd been misdiagnosed and she was going to live after all. Evelyn whooped and danced around a confused Gray.

With a huge grin, she handed a picture to Gray. "Here, give this to Camilla. Proof that I won the bet."

He stared at his image. It was all there. The little smirk, the black hair, the muscular arms, the whole hot package.

"Is this me?" he asked, gazing at her in shock.

"Yes. Don't you recognize yourself?"

"It's been over a century. And the transformation changes you. I've seen it happen to others, but never really thought about how I'd changed. I look..."

"Gorgeous."

He smiled. "Young. I was close to fifty when I transformed."

As Evelyn watched him, she wondered what it would be like to never see your refection in a mirror. Rather difficult, she guessed.

She gave Gray all the photos. "You only need to show

Camilla one. You can keep the rest. Will she be upset?" Fear dampened her high spirits.

"About losing?"

"Yes, and about me knowing your secrets."

"Oh yes. Camilla has never lost a bet before."

Despite her unease, Evelyn noted how he had used her name. Interesting.

Gray tapped the picture. "How did you do this? She'll want to know."

"Trade secret."

"She's not going to be happy."

"Too bad. It's business," she said with more bravado than she felt.

After Gray left, she picked up her hybrid camera. Popping open the back, she picked up a pair of tweezers, and extracted her life-saving lens.

The human eyeball had started to dry and was nicked where she had secured it inside the camera. She grabbed a glass jar filled with formaldehyde and dropped the eye in. It sank to the bottom, turning so its lifeless brown iris stared at her. Thank God Antonio still worked at the funeral home.

Despite her knowledge of photography, the solution had been simple. After all, she could *see* Gray.

MONDAY

Getting back to her routine, Evelyn felt good about the day's work. She even handled Vee's resignation with professional aplomb. However, her brush with Camilla taught her that there was more to life than photographing models. She planned to cut back her hours, travel more, and visit her mother.

Evelyn was in the process of cleaning up the mess from the week before, sorting equipment into boxes when Gray appeared in her studio.

She straighten as a sick feeling swirled in her stomach. "Are you here to—"

"No. Relax. Camilla's angry, but as long as you don't cause trouble, she'll leave you alone."

Not convinced, she waited.

"I called in that favor," he said.

"Then why are you here?"

"I brought a few friends with me."

"Friends, as in—"

"Yes."

Not good. "What do they want?"

"They want you to take their picture."

NEW GIRL

A friend of mine was putting together an anthology of tales involving spirits. She asked if I would donate a story because all the profits from the book sales would go to 826 National, a non-profit organization that helps students with their writing. I'd never written a ghost story, but thought it would be a fun challenge. Plus it was for a good cause. The story didn't turn out the way I planned; they never do, which is one of the things I love the most about writing.

NEW GIRL

I'm the new girl. Always am. Don't worry, it doesn't bother me anymore. I'm a pro. It's so easy to ignore the stares of the other students as I stand on the steps leading into the main entrance of another Dead President High School. I'm in some town in Wisconsin. Or is it Minnesota?

All I know is, it's cold and bleak here, my mother's still dead, and there's nothing to distinguish this place from any other town in the Midwest. Just like the school. It resembles the one I attended before and the dozen I attended before that. I can predict my first day here without fail.

One of the type-A cheerleaders will show me around. She'll be friendly, bubbly, and introduce me to all my teachers. And then she'll abandon me 'cause I'm not one of her "people." She will have determined my place in the high school hierarchy thirty seconds after meeting me by assessing my average—i.e., not designer—clothes, my generic backpack, and well-loved purple sneakers. She'll rate me slightly better than the freaks, geeks, and invisible types, but far below her own exalted station.

I'll try not to laugh at her, 'cause I've seen her type in every high school across the United States. There's nothing special about her or anyone in this place. Millions just like them are forming the same cliques, dealing with the same problems, and all believing they're special.

In fact, nothing will surprise me today. The jocks, the goths, and the teachers will meet my low expectations. The faces and names might be different, but that's it. I'll attend my classes amid whispered speculation, rude stares, and I'll see that hopeful gleam in a few girls' gazes. You know the type—the fringers who don't have any friends. They'll see the new girl as a potential new BFF.

I'll ignore them. It's kinder this way, trust me. If we become BFFs, I'll only break their hearts when I leave to attend the next Dead President School or Dead Humanitarian School. 'Cause I will leave. That's a guarantee.

Maybe not for a month or two, but my dad will find another job that will be too good to pass up, and off we'll go.

So I know you're wondering why I still bother with school. I'm sixteen and could just quit. But, you see, attending college is my goal. Why? 'Cause college means I get to stay put for four whole years! When I'm in college, I won't be dragged from place to place, and I can make a friend without worry.

And as I predicted, my day plays out like it has too many times to count. At the end of the first day, I retreat to the library. Sorry, I guess I should say the Learning Resource Center, or the Media Center, or the IMC. Doesn't matter what it's called, it's my place to study and hang out until my dad picks me up.

I'd rather be here than in some hotel room. Wouldn't you? I find a spot that's hidden and quiet and make it my temporary home.

Except this time, my spot isn't quite as hidden as I thought.

"Hey, you're the new girl, aren't you?"

I stare at the "genius," deciding between a sarcastic reply or cold silence to drive him away. He looks like a fringer, but he could be one of the invissies. I opt for silence, but he doesn't get the hint.

"I'm Josh Martin." He plops in the chair on the opposite side of the table. He points to my open textbook. "I have Algebra Two with Mr. Kindt."

When I don't respond, he leans forward and says, "So what do you think about our school?"

I consider my options. What will drive him away the fastest? "Did you know there are forty-seven other high schools with the same name across the US?"

"Really? Wow. How do you know that?"

I suppress a groan and shrug. "Internet."

"Cool." He smiles at me.

Josh has freckles, a few pimples, and grayish green eyes. His shaggy brown hair curls at the ends. He's wearing generic jeans, sneakers, a gray hoodie, and an L.L. Bean backpack. At least he doesn't have his initials stitched on it—that's so lame.

Before I can tell him to get lost, he asks my most hated question, "So where are you from?"

I refuse to answer. Always will. Instead, I say, "Look, John—"

"Josh."

"I have lots of work to catch up on."

But he's sixteen and male. Which means he's denser than a white dwarf star and unable to pick up on subtle hints. I try a more direct brush off. "Jack—"

"Josh."

"Go away. Shoo!" I wave my hand.

But the idiot just gives me a goofy grin. He pulls out his Algebra Two textbook, flips the pages, and works on the assigned problems.

Whatever. I ignore him and concentrate on my own work. But he can't keep quiet.

"Number five is tricky," he says.

"What did you get for number nine?"

"Avoid the taco salad. It's poison. But make sure you try the school's French fries," he says.

I don't answer, but that doesn't seem to matter to him. He gossips about the other students despite the fact I have zero interest.

"Uh, Jake—"

"Josh."

"Don't you have to go home?" I ask.

A brief flash of pain creases his face before he shrugs. "Not really."

"Oh."

At five o'clock the librarian kicks us out, and Josh disappears. Typical. When my father arrives, he knows better than to ask about my day. We eat at a local diner and return to our hotel room. I sit by the window reading my book and watching traffic as my dad laughs at one of those ridiculous reality TV shows. Reality is *not* entertainment.

You'd think Josh would ignore me after my very rude behavior, but you'd be wrong. He shows up in the library after school again.

I don't say a word or encourage him in any way as I do my homework. His stream of chatter seems endless.

"Michael Klein asked Jenna to the prom, and she said no," he says.

"Do you know Mr. Hedge can do fifty one-arm pushups? That's awesome for an old dude."

"Death Kombat Ten is coming out this Friday. And I'm gonna have the whole Prez's day weekend to play it. Three days of heaven. I can't wait."

I look up at this last comment. "Uh, Joe—"

"Josh."

"President's Day was two weekends ago. Today's February 28."

"Oh." He stares at me for a few uncomfortable seconds. "My friend Matt's addicted to video games. You're sitting in his favorite seat. He says it's the only place where the librarian can't see you."

A rough edge in his voice catches my interest. And despite my promise not to encourage him, I ask, "Matt? What's his last name?"

"James."

"Is he in any of my classes?"

"He used to be the captain of the swim team, and it bugged him I never learned how to swim."

He didn't answer my question. "Did he quit the team?"

Josh fiddles with his pencil. "No."

"Did he get cut?"

"Oh, no. He made the state finals last year." He notices my confusion. "He just doesn't swim anymore."

"Why not?"

"There was an...incident." Josh looks down at his homework. "What did you get for number ten?"

Matt was probably caught doing 'roids or drugs. And since I've learned it's best to stay uninvolved, I flip my Algebra folder open.

After a few weeks in town, my father rents an apartment with a loft. Now before you get too excited, he's done this a few times in the past, and it doesn't mean anything. It's not a sign that he might want to stay here for more than a couple months. Not at all.

"Look, sweetie," he says, raising the blinds in my "new" room, which is basically the loft. "You have a view of the river. I know how much you love a view."

I do. Tight quarters don't seem so bad with a decent view. And I'm surprised by how much I like the loft and having my very own level. I'm missing it already.

~

Despite my best efforts Josh doesn't give up, so I now have a friend. He manages to pry a few personal details from me. Only child. Mother dead. Father unable to stay put.

In the library after school, I warn him. "Look, Jim—"

"Josh."

"I won't be here long. And when I leave, I'm not going to do the whole text/Facebook thing. I know how it goes. Lots of texts at first, and then more and more time will pass between replies until we're apologizing for not getting back to each other sooner, and then the messages will stop all together. Not worth the effort."

"Cold turkey, huh?"

"Yep."

"Do I get a warning, or will you just not show up one day?" he asks.

"You'll get a couple days notice. That's all I get." I try to keep the bitterness from my voice.

Josh looks glum and twirls his pen on the table. "Better than no notice. It sucks when you don't get a chance to say good-bye."

The librarian rounds the bookcase. Her annoyance causes the wrinkles on her face to multiply. Considering she's at least a hundred years old, I didn't think she had room for more lines. Go figure.

"Cell phones are not allowed in the Media Center, miss. Please turn yours off or leave." She stabs a gnarled finger at the exit.

I spread my hands wide, showing that they're empty. "I don't—"

"Don't get smart with me, young lady. I might be old, but I know all about those ear things."

But she can see my ears, because my hair is pulled into a ponytail. It's straight and brown, so there's not much else I can do with it. I turn so she can see my other ear.

She squints and huffs. "I heard you back here talking so don't play cute with me."

She's lost her mind. I glance at Josh. But he's gone. Stifling a laugh at his cowardice, I apologize to her. She leaves muttering about "kids these days." Josh doesn't come back. Chicken.

"So why won't your father stay in one place?" Josh asks.

We're at our table in the library, doing homework. I consider ignoring the question—he's getting better at reading my moods and won't press the issue. But I'm curious to see what his reaction will be. Especially since I've never shared my theories with anyone.

"I think he's running away from grief," I say, keeping my

voice low so the librarian doesn't accuse me of using my cell phone again.

Josh sits a little straighter in his chair. "Really?"

"Our nomadic existence started right after my mother died and I recovered from my head injuries. I think the...excitement of moving, meeting new people, and starting a new job keeps him from thinking about my mom. But after the newness wears off, he has nothing to distract him and so...we move again."

"Wow. That sucks for you. Running from grief..." He pulls a sketchpad from his backpack. The cover is almost torn off, and the metal spine has seen better days.

"I didn't know you liked to draw," I say 'cause this isn't what I expected.

"I don't. I doodle." He sketches two figures. One looks like a zombie-wolf hybrid that you'd see in a manga comic book. It's chasing the other who appears to be a normal guy.

"Who's that?" I ask, pointing to the monster.

"It's Grief."

I lean back. He's lost his mind.

"Like a personification," he says. He gives me his goofy grin. "I learned that in Comm Arts last week. A personification is...like Death. He's always a skeleton wearing a hood and black robe, carrying a scythe. Grief is his...younger brother. What weapon do you think he'd carry?" Josh looks up. "A knife?"

He sees the answer in my expression.

"Dumb question," he acknowledges. "Of course he'd have a knife. 'Cause Grief always goes right for the heart. One thrust and you're done." He gives Grief a long, wicked-looking dagger.

Josh has had some personal experience with grief. My mom's been gone two years, and when I think about her, it's like Josh says, a cold steel blade stabbing right through to my backbone. But I don't want to commiserate with him or anyone.

So I quickly backpedal. "The whole running-from-grief thing is probably nonsense. I'm sixteen. What do I know?"

My joke falls flat. There's a strange shine in his eyes. "A lot can happen in sixteen years. For some people, it's all they get."

Oh crap. Is he talking about his ex-swimmer friend Matt? Maybe the "incident" wasn't 'roids, but something more dire. I decide to stick with the original topic. "Well, I learned about people avoiding their feelings from the Internet. My dad fit the profile for someone in denial. But that's just some website. It's probably wrong."

"The Internet knows everything," Josh says with a reverence only a sixteen-year-old boy could have. "Humanity is so screwed when the Internet becomes self-aware. You do know that, don't you?"

He sketches another mutation that's half human and half computer with big pointy teeth.

"You do know you're insane, don't you?" I ask.

"Oh yeah." He gives me a sad smile. "My friend Matt used to tell me that all the time. He also called me a genius." Full-out sorrow erases his smile. "Too bad I can't talk to him anymore."

Awkward. Very awkward. I don't want to know anything about Josh's personal life. That makes it harder when I leave. So instead, I say, "If you're such a genius, then why are you failing Algebra Two?"

"Albert Einstein had trouble in school."

"You're no Albert Einstein. At least, not yet. You need bushier hair."

"Tell that to my mom. She's always nagging me to get it cut."

With that, we return to normal.

The next day, he asks, "Why don't you tell your dad how much you hate moving?"

"He knows how much I hate it. Doesn't matter."

"How does he know? Did you do the girlie thing?"

"What girlie thing?" I demand.

"You know. The silent treatment. Pouting. My mom does it all the time. Well, at least that's what my sister says she does."

"No. I'm not like that."

"Then how does he know? We guys can be pretty dense sometimes."

"I already know *that*, Jeff—"

"Josh." He grins.

I think back to all our moves and really can't recall telling my father how unhappy I am. We also never talk about Mom. Am I running from grief too?

That night during dinner, I tell my dad about Josh. Since I never talk about school, he's surprised. But he's smart enough not to make a big deal about it or question me too much.

"Why don't you invite him over to watch a movie or something?" Dad asks. "We'll order pizza and wings."

"I can't."

Dad waits. His bushy eyebrows hover at the midpoint of his large forehead. Poor guy has only a few hairs doggedly clinging to his scalp. The silence goes on a little too long. I didn't realize how hard this would be.

"I can't be friends with Josh," I say. "'Cause, you know." I wave a hand.

"No, I don't know."

He's denser than Josh, and I didn't think that was possible. I huff. "'Cause we'll be moving in a couple months. No sense making friends. It's pointless."

"You can always email."

"And how many of *your* friends do you email?" I ask.

The answer is in his haunted gaze. Communicating with friends reminds him too much of Mom.

"As I said, pointless. Unless..."

He focuses on me.

"Unless we stay. I really like this place and the school. And I really...hate moving." There I said it!

"We'll stay...for a little while at least." He bustles around the kitchen, cleaning up the dinner dishes.

"How long?" I rub my temples.

Dad won't say.

The next day, I wake up with one of my migraines. Since the accident, I get them from time to time. Stress-related, or so the doctors claimed. They might not be too far off—talking to my dad is always stressful.

After downing mass quantities of caffeine and aspirin that will dull the pain from OMG-I'm-ready-to-spew bad to just plain rotten, I head to school. It's better than hanging out in our lonely apartment all day.

When classes are over, I round the bookcases at the library and say, "Well, I took your advice—"

I stop. Josh isn't there. Some blond-haired guy is sitting in my seat.

"Took my advice?" he asks.

He's wearing a blue swim team hoodie, black jeans, and high tops. A jock. So what's he doing here? Is he Josh's friend?

"Sorry, I thought you were someone else."

He gives me the once over. His blue eyes are as pale as the winter sky. "Are you the new girl?"

"No, I'm the *newer* girl. The new girl is now the old girl."

Completely missing my sarcasm, he smiles and pushes the chair across from him out with his foot. "Have a seat."

"That's Josh's seat." Yes, I know it's a stupid thing to say.

His humor is gone in an instant. He surges to his feet. Anger pulses off him as he stares at me. I shrink back. He's tall, and the only other person in the library is the hundred-year-old librarian.

"You're one sick girl." He hefts his backpack and strides away.

I watch him go. That was...odd.

Josh doesn't show up the next couple of days. I'm not worried. I never see him during the day. Well, I don't usually look for him. I was just...concerned. I pay more attention to the school gossip than I usually do, hoping to hear if Josh is sick or something. But talk about an upcoming swim meet fills the halls, and how losing Matt really hurt the team.

When I spot Josh at his usual seat in the library, I pause a moment in relief before joining him. He's been gone three days.

"Hey, where've you been?" I ask.

"Did you miss me?"

"No. I enjoyed the quiet."

"Yeah, right. You were bored."

Pretty much, but I'm not gonna admit it. "Oh, not at all. Some jock was here. He asked me to the prom."

Josh laughs. "Yeah, right."

"He was sitting in my seat. Maybe it was your friend Matt?"

His humor disappears. "No. Matt doesn't come around here anymore."

I think back to Josh's earlier comments—the ones I paid attention to anyway. "Why not? Isn't Matt's your friend?"

"He was."

"Why aren't you friends anymore?"

"I did something...really stupid." Josh doodles on a clean page of his sketchbook. The jagged lines resemble waves.

"Does it have to do with the incident with the swim team?"

"Something like that," he mutters.

I know what I said about not getting involved, but I like Josh. "Is there some way you can apologize? If you've been good friends, I'm sure he'll forgive you."

"No. I ruined...everything." He shakes his head. "It's not possible." His pencil point breaks off. "Crap." He pulls out a pencil sharpener.

"What did you ruin?"

Concentrating on his pencil, he ignores me. I shrug and pretend to work on my homework as I listen to the crunch-squeal of the sharpener. The smell of pencil shavings reminds me of my childhood. Getting ready for my very first day of school, I filled my pencil box and tucked my favorite book into my backpack. I love books. My mother used to read to me when I was little. All my childhood books are packed in a box that we lug from place to place. I never have time to unpack them.

As if Josh can read my mind, he asks, "Did you tell your dad that you hate moving?"

"Yeah."

He waits.

"Didn't change anything."

"Did you say it like a dozen times?"

"No, why?"

He rolls his eyes. "It takes at least that long for stuff to sink in. Even when my mom makes me repeat back to her what she just said, I've no idea what she wanted me to do."

"My dad was paying attention."

Josh flips to the page where the mutant zombie/wolfman is chasing my dad. "Did you explain your theory?"

"No. He's not gonna listen to me and my Internet diagnosis."

"How about talking to the school counselor? I hear she's pretty good, and she can—"

"Not gonna happen."

"Then you'll be moving soon. And when you're in your *new* school, talking to another nobody, you'll be sad that you didn't listen to my advice."

"I'll make sure to note it in my agenda that day." I pretend to write. "Jay. Was. Right."

"Josh." He smiles. "You're gonna run out of *J* names pretty soon."

"Not gonna happen."

The boxes show up after I've been at Dead President High School for three months. They're scattered around the living room. Some are half full. Others packed and piled. I stand in the doorway half expecting to see Josh's mutant zombie/wolfman hiding behind the pile, waiting to ambush my father.

Dad strolls from his bedroom carrying two more packed boxes. He pauses when he sees me, but drops them onto the floor before he starts in with his lame excuses.

"...better opportunity for advancement...benefits...exciting challenge...almost double the salary..."

"I don't want to move," I say.

"Sweetie, this job—"

"Sounds like the one you have now. I like it here. Can't we stay until I graduate high school? Please?"

A queasy expression creases his face. He glances at the pile of boxes and tugs on his shirt. "No, sorry sweetie, but we have to go. We can't stay."

"You can't stay, but I can." I rush to explain. "With the next job, you can afford to rent this place and your next...whatever. I'll finish high school and then hang out with you the summer before I go to college. I can even get a part-time job!"

So many possibilities! I can get a library card and join a school club or team. My excitement rises until I see my dad twisting the bottom of his shirt as he stares at me in panic.

"You can't stay here all alone," he says

"I'll be seventeen soon. And you know I'm responsible."

"But...but...you'll be *all alone*."

Which means, *he'll* be all alone, and the answer is *no*. I swallow the lump of emotions lodged in my throat. College. I console myself with the knowledge that I can do all those fun things when I get to college.

"When are we leaving?" I press my fingertips into my temples, hoping to stop the migraine from building.

"Friday morning."

Three days to pack. Josh's words, *it sucks when you don't get a chance to say good-bye*, sound in my mind. At least, I'll be able to tell Josh.

∼

Except the next day my migraine and Matt are back, and Josh is nowhere. I search the library just to be sure. Nope. Matt is sitting in my seat, but he's staring at the floor and playing with a blue and yellow scarf—the school's colors—pulling it through the fingers of his left hand.

I retreat to another table and take out my homework. I'm worried Josh won't show up before I leave. Then I won't get a chance to say good-bye. I realize I don't even have his cell number, home phone, or an address. What's the point in getting all those when you have no intention of using them?

"Hey, New Girl," Matt says. He's standing next to my table. "Sorry I yelled at you last week. When I heard Josh's name..."

"That's okay." What else could I say?

"Yeah, well..." He looks around. No one's here except the ancient librarian. "Lots of kids are named Josh." He shrugs. "I shouldn't have gotten mad."

"That's okay." Yep, I'm the queen of conversation.

"I should have known better. I mean, you're like a ghost around here. You wouldn't know Josh Martin."

"I'm a ghost?" It's all I can manage. I'd like to see you do better.

"You don't talk to anybody. Hiding in the library, talking on your cell phone. Friends from your last school, right?"

Too surprised to do anything else, I nod.

"You should try and make friends here," he says.

"I have a friend, and I do know Josh Martin. You used to be good friends. Right? But now you're mad at him."

His mood changes in an instant. "I could never be mad at Josh. You're crazy." He storms off.

Confused is an understatement.

But Matt's comments won't disappear, and when I combine them with Josh's, a scary thought forms in my mind. A shudder rips through me, sending my migraine to stratospheric levels of pain. I rest my head in my arms. Matt is right. I'm crazy.

The next day, I ask a couple of fringer girls about what happened between Josh and Matt.

They give me these shocked looks.

"Something about the swim team?" I prod.

"You've been here three months and don't know? How lame is that?" the redhead with five nose piercings asks.

"Did you even *see* the memorials?" the other girl demands.

Fear curls inside my stomach. "Uh, no."

Redhead rolls her eyes. "You want to know what happened between them? A fall through the ice and death happened over Prez's Day weekend last year. Death tends to end a friendship *permanently*. Come on, Sara." She pulls her friend away.

I've been talking to a dead guy. *Yikes* isn't a strong enough word to describe how I feel. And I know what you're thinking. It's impossible. Yeah, well, I'm not going to worry about it right now. If I'm crazy, they'll put me away, and I won't have to move. Win-win.

My father isn't the only one running from grief. Josh has been running, too. That's why Josh liked talking to me—'cause I didn't know about Matt.

After school, Josh is once again missing in action. And I'm frantic. Which is funny, considering I didn't want to get involved.

But I have one day of school left, and I need to say good-bye to Josh. Yes, *need* to. For all my disdain about nobody being special, Josh is special.

He should know Matt isn't mad at him. Maybe then he won't pretend his friend is still alive. I log onto the library's computer to find Josh's address. Google, the search engine of last resort.

~

"Most of your stuff is packed, but you'll need to finish up tonight, so we can get an early start in the morning," my dad says when we get home.

"Tomorrow? But what about school?"

"I'll call them in the morning."

"No," I tell my father. "Not tomorrow, I need—"

"I'm not asking. We're leaving. Go pack." His tone borders on anger.

My own fury rises. I see red. It's way more than a visual thing. Although everything appears to have a reddish tint, my blood boils, and an intense surge of energy consumes me as well.

I yell and call him a coward for running from grief. "Eventually, Dad, it will catch up to you. By then, I'll be gone, and you'll be all *alone*. No friends. No family. Nobody!" I throw my backpack down and rush out the door.

Sprinting through the streets, I have no idea where I'm going. I ignore the dull throb in my head, hoping it won't explode into another migraine. Eventually I end up walking along the river. Chunks of ice tumble in the quickly moving current. The edges of the river are slushy. Our neighbor last year warned me not to trust a frozen river, even if the crust appeared to be sturdy. I was polite enough not to tell her that every northern Midwestern school I've attended made sure students are aware of the dangers of thin ice.

Up ahead, a white cross stands out against the surrounding gray twilight. My insides clench as I draw close. Plastic flowers, stuffed animals, and half-burnt candles cluster around the base of the cross. I glance at the name carved into the wood. A memorial for—

"Hey, New Girl."

I yell and jerk in surprise. Matt is standing behind me. His hands are tucked into the pockets of his hoodie.

"Sorry," he says. "I thought you heard me."

Too scattered to reply, I just gape at him.

Matt squats next to the memorial, straightens a couple teddy bears, and fixes a bouquet of flowers. "Why did you think I'd be mad at Josh?"

The big block letters on the cross consume my vision as black and white spots swarm in front of me.

"Are you all right?" Matt grabs my arm as I sway. "You better sit down."

My legs fold under me. I suck in deep breaths, hoping I don't pass out.

Josh's name, not Matt's marks the cross.

I've been talking to the wrong dead guy.

"You're an odd chic...girl," he says, settling next to me. We're near the edge of the steep bank.

He gazes at the river. "I've been thinking about what you said. And, you're right. I'm pissed at Josh. He knew better than to fool around on the ice. And he should have learned to swim." Matt picks up a rock and flings it into the water below us.

I regain my composure. "It wouldn't have mattered. It would have been too cold to swim. You only have—"

"That's bull. I get hot when I swim. I should have—" He fires another rock as if he can punish the water for taking Josh's life. "I should have jumped in after him."

"But you would have—"

"No, I wouldn't. I'm the fastest swimmer in the state. I could have pulled him out in seconds." He launches a few more rocks. "Instead I called 911, like an idiot, flagged down help." Sighing, he looks at me. "And why am I telling *you* all this?"

"'Cause I'm the new girl?"

He huffs in amusement before standing up. Wiping the dirt off his butt, he offers me a hand. "My mom will freak if I'm not home soon."

If Matt doesn't forgive Josh, Josh will be miserable and all alone when I leave.

"Wait," I say, stopping him before he walks away. "Josh is upset that you're mad at him. I know. You think I'm insane, but I've been hanging out with Josh—or rather his ghost in the library these last three months."

"No, you're beyond insane. You're a grade-A sicko." He turns.

"Then how do I know Josh liked to draw manga figures and play Death Kombat?"

He pauses. "Someone at school told you."

"Who? I haven't talked to anyone but you and Josh. You said it yourself."

"You're lying."

"Why would I lie? I'm leaving tomorrow to I-don't-even-know-where."

He spins back to me. "Then why do you care?"

"'Cause in the last two years, I haven't met anyone I've wanted to say good-bye to. And he won't come back until you're not mad at him."

"Stay away from me." He growls before striding away.

But I won't give up. I'm not going to slink back to the apartment to finish packing and leave without saying goodbye. Not this time. I'm done running from grief.

I race after Matt and grab his wrist. "Just listen, please."

"Get lost!" He breaks my grip with ease and pushes me away. Hard.

My feet slip on a patch of ice as I move to chase after him, throwing me off-balance. How did I get so close to the edge? I pinwheel my arms, but the next thing I know I'm falling, and waves rush to greet me. The shock of the impact steals my breath.

I flounder before I remember I know how to swim. Except the icy water saps my strength. My legs turn numb as the river tosses me around. Panic sets in. I thrash, but with frozen limbs, it's too hard to swim. My soaked clothes pull me down.

"Hey, New Girl," a voice calls over the drum of the river.

Matt is cutting through the waves as if he's Michael Phelps. "Come on, move," he orders, grabbing my arm.

I make a few weak attempts.

"You going to give up, New Girl? Can't hack it, can you? You're beyond lame!"

I know *exactly* what he's doing. But it works. Anger fuels my efforts, and I kick to keep our heads above water.

The current drags us along as if we're a couple of bath toys. Matt holds me tightly, and we try to swim for shore. But the river is stronger. We're in trouble. My fear is dulled by the bone-aching numbness. All I want to do is give up and go to sleep.

A yell cuts through my icy stupor. People on the bank are waving and calling to us. A rope flies through the air. Matt catches it, but when the men on the bank pull, it slips from his hand.

Another attempt fails. But on the third throw, we both catch it. Clinging to the rope, we're fished from the river and wrapped in blankets by our rescuers. Shivers take control of my muscles. I plop onto the ground so I don't fall down.

Matt pushes through the press of people. He kneels next to me with an alarmed expression. "Did I—"

"No...I slipped." My teeth chatter. "You...c-couldn't...have saved him."

A wild look shines in his eyes.

"Water...c-colder last year. Josh...c-couldn't swim. I *can*."

A smile tugs at his lips. "You call *that* swimming?"

"I'm out...of practice."

"You. Are. Insane."

You know what happens next. Police, ambulance, hospital, and my father's panicked face as he barges into the ER. Questions, questions, and more questions. I make sure everyone knows Matt saved my life. I stay overnight in the hospital and spend the next day at home. The upside to all this is my dad stops packing. The downside is he keeps asking me questions about the swim that wasn't.

And a strange thing happens. We stay. My dad keeps his current job. The only annoying thing is we have weekly sessions with the school counselor. Boring.

The rest of the week, I go to the library, but Josh hasn't returned. It's quiet and lonely until Matt's swim practice is over. Then he shows up smelling of shampoo and chlorine. We attempt to do our homework, but always end up talking or going to the coffee shop down the street instead.

Two weeks later, I head toward my spot in the library and stop. Josh is there. I'm not sure if I should be scared or glad to see him. "Hey Jared—"

He laughs. "Josh."

"So where ya been?" I ask.

"Around."

I sit and take out my Algebra Two textbook. Just because he's dead doesn't mean we can't hang out. "How did you do in last week's chapter test?"

"An epic failure. You?"

"Not bad."

He looks at me. "So I guess you took my advice," he says. "You're no longer the new girl."

"Yeah. Thanks, Joel."

"Josh." Grinning, he pulls his sketchbook from his backpack and rips out a page. Josh pushes the sheet across the table toward me as if it's a huge effort. When he lets go, a high-pitched pop sounds. "For you."

I pick it up. It's a drawling of Grief lying on the ground with a dagger through its heart. Standing over it is a girl with her fist raised in triumph. I meet his gaze.

"Grief's not dead," he says. "But round one goes to you."

"What about you and Matt?" I ask.

"We're good. Thanks for your help."

I shrug. "That's what friends do, right?"

"Right. And you'll soon have lots of friends. Matt knows everybody." He glances at my Algebra textbook. "So what did you get for number three?"

A couple things click together and I realized that Josh isn't hanging around to copy my homework. I swallow, missing him already.

"Do your own work, Josh."

"You called me Josh!"

"So?"

"You know what that means, don't you?"

"That you don't have to worry about Algebra Two anymore?"

"Yeah, and it's time for me to say good-bye."

"Thanks for the picture and for...everything." Tears threaten to spill.

"That's what friends do, right?

"Right."

"Good-bye, Emma."

"Bye, Josh."

NIGHT VISION

At the time I wrote this story, my fantasy novels were selling well and, I was "hot." Which meant I was getting a bunch of anthology invites. One of those was for The Mammoth Book of Paranormal Romance. My novels all have romantic sub-plots, but not much romance overall. The challenge was to incorporate more romance. The idea for Night Vision came from one of my readers who has a rare disease called Erythropoietic Protoporphyria or EEP for short. Those with EEP have to avoid all light because it kills their red blood cells. Living in the dark has to be extremely difficult. As I contemplated the logistics of their lives, my writer's imagination kicked in. As with all my stories, the initial idea twisted and changed as I wrote. I also pulled from my biker days, when I used to go off-roading, riding a three-wheeled All Terrain Vehicle (ATV) with my ex-boyfriend, who rode a Honda 250X dirt bike. Unlike, Sophia, I needed a headlight.

NIGHT VISION

Sophia started the Honda 250X dirt bike. The roar of the engine cut through the quiet darkness. *A perfect September night for a ride*, she thought. The air smelled of living green. No moon. No wind.

She swung on her backpack, strapped on her helmet, and checked her safety gear before pulling on a pair of padded leather gloves. She straddled the bike.

Where too? Sophia glanced at the surrounding forest. She lived near the Great Smoky Mountains in North Carolina. Basically, the middle of nowhere with not a soul around for miles. Which suited her just fine. No neighbors. No annoying questions. No light.

She decided to ride to Standing Indiana Mountain near Georgia's northern border. It had been a couple months since she last visited. The old glider landing strip near the peak would be a nice place for a midnight snack.

The bike jumped to life as she feathered the clutch. Following the narrow trails, she rode hard. Low-hanging branches smacked against her chest protector. She ducked thicker limbs, navigated around trunks, splashed through streams and motored up inclines. Her heart raced with pure adrenaline as the bike chewed up the miles.

Sailing over the last mound, Sophia whooped in mid-air. The bike landed with a solid thud. She stopped at the edge of the airstrip and removed her helmet and backpack.

It took her a moment to realize the long grass that had grown wild on the strip had been cut to stubble. Tire tracks grooved the ground. The glider port was no longer abandoned, but no aircraft was in sight.

Curious to see if the farmhouse nearby was also in use, Sophia hiked to the dilapidated two-story building. Sure enough, light gleamed from the windows despite the late hour. A blue Ford F150 pickup with Virginia license plates rested in the weed-choked driveway.

Not a weekender—Virginia was too far. Perhaps the new owners were glider pilots.

The brightness from the house burned her eyes. She averted her gaze and headed to her bike. But the sound of tires crunching over stones enticed her back. Crouching nearby, she vowed to leave as soon as she spotted the car's owner. After all, they were technically neighbors.

Face it, Sophia, this is the first bit of excitement you've had since Dad died.

A Land Rover bounced and bumped along the dirt...well, calling it a road would be an exaggeration. Clouds of dust followed in its wake. Keeping out of the headlight's beam, Sophia watched as the Land Rover stopped in front of the house with a squeal.

Two men stepped from the vehicle. A tank-sized, muscular man pounded on the front door. "Hey Rick, come out. We caught a big fish."

The driver unlocked the back gate of the Rover. The door swung wide and Rick came out of the house to join his friends.

"Who the hell is that?" Rick demanded.

"He's a fed, man," the Tank said. "Special Agent Mitchell Wolfe."

An icy chill crawled up Sophia's spine. The cliché about curiosity and dead cats churned in her mind.

"Shit. How much does he know?" Rick asked.

"He knows we've been collecting treasures, but he doesn't know the pick up location," the driver said.

"Shit. What did you bring him here for?"

"He hasn't reported in yet. We didn't know what to do." Keys jangled as the driver gestured.

"How did you know he didn't talk to the feds?"

"We threatened to harm *his* treasure. He blabbed like a baby."

"Did you get it?"

"Yep." The big man yanked a long mesh bag from the back seat of the Land Rover.

Rick jerked a thumb toward the house. "Inside. Wake Glenn. We're gonna need him." A resigned annoyance colored his tone.

While living in the middle of nowhere had its benefits, it also had its drawbacks. No wireless signals. No authorities within fifty miles.

The two men discussed delivery times as they waited for Glenn. Sophia heard "four a.m." and "three treasures" before Glenn slunk from the house.

"This better be good," Glenn said.

"We have a problem," Rick explained.

"No problem." Glenn gestured. "We're in the middle of bloody nowhere. Nobody'll find him." He pulled a gun from behind his back and aimed.

Sophia jumped to her feet. Ready to...what? Scream?

Rick shoved Glenn's arm down. "Not in the Rover, you idiot. Blood evidence stays behind even after you clean up. Don't you watch CSI?"

Glenn shrugged. "Whatever."

"Go ten miles out and shoot him in the woods. Leave him for the cougars. Ed, you drive."

The driver closed the back. He slid behind the wheel. Glenn hopped in beside him.

Watching the Land Rover U-turn, Sophia's thoughts raced. There was no doubt she had to help, but Glenn was armed. She had a tool kit, but no weapons. Tonight had been a fun ride, not a hunting trip.

She had her Honda. The two hundred and fifty cubic centimeter engine would keep up with the vehicle, and she had her...other talent if desperate. Running to her bike, she jammed her helmet on, and mounted.

The beams of light from the Rover sliced the darkness, making it easy for Sophia to follow. Since she didn't need a headlight, the men should be unaware of her presence.

After bouncing and crashing along the tight trail for thirty minutes, the vehicle swung to the side, illuminating a thick patch of underbrush.

Sophia silenced her bike and coasted to a stop about a hundred feet from the Rover. Propping the bike, she crept closer. The men stepped from the vehicle, leaving the engine running.

"Perfect spot," Glenn said. "He's starting to wake. Take him out to those briars." He checked his weapon.

Ed pulled the captive out. The man staggered. Ed steadied him. The agent's wrists were handcuffed behind him. Cuts lined his face and a purple bruise covered his swollen right eye.

He looked groggy, but when Glenn flashed his gun, he snapped awake.

"Easy there, Mitch," Ed said. "We're just going to leave you here to find your own way home."

"Right," Mitch's voice rasped with sarcasm.

"Come on." Ed dragged him toward the briar patch.

With her heart doing gymnastics in her chest, Sophia bent the light around her, rendering herself invisible to the men. She reached the vehicle and crawled toward the front tire, keeping her gaze on the men and away from the burning brightness. When the two men stepped into the Rover's headlights, they disappeared from her vision.

One chance. Sophia opened the driver's side door and switched the headlights off, plunging the three men into total darkness. Points scored for middle of nowhere.

Mitch used the sudden blackout to kick the side of Ed's knee. Ed crumbled to the ground in pain.

"Shoot him," Ed said.

"I can't see, you idiot!" Glenn shouted. He fumbled for the Rover.

The agent ducked and ran, but tripped and crashed. Without light to bend, Sophia became visible. She darted after the agent. He regained his feet as she caught up to him.

"I can help you," she whispered.

He jerked in surprise, but thankfully stayed quiet.

"Follow me. I have excellent night vision." She put a hand on his arm and guided him toward her bike. "Hurry."

They reached the bike as the Rover's headlights lit up the area. Silently thanking Honda for electric starters, she thumbed the switch.

"Over there!" Ed yelled. "What the hell?"

A gun fired.

"Jump on," she ordered. Panic threatened to scatter her senses, but she bit her lip.

The bike sank as Mitch's weight compressed the suspension. He wouldn't be able to hold on to her with his hands cuffed behind him.

Another gunshot cracked through the air. Mitch grunted.

"Lean on me." She put the bike in gear, taking off down the road and away from the Rover. Mitch's stomach and chest pressed against her back.

Behind her, doors slammed and tires spun on gravel.

"They're chasing us," Mitch said. His voice was strident with urgency.

Great. Her heart dropped to her stomach to do a floor routine. Sophia reviewed her options. With his hands bound, she couldn't ride off-road with him. The Rover's headlights behind her caused sections of the road to disappear from her sight, making it difficult to navigate. She could bend the light around the bike, but if the headlights aimed directly at them, they would be suddenly visible.

She maneuvered around a turn. Mitch leaned with her. *He's been on a bike before.* Perhaps she could cut through the mountains and lose the Rover. She searched for an appropriate path.

When she spotted a tight trail, she turned so Mitch could hear her. "I'm going off-road. Match my movements."

"Jesus Lady, you don't even have a headlight."

"Would you rather stay?"

"No."

Slowing to half speed because of her passenger, she struggled to find a path that wouldn't unseat him. Curses, yells and a few more gunshots sounded. She concentrated on riding, pouring every ounce of energy into it. Time blurred.

"We lost them," Mitch said, breaking her concentration.

With her arms shaking from fatigue, she stopped. Mitch dismounted and dropped to the ground.

"That was close," he said. "You saved my life. Where the hell did you come from?"

She removed her helmet. Her long ponytail snagged in the strap. Sweat stung her eyes and soaked her shirt under the chest protector. "I was riding and saw you needed help."

"In the middle of the night *without* a headlight?" His tone implied disbelief. "It's pitch black out here."

"I told you I have good night vision. Besides, I grew up around here. I know these hills like a bat knows its cave."

"What's your name—Bat Woman?"

"No. Wonder Woman. My invisible plane is in for repairs so I had to use my super bike."

His shoulders sagged. "Sorry. It's been a hell of a day. I'm Mitch Wolfe—a federal agent, and I'm going to need more of your help."

"Sophia Daniels. I'll do what I can."

"First, I need to get these cuffs off."

"My tool kit—"

"I have a key in the..." he cringed, "...waistband of my underwear."

She couldn't suppress a chuckle. "Are they special spy underwear?"

"Yep. They're bulletproof, too. A man can't be too cautious when it comes to personal safety." He laughed with a deep, rich rumble that rolled right through her. "It's a master handcuff key. It's along my left side." He re-gained his feet.

His gray T-shirt was ripped and stained with blood. Too much blood. She gasped. "You've been shot."

"I felt a nick."

She pulled his shirt up. A deep gash oozed near his ribs on

the left, cutting across the ripple of muscles along his abdomen. "It's more of a slice. You're going to need sutures."

"Sutures? Don't tell me my nocturnal rescuer is also a doctor because that would be another hell of a coincidence."

"My father was a paramedic. I have supplies—"

"Later. Key first."

Sophia tried pulling the waistband up past his jeans.

"You need to unbutton the pants," he said in a matter-of-fact tone.

She hesitated before fumbling at the button. *Wonderful, Sophia,* she chided. *You're coordinated enough to jump a dirt bike over Ranger's Gap, but you can't undo one button.* An eternity later, she ripped the key from his waistband and unlocked the cuffs.

He groaned with relief, rubbing his raw wrists. Sophia realized she stood rather close to him, and he was a stranger. He was about six inches taller than her own five foot eight, and had arms like a professional quarterback. He looked about thirty, a few years older than her. Mitch claimed to be a federal agent, but she didn't have any proof.

She remembered his injury and reached for the first aid kit in her backpack but stopped. Her pack! She had left it by the airstrip. A quick mental scan of the contents made her relax. No personal information, but she didn't have the kit, food or water.

He tapped his pockets. "Shit. They took my wallet, phone and gun. Do you have a cell?" Mitch rebuttoned his jeans.

"No signals out here."

"Where then? I need to make a call. The sooner the better."

She sighed. No other choice. Her house was the closest. "I have a land line."

"Within walking distance?" A hopeful note crept into his voice.

"No. About twenty miles off-road."

"And on the road?"

"Fifty."

"Damn. I'm going to have to trust your night vision again, aren't I?"

"Yep." Buckling up the chest protector, she donned her helmet.

A queasy expression creased his sharp nose and he rubbed his hand along his five o'clock shadow. Long black eyelashes matched his almost military-style short black hair. His uninjured blue eye stared at her in concern.

"Relax, Mitch. I'll get us there in one piece. After we jump the chasm of death, we're home free."

"Funny." He deadpanned. "I don't suppose you have another helmet?"

"Nope. But if we do crash, I'll aim for the right side to even out your injuries."

He gave her a wry grin. "Enduring poor attempts at humor is better than being dead. At least, you have a decent bike. My fragile male ego wouldn't be able to handle being rescued by a lady on a scooter."

With a passenger onboard, the trip to her house lasted twice as long as normal. Mitch clutched her waist with a vise grip. He cursed and muttered under his breath, but matched the rhythm of the bike's motion.

When they arrived at her small log cabin, he slid off on unsteady legs. The blood stain on his shirt had spread. Sophia tossed her helmet and gear into a pile. Leaving the bike next to her shed, she led him into the living room.

The place followed the standard mountain cabin décor—comfortable recliners, plaid-patterned couch, faux bear rug, and animal paintings.

"Sit down before you fall down." Sophia guided Mitch to the couch.

"Are you going to turn on the lights or did you forget to pay your electric bill?" he asked with a nervous edge.

She closed her eyes for a moment, summoning the strength for a difficult explanation. If there had been a phone anywhere else, she would have avoided this.

Working up the nerve, she said, "I can't tolerate visible light."

"Can't tolerate light? Like a vampire?" His confusion turned into alarm.

She huffed with exasperation. "I wish! At least vampires can go to a movie."

Mitch gestured as if calming a crazy person. "Look, all I need is to use your phone."

She sighed. *Shouldn't have made that vampire crack.* "I'm sorry. I'm not explaining it well. I'm out of practice." Sophia drew in a breath. *Time for the standard spiel.* She would love to tell the truth, but who, except the wrong people, would believe her? Instead, she said, "I have a rare disease called Erythropoietic Protoporphyria or EEP for short. Light kills my red blood cells, so I have to avoid *all* visible light, which means I live in the middle of nowhere with no TV, computer or..." Human contact. But that sounded pathetic.

If anything, her story made him more uneasy. She wondered why.

"What do you do when the sun comes up?"

Retreat to my coffin. "I sleep during the day."

He had an odd...queasy expression. Perhaps he searched for words of regret or encouragement that she didn't deserve to hear. Before he could speak, she said. "There's a phone and a lamp in the guest room, and a light in the guest bath. You can make your call and at least clean that gash before it becomes infected."

"Phone call first." He surged to his feet, but paused. "Where are we?"

"North of Shooting Creek, North Carolina."

"North Carolina! I didn't realize..." He rubbed his hand on his swollen temple. "How far to Knoxville?"

"One hundred and thirty miles."

"Damn." He considered. "Do you have an address?"

"I have GPS coordinates. Will they work?"

"Yeah. I just wish I knew where *they* were heading," he muttered more to himself than she did.

"Your friends?" she asked.

"Yes."

Sophia realized he didn't know about the farmhouse. She explained. "It's isolated, but I can pull the GPS coordinates off a topo map for you." Strangely, her offer increased his apprehension.

"Good." He seemed distracted. "Where...is the phone?"

She took his hand in the pitch dark and guided him to the guest room. The cabin's first floor contained a kitchen, living room, bedroom and bathroom. Her room and another bath were down in the basement.

Handing Mitch the cordless phone, she put his other hand on the lamp switch. "Wait until you hear the door close before turning the light on. I'll go pull the coordinates for you."

"Thanks," he said.

A strange hitch in his voice worried Sophia but, considering what the man had been through tonight, she didn't blame him. She was halfway to the door when he flicked the lamp on. Blinding whiteness obscured her vision. She stumbled and bumped into a chair.

"What did you do that for?" she demanded, fumbling

around. *Where was that door?* The light was too strong for her to bend.

Instead of answering, Mitch grabbed her wrists and pushed her against a wall.

"Let go!" Fear flushed through her. *Idiot.* Why didn't she ask for identification?

She tried to kick him, but missed. He pressed his weight on her, pinning her legs.

"You can't see me, can you?" Accusation laced his voice.

"Turn off the light."

"You're working with Ed. What's the purpose of your mock rescue?"

"I'm not working with anybody. Get off!"

"Don't lie. I just have to look at your eyes to know you're one of *them.* I suspected, but when you said you were 'out of practice' I knew for sure."

"What are you talking about?"

"You're one of those...Blind Assassins."

Anger flared. "Guess I couldn't fool a *federal* agent. You're right, Sherlock, I'm an assassin. I saved you from those goons just so I could bring you back here and kill you!" She tapped her head against the wall. "Oh damn! I left my Glock in the other room."

"You know what I mean," he said. "Your so-called night vision is physically impossible without goggles. I've trained for night ops. You can see in the dark, but are blind in the light. Who are you working for?"

She struggled to free herself, but his body trapped her. He knew about her condition. Not only could she even see colors in the dark, but read, too. The blacker the night, the better her vision. She had been born with this strange power, and, as far as she knew, there were only a handful of people born in the United States with it.

"Tell me now or I'll take you into custody for questioning."

An image of being blind and helpless in an unknown place filled her with dread. Avoiding that situation had been the whole reason she lived here. She was out of options. *Shit.* "I'm not working for anybody. That's the whole point of living miles away from civilization."

That made him pause. "You're in hiding?"

"Give Mr. Super Detective a gold star."

"From who?" The suspicion was back.

"Everyone!" Her father would be livid if he were alive. She had just undermined all his efforts to keep the government from knowing where she hid. Sophia would never forget the day the federal agents had visited them. They had called her special, and wanted her to train at an exclusive school to become an agent. Her father promised to take her. Instead of driving to the school, he headed for the hills. When she questioned him, he had explained the government would train her to sneak around in the dark, stealing, spying, and killing people for them. "And you're the worst."

"Me?"

"Yes. You said it yourself. The government wants to exploit people like me. We can see in the dark. That's a handy skill for an agent. Do you think we...what did you call us?"

"Blind Assassins, but they do other...jobs as well."

"Do you think the members volunteer?"

"No, they don't," he said in a quiet voice. "In fact, I thought the Blind Assassins were just an urban legend. Agents would blame them for unexplained events like you would blame a ghost for rearranging your knickknacks. An agent even joked Bin Laden used a Blind Assassin to help him escape through the caves in Afghanistan. At least, I thought he was joking until..."

He released his hold. She didn't wait. Inching along the

wall, she searched for the doorway with her hands. Was she even going the right way?

The lamp switched off, flooding the room with darkness. She sagged with relief. Mitch sat on the edge of the bed with his hand on the lamp.

She darted to the doorway, but paused at the threshold. "Until what?"

"Until tonight," he said.

"Are you going—"

"No. I won't tell anyone about you." He gave her a sad smile. "But I might try to recruit you. *You* could find Bin Laden's hideout and—"

"Not interested."

He frowned. "Could you get the coordinates of the farm-house for me?"

"Sure. There's a first aid kit in the linen closet, clean T-shirts in the drawers. They're my father's, but he's dead. The shirts should fit you; he used to be a firefighter before he was a paramedic." She babbled, but couldn't stop. "There's food in the kitchen and flashlights in the closet. Help yourself."

Sophia ran downstairs to her bedroom. Embarrassed and upset, she had a whole gymnastic team of emotions doing twists and flips in her chest. He attacked and threatened her and she had transformed into Miss Manners. She should have kicked him out. *One phone call, buddy and go.* Was she that desperate for company?

Before tonight she thought she didn't need anyone. She had her books, her dirt bike, her pen pals, and was learning how to paint.

God, you are pathetic.

She wanted to hide under the blankets, but she needed a shower and had promised Mitch those coordinates. Kicking off her motorcycle boots, she headed for the bathroom. She peeled off her long-sleeved riding shirt and padded bike pants. *Not very sexy.*

Her father had threatened to pull the spark plug from her bike if she didn't wear all the gear. Mr. Safety. She missed him like crazy. He had changed his lifestyle for her, sleeping in the daytime so he could be with her at night. He taught her how to hunt and how to ride.

He saved her from being taken by the government or by one of those other alphabet agencies of questionable repute. *Someone with my skills can be beneficial to all types of organizations. Drug smugglers, weapons dealers, and the military.*

Sophia shivered and jerked her thoughts to the present. She hesitated before removing her underwear. The idea of being naked with a strange man in the house unnerved her. She snorted. *Unnerved. Wonderful.* Considering how long ago it was that her last boyfriend declared he was too 'freaked out' by her whole nocturnal existence and left, she should be seducing the handsome agent by now. She was pathetic and spouting clichés. *Handsome agent. Pah.*

After a quick shower, she changed into jeans and another long-sleeved shirt. Sophia combed her hair. With her pale skin, dark hair and silver eyes, no wonder he thought she was a vampire.

Her hair used to lighten in the sun. She had an almost normal childhood. That was the hardest part of her condition. Her eyesight had deteriorated as she aged. When she turned twelve, she was blind in bright light but, with a concentrated effort, she could bend the dim or indirect light rays around her body so she could see, but it had an unfortunate side-effect. Her father had jumped out of his skin the first time she had turned invisible. She was well aware of the irony—could see but not be seen in the light. A Light Bender. *Better than being called an assassin.*

Sophia rummaged through her desk for Standing Indiana Mountain's topographical map and pulled the coordinates of the farmhouse.

She crept up the stairs. A thin line of white shone under his door. The deep murmur of Mitch's voice sounded. She slid the paper underneath and retreated to the kitchen. One a.m. already. Her stomach grumbled. Slicing apples, she wondered if Mitch was hungry. Should she make him a sandwich? *No.* Miss Manners had told him to help himself.

Light illuminated the hallway as his door opened. He replaced the bright lamp with a flashlight's beam.

Not wanting to surprise him, she said, "I'm in the kitchen."

He stopped at the threshold, aiming the flashlight down. Water dripped from his wet hair onto his bare muscular chest. A whole new slew of clichés jumped up and down in Sophia's head. Her heart threatened to join in.

"Um. Could you help? I think it needs to be stitched." He held bandages and her father's fire department T-shirt. The gash below his ribs oozed. "Can you do that?" At least this time he tried to mask his suspicion.

She bit back a sarcastic reply. "As long as you're not allergic to lidocaine."

"And if I am?"

"Then I'll give you a shot of whiskey and a rolled-up wash-cloth to bite down on."

He laughed. "I'll pass on the washcloth, but the whiskey sounds good."

After she collected the supplies, she told him to sit side-ways on the couch. He settled into position then doused the flashlight.

She crouched next to him, filling the syringe. "This is going to pinch, but it will numb the area." He smelled of soap and

Old Spice—an intoxicating mix. To distract her senses, she asked him if he finished making his phone calls.

"Yeah. My team will pick me up, but it'll take them a while to get here."

"How long?"

He squinted with suspicion. "Why do you want to know?"

"So I can tip Rick off." Sarcasm dripped, but his reaction surprised her.

He grabbed her arm. "How did you know Rick's name?"

"I overheard them talking."

"And you waited until *now* to tell me," he said with an outraged disbelief.

"Since we've just been sitting around doing nothing all night, I didn't want to ruin the mood." She knocked his hand away. Finishing the sutures, Sophia tied off the thread and bandaged his wound a little more harshly than necessary.

Mitch touched her shoulder. "Sorry." He pulled her beside him on the couch.

A strange tingling rushed through her as she realized his warm fingers still rested on her.

"It's disconcerting to hear your voice, but not be able to see you. I need a...physical connection. Okay?"

"Sure." Her voice rasped. *How embarrassing!* But she relaxed and left his fingers on her arm.

"Could you please tell me everything you heard?" he asked.

As Sophia recited, Mitch stiffened. She felt his anxiety vibrate through his touch.

"A mesh bag? Are you sure?" he asked.

"Yes."

He swore. "And..." His voice cracked. "A four a.m. pick up tonight?"

"I don't know if they meant tonight."

He covered his eyes with his other hand. "My team won't

be here in time. Maybe we can intercept the vehicle. Is there another road out?"

"The airstrip."

"What?"

"There's a landing strip next to the farmhouse."

Mitch shot to his feet. "I need to get there. Now!"

"What *treasures* are worth risking your life for?"

"Classified. I need a ride—"

"Not until you tell me."

His hands balled into fists. She scrambled away as he stepped forward. Mitch stopped and drew in a deep breath. "Those guys are kidnappers. They smuggle young girls to foreign countries to be sold to organizations seeking Blind Assassins."

The information sank in. "They threatened a girl to make you talk! How awful."

Emotion roughened his voice. "They threatened *my* little sister. Who I had sent to a special needs boarding school after our mother died. A school she insisted she didn't belong in because she could *see* in the dark. I didn't believe her, but did a little research to mollify her. Big mistake. When the agents with the scary questions finally left my house, I drove to the school to get her, but encountered Ed and his large friend."

After Sophia connected the contents of the mesh bag to Mitch's sister, she bolted from the couch. "Why didn't you know they had her before?"

"I thought she had escaped. She disappeared while I fought with Ed's friend."

His sister was a Light Bender like her. "Let's go."

Mitch donned the T-shirt and ran to the phone to update his team. She dashed out the back to prep her bike. When Mitch joined her she said, "My father's helmet is in the shed."

"Any weapons?"

"Hunting rifles."

"Ammo?"

"In the cabinet in the living room. Grab the thirty-thirty and my Winchester."

"Yours? Oh no. You're just giving me a ride. After you drop me off, you're coming back here."

"Don't be ridiculous. I can *see* in the dark."

Although unhappy, Mitch agreed with conditions. "You are to do *exactly* what I say. No free styling. Understand?"

"Yes, sir."

Grumbling, Mitch used the flashlight to find the guns and helmet. He strapped the rifles on his back. The trip to the airstrip wasn't as exhausting as the ride home. Mitch's hold stayed loose. He molded his body to her back. Although his warmth distracted her at times, the connection helped him match her movements faster. She realized he trusted her.

The Honda chugged up the mountain and crested on the far side of the runway. She cut the engine and coasted to a small dip. Mitch handed her the Winchester.

"Here's the plan," he said. "We'll approach the house from the east side. If they're still there, I'll get in close to see *who* is where. You stay put. You're my sniper. If the guys try to drive away, shoot out their tires. *Only* if you have a clear shot."

"What are you going to do if they stay?"

"Wait. It's three thirty. If the plane comes at four, they'll leave the house with the girls and I'll surprise them. Otherwise, I'll wait for my team."

His plan sounded simple. The element of surprise combined with her night vision should work well together. Something about famous last words echoed in her mind, but she squashed all doubts. She remembered listening to her father lecture the rookies at the firehouse before the blindness forced her into isolation. He'd tell them to switch off their emotions, to think and act now, and leave the worries and the panic for later.

Good advice, Dad. But how do I get the rest of my body to comply? Her insides felt jittery and her palms left wet prints on her rifle.

Sophia led Mitch to the east side. Both vehicles were parked in the driveway and lights shone from the first floor windows. The kidnappers hadn't left.

Mitch's relieved expression matched hers. He had enough light to navigate on his own. He pointed to the ground and mouthed the word "stay". She saluted. He flashed her a grin, turned away, then paused.

Something wrong?

Her heart decided to go for a gold medal in the hundred yard dash. *I spent way too much time listening to the Olympics on the radio.*

Mitch moved to whisper in her ear. "Just in case I don't get a chance later, thank-you for saving my life."

"Make sure you hold on to it. I doubt the next time you're in trouble a Blind Assassin will ride to your rescue."

Another smile. She liked the way his eyes crinkled when he grinned.

He cupped her chin and peered at her. "A supernatural beauty." His gaze met hers.

Her body turned to stone as all her nerve endings rushed to where his fingers touched her jaw. He leaned in and kissed her. Sensation flared on her lips and she returned the kiss.

He pulled away. Sophia watched him for as long as he remained visible. Once he neared the house, she lost him in the light. She scanned the second-floor windows and thought she spotted movement, but couldn't be certain.

Glad the night air stayed calm Sophia practiced aiming at the tires with her rifle. Scanning the black sky, she searched for signs of an approaching airplane. All quiet. After a few more minutes, she decided waiting sucked.

When the grunts and sounds of a scuffle reached her, she changed her mind. Waiting was better. A thud followed a curse and she heard voices, but not Mitch's.

"Told you the ambush would work," Ed said.

"Bring him inside," Rick said.

A door slammed. They had expected him. *How?* Didn't matter at this point. Mitch and the girls were in the brightly lit house. Panic bubbled up her throat, but she gulped it down.

Think now, freak out later.

Option one; wait until they left the house to meet the plane at four a.m. She would play sniper, incapacitating them one by one. *Won't work. They would scatter at the sound of the first shot.*

Option two; hit the airplane when it landed. Unable to fly, they would be forced to drive out and, best case scenario, run into Mitch's team. *No. They would kill Mitch. No reason for them to take him along.*

Option three, cut off the electricity and tip the playing field in her favor. Not the best plan, but she had a winner.

Sophia moved with care, circling the house. She searched for the electric box. The light from the windows made it impossible to find. She would have to crawl around the outside walls and explore with her hands. Approaching the house from the back side seemed logical; she held out a hand and entered the whiteness. She tried to avoid the direct light.

When her fingers touched the wood siding, she began the hunt. Two hands would be faster, but she wasn't stupid enough to put her weapon down.

On the west side of the house loud voices came through the window.

"...your friend?" Rick asked.

"Dropped me off and went home," Mitch said.

He was conscious and alive. Sophia let out a quiet breath as relief washed through her. The feeling didn't last long.

A high-pitched squeal of pain sliced the air. "Mitch!"

His sister. Sophia wilted.

"Let's go over your story again," Rick said. "We know your biker friend was near the house and heard us talking about you because Ed found a backpack and tire tracks nearby. Biker then follows the Rover and rescues you in a blaze of glory. Here's where *your* story gets...creative." He chuckled without humor. "You claim the biker took you to a rustic cabin with no electricity or phones, helped you clean up, and then brought you back here. Is this correct?"

"Yeah."

"Glenn," Rick said.

A heart-breaking scream erupted. Sophia rolled into a ball to keep from pounding on the window and surrendering.

"You won't hurt her," Mitch said in a flat, deadly tone.

"We already have," Glenn said.

"Surface bruises. You won't damage the merchandise or you'll lose thousands of dollars."

Mitch just bought her a few extra minutes. She hurried. She found the box and pulled out her Swiss Army Knife. Silently thanking her father for teaching her another fireman's trick, she unlocked the box and turned off the electricity.

Her night vision returned as cries and curses sounded. She ran to the window and peered in. Ed and the Tank held Mitch tight. Glenn had one arm wrapped around a young girl. He had backed into a corner with his other hand pointing a gun. Rick told everyone to calm down.

"The biker only knows one trick," Rick said. "Stay put, I'll get the spotlight." He felt his way from the room.

Sophia aimed her rifle. A million worries and doubts boiled

in her stomach. What if she missed? *Act now, panic later.* She held her breath, braced for the recoil, and squeezed the trigger.

The window shattered, the noise ricocheted around the room, and Glenn slammed into the wall. The bullet pierced his shoulder right at the joint of his shooting arm. The force knocked him out. He slid to the floor with a thud.

Bingo! One down, three to go.

The girl yelled and threw herself flat, covering her head with her arms. Her brother taught her well. Sophia swung the rifle toward the others. Ed dove into the hallway, but the Tank had his arm around Mitch's neck, pinning the agent in front of him as a shield.

"Shoot him," Mitch called.

Where? Mitch covered almost all of The Tank. And she wasn't a sharpshooter. Then she realized Mitch's hands weren't bound. One grasped The Tank's meaty forearm, but the other pointed down. The guy's knee poked out between Mitch's legs.

Oh shit. She aimed. *I'd bet Mitch is wishing for a real pair of bulletproof underwear.* Firing the gun, the bullet hit the Tank's knee, obliterating it. *Yuck.* Mitch broke away as the Tank screamed.

"Jenna?" Mitch called, searching for his sister. They connected. The girl wrapped her arms around him and sobbed.

"It's okay," he said over and over.

I wish. She kept watch for the two men who escaped. The sound of an engine turning over came from the front of the house. Headlights stabbed the darkness.

"Mitch, they're in the Rover," she said.

The noise grew louder as the light brightened.

"Go!" Mitch ordered.

Sophia sprinted around the back of the house, hoping to

loop behind them and shoot out their tires. When she reached the front, light blinded her. She forgot about the pickup truck.

A shot boomed. Wood splintered. She dove to the ground, dropping her rifle, but kept moving, pulling herself along as if the air was filled with smoke. Gravel scraped her forearms as she sought the edge of light.

She bumped into a solid object. *Please be a tree trunk*, she prayed. But even blind there was no mistaking the touch of cold hard metal on her temple. A wave of terror swept through her.

"Stand up," Rick said.

She stood. The gun remained.

"Son of a bitch. No wonder you've been giving us such trouble. Are you working for the feds?" he asked.

"Yes, and my team will be here any minute."

He laughed. "Nice try." He shoved her forward. "Up against the house."

Rick pushed her into the wood siding. The peeling paint chips scratched her cheek, a minor thing considering the gun's barrel now pressed on the back of her neck. She heard the Rover squeal to a stop.

"Did you get him?" Ed asked.

Rick snorted. "Our biker's a *blind* lady."

"No shit!"

"Take the rifle and check the house. Let Mitch know we have his friend. One we *can* hurt."

Rick must have turned the lights back on. Time flowed like sweet tea—the kind with so much sugar it had the consistency of syrup. Sweat collected and dripped down her back. *Why didn't I ride over to Nantahala Lake tonight?*

Finally, Ed returned. "Mitch and his sister have disappeared. Glenn's gun is gone and he and Max are in bad shape."

The tightness in her chest eased a bit. She hoped Mitch took his sister far away.

"The other girls?"

"Gone, too."

Rick cursed. "Get the spotlight and go find them," Rick ordered. "They couldn't have gone far." He grabbed Sophia's arm and propelled her into the house. "You saved his life and he left you behind. That's gotta hurt."

"I'm glad," she said. "I'd rather he save those girls than me." And she meant it. They could have full lives ahead of them—high school, graduation, college, romance, marriage and babies if they weren't forced to become night-time operatives for some government. Her existence was just that, an existence. She had retreated from the world, but...

She didn't have to. Suddenly a whole list of things she could do scrolled through her mind. If she had a second chance, she wouldn't hide anymore. If not, then exchanging her life for the others would be consolation enough.

The fear left her, leaving behind a peaceful confidence.

Rick kept his hold and the gun on her. The hot scent of blood filled the air, gagging her. A man moaned in pain.

"Damn, lady. You sure did a number on them."

"They're survivable injuries," she said.

"But they're no good to me now. I can't take them with me and can't leave them here."

The gun moved. "No!" she yelled. She spun, knocking his arm away as the gun fired. They fell together.

He rolled on top of her, pinning her down with his weight. Rick pressed the red hot barrel into her neck. She cried out as the smell of burning flesh replaced the cloying blood scent.

"You're dead," he said.

She jerked as the gun roared. Sophia struggled to draw breath as a heavy weight settled on her chest. Warm liquid soaked her shirt. *Can't breathe.* She felt light as her father called her name. Then he shook her shoulders...hard. When he slapped her, she tried to punch him, but he grabbed her wrist.

"Are you all right?" Mitch asked.

She felt her neck. Aside from the burn, it remained whole, but the metallic tang of blood dominated her senses. Her hands were sticky. "Rick?"

"Dead. Come on." Mitch pulled her to her feet.

She wobbled. "The girls? Ed?"

"Oldest trick in the book. I hid the girls in the basement, and left the back door wide open. Ed's out cold." He wrapped her in a hug. "I've done a number of stupid things today, but I wasn't going to leave you."

She clung to him, enjoying his warmth and strength.

"Thanks for saving—"

He silenced her with a kiss. All too soon he broke away. "Just returning the favor."

Mitch kissed her again, but this one had a feeling of finality about it. He led her outside. The darkness embraced her and she fanned her blistered neck.

"My team will be here in an hour. You need to go." He was all business.

Despite the ache chewing holes in her heart Sophia understood he was protecting her.

Her moment of clarity had given her plenty of ideas of how to use her talent to help people. Even though she could see in the dark, it didn't mean she had to live there.

I won't. She took her first step. "Mitch, your sister—"

"I know. I'll keep her safe. Don't worry."

"Not that. She's what I prefer to call us—a Light Bender." Sophia explained why Jenna had disappeared. "Those Blind Assassins can do more than just see in the dark. And if the light was bright, her powers are stronger than mine."

He scowled. "Than yours? You can bend light, too?" Anger fueled his words. "What else are you keeping from me?"

"Nothing. Look, I can help her if—"

"No. Go home, Sophia. Go back to hiding in your cabin." He left.

An icy chill gripped her. She slogged to her bike. The ride home blurred into one long endurance test, ending with a collapse on her bed.

Months passed. Sophia ventured back into society. The Association for the Blind taught her how to live in the light. She reconnected with the people at her father's firehouse. At night, her activities became more clandestine. She aided a search and rescue mission, helping to find a lost boy scout, and she followed a potential arsonist, stopping him before he set another barn fire. These excursions were made well away from her home town.

Sophia was painting when headlights swept her cabin. The Association was delivering her guide dog tonight. Eager to meet her furry companion, she hurried outside. Caught in the headlights, she clutched a post on her porch to keep from tripping. When the lights extinguished, she saw a huge pickup truck with a Suzuki Z250 in the bed parked in her driveway. No dog.

Mitch hopped down from the driver's seat. She blinked, but he remained.

"What do you think?" He gestured to the bike.

"You should have bought a Honda instead of a suck-zuki," she said.

"They're fighting words. You'll change your mind when you're eating my dust."

She laughed. "You think you can keep up with *me*?"

He reached into the cab, pulling out a helmet. "State-of-the-art night vision visor." He glanced at her. "Want to go for a ride?"

"I can't. I'm waiting for a dog."

"A dog's more important?" he asked with a neutral tone.

"The dog's here to stay, and isn't just visiting for a joy ride."

He set the helmet on the seat, and strode toward her. He wore her father's T-shirt. The bruises on his face were long gone, and her insides flipped when he reached her.

"I couldn't stop thinking about you. I've been keeping track of this area, reading the local papers, and doing Internet searches." He touched her neck, rubbing a thumb over her burn scar. "Seems a few unexplained, yet happy incidents have occurred in the Smoky Mountains these past three months." He dropped his hand. "Guess I was wrong about you."

"No. You were right. I've been hiding for a long time. Afraid to use my talents."

"And now you're not?"

"No. I'm still afraid, but I won't let it stop me."

"Admirable." He smiled. "Are you brave enough to expand your nocturnal activities, and work with a partner?"

"It depends."

His smile faltered. "On what?"

"On how close of a partnership you're talking about."

He pulled her toward him. Wrapping his arms around her, he kissed her. "Is this close enough?"

Instead of answering, she led him to her dark bedroom. "You can get closer. How's your night vision?"

Mitch grinned. "Excellent."

THE COLDEST GAME

I had fun writing about werewolves, but could I write about another were-creature for the anthology, Bewere the Night? *If so, then which one? Every culture has stories of humans shapeshifting into animals, so it was a challenge to pick one. Then I needed a setting for this story. I had just visited my alma mater, Penn State University, where I'd earned a Bachelor of Science degree in meteorology. Lots of good memories from my Penn State days filled me and I decided to dip into my past for this story. Much of the story has some truth to it. I did work a five a.m. shift in the campus weather station, which is a ghost town on the weekends. Ben Bernstein is still a good friend of mine, although the "he-man women haters club" has been disbanded as all the members are now happily married. Yes, I lived in 233 Runkle Hall with a freshman beauty pageant contestant who I nicknamed Bubbles (shhh...she still doesn't know). And I struggled with thermodynamics.*

THE COLDEST GAME

The screech of a small child being tortured woke Lexa. At least, that was what her alarm sounded like at four in morning. *I feel your pain, girlfriend,* she muttered under her breath as she swatted the clock before her roommate could growl.

Why? Why did I ever *volunteer for the five a.m. shift?* Lexa asked herself this every single Friday morning. The answer remained the same. *Because I'm an idiot and fell for Ben's bullshit claim that the morning shift is the most exciting.* It wasn't.

Grabbing her shower basket, she schlepped to the bathroom down the hall. Her choice of shower stalls remained the best thing about this time of day. *Ah, dorm life.*

After a scalding-hot shower, Lexa returned to her room. She dressed in the dark—jeans, sneakers, and a shapeless navy Penn State University hoodie. Twisting her long brown hair into a knot, she tucked it under a navy baseball cap before leaving.

An early November fog blanketed the silent campus. Street lights reflected off the white mist. No one was around—the only time Penn State's main campus was this quiet. It matched her gloomy mood.

She'd been in a funk since Lauren, her younger sister had been killed by a drunk driver last year. It deepened when Jason, her boyfriend of three years dumped her in September. Now failing thermodynamics, Lexa thought she'd never see daylight again.

Lexa headed toward the Walker Building on the western edge of campus. At least she had her own key now. Last week Ben had forgotten his, and they had botched the forecast in their haste. A couple radio stations had complained. What did they expect anyway? They were getting free weather forecasts from a bunch of student meteorologists after all.

When Lexa cut through West Halls, a strange icy feeling slipped down her spine. The campus was relatively safe, but her imagination conjured up all those horror movies that Jason had dragged her to see.

Perhaps she should have arranged for a security escort— some jock doing his good deed for the day, but she'd never felt unsafe on campus until now. She dismissed her anxiety as a product of her overdramatic imagination.

Just before she entered the short cut between Irvin Hall and Jordan Hall a low anguished growl emanated from the shadows. Logic urged her to run. But she savored the feeling of fear for a moment. Since Lauren's death, she'd been going through the motions of living, trying to keep the painful storm of grief contained inside her. She'd felt nothing else.

Lexa lingered a moment too long. A black mass launched from the shadows. She fell back, banging her head on the cement as the heavy beast landed on her chest. In a flash, white pointy teeth dug into her neck. Burning pain squeezed her windpipe closed.

Black and white spots clouded her vision. Then the creature paused. It released her and bounded away as fast as it had appeared. She caught a glimpse of a four legged creature with gray fur stripped with black. A big fucking dog.

Blood gushed from her throat, soaking the collar of her hoodie. Dizziness and nausea swelled as she explored the ragged skin. A strange concern over the location of her cap floated through her mind before she passed out.

Unfamiliar voices woke Lexa. She squinted into a bright whiteness. The antiseptic smell matched the room's décor— curtains hanging from a U-shaped track on the ceiling, florescent lights, and cabinets with glass doors.

Lexa touched her neck. Bandages covered her throat. A sharp ache pulsed from underneath the dressing.

The curtains parted and a tall young man entered. He skidded to a stop in surprise. Large splatters of blood covered his ripped white Penn State T-shirt and dotted his white sweat pants. Lexa's first thought—college student was followed by —jock.

"You're awake," he said.

"Who..." Her voice rasped painfully.

"Don't talk... Wait." He dashed away, calling to another.

A nurse bustled in and Lexa wondered if nurses ever just walked or sauntered. The student trailed after her. Concern creasing his forehead, he raked his fingers through his short spiky black hair.

"What--"

The nurse cut her off. She sent the student to the waiting room before asking Lexa questions. Lexa explained about the oversized dog. It didn't take long.

"Was the dog foaming at the mouth?" she asked.

A vision of sharp teeth flashed in her mind. "No."

"We'll test for rabies just in case." The nurse clicked her pen and wrote on her clipboard. "Miss Thomas, you're in the Mount Nittany Medical Center's emergency room. You have a mild concussion and four lacerations in your neck. We put in sixty sutures, administered a tetanus shot, and contacted your parents."

She groaned. *Mom probably freaked.*

The nurse continued with a more scolding tone. "You're extremely lucky. One of the lacerations *exposed* your jugular. If it had been torn, you'd be dead."

Upset parents no longer seemed so bad. "How did I get here?" Lexa asked.

"A student found you and called an ambulance. He's been here all morning."

"Can you ask him to come back?"

"Sure. The doctor and the police will also be in to see you." The nurse left.

The police? Lexa searched for her phone. It was in a plastic bag under her bed along with her clothes. No baseball cap. Ignoring the fifteen text messages and three voice mails from Ben, she called her mother, and endured the hysterics. Calming her mother. Lexa noted the irony of how *she'd* been injured, but her mother needed to be soothed.

"No need to come, Mom," Lexa said for the seventh time. "I'm fine. It's a couple of scratches, and I'll be home in two weeks for Thanksgiving." The first anniversary of Lauren's death—hell with turkey and stuffing.

Finally, her mother agreed. Lexa read through Ben's texts. He'd teased her, assuming she slept in, but when she missed classes, his texts became more frantic. Avoiding another phone call, she texted Ben. Two seconds after she hit send, her phone vibrated with another message from Mr. Lightning Thumbs.

I'm coming.

She didn't have the energy to argue. Besides, she'd need a ride home. Lexa tossed the phone on the table. There was no one else to call. Her roommate, Bubbles the aspiring freshman beauty queen, wouldn't even notice her absence.

The curtain to her room parted, and the black-haired student entered. A wary concern lurked in his blue eyes as if he was afraid she would yell at him.

"Uh...the nurse said you..."

"Thank you for helping me," Lexa said. She gestured to the dried blood on his clothes. "Sorry about bleeding all over you. If the stains don't come out, I can buy—"

"Don't worry about it. I get blood on my clothes all the time."

"Really?"

"Man, that sounded weird." He crossed then uncrossed his arms as if he wasn't sure what to do with them. "I play hockey."

Her first impression of jock had been right. Plus only an athlete would have biceps that defined. "Are you one of Penn State's Ice Men?"

"Yeah, I'm—"

A police officer stepped into her room. "Miss Thomas? She nodded.

"I'm Officer Reed of the State College Police. I'd like to ask you a few questions." The officer addressed the hockey player. "You can wait at the nurses' station. I've questions for you, too."

"Yes, sir." He retreated.

"Are you sure it was a dog that attacked you?" Officer Reed asked.

"Yes. It was gray with black stripes. It was wide and solid, not tall. Big teeth."

He wrote a few notes in a small book. "Do you know Aiden Deller?"

The name sounded familiar, but she couldn't place it. "No. Who's he?"

The officer gave her a tight smile. "He called the ambulance."

"Oh." She made the connection. Aiden Deller was a senior forward, and one of the top scorers for the Ice Men. The nickname Ice Men came from the precise, emotionless way they played.

Officer Reed's next set of questions focused on Aiden and his timely arrival.

"It was an animal," Lexa repeated. "Ask the doctor who stitched me up."

"No need to get upset. I'm just eliminating all the possibilities. Dog attacks of this magnitude are extremely rare." He handed her a card. "Call me, if you remember anything else." Officer Reed left.

After twenty minutes, Aiden returned. "I overheard the nurses." He pointed at her neck. "They mentioned a dog?"

"You didn't see it?"

"No. As I told Officer Reed, I found you lying on the ground. Alone."

She shivered at the memory. "I don't think they believe me."

"What were you doing out that early?" he asked.

Lexa explained about her forecasting shift.

"Meteorology, that's cool."

"Most people think it's geeky." Including Jason. "What's your major?"

"Architectural engineering."

"Wow. I thought—"

"Jocks aren't smart?"

"No." She rushed to assure him. "I thought you'd be doing something sports related."

"Odds of me being drafted in the NHL are slim."

"But you score a hat trick every game, and last year, you had the best record in the league."

He raised his eyebrows. "Hockey fan?"

"Sort of."

Aiden waited.

Lexa felt self-conscience, but she couldn't let him think she'd lost her mind. "My ex-boyfriend is a big fan. He dragged me to all of the home games over the last three years, but I haven't gone this semester. Besides," she added to avoid sounding pathetic, "it's impossible to score tickets this season, and I don't want to be one of those fair weather fans."

He laughed at the weather pun, but paused as if surprised by his own response. "If you've sat through those three horrible seasons, then you're not at all like those filling the stands now."

A smile tugged. "It was painful to watch."

"It was painful to play."

"The new coach made a big difference."

Aiden sobered. "Yeah, Coach Hakim...who'd of thought a guy who grew up in Indonesia would know so much about hockey."

Lexa detected bitterness in his voice.

"If I sent you a ticket to tomorrow night's game, would you come?" Aiden asked.

"Of course, but—"

Ben arrived with two security guards in tow. "Can you please tell these goons that I'm allowed in here? I'm practically your next of kin!"

Lexa grinned at Ben's disheveled appearance—mussed brown hair in need of a cut, flannel shirt untucked and two days of stubble. They'd been best friends since freshman physics. He was the first person she'd called when Lauren had died. "It's okay. He's my ride home."

He sputtered, but couldn't complain since the guards left. "What happened? Your text—" Ben noticed Aiden standing on the other side of her bed.

The two men sized each other like warriors preparing to battle. Stocky but not fat, Ben was shorter than Aiden, who was all lean muscles.

Lexa introduced them. "Aiden, this is my *friend*, Ben Bernstein. Ben, this is Aiden Deller." She explained Aiden's rescue.

"What were you doing out that early?" Ben asked him.

"Running."

"At four thirty a.m.?"

"Ben," Lexa admonished.

"I better go. Coach has a fit if we're late for practice," Aiden said. "Where should I send the ticket? Or should I send you two?" He glanced at Ben.

"One's fine. Ben hates hockey. I'm in 233 Runkle Hall."

Ben huffed. "I thought you hated hockey."

Lexa wished Ben would shut up. "You're thinking of horror movies."

"Uh-uh." Ben looked unconvinced.

Aiden said good-bye. Lexa felt suddenly fragile as if he had taken a part of her with him. Silly nonsense. She touched the bandages. What would have happened if Aiden hadn't shown up? Would the dog have killed her? At least she wasn't disappointed about surviving.

Ben kept her company until the doctor discharged her. With instructions and prescriptions in hand, she followed Ben to his Ford Ranger pick-up.

He slid behind the wheel and started the engine. "You shouldn't be alone. You can stay at my apartment tonight."

"And listen to the 'he-man women haters' club while I try to get comfortable on your cushionless couch? Thanks, but no thanks."

"Hey, you're a member, too, and you haven't missed a single meeting at the Gingerbread Man." He pulled into traffic.

"I'm not passing up free beer and hot wings."

He gasped. "I should have suspected. You swore off dating women too easily."

Lexa laughed, but stopped as pain ringed her neck.

Ben glanced over. "Wow. That's the first time you've laughed in...months."

"Don't start."

"Fine. Humor me and stay tonight. You can have my bed."

"Bubbles is going home, and I have the room to myself."

"Are you sure it's not because you're hoping Mr. Knight-in-Shining-Armor delivers that ticket himself?"

"Don't be ridiculous."

"Just don't go all Florence Nightingale over him."

"You have that backwards. *I'm* the patient."

"You know what I mean."

"No, Ben, I don't know."

"He probably has a dozen girls drooling over him. I don't want you becoming Depressed Girl again."

"You're worse than my mother. It's just a ticket to a hockey game."

Yet the next day, a thrill of excitement rolled through her when she found an envelope under her door. Inside was one ticket to the game.

~

Lexa gawked at the packed stands. The Ice Pavilion's bleachers stretched along one side of the rink. It appeared as if every seat was filled.

She glanced at her ticket. Section C. Row 5. Just as she suspected, the seat was one of the best in the pavilion. Dead center and high enough to see over the Plexiglas.

Sitting next to a beautiful blonde, Lexa scanned the small roped-off area. Many of the seats remained unoccupied, but a few pretty girls and two older couples sat around her. *Ah, the girlfriend and parent section.*

The blond gave her the once over. Lexa tucked a hair behind her ear, feeling inadequate in her navy turtleneck and jeans. Wearing Ugg boots, a pink Eddie Bauer sweater, and a sorority pin, the blond was probably the homecoming queen.

"Who are you here for?" the blond asked.

"Aiden Deller."

The blonde's thin eyebrows rose slightly. "That's surprising."

"Why?" Lexa demanded.

"Oh, no offense. He just never invites anyone. Even his parents stopped coming."

"Really?"

She gestured to the empty seats. "Most don't. Ever since the guys have been winning, they've ignored everyone. Hockey is all they care about."

Lexa watched the team warm up. A dead serious expression covered all their faces as they passed the puck with precise motions. She had heard the rumors, and the nickname, but to see them in action sent a chill along her spine. Aiden matched the other's mechanical movements, but when they circled to return to the bench, he met her gaze and winked.

Feeling a little better, Lexa asked the blond who she was rooting for.

"Ryan Collins, but not for long."

"Why?"

"He's lost interest in life. Ryan's turned as cold as the ice he skates on. If you're smart, don't get involved with Aiden."

"Oh. No, I'm not... He just..." The game started, saving her.

With the blond's comments fresh in her mind, Lexa paid attention to the Ice Men. Since she had seen them last, they had improved in every way—skating, passing, working as a team. Yet when they scored a goal, they didn't celebrate. No one raised a stick or smiled or slapped each other despite the crowd's roar.

Deep in the third period, Aiden scored his hat trick. He pumped a fist and smiled at Lexa.

The blond leaned close to her ear. "Maybe you should stick around. Aiden's showing signs of life."

The buzzer signaled another win for the team. Spectators filed out as the players lined up to slap hands. Lexa debated. Should she go?

As the teams broke apart and headed off the ice, Aiden caught her eye. He put his hand up in a stopping motion and pointed down as if he wanted her to wait for him. She nodded. He gave her a thumbs up.

A strange tingling on her skin caused her to look across the ice. Coach Hakim stared at her. His hard expression unreadable, but she sensed trouble in his gaze. She shivered, and pulled her jacket closer. When she risked another peek, the Coach had disappeared.

The stands were almost empty when a familiar voice called her name. Jason and his new girlfriend stood a few rows down from her. They held hands. *How cute.* She braced for the dagger of pain, but felt nothing.

"I thought you didn't like hockey," Jason said.

She shrugged. "It grew on me."

"Sure it did." His sarcastic tone suggested otherwise. "Don't you think this is a little pathetic?" He smirked.

"What is?"

"Coming here so you'd run into me, hoping I'd see you and regret dumping you."

His girlfriend giggled.

When they'd been dating, they'd always done what Jason wanted, and never did anything she enjoyed. She studied him and wondered how she could have fallen in love with him.

"Get over yourself, Jason. I didn't come here for you," she said.

"Yeah? Then why did you come?"

"Because I invited her," Aiden said. He held a hockey stick, and his hair was still wet from the shower.

Jason gaped and stammered.

"Ready to go?" Aiden asked her, holding out his free hand.

"Yep. I'm so done." Without hesitating she took his hand. They left the rink as if they were a couple. From the moment she touched him, she felt as if they'd been together for years. That kind of thinking would only lead her in one direction, back into the valley of pain where she'd been wallowing since last year.

When they reach the parking lot in front of the pavilion, Aiden let go. "Sorry about that, but when I heard that son-of-a-bitch gloating... It was either that or I was going to punch him."

"And ruin another shirt for me? I couldn't handle the guilt."

Aiden laughed. He stopped next to a black Honda Accord and unlocked the trunk. Tossing the hockey stick in, he closed it. "I'm starving. Do you want to go get something to eat?"

Her heart danced in her chest, but she replied with—she hoped—a casual tone. "Sure."

"Great. Hop in." He opened the door for her.

So polite. She slid into the passenger seat.

He settled behind the wheel. "Almost forgot." Reaching into the back, he grabbed her baseball cap. "I picked this up after the paramedics left. Yours?"

"Yes. Thanks."

"You don't seem the baseball cap type," he said.

"I'm not, but it helps disguise me." She took the cap. "So I don't appear to be a woman."

"You could arrange for an escort if you're afraid of being assaulted."

"I could."

He shook his head. "Do you mind if we go to Bellefonte for dinner? If I eat around campus, I get a bunch of drunk guys telling me how fabulous I am." He gave her a wry grin. "I don't mind being told I'm fabulous by drunk *girls.*"

"It must suck to be famous," she said.

"Yep. Poor me."

Lexa laughed. For the first time in a year her stomach growled with hunger instead of swirling with nausea. For the first time the thought of her sister didn't cause intense pain.

"Did you enjoy the game?" Aiden asked.

"Yes. But the players looked too serious."

Aiden kept his focus on the road. "Coach doesn't like us to celebrate goals. He thinks it's poor sportsmanship. Actually, he tells us to leave all our emotions in the locker room. He says pre-game jitters, anger, or just stressing over a test can all get in the way of our performance."

"That strategy is definitely working. No penalties, fights, plus the bonus of being undefeated."

"Yeah. It's nice."

She sensed a but.

"How's your neck?" he asked, changing the subject.

~

After dinner, Aiden drove her home. Before she opened the car door, he handed her a stack of hockey tickets.

"This isn't going to help my thermodynamics grade," she said.

"No problem, I got an A in thermo last semester."

"Of course you did. Can you turn metal into gold, too?" she teased.

"All the time. Except for my hockey skates, they're platinum—gold is too soft."

She stood there grinning like an idiot as he drove away. She knew it couldn't last, that he would leave her, too. At least when she hit bottom this time, it would be at full speed and would cause major carnage.

She saw Aiden every day over the next five days. They either went to dinner after a game, or he helped her with thermodynamics. Officer Reed called her mid-week to report that they had caught a wild dog on campus. He wanted her to identify it. Aiden skipped practice to drive her to the pound on Thursday afternoon.

"Won't your coach be upset?" she asked.

"Not for this."

"Why not?"

His grip on the steering wheel tightened. "Lexa, I need a favor."

"Sure."

"You don't even know what it is."

She shrugged. "Considering all you've done for me, it would have to be a crime for me to say no." She kept her tone light.

Instead of smiling, Aiden grimaced. *Uh oh.*

He stopped at a red light. Meeting her gaze, he said, "I

want you to tell Officer Reed that the dog they caught *was* the one that attacked you even if it isn't."

"Why?"

"I'll explain later, although it'll be hard to believe. Christ, I don't believe it myself sometimes."

"But if it's the wrong dog, then the right one might attack—"

"Won't happen. I promise no one will be harmed again."

The light turned green. Aiden released Lexa from his intense scrutiny. Her emotions balanced on the edge, teetering toward the plunge. She touched her neck. Another turtleneck covered the bandages. The stitches would come out next week.

As the silence lengthened, she puzzled out the only logical explanation for his request. "Your dog attacked me."

"I don't have a dog."

A painful knot tightened her throat. "Did you see what attacked me?"

"No. Yes. It's complicated."

Shit. The bottom rose to meet her.

Aiden pulled into the pound's lot. "Please do this, and I swear, I'll explain everything."

Officer Reed met them in the lobby. "Ready?" he asked.

Lexa nodded. It was all she could manage. They entered the back room, and the dogs immediately started barking.

The volunteer seemed surprised. "Must be the uniform," he muttered.

The accused dog matched Lexa's description. The huge Mastiff had a black muzzle, and it had black stripes on a fawn-colored coat, which could be mistaken for gray in the dark. It growled, baring its sharp teeth when it spotted them. Its tail tucked under its body.

Without warning, a clear image from the attack flashed in her mind. This dog didn't match at all. The muzzle was too droopy, the ears weren't cropped, no white on its face, and it didn't have long whiskers. *Whiskers?*

Aiden stood behind her. His hands rested on her shoulders as if he lent her support. Officer Reed eyed him with interest. Conflicting emotions struggled for dominance, Lexa didn't know what to do. However, she believed Aiden when he promised no one else would be hurt.

"That's the one," she said.

"Really?" The volunteer scratched his goatee. "Normally, he's a real sweetheart."

"It's obvious he doesn't like her," Officer Reed said. "Case closed!"

Aiden kept quiet as he drove toward campus.

Unable to endure the silence, Lexa said, "You were going to explain."

"I will in Coach Hakim's office. You—"

"Take me home." The blond at the game had been right, it's all about hockey. Aiden had probably been running with the Coach's dog that morning.

"But don't you—"

"No. I don't care. I just killed a perfectly good dog for you. We're done."

"But you *need* to talk to Coach."

Fear's icy fingers squeezed. "Are you kidnapping me?"

"No." He drove her back to Runkle Hall.

Returning to her dorm room, she plopped on her bed, feeling numb. Her phone rang. *If that's Aiden...* It was Ben. Disappointment stabbed. *How crazy is that?*

"I'll pick you up at four twenty-five tomorrow," Ben said.

"Tomorrow?"

"Campus weather. Remember?"

Barely. "Don't worry about me."

"I don't mind."

"I have pepper spray, and I need to do it myself. Like that old adage about getting back on the wagon."

"Getting back on the horse," he corrected. "Are you sure?"

"I'll be fine."

Except she wasn't fine. Not at all. She stood outside Runkle Hall the next morning, holding her phone in one hand and the pepper spray in another. Convinced a huge dog lurked in every shadow, she couldn't move.

"Lexa?"

She spun ready to push buttons when she recognized Ben. "Don't scare me like that!"

"Sorry."

"What are you doing here?"

He gave her a don't-be-stupid look.

She drew in a deep breath. "Sorry. Thanks for coming."

"I'm surprised Mr. Knight-in-Shining-Armor isn't here. You guys have been spending all your time together."

They headed west on Curtain Road.

"You were right about him," she said. "But you're not allowed to gloat."

"Not even a little?"

"Nope." After a couple minutes, she asked, "Do you know if there are any 'she-woman men haters' clubs around that I can join?"

"Nope, but I'm sure my fellow he-mans won't have any trouble swearing off men."

The morning weather shift flew by. Lexa had an hour before her first class. She wasted time surfing the net instead of working on her thermo homework. Curious, Lexa pulled up pages on various big cats found in Pennsylvania, searching for one that matched the image in her mind. None. Remembering a neighbor who owned an exotic pet shop, she expanded to panthers and tigers. She leaned forward, clicking on the pictures of tigers on Wikipedia to enlarge them. A wave of nausea hit her. *That's close.* Except the creature that attacked her wasn't orange, but gray.

Following a few links, Lexa found an article about a subspecies of the South Chinese Tiger which was rumored to have a slate-gray coloration called a Maltese Tiger. She swallowed as she peered at the artist's rendering. *Bingo.*

What was Aiden doing with a tiger? He had wanted her to talk to Coach Hakim. She read Coach Hakim's bio online. He was born in the city of Surabaya, East Java, Indonesia. He spent every free moment of his childhood playing hockey. In 1980, he started skating for the Hong Kong Tigers.

The team's name triggered a connection. Hong Kong was near South China. She read on. Hakim became head coach of the Tigers in 2003. After the Tigers won every single tournament in Asia, Coach Hakim was hired by Penn State.

When asked why Hakim moved half way around the world, he replied that he loved a challenge, and wanted to show Penn State fans that hockey was, "the coldest [coolest] game on earth." The brackets translated the Coach's meaning since English wasn't his first language. From what Lexa knew about Hakim's players, perhaps he had meant coldest.

She mulled over all the information. Did the coach own a Maltese Tiger? A tiger breed that had never been seen before? *The World Wildlife Foundation would freak.*

She startled when Ben tapped her on the shoulder.

"You missed thermo again," he said. "Do you want to copy my notes?"

"Uh. Sure."

Ben studied her. "Is Depressed Girl back?"

Lexa examined her psyche as if probing a sore tooth with her tongue. An ache for her sister flared, but nothing like the all consuming grief. "No. Depressed Girl is gone."

"That calls for a celebration."

"No time. I have to work on thermo for Monday's test or I *will* fail the class."

"I can help you with thermo. After all, I nursed you through meteorological instrumentation."

"Thanks. Where?" she asked.

He gestured to the weather center. "This place is a ghost town on Friday nights. We'll start right after dinner."

After Ben left, she searched a few more sites on Asian ice hockey and tigers. She uncovered an odd link to a write up about a folk legend popular in Java, Indonesia that claimed were-tigers existed. When killed by a were-tiger, a man would lose his soul. The victim couldn't reclaim his soul until he, in turn, killed another. Villagers in Java would watch the men closely, seeking the signs of soullessness—cold, emotionless, and without joy.

That description could easily describe the Ice Men. Which was ridiculous—another example of Lexa's overactive imagination. Besides Aiden hadn't acted like that at all. Without thought her fingers stroked her neck.

Even with thermodynamics to occupy her mind, Lexa grieved over Aiden's absence. She couldn't focus at all on Saturday night especially not during game time. Exasperated with her lack of concentration, Ben called it a night. They headed to the G-man to have the first 'she-woman men hater's' club meeting.

During the week, the hockey team had a series of away

games. Lexa ached as though she had lost a limb. She wasn't Depressed Girl, but she couldn't sleep or eat or concentrate for more than two seconds. Her symptoms resembled withdrawal.

Perhaps she had been too hasty in sending Aiden away. Athletes were loyal to their coaches. Maybe Coach Hakim's tiger escaped and Aiden had been trying to find it. Just bad luck she happened to find it first. Of course all this was pure conjecture. She needed to confirm the tiger's existence.

After her thermo class on Friday morning, Lexa hiked out to Coach Hakim's house. The team had an afternoon game at West Chester University and wasn't due back until late. Lexa circled his house, but found no evidence that a tiger lived there. He didn't even have a fenced in backyard. She returned to campus.

Instead of heading home, she entered the Ice Pavilion. She found Coach Hakim's office, but the door was locked. Peering through the translucent glass, Lexa couldn't see anything.

"What are you doing?" a deep male voice asked her.

She turned. Coach Hakim stood with Kyle Gant and Mike Miller, both defensemen behind him. He scowled.

"Uh... Shouldn't you be with your team?"

"I came back early. But I'm glad you're here, I need to talk to you." He unlocked the door and drew her inside, motioning her to the seat facing his desk.

The defensemen followed. They stood in front of the closed door as if guarding it. Lexa glanced around. Equipment, trophies, binders, stacks of papers, and posters of tigers decorated the office. *There's a clue.*

Hakim settled behind his desk, looking unhappy.

Fear bubbled up her throat. "Look, if this is about your pet tiger, I won't say a word to anyone. I promise."

He grunted. "Did Aiden tell you that?"

"No. I guessed. Isn't that what attacked me? What you didn't want the police to know about?"

"Sure. Let's go with that."

Confused, she said, "Is that what you wanted to talk to me about?"

"Not really. I'm more concerned about Aiden. He hasn't scored a goal since last Saturday night."

"Oh. What—"

"You're the reason, and we're going to fix it tonight." He stood. "Give me your phone."

"Uh... I'd better go. I've a class—"

"Kyle, take her phone. Keep her here until the team returns." Hakim left without another word.

She jumped to her feet. "Hey!"

Even though she fought, Kyle confiscated her phone, shoving her back into the chair. When she stood again, he pushed her down and said, "Tape," to Mike who moved to grab the duct tape.

"No," she said. "I'll stay in the seat." She met his gaze and true terror exploded in her chest.

Kyle stared at her with dead eyes. No compassion or emotion of any kind shone from his face. Mike's was also as cold as the ice they skated on.

Holy shit, they're zombies. Except they were in the peak of health. *Brainwashed.* She couldn't decide if that was better or worse.

She spent an eternity in that chair. They wouldn't answer her questions and she stopped asking when they held up the roll of tape. Every emotion, every horrible scenario ran through her mind until she was numb.

Hakim returned after dark. "Bring her."

Kyle and Mike each grabbed an upper arm and dragged her to the ice rink. The dark arena didn't bode well for her future.

Four more players waited on the bleachers. Lexa recognized them all.

Coach Hakim sat on the bleachers. "Did you text him?" he asked Tim.

"Yes, sir."

"Good."

The door banged open and in rushed Mr. Knight-in-Shining-Armor. Too bad he was outnumbered seven to one. Aiden glanced at Lexa, but focused on his coach.

"Finish it Aiden or I will," Coach Hakim said.

"No. It can work." Aiden's voice held a note of pleading.

"You haven't scored a goal in three games. It's not working."

"That's only because we were apart. I scored four goals Saturday night when she was there."

"Can you tell me what's going on?" Her voice sounded as it should—petrified.

"Aiden attacked you," Hakim said. "He should have killed you, but his mother raised him too well."

"Kill me?"

"I lost control," Aiden said. "I'm sorry. I couldn't stand being...dead inside anymore." He gestured to his teammates. "Like them."

"If you don't kill her, I will have to kill you both. You know how it works," Hakim said.

Aiden closed his eyes for a moment. "Okay. I'll do it."

"Good. Go change."

Lexa watched Aiden walk away. He entered the locker room without looking back. Pure fear pumped through her veins. Panic jumbled all logic, but she managed to snag one coherent thought. Why would Aiden kill her? He wasn't dead inside. Not anymore. Was the Javan legend true?

"Will I come back like you?" she asked. "A soulless were-tiger until I kill someone?"

Coach Hakim peered at her in surprise. "How do you know?"

"Internet. Plus it's the only thing that fits...this."

A big gray tiger with black stripes stepped from the locker room.

"Sorry, but only men can survive the change. And they come back stronger and faster."

Mike and Kyle let her go, stepping away.

"Run," Hakim said. "Cats can't resist the chase."

Instead she backed up as the tiger...Aiden neared. Powerful muscles bunched and he crouched just like a house cat ready to pounce. Her muscles liquefied in terror.

In a heartbeat, he launched. Roaring, Aiden landed on Hakim's chest. The others moved to their coach. After the initial shock, Lexa didn't linger. She slipped out the doors and ran. Then stopped. She couldn't leave Aiden. He had the upper hand now, but the others could change into tigers as well. He'd be tiger food.

Think! She spotted Aiden's Accord in the lot and raced to it. *Please let the keys be inside.* Yanking open the door, she almost fainted in relief. His key ring glinted from the cup holder. Lexa jammed the key in the ignition and drove the car straight into the front doors.

The screech of metal and cracks of shattered glass echoed throughout the rink. Four of them sat on Aiden. Two hovered over their unconscious coach. She aimed the car at the four. They scattered. She pressed the window button. The back one went down. Aiden sailed through the opening.

Throwing the car in reverse, she backed out, turned around and headed north on University Drive. They didn't get far. The front tires were flat, and the radiator was damaged. She pulled over near Jeffery Field.

Aiden hopped from the car and pawed at the trunk. She opened it. *This is insane.* Aiden reached inside and pulled out a duffle bag. He moved away, glancing back at her.

"I'm right behind you," she said. *Might as well embrace the insanity.*

They crossed the street, cut through the Intramural fields, and entered the Arboretum's grounds, stopping behind the Schreyer House.

Lexa puffed as she plopped on the ground. "Now what?"

Aiden dropped the bag in her lap. She unzipped it. Men's clothes had been packed inside.

Holding up stripped boxers, she said, "You don't seem the boxer type."

He growled with impatience.

"Okay, I get it. You're going to change back." She turned around. "And I think I get the other stuff too. You lost control, attacked me, but when you saw I was a girl, you stopped. Please thank your mother for me. Instead of getting my whole soul, you only got a portion—that's why I stopped being Depressed Girl and why when you're with me I feel so complete. And why, when you were away, I failed my thermo test. And, yes I'm babbling. Considering the circumstances I'm allowed."

Lexa sucked in a breath. "So your teammates are soulless and your coach must be the one who killed you. That's why he has emotions. Although he didn't seem upset about my future demise. And now they're going to hunt us down and kill us both. Unless we can figure a way to get the hockey team's souls back without killing anyone. And we need to stop Coach Death, but I don't think Officer Reed and the State College police can handle something like that. He seemed so happy to have found a wild dog. Imagine—"

"Lexa." Aiden wrapped his arms around her.

She leaned back against him. "What are we going to do?"

"Just what you said."

"How?"

"I'm going to do some recruiting."

Aiden led her through the quiet campus. "Those six guys are Coach's favorites. But if we can get the rest of the team on our side—"

"Won't work." Lexa would never forget Kyle and Mike's dead stares. "They need souls."

"We're not going to kill anyone."

"Of course not. But..." An answer bubbled to the surface of her mind. "They can share."

Aiden stopped. "No. That's too much to ask. After this is all done, somehow you're getting yours back."

"No. I don't want it. I'm happy for the first time in years." Lexa realized she had assumed he felt the same. "Unless, you'd rather not be... I'm sure there are others..."

He drew her close. "I'd be an idiot to want anyone else. Look at what you've done tonight. Rescued me. Took the whole were-tiger thing in stride. You're awesome. I love being with you." He kissed her.

Her muscles melted again, but this time for a better reason.

Too soon, he pulled away. "We have to talk to the guys before Coach does."

"Not going to work. Talk to Ryan Collins' girlfriend. I'm positive she'd be willing to do anything to bring him back to life."

"Chelsea Belham? Really?"

~

Despite the late hour, convincing Chelsea was easier than expected. All she needed was to see the change in Aiden.

"I'm in. What's next?" Chelsea asked.

Lexa glanced at Aiden. "I haven't figure that out yet."

"I have. I thought of nothing else during that horrible week we were apart," he said. "It's an exchange of blood and saliva."

Chelsea drove them to Ryan's apartment in her silver BMW. He shared it with Doug Vett, a forward. When Ryan opened the door and saw Aiden, he grabbed him, pulled him into the apartment, and slammed him into a wall. Aiden crumpled to the floor.

Lexa and Chelsea jumped on Ryan, but he shrugged them off with ease. Doug Vett stood in the threshold of his bedroom. He didn't seem inclined to help, but he texted on his phone.

"Coach called," Ryan said in a monotone.

"Already figured that out big guy," Aiden said from the floor. He lumbered to his feet. "Wait," he said when Ryan moved. "Listen to me." Aiden rushed to explain.

"Coach said to hold them here until he arrives," Doug said.

Ryan blocked the door.

"I guess that's a no," Aiden said.

Chelsea hadn't moved since Ryan tossed her onto the ground next to Lexa. Her expression hardened into what Lexa would describe as bitch-mode. Opening her Prada handbag, Chelsea yanked out a thick nail file.

Figures. Although, a cell phone would have been confiscated right away.

Instead of filing her nails, Chelsea flicked her thumb and a blade shot out. Everyone froze in surprise. It was enough time for her to cut her wrist, stand, and cross to Ryan. She offered her bloody arm to him.

A predatory glint transformed his eyes into tiger eyes. Ryan clamped onto her wrist as if she was fresh kill. He sucked greedily.

Aiden pried Ryan from her. "Not too much or you'll kill her."

Ryan sank to the ground and put his head in his hands. Aiden knelt next to him.

Lexa wrapped a paper towel around a paler Chelsea's wrist.

"How long?" Chelsea asked.

Aiden said, "For me, it was pretty quick, but—"

"Chel?" Ryan glanced around.

The girl didn't hesitate. She threw herself into his arms.

One down, twenty-four more to go. Lexa glanced at Doug.

"Uh, Aiden." She pointed to Doug. He held his phone to his ear.

"Doesn't matter. Coach is already on the way," Aiden said. "We need to leave." He helped Chelsea and Ryan to their feet.

"Mark? It's Doug."

Aiden and Lexa exchanged a grin.

"Where can we go that Coach doesn't know about?" Aiden asked.

She felt her pockets. Despite all the running around, her keys remained. Holding up the key to the Walker building, she said, "This place's a ghost town on Friday nights."

The five of them crammed in Chelsea's BMW. They picked up Mark on the way.

~

It was a long exhausting weekend. Not all the players had girlfriends or boyfriends, and a couple weren't as understanding as Chelsea and Mark. Aiden and Lexa played matchmaker.

"I don't know about this," she said to Aiden as they waited for a potential mate. "What if they don't like each other, or have opposite personalities?"

"They won't afterward," Aiden said. "They'll be soul mates. It's what every single couple in the world hopes for, and only a tiny percentage achieve."

"But we're manipulating it with the tiger magic."

"We were manipulated. Do you have any complaints? Regrets?"

She stepped into his arms. "None."

The Coach remained a problem. And there was a game on Sunday afternoon. By that time, they had converted fifteen players.

"We play," Aiden said. "He's not going to do anything in public and we outnumber them. Once he sees we can still win, he'll back off. Winning is all he cares about."

En masse, they arrived at the Ice Pavilion. They met with a token resistance, but the ten remaining players didn't have the heart to fight. Lexa kept an eye on Coach Hakim during the game. He tried to prevent Aiden and the others from playing, but they ignored him. The team won seven to zero.

After that, the Coach cooperated. He even allowed the girls and guys to travel with the team for away games. The rest of the players found soul mates. The Ice Men had thawed.

"Coach Hakim can't walk away," Aiden said to Lexa after finals week. They were headed to the Gingerbread Man to celebrate the end of the semester and an early Christmas with the he-man club. Ben hadn't been supportive of Mr. Knight-in-Shining-Armor until he realized Depressed Girl was gone for good, and Aiden wasn't leaving.

"Nothing's stopping him from going to another school and creating another team filled with soulless were-tigers. We all swore not to attack anyone, but Coach didn't."

She mulled it over. They needed something that would ruin his reputation to a point where no one would hire him. Jail time would be a bonus. The answer clicked.

Aiden laced his fingers in hers. "I sense from that evil gleam in your eyes there's a solution?"

"Isn't Ryan a computer science major?"

"Yeah, going into cyber security."

"Even better. I'd bet he could hack into Coach's computer and plant evidence that the Coach has been betting money on the hockey games. An anonymous tip to the NCAA and his career as a hockey coach would be over." Perfect, except the coach was still a dangerous were-tiger. "But what if he seeks revenge?" she mused aloud, worried he'd attack Aiden or his teammates. "Or changes his name and moves to another country before we can ruin his career? More people will be in danger."

He grinned. "Haven't you heard? Coach's ex-wife is in town to pick up the rest of her things. The boys thought they'd supervise a reunion."

"Wow, that's devious."

"Yeah. We have it all figured out. Except what we're going to do in the off-season."

Lexa considered. "Play baseball?"

He pressed a hand to his chest in mock horror. "Please never mention the b-word ever again."

She laughed, but then thought, what else could a group of

super-brawny guys, who could change into tigers, do during the off-season? Her gaze snagged on the headlines of *The Collegian*. Yet another article about the Jerry Sandusky scandal.

"Perhaps you and the team could help the helpless." She tipped her head toward the pile of newspapers on the sidewalk.

"As vigilantes?"

"Not that extreme, but more like finding the abusers and then calling in the police to arrest them."

"I like the idea of helping the helpless. I'll see what the rest of the team thinks."

When they reached the entrance to the Gingerbread Man, Aiden pulled her close. "Forgot to ask. How did you do in thermo?"

"Terrible. I'll have to take it again, and the F sent my GPA into the toilet."

"But you were getting the hang of it."

"Way too late to save my grade. On the bright side, I know a really good tutor."

"Oh yeah?" He smiled. "First lesson, thermodynamics is all about the transfer of heat. Let me demonstrate." Aiden kissed her with all his heart and soul.

A flame ignited in her core and sizzled on her skin.

He broke away, leaving her gasping. "Understand?"

"I'm still a bit...fuzzy on the concept. Can you go over it again?"

Laughing, he recaptured her lips for another heated exchange. Then he said, "Best make it a hat trick," before dipping in for a third scorching demonstration. "And now?"

"Yes. I see an A plus in my future."

GODZILLA WARFARE

An anthology of stories written by female science fiction authors titled, No Man's Land. *Where do I sign up? It was an honor to be invited to participate in this unique opportunity. One problem, the stories had to be military science fiction. Well, shoot. I've written dystopian SF and near-future SF. But military? Not in my wheelhouse. I'd no idea where to start and the alien invasion trope had been done to death. Good thing Danielle Ackley-McPhail, one of the editors, didn't accept any of my weak excuses. She was determined to to have me listed in the table of contents. I was overwhelmed by the genre, thinking I had to create this entire empire and learn military tactics for this story. I was certain this challenge was beyond my skills. However, Danielle told me to think small. Just pick a cog in the wheel—someone like an expert on bombs or a bomber pilot and go from there. I took her advice to heart and ended up with a story, and a character who is one of my favorites of all time. Can you tell who?*

GODZILLA WARFARE

Val's comm link buzzed in her ear, waking her. *Not another problem with the simulator*, she thought. *Damn thing breaks more than the mining trolls on Mars Seven.*

She toggled it on with a little more force than required, hurting herself which just added to her annoyance. "Harris here, this better be important."

"Sergeant Harris, report to Captain Bachman's office immediately," a mechanical voice said.

Oh shit. Val rolled out of bed, sorted through the pile of uniforms, searching for one less wrinkled than the others. An impossible task. Finally, she found a pair of fatigues that didn't look like it had been on the losing side of a fight. She dressed, tied her long auburn hair into a regulation knot, and sprinted for the Captain's office.

This is it. Time for the you've-outlived-your-usefulness-talk. Time for the let-the-younger-generation-take-over speech. Even though, at forty-two, she was still able to outsmart the newbs, the invention of the planet-wide shields had rendered her expert skills obsolete.

She paused outside the Captain's door to compose her expression before peering into the retinal scanner for identification. The base on Mercury Three was far enough away from the action to be safe from a direct attack. Indirect was the new strategy. Thus the time-to-retire talk.

The door slid open, revealing a waiting area with a receptionist. Val fully expected to be gestured to a seat in the typical army hurry up and wait manner, however the Private working the desk admitted her into the Captain's office without delay.

Double shit.

The Captain sat behind her desk and watched Val approach and salute. Bachman's immaculate uniform lacked a crease. The knot of her blond hair had been twisted into perfection. Val resisted the desire to yank at her semi-wrinkled shirt.

"Sergeant Harris, I have an assignment for you," the Captain said.

Biting down on her surprise, Val waited.

Captain Bachman glanced at the collective's screen. "There's an unexploded MFG-66 on Jupiter Nine and since you're the expert in disarming those...what do you call them?"

"Godzilla bombs, sir."

"Why?"

"It's a reference to a mythical Earth creature that can destroy a city, sir. Since the MFG-66 has enough energy to flatten a city with an approximate population of thirteen million, we've code named it the Godzilla, sir." And it managed it without using nuclear energy. No sense contaminating the planet you're fighting over.

"Interesting." The Captain tapped on the screen. "There is a bullet waiting to take you to Jupiter Nine. Please report to deck twelve, barrel two right away."

Val hesitated.

"Sergeant?"

"We're at war with J-9, sir." And a whole list of other ungrateful colony planets.

"Not at present. We have signed a cease-fire agreement with them, and are currently involved in treaty negotiations. This mission is an act of good faith on our part Sergeant, so don't screw it up or UFoP will come down hard on us."

"Yes, sir."

The Captain confirmed what Val had surmised on her own. The war with J-9 and the other colony planets hadn't been going well these last few years.

Val swung by her tiny office next to the beast, a.k.a. the simulator to gather her equipment. She hadn't been assigned a field job in over seven years. A few of her instruments were out of date, but so was the Godzilla. Odd. This whole mission felt...off. Not much she could do about it. Val sent a message to her second, putting her in charge of the newbs' training and nursing the temperamental simulator. *Good luck.*

She reported to barrel two. The bullet to J-9 was piloted by a scruffy-looking Lieutenant whose skin had the grayish tinge of someone who hadn't seen sunlight in years. *Another old soul. Wonderful.*

He flashed her a toothy smile when she saluted. "No need for formalities on my ship, Sergeant. Call me Leo." He eyed her gear bag. "How much does that thing weigh?"

"About three kilos."

"And you?"

"Fifty-four. Why?"

"This baby's stripped down for extra speed not comfort. Let me ditch about sixty kilos and we'll be all set."

Leo piled various gadgets on the deck. He held a stack of vomit bags, debating. "Do you get Kasner-speed sick?"

"No."

"Great." He tossed them onto the pile. "Let's go."

Val wedged herself into the back seat, strapping in even though, with this conveyance, you either arrived or you didn't, there was no in between. The ship's name came from the simple fact that it resembled the old projectiles that had been used on Earth. Cone full of navigational equipment and controls, a seat for the pilot, followed by a seat for a single passenger, a small cargo area, and ended with the Kasner-Phillips engine. Constructed for the sole purpose of getting from one place to another as fast as possible, the bullet was literally shot out of a barrel and into space.

They hit Kasner-speed as soon as they broke Merc-3's gravity. Val had forgotten how truly awful the experience of traveling at Kasner-speed was. The destroyers she'd been assigned to before baby-sitting newbs traveled at the more leisurely pace of Phillips-speed.

By the time they arrived near J-9 and her body coalesced, Val wished she'd kept a few vomit bags. *Getting too old for this shit.*

"How ya doing?" Leo asked.

"Fine. How much longer until landing?"

"As long as the Jups open their shield, we should be on terra firma in twenty."

"And if they don't open the shield?"

"We'll go skating, baby. Put on a nice fireworks show for the Jups as we burn!"

Val sighed. *Fly boys.* "I meant what's the plan if we're refused entry?"

"Oh. Turn around, go home. They're the ones with the pimple."

The dimple. Bombs that crashed but failed to explode left craters that the explosive experts called dimples. But she wasn't going to correct an officer even if he had spent too much time at Kasner-speed.

Despite Leo's personality quirks, they landed with nary a bump twenty minutes later. When they finished decontamination, Val and Leo entered the port and were surrounded by a dozen armed soldiers.

"Ah, the welcoming committee," Leo said. "Let me handle this, Sergeant." He introduced himself to the squad's leader. "I believe you requested an ED expert? I'm just the pilot, but I've brought Sergeant Harris. If you have an ED to disarm, she's your girl."

Val kept her expression neutral despite the desire to cringe over the Lieutenant's intro. The J-9 Sergeant's hard gaze swept over her with frank appraisal. She reciprocated. About her age, he had the weathered look of someone who'd been in one too many skirmishes. Buzzed black hair and blue-colored eyes, he stared at her with open suspicion.

They confiscated her gear bag and "escorted" her to a conference room, while they led Lieutenant Leo...elsewhere. She sat on one side of a square metal table that had been bolted to the floor. No windows, no decorations—other than six chairs all secured to the floor—Val realized the purpose of the room probably wasn't to confer, but to interrogate.

If they think I'd make a good POW, they're in for a surprise. I haven't been relevant since those damn planet-wide shields. The civil war with J-9 and a number of other planets had gone on far too long. She understood that they desired their independence from Mother Earth. But they didn't want to pay Mother back the octillions of dollars she invested in equipment, supplies, and labor needed to colonize a raw planet. Nope. They wanted a free ride.

Mother didn't have a problem with the colony planets that signed the pay-their-way-to-freedom contracts. Although these semi-free planets had formed the United Federation of Planets (UFoP)—a laughable tiny group for such a big name. Too bad they didn't remain small and insignificant. The UFoP agreed to stay out of the civil fights as long as Mother Earth adhered to fair warfare tactics. They also now had enough member planets and firepower to enforce the rule.

The Sergeant from the port entered the room with two of his men. The door closed with a distinctive click. The men stayed near the door as the Sergeant approached. She stood.

"Sergeant Harris, I'm Sergeant Gideon. I'm to brief you on the situation." He didn't offer his hand.

They sat on opposites sides of the table. Gideon tapped on the surface of the table. It glowed as it accessed the J-9 collective. A live picture of a barren landscape showed a number of small dimples. As the view zoomed closer on one, it revealed the crater the bomb had created. The MFG-66 had made an impressive scar, digging deep. The view followed the impact path and then the bomb itself—a melted distorted mass, but still deadly. Val wondered how the Godzilla ended up in the middle of nowhere. Here it couldn't do any damage even if it had detonated on impact.

"I'm leading a team to the crater. You'll remain here and give me instructions to disarm it. I have experience with explosives," Gideon said.

Interesting brief. At least he wasn't planning on using a remote robot. Those things had a twenty percent success rate with the Godzilla. "No," she said.

"It isn't up for debate, Sergeant."

"Sergeant Gideon do you want to die?" she asked in a reasonable tone. "Do you want that MFG-66 to detonate because your expert can't smell, touch or get a sense of the bomb through a screen? Now, I personally don't care if you blow your team to little tiny bits, but my boss ordered me not to screw this up. So unless you take me out there, I'm not going to cooperate."

Gideon stood. "I'll discuss it with my superiors."

"Good. And make sure you tell them that, when *we're* onsite, *I'm* in command. It's not negotiable."

His demeanor remained dispassionate, but anger burned in his gaze. She almost laughed. Working with unpredictable explosive devices in hostile environments over the years, Val couldn't be intimated by one man's ego.

The three soldiers left. Val tried to get a better view of the Godzilla, except the screen turned off at her touch. *Probably set off an alarm. Good, it will keep them on edge.*

An hour later, Gideon returned Val's gear bag and led her to a shuttle along with six armed guards.

"Tell your pilot to land two kilometers from the crater," she ordered Gideon.

After they reached cruising altitude, Gideon sat across from her with his STR-23 rifle in his lap. Val ignored him as she prepped and calibrated her instruments.

When they landed, Val had them wait thirty minutes before opening the hatch. Not that they could out fly an explosion, but the vibrations from the landing should have settled by then. Gideon's impatience grew, causing his men to tense up as he bore the wait with ill humor.

At the end of thirty minutes, Val said, "Your men will stay here, Sergeant." She paused to let him refuse. He didn't disappoint.

"It's not up for debate," she said, keeping her tone even. "Normally, this is a one person operation. Explosives are temperamental, and ones that have burned through an atmosphere and crashed are overly sensitive to the slightest vibrations. The more feet tromping around, the higher the risk of setting the damn thing off." Val rummaged in her bag. Pulling out two pairs of soft-feet, she handed one set to Gideon. "Put them on the bottom of your boots. They're hard on the ankles, but sore ankles are worth not dying."

They exited the shuttle and covered the two clicks in silence. Val noted the air was cool and dry. A breeze blew from the east, stirring the lifeless soil. Nothing except a few clumps of rocks and a couple smaller indentations marked the empty expanse.

When they reached the edge of the crater, Val surveyed the damage. "How long ago did this hit?"

"That's classified," Gideon said.

"You're going to make this as difficult as possible for me, aren't you Sergeant?"

"I have my orders, *Sergeant*," he shot back.

And that would be a yes. She climbed down the steep side of the crater. Grabbing a handful of scorched dirt, she rolled it around her palm and smelled it. She moved to another area and repeated the test. Val wiped her hands and followed the path of impact until she neared the Godzilla. It was half buried.

Opening her pack, she removed her sniffer. She stood downwind from the MFG-66, testing the air for chemical leakage. Then she sampled the soil. The Godzilla's casing hadn't ruptured on impact, the good news. The impact had happened a few weeks ago, the bad news. An already old bomb—the

Godzillas hadn't been manufactured in the last seven years—combined with chemicals degrading on the ground created one twitchy bomb.

Which raised the question, why didn't they just set it off with one of their own explosive devices? She asked Sergeant Gideon.

"Classified," he said.

Something stank. And it wasn't the burnt fuel.

Val mulled over the few facts and watched Gideon's expression as she theorized aloud. "You tried to trigger it, but the Godzilla's defensive scrambler sent your bombs wide which explains the other two impact craters."

He kept his neutral demeanor, but a slight twitch in his jaw gave him away. She was on the right track. Val gestured to the bomb. "This is a recent hit. Which should be impossible due to your shield. Our ships no longer carry the Godzilla. It could have been launched from a Hermit ship. But, again your shield should have destroyed it."

His eyebrows rose, but he smoothed them just as quick. "Is that what the G stands for in MFG?"

"That's what we call it. There is a technical name the higher ups use."

"What does the MF stand for?"

"Official or ours?"

"Yours."

"We refer to that device as the Mother Fucking Godzilla."

Gideon laughed, and the tension between them slipped a few notches. Until Val realized he had been trying to distract her from putting all the clues together.

She picked up the thread of logic and gathered it. "Someone sliced into your collective and turned off your shield just long enough for the Godzilla's entry. Didn't they?"

"That's impossible. No one has sliced into our collective."

Yet he had stiffened as if she had hit a nerve.

With Gideon a step behind her, she approached the bomb. The vibrations in her chest increased ten-fold as sweat dampened her uniform. The number of times she'd defused a bomb didn't matter. Each had its own quirks and challenges. Each one could be her last. Each caused the adrenaline to rush through her body.

The bomb appeared to be far bigger than the standard Godzilla, but the outside markings matched. After confirming the absence of dangerous chemicals, she located the access panel.

Val handed Gideon the sniffer. "If this reads over ten parts per million, tell me."

He nodded.

Glad her hands remained steady, she opened the panel, revealing the bomb's innards. She stared at the complex twist of wires, circuit boards and switches. Except she didn't recognize the configuration. Not right away. When she understood just what sat in front of her, she cursed.

"What's wrong?" Gideon asked.

She replaced the panel and backed away, pulling the Sergeant with her. Val didn't stop until they reached the crater's edge.

"What's—"

"I need to speak with my colleague," she said.

"The bullet pilot? Why?"

"It's classified."

Now it was Gideon's turn to curse. "This better not be some stunt or attempt to influence the treaty negotiations."

"It's not."

He stared at her. "I'll hold you to that."

~

"It's a Death Star," she whispered to Lieutenant Leo. They were in the conference room and she suspected it had been bugged, but she needed to talk to Leo.

"Holy shit with a halo and a white robe! Are you sure?"

"Unfortunately. Are the treaty negotiations going badly for us?"

"I don't know. You can ask the Ambassador, he's at the J-9 capital. That is if he'll talk to you." Leo swept a hand through his non-regulation shaggy hair. "Damn girl! Can you disarm it?"

"No. Not alone. It's wired so you need two people, working in tandem."

"But you've done it before. Right?" A crazed hope shone in Leo's eyes as he clutched her sleeves.

"In the simulator, with my assistant. We had one successful session." And only one other team had managed to duplicate it. Not a real achievement since they stopped training on it when the planet-wide shields proved to be an effective defense against the Death Star. Which had been the point. Intel on the Death Star's incredible power had leaked before the device was ready to launch. The panic had been epic.

"Out of how many practice sessions?" Leo asked.

"You don't want to know."

"Time to vacate the premises." Leo stood.

"They won't let us go." Val went up on tip-toe and whispered in his ear. "The Death Star is in delay-action mode."

Leo's face paled to pure white. He swayed. "Why bother to send us?"

"Think about it," Val said. She had. During the trip back to the base, she did nothing but mull it over.

Her theory wasn't pretty. Mother Earth had signed a cease-fire with Jupiter Nine because the colony had been winning the war. The planet-wide shields had countered Mother's one effective offense. With J-9's new guerrilla attacks on Mother Earth's bases, Val suspected Mother had to be desperate. So Mother played nice with J-9, sending an Ambassador and his retinue to negotiate terms and conditions. Once inside the shield, one of the team had probably managed to shut the shields down long enough for a bomb to slip through.

Mother probably acted surprised. *How did that happen? Must be from a Hermit ship from the past since it's an old MFG-66. We'll send our best expert to take care of it for you.* Except the expert wasn't qualified to disarm a Death Star—no one was. And after the expert "triggered" the bomb, Mother would be all apologetic to the UFoP. *Oops, our mistake. Sorry. Someone must have stolen the schematics to the YFS-97, a.k.a. Death Star or as the late Sergeant Val Harris liked to say, You're Fucking Screwed in ninety-seven different ways.*

Val admitted it was an elaborate ruse to appease the UFoP, but she suspected Mother Earth would rather turn J-9 into an asteroid belt, than turn it over to the Jups without a pay-back contract. She was a spiteful bitch that way.

Val could almost hear the gears and switches humming inside Leo's head as he put the clues together.

"And here I'd been worried I'd be forced into retirement. Far better to retire than be a flipping martyr," Leo said.

"Actually, to be a martyr, you have to be the one to decide. In this case, we're being sacrificed."

"Thanks for taking away the only shred of dignity I had left. Did you torture animals when you were little, too, Sergeant?"

"What do we do?" she asked.

"Kiss your ass good-bye and find someone willing to fuck your brains out before the big bang."

Val frowned at the Lieutenant. He was not helping.

Conflicting emotions churned inside her, Val had been glad the Death Star program had never been activated—the loss of life would have been astronomical. Plus it sickened her. But she was loyal to Mother Earth and felt she was right to expect to be compensated for all that hard work in colonizing a planet. Her warring thoughts connected and produced a blast of inspiration.

"Lieutenant, can you contact the Ambassador and tell him I *need* to speak with him?"

"You have a plan?" Leo asked.

"I have an idea."

"Bless your wicked little heart." Leo pounded on the door and demanded they be taken to the Ambassador.

Surprisingly, Sergeant Gideon agreed, escorting them to another interrogation room thinly disguised as a conference room.

The Ambassador swept in a couple hours later with a scowl already deepening the lines on his wide forehead. "Report, Lieutenant. And it better be important or you'll both be court marshaled for interfering."

Val studied him. A thick, but powerful build, receding hairline with enough gray to appear respectable. His agitation seemed genuine. Leo glanced at her to begin. Time to test the extent of his knowledge. Did he know he was on a suicide mission?

Keeping her voice pitched low, she explained the situation.

At first, the Ambassador huffed in disbelief. "No one on my team could have taken down their shields." But soon his survival instincts kicked in. "There was mention of a Hermit when we flew in. Are you one hundred percent sure it's a YFS-97, Sergeant?"

"Yes, sir. No doubt."

"I never should have pissed off General Reffan," the

Ambassador said. "The old bastard never forgot and here I am, thinking I'd been promoted."

And Val had thought she was useful for the first time in years. Leo's sad gaze matched hers. Another old soldier who had outlived his usefulness. She let the bout of self-pity run its course, then shook it off.

"Ambassador, you need to inform the Jups of the situation," she said.

"So they can tell the UFoP before we're blown to smithereens? How much time do we have?"

"Not enough to argue with me, sir." She ignored his outrage. "They have the right to know, and I need the complete and unquestioning cooperation of Sergeant Gideon. The only way he'll give it to me is if he's ordered to by a superior officer. Plus he should know what he's dealing with."

"You're going to try to disarm the cursed thing?" Leo asked.

"Yes. There's not enough time for an evac, it's either try or do what you suggested earlier Lieutenant."

Leo leered at Val. "I knew you'd see it my way eventually."

The Ambassador, though remained confused. "Why not have the Lieutenant help you? That way we don't have to say a word to the Jups."

Val poured a glass of water. She handed it to Leo. "Please take a drink, Lieutenant."

He lifted the glass and downed the contents in one gulp. When he handed it back, Val took it from his shaky hand. Too much time spent at Kasner-speed affected the nervous system. He was okay to fly, but disarming the Death Star would take a steady hand.

"What are the odds of success, Sergeant?" the Ambassador asked.

"Does it matter?"

"That bad?"

"Yes, sir."

~

"A what? Sergeant Harris, you're not making sense," Gideon said. "What the hell is a Death Star?"

She suppressed a sigh. His superior officer had ordered him to cooperate with her without hesitation or question, but failed to state a reason, leaving that bit of nasty news to Val. "The bomb buried in your planet is a YFS-97 not a MFG-66. It's carrying enough energy to destroy your *entire* plane, and it's set to go off in twelve hours." They had wasted six precious hours talking with the J-9 authorities.

He rocked back on his heels as if she had punched him. "You're wrong. They've been obsolete since the shields."

"According to *your* people, it managed to slip through when the shield opened to allow a supple ship to land. With the right timing, dead accurate maneuvering, and the bomb's special coating, which makes it invisible to your sensors, it is possible."

"But it was shot from a Hermit ship sent over a decade ago. It wouldn't have the latest tech."

She waited, letting him realize the Hermit either had been a decoy or another ship disguised as one. Unlike Val, Mother Earth hadn't given up on the YFS-97 program.

He blanched as fear widened his eyes and his lips parted. "Shit."

Val watched as Gideon swiped a hand over his face, wiping away the horror and transforming into a soldier. He straightened and met her gaze. Black stubble peppered with gray darkened his strong chin. She wondered if he had a wife and kids or a girlfriend waiting for him at home. Or if he was like her, married to the job.

"What do you need from me, Sergeant?" he asked.

"Hold out your hands."

He did. They were rock steady.

"I need you to make the impossible possible."

Gideon quirked a smile. "Is that all? And here I was worried."

They returned to the crater. This trip was completely different than their first. Gideon sat next to her and she explained everything she could remember about the Death Star. Since a delay-action device was a different beast than an unexploded one, the shuttle could land right at the crater's edge.

Val removed both access panels. They were located on opposite sides. Pointing out the important circuits and wires to him, she said, "At times, my instructions will seem counter-intuitive, but you need to do exactly what I say. Understand?"

"Yes."

When Gideon called that he was ready, a cold wave of terror washed through her. The only successful disarms had been with teams of two women. She should have requested a female sergeant.

"Harris?" Only Gideon's face could be seen above the bomb's body. "Let's do this."

Pulling in a deep breath, Val stared at her hands. Despite her out of control heart rate and her guts turning to liquid, they remained still.

"All right, Gideon. Located the red and black wire that has been twisted with a green and yellow one. On the count of three, cut the red and black wire." She positioned her wire cutters then glanced up. Gideon stared at her, waiting.

She said, "One. Two. Three." Snip. Val braced for the roar, the flash of light, but nothing happened.

This is going to be pure hell. Consider the alternative, Val. Right.

"Okay, now I want you to cut the green and yellow wire on three."

Once again he met her gaze while she counted, cutting the wire without looking at his wire cutters. Her assistant hadn't done that. Anxiety boiled in her stomach.

She continued with the initial sequence. If the steps weren't done in order and in tandem, the Death Star would detonate. The device's internal clock couldn't be stopped or disconnected without severing the contacts with the explosives. In other words, there were no short cuts.

Val had lapsed into a rhythm, when Gideon broke her concentration.

"Harris that's insane. You're sending current *into* the pads. It should be diverted." Little streams of sweat ran down the sides of his face.

"Twist the wires together on my count."

"No. You're a Godzilla expert. They sent you to fail, remember?"

Ouch.

"You're going to kill us all," he said with a voice pinched tight with panic. "There are over five million people living on this planet. I won't do it."

She tried logic. "We're all going to die anyway."

"But I *won't*...can't be the reason." Gideon stepped away from the panel.

"Damn it, Gideon. We were working. Ninety-five percent of the simulated sessions had failed by this point." She made up the statistic, it sounded reassuring and was close enough to the truth.

He paused.

"Stop thinking. This baby is unlike anything you've dealt with before. But I have experience. Now twist those wires on three, Sergeant."

Gideon nodded and returned to the bomb. Val allowed a second of cool relief to flow through her burning muscles before she counted.

As they worked, Val disconnected from what might happen to the task at hand. But statistics caught up to her. Two people cutting, splicing, and re-wiring circuit boards at the exact same time was near impossible.

The YFS-97 shuddered and activated with a series of clicks. She jumped back.

"What happened?" Gideon asked.

"We're done."

"But we were so close!" His voice rose in panic. "Why didn't it explode?"

Her thoughts jumbled, twisting until they resembled the pulled out guts of the Death Star. *Kaboom, kaboom—where's the kaboom? Leo had the right idea, I should be on the floor with Gideon, spending my last minutes—*

"Harris." He shook her shoulders. "It's not over. Finish the mission soldier!"

She blinked at him. "They sent me to fail. I've achieved my mission."

"Yes, they did send you to fail. After years of loyal service, you were deemed disposable. How does that make you feel soldier?"

"Mad as hell."

"What are you going to do about it?"

The clicking increased in volume and speed. *Kaboom come soon.* Val almost giggled, but a chunk of vital information formed in the middle of her spinning thoughts. *No kaboom. Why not?*

They had been near the end. Only a few connections were left, which meant the YFS-97 had to find another way to detonate.

"Go!" She pointed to his panel. Grabbing her pliers, she shouted instructions to Gideon over the noise.

It didn't matter if they worked in tandem as long as they both finished the last step before the Death Star re-routed its ignition. Sweat dripped and she panted with the effort.

"Last cut, Gideon," she yelled. "Blue wire, snip it off before it enters the boxes on either side and pull it—" A shower of sparks arched across her wire cutters. Then a huge fireball slammed into her, knocking her off her feet.

Kaboom. Mission accomplished. She crash landed. All thought disappeared.

Pain and semi-consciousness returned at the same time. Every centimeter of her body hurt, and she had lost her vision and hearing. Val swore. Except it didn't help when she couldn't hear her own cursing. She also couldn't move, which would be alarming if she had the energy to care.

Real consciousness came with some serious pain, but the meds helped blur the sharp edges. And the return of both her hearing and vision aided in her recovery.

Gideon visited. "Welcome back, Sergeant."

"But...the fire. What..."

"I've no idea. I yanked the blue wire just as the fireball hit you. It dissipated. The clicking stopped. I'm here and not blown to bits. So I'm not complaining."

"How long..."

"You've been out of it a couple days. Leo's beside himself. He wants to go home, and is driving us all crazy."

"Pilots have...a harder time...being a POW. There's been... studies." *And I probably won't do much better.* However, when she considered the alternative, being a POW didn't seem so bad.

Gideon smiled. "While you're welcome to stay—you are a hero, after all—of course only a few people will ever know about it—however, you don't *have* to stay. As soon as you're feeling better, Leo will fly you back to your base."

Confused, Val asked. "What did I miss?"

"Your Ambassador made a deal. If you saved our planet, you would be allowed to leave. But there is one condition."

"Home sweet home," Leo cried as he landed the bullet.

"Leo, it's a barren rock with a military base. Not what I'd call home," Val said as she tried not to get sick in his ship.

"Better than some foul swamp with huge creatures that consider us dessert."

"Ugh. You've been to the base on Venus Five?"

"Spent two years there." He shuddered. "I'll take a barren wasteland any day."

Her sore muscles protested as Val climbed from the bullet and entered the decontamination area. But she forgot all about her aches and pains when she spotted Captain Bachman and four MPs waiting for her on the platform.

"Sergeant Harris, come with me," the Captain ordered. "Lieutenant Leo, please report to your commanding officer."

"Yes, sir." They both snapped a salute.

Leo shook her hand good-bye. Grinning, he headed in the opposite direction. *I'd grin, too if I could claim ignorance, telling everyone I'd hung out in the pilot's lounge drinking the entire time.*

The Captain led her to a debriefing room and gestured to a chair. Val scanned the room. The place had been rigged with video and audio sensors.

"Report, Sergeant," the Captain ordered.

"I disarmed the bomb as requested, Captain. I've nothing else to report."

"You disarmed a MFG-66?"

So she had known. "Yes, sir."

"Are you sure?"

Val feigned confusion. "Of course, sir. The explosive device was clearly labeled. There is even video footage—"

"Sergeant Harris, I don't care what the video showed. I want an honest report."

Then you shouldn't have lied to me, bitch. Swallowing the bitter taste in her mouth, Val detailed a textbook disarming of a Godzilla bomb for the Captain.

Clearly impatient, the Captain banged her hands on the table. "What took you so long to return?"

"After I disarmed the bomb, I supervised the proper dismantling and safe storage of the explosives, which required a few days."

"That wasn't part of your mission, Sergeant."

"Sorry, sir. I misunderstood. Since you informed me that my mission was an act of *good faith*, I felt it was my duty to ensure the safety of the Jups."

The Captain kept trying to trip Val up. However, Bachman wouldn't directly ask about the Death Star. And with the Ambassador's report, confirming Val's statement, Captain Bachman couldn't charge Val with treason.

The Jups had been smart to pretend all had gone as planned. They kept Mother Earth wondering and worried about what happened to that Death Star. *Good, it will keep them on the edge.*

～

Val tendered her resignation a few months later. Although upset, Captain Bachman couldn't stop her. She packed her few belongings and met Leo on deck twelve.

"Free at last?" he asked.

"Yep. What about you?"

"I'll never retire. I'm a speed junkie." He grabbed her bag and shoved it in the cargo area of his bullet. "Where to, my dear?"

"Jupiter Nine."

"Oh?"

"I hear they're looking to hire an explosives expert."

"Really? Are you sure it isn't because of a certain yummy Sergeant Gideon?"

"I wouldn't use the word yummy to describe the Sergeant."

"What word would you use?"

But Val only smiled at her friend as she settled into the passenger seat. While she waited for the bullet to fire, she thought of the perfect word for Gideon.

Kaboom.

SAKE AND OTHER SPIRITS

When I was invited to submit to After Hours: Tales from the Ur-Bar, *there were three requirements: the story must be set in a bar, it must have the original clay tablet with the Sumerian beer recipe somewhere inside, and the bar must be owned by the immortal Gilgamesh who couldn't leave the bar. Time and place didn't matter as this magical bar traveled through time. As long as, "...drinks are mixed with magic and served with a side of destiny and intrigue." Oooh, I was immediately interested. At the time, I'd been teaching a fantasy writing class about choosing settings that are outside the classic medieval European box, challenging my students to find unique settings. For this story, I followed my own advice. Drawn to the stories of samurais in feudal Japan, I did some research and discovered their wives were also well trained in order to protect their home and children while the samurais were off fighting. This sparked an idea that involved a sake house, included a mythical Japanese creature, and ended up being one of my favorites in this collection.*

SAKE AND OTHER SPIRITS

The paper lanterns swung as cold air gusted from the open door. A group of traders bundled in furs hurried into the sake-house. Flakes of snow swirled around them. Azami noted the lack of excited chatter and boisterous calls to Gilga-san, the owner of the establishment. Concerned, she stuffed her bar rag into her kimono and helped the men remove their heavy coats and leather boots.

She caught Saburo's gaze. Usually so quick with his smile, his lips were pressed tight. His movements were stiff with tension as he shrugged off his fur. His fellow traders kept their somber expressions as they ordered sake and shabu-shabu stew.

"What happened?" Azami asked Saburo in a whisper.

"Two traders have died and Toshi's caravan is missing. I'll tell you more later," he said as he joined the men around a low table, dropping onto a cushion as if defeated.

Gilga-san, always alert to the mood of his customers, crossed the room with a seasoned fighter's grace. He managed to fold his tall body into an open space at the table. Even sitting he towered over the traders.

As she served bowls of steaming stew and cups of sake, Azami heard snippets of the traders' conversation.

". . . white as snow, not a drop of blood . . ."

"Disappeared for days, then . . ."

". . . on the western bank. . . "

". . . Toshi and four others . . . gone . . ."

Each one caused her greater alarm. Besides being horrified for the men and their families, the strange happenings might bring the samurai to town. And if they came, Azami would need to flee.

When the night grew late and only a few customers remained, Gilga-san assisted in the clean up despite her protests.

"This is what you pay me for," she said. "Go and entertain your guests."

Gilga-san enjoyed regaling his customers with stories that put the best Rakugoka to shame. But tonight he seemed preoccupied, and his gray-green eyes peered through her. "Not tonight. No one is in the mood for frivolous stories."

"Is it because of the traders who died and the missing men?"

"Yes. The first two disappeared three days ago from Yukio's caravan while they traveled around Lake Biwa. A fisherman found their bodies today, washed up on the shore."

"Drowned?"

"Hard to tell. Their lungs were full of water and their throats were shredded."

Azami's hand went to her neck as she glanced at Saburo. Since the snows had closed the mountain passes, his caravan also passed the lake. He remained at the table with three others. The rest had gone home.

"Murder?" she asked.

"Perhaps."

"The other five?"

"Toshi's caravan was due back this afternoon."

"That's terrible. Their families must be upset."

"They are. You should keep your kaiken close at hand when you leave tonight," Gilga-san said.

She jerked in surprise. No one knew about her dagger. Or so she thought.

He shot her a slightly amused smile. "We've been working together for over a year."

A year? Already? She had taken the job in his sake-house to earn enough money to leave Hokuga. Azami needed to increase the distance between her and her former life. The small fishing village of Hokuga had just been a temporary stop. Except Gilga-san treated her as an equal, and his bookkeeping had been an utter mess until she had taken it over. Then there was Saburo with his kind heart, good intentions, and sweet smile.

As if he could read her thoughts, Gilga-san said, "Saburo won't let you go home tonight unaccompanied. But he has no fighting skills."

Azami searched his expression. Most men would forbid a woman of her station to carry a weapon. Did he suspect her former identity? He must, otherwise he would send along another protector who could defend them both.

Aware of her assessment, he waited. His foreignness used to unnerve her. With his oval eyes, black curly hair, pale skin and muscular build, he stood out among the locals who were mostly thin with straight black hair, olive-colored skin and brown eyes. Like her.

She glanced away, stacking clean cups under the bar. "Why didn't you mention my kaiken before?"

He gestured to the room. "Men inebriated by sake plus a beautiful serving girl equals trouble."

She snorted. "You can handle trouble."

"But I can't protect you when you leave here."

Gilga-san lived upstairs and had never been seen outside the building. Azami stifled the desire to question him. He hadn't pried into her past so she would respect his privacy as well.

Saburo, on the other hand had been curious. She had told him a fire killed her family and she wished to start a new life someplace else. As Gilga-san had predicted, Saburo insisted on walking her the few short blocks to the room she had rented. They bundled in heavy coats before muscling their way through the icy wind. No others walked the streets of Hokuga, which was odd, considering the town was a popular stop-over for caravans traveling to the western sea ports.

"Until the criminals are caught, you shouldn't be out on your own," Saburo said.

"Did you know the men who died?" she asked.

"Only in passing. Do not worry." He took her hand in his. "I will protect you."

She kept her tongue as frustration boiled. Years of tradition could not be undone by one outburst. Women were wives and mothers. They were protected and cared for. As Saburo talked of other topics, Azami realized if she truly desired independence she would need to disguise herself as a man.

It was a prospect she had toyed with this past year, but it galled her to no end. She had been taught how to fight and defend herself. Yet her skills could only be used to serve another—her future husband. To keep his house and children safe when he was away from home.

Azami hated the need to be connected to a man—a father or a husband—in order to be accepted as a member of their society. Women without a family had no rights. They were frequently arrested and sent to be yūjo in the walled pleasure cities.

But she didn't hate men. In fact, some, like Saburo treated her almost as an independent person. He also didn't act stoic and emotionless, mimicking a samurai. She wished she could spend more time with him.

Wished she could stay in Hokuga.

Wished to no longer be afraid.

Two days later, the five missing men surfaced in Lake Biwa. Their bloodless corpses and shredded throats matched the first victims. To add to the general panic, Saburo's caravan was attacked in broad daylight. A few traders had been injured and others taken, but no one who came into the sake-house could name them.

When she heard the news, her chest felt as if she'd been skewered by a katana. Time slowed and each breath she pulled hurt.

Azami kept busy, serving stew and sake to customers. The hushed conversations had turned from speculation of robbers and murders to the belief that a malevolent water spirit had taken up residence in the lake.

"... greenish-yellow skin like seaweed ..."

"... scales and webbed toes ..."

"... misshapen head ..."

"... small, like a child but stronger than a sumo ..."

"... kappa ..."

This last comment stopped Azami. Did they really believe a kappa haunted the lake? Gilga-san had told tales about the creature before. She glanced at the far corner of the sake-house. Gilga-san had drawn the screens around his biggest table. The town leaders had assembled to discuss the situation.

She fretted about Saburo until he strode through the door late into the evening. He sported a deep gash and a nasty bump on his forehead.

The tightness in her heart eased and she rushed to him in relief. She remembered her place, stopping short and stifling the desire to crush him to her. Instead she bowed politely and took his coat. They locked gazes for a moment.

Near closing-time, Gilga-san gestured for Azami to follow him. He pushed open the screen and offered to bring the leaders fresh food. They declined.

"Have you made a decision?" Gilga-san asked.

"We will appeal to the daimyo and request help from his samurai," Moyama, the oldest and therefore wisest man of Hokuga said. "We cannot fight a kappa."

"If a water vampire does prey on your shores, then all you need to do is—"

"What do you know of fighting a kappa?" Moyama asked, but he didn't wait for a reply. "You're gaijin. And too afraid to leave your sake-house. Let the samurai deal with it."

Gilga-san bowed to the men and retreated. Azami collected the used stoneware and carried them to the kitchen to wash. Once again, Gilga-san helped her, but his sour mood and frequent outbursts about the stubbornly traditional locals made her wish he had chosen to brood in his office.

"How long until the samurai arrive?" she asked him.

"Three days at most."

Azami had to leave Hokuga. The only way to avoid the incoming samurai would be to head west—past the water vampire. If it existed. Yet Saburo and the survivors of the attack had been convinced a kappa haunted the lake. Azami couldn't risk leaving now. That was the reason she clung to, and not because of her reaction to seeing Saburo alive. She would endeavor to blend in and hope the samurai wouldn't recognize her. They shouldn't as they lived in another district than her hometown.

Despite his injuries, Saburo walked her to the inn that night. Azami's kimono flapped in the cold wind. The night sky sparkled and a three-quarters moon illuminated Hokuga's wooden buildings. The weathered structures huddled together like lost children.

When they neared the ryokan, Saburo paused. "Azami, I. . . ." He played with the toggles on his coat. "The attack made me worry about the future. I'd always assumed I had more time."

He turned to face her, taking her hands and pulling her close. Her heart thumped against her chest.

Saburo's intense gaze met hers. "Today I learned the future could be gone without warning. Time has become precious and I do not wish to waste it. Will you do me the honor of becoming my wife?"

She had known he cared for her, but respectable traders didn't marry sake house servers. Or liars either. They married the daughters of other traders. These thoughts weren't helping her sort out her chaotic feelings, but they gave her a place to start. "Your family—"

"Already approved."

"But I'm—"

"Not anymore. Gilga-san has offered a dowry for you."

Shock silenced her. Then fury at her boss's presumption warred with affection for the meddling man. She pushed those emotions away. Marriage had been the reason she ran away in the first place. Granted it was a different type of union, but still.

"I would wish to continue my work for Gilga-san," she said.

"You won't need to. I will provide—"

"For me, I know. I love you, Saburo. I do. But I cannot be a traditional wife."

He stiffened as if she'd slapped him and dropped her hands. "You'd rather be a serving girl than a respectable member of this community?" His harsh tone cut through her.

"I'd like—"

"Do not say another word. I will inform Gilga-san his offer was rejected." He strode away.

The desire to run after him and explain pulsed in her chest. However if she told him the truth, he would no doubt report her to the daimyo, his honesty another admirable quality. Deep down, she'd always known nothing could come of their relationship. But it had been nice to delude herself for a little while.

The samurais' arrival injected hope back into the terrified townspeople. The sake-house filled with relieved traders, fishermen, farmers, and a company of samurai. Saburo wasn't among the customers. No surprise.

"The boy's an idiot," was Gilga-san's only comment to her regarding the marriage proposal and he ignored her questions about the dowry.

Azami wove her way through the crowded tables, but kept clear of the warriors. Gilga-san waited on them. They livened the mood with their boisterous laughter and confident manner. And the best part was, she didn't recognize any of them.

But they lingered until the other customers had gone. Gilga-san told her to go home; he could handle a dozen men. Before she left, the front door swung open and the rest of the samurais entered. Azami returned to the kitchen with dread pushing up her throat. They were the warrior elite and by law the sake-house would remain open until they chose to leave.

Thirty men gathered. They kept her and Gilga-san busy with orders. Their conversation focused on the village's rumors and the survivors' stories, comparing information to create a plan of attack.

Gilga-san approached the leader. He bowed slightly and introduced himself. The men shook hands.

"May I offer a suggestion on killing this kappa?" he asked.

Azami suspected he was being polite for her. This was his place and if he wished to speak his opinion, he could.

Amusement quirked at the samurai's lips, but he invited Gilga-san to join them.

"The water vampire is strong and quick. Before engaging him, I suggest you show him the proper respect and bow to him. The lower the better."

Laughter rippled through the men.

"We do not honor a malevolent spirit," the leader said.

"In this particular case, it is vital that you do."

The leader scoffed. "Ridiculous advice, gaijin. Samurais do not bow to evil."

"Then you will die." Gilga-san walked away as another wave of mirth erupted.

Azami hurried after him. In the kitchen she asked, "Will they succeed?"

"No."

"How do you know?"

"These things are not limited to the waters of Nihon."

"Can it be killed?"

"No, but it can be . . . reasoned with."

"You need to tell the samurai."

"I tried. Twice."

Her stomach twisted with fear. "Try again."

"They will not listen to me. I'm gaijin."

Late into the night, the samurai meeting finally ended. As the warriors filed out, Gilga-san asked his chef to accompany Azami back to her room. The pre-dawn silence chilled her more than the air. The wind had died. An ill omen.

Azami thanked the chef and entered the quiet inn, surprising since the samurais filled every room except hers. Too bad they didn't pay for their lodging or their meals. Then again, they had come to help. And if she had thought about it beforehand, she should have spent the night in the sake-house. Now who was the idiot?

She crept up the stairs, slipped into her room and shut the door without incident. The floor creaked behind her. She spun, pulling her kaiken.

A dark shape stood near her window.

Brandishing her weapon, she said, "Get out or I'll make the kappa seem kind."

He chuckled. "Well said, Run Away."

Caught. Her insides turned to stone. Nothing to blame but her own fear.

"Did you really think we wouldn't notice you? A beautiful woman? Our brothers in the north sent us a message months ago, asking to keep an eye out for you. We will return you to your proper home when our business with the kappa is finished."

She stepped into a fighting stance and held her weapon close. "No."

With a ring of metal, he drew his katana. The sharp blade reflected the weak moonlight. "Do you think you can refuse me?"

If she had her naginata, her odds of beating him would be much higher. The long pole and curved blade would keep his katana from reaching her.

"No." She returned her dagger to her belt. Azami had been forced to train in tantojutsu, the skill of the knife. The intended wife of a samurai needed to protect his home and children from his enemies. Educated as well, she'd been taught how to run a household and, in the process, how to think for herself. Unfortunate since she realized she had no desire to become a samurai's wife. To be, in essence, owned by another.

The samurai pointed to the floor with his katana. "You will remain here. There will be a guard at your door." Confident she would obey, he didn't wait for a reply. He left and ordered a colleague to stand watch.

No need to confiscate her weapon. She had earned the right to carry it, and it was useless against a skilled warrior. Sitting on the edge of her bed, she considered her options. Azami had prepared for an escape, but her plans hadn't included an evil spirit. She would bide her time. For now.

The next morning the warriors talked and laughed as if they faced a kappa every day. When they left to hunt it down, Azami didn't waste a moment. She pulled a box from under the bed. Emergency escape supplies had been packed inside.

She changed into the loose pants and tunic that the local fishermen wore, tucked her kaiken into the belt, and wrapped her hair in a tight bun. Donning a fur hat, she grabbed a heavy coat.

The inn's owner had been asked to provide a guard outside her door. However, she didn't plan to use the door.

Taking the rope from the box, she secured one end to the heavy bed frame and tossed the other out the window. Azami removed the last item from the box--a satchel already filled with all she would need on the road. She dropped the bag and coat out the window. They landed with a soft thud.

Not waiting to see if the guard noticed the noise, she climbed out the window sill and wrapped her legs around the rope, sliding to the ground. She collected her belongings and ran to Gilga-san's sake-house.

Slipping in through the back entrance, Azami surprised the chef, who ordered her to leave. Gilga-san, though, recognized her right away. He brought her to his office and closed the door.

Exotic antiques and strange metallic objects filled the shelves of the room. Keys of all shapes, sizes, and metals— gold, silver, iron—littered every surface.

As she perched on the edge of the chair facing his desk, Azami marveled. The room shouldn't be big enough to hold the massive collection, yet it did.

Gilga-san half sat on the edge of his desk. He tugged his braided beard while she explained her predicament.

When she finished, he rested a hand on her arm. "I can hide you. You do not need to leave."

His offer touched her, but the risk was too great. "This town is too small. Even disguised as a man, they would find me. You would be arrested."

He laughed. "I'd like to see them try."

"No. You've been so kind to me, I won't endanger you."

"But what about that kappa? I doubt the samurai killed it today."

Icy fingers of fear stroked her back, but she considered the alternative. "I would rather lose my life than my freedom."

Gilga-san sobered and stared at the red clay tablet that hung on the wall opposite his desk. Pictures had been scratched on it and it appeared as if someone had used a chopstick to poke round dents into the clay before it had hardened. According to Gilga-san, it was an old drink recipe. No one was permitted to touch it.

He played with the braid hanging from his chin. Then he surged to his feet. "I agree. Losing your freedom is a hardship you do not deserve. Before you go, I have something for you. Wait here."

Unable to remain sitting, she paced. She hoped to leave before the samurai returned. If they were busy fighting the kappa, they wouldn't notice a fishing boat leaving the dock. And if the kappa remained engaged in battle, it wouldn't bother chasing after her.

Gilga-san returned with a plain white cup. He handed it to her. She sniffed the warm contents. It smelled like jasmine tea but resembled milk.

"Your features are too elegant to pass for a man," he said. "If you truly wish to live as a man, drink the . . . tea and you shall be transformed. However, once done, it cannot be undone."

Azami's hand shook. An impossible offer. A jest? She had never known him to play pranks. No. Deep down in her heart, she felt it. He meant it. She sank into her chair and clutched the cup with both hands, resting it in her lap.

Afraid to spill it. Afraid to drink it. Afraid to refuse it.

A knock broke the silence. Gilga-san cracked open the door.

"The samurai have returned," a voice said.

"Stay here," Gilga-san said to her. "No one will find you." He left.

Azami's thoughts swirled. To transform into a man. To have the freedom and the privileges men enjoyed. To no longer be afraid someone would force her to marry and bear children. She could walk among the samurai in the sake-house without worry. Her problems solved.

Then her musings went deeper. Would her personality change? Would she desire women? Or would she still desire men?

It had been easy to wish, but making a choice wouldn't be as straightforward. Gilga-san slipped into the room. His expression troubled.

"What happened?" she asked.

"Six samurai died, ten injured, and the kappa remains at large."

"You were right."

"Poor consolation, considering the cost." He eyed the cup in her lap. "They're searching for you. If you become a man, you can stay here and work for me. Otherwise, I'll hide you."

She stared at the white liquid. Hiding was another form of imprisonment and it didn't sit well with her. Transforming felt wrong as well. As if she were cheating.

"What do you truly desire Azami?"

"A partner." The words popped out without censure and kept coming. "Someone I can share my life with and who won't direct my life. Someone who treats me as an equal despite my gender." Like Gilga-san did. Why? Because she had worked hard for him, sorted out his messy bookkeeping, and helped create a few new drink recipes. She had earned his respect and friendship.

Sudden understanding zipped through Azami, energizing her. She thrust the cup into his hands. "Thank you for the offer, but I don't need it. I'm not hiding any longer."

A strange expression crossed his face. Not quite amusement, although gladness did spark in his eyes. He seemed proud and that added to her determination.

"What are going to do?" Gilga-san asked.

"Go fishing."

"And you will show this fish the proper respect?" he asked.

"Unlike the samurai, I do not have a delicate male ego," she said.

His deep laughter followed her out the door.

Her bravado and determination leaked from her as she crept from shadow to shadow, heading west through Hokuga. The idea she could prevail when the samurai could not seemed ridiculous in the cold darkness. Doubt and terror swirled in her chest.

She scanned the small town, committing its quirks-- Toshi's half completed fence, fishing nets hanging from Futsu's back door, and the family of cats living under Oda's bamboo hut—to memory. Fondness for these people pulsed in her heart. She would have been content to serve customers and listen to Gilga-san's stories until the end of her days.

When she reached the last building, she gauged the distance to the thin cover of the winter woods. Could she do this? She considered the alternative—dragged back to Yamakage, punished and forced to marry.

Gilga-san believed in her. It was time to trust herself. Azami shoved her misgivings away.

As she dashed to the tree line, hurried footsteps sounded behind her. She spun in time to see a figure running after her, hissing her name in a loud whisper. Drawing her kaiken, she slid her feet into a fighting stance. But the man skidded to a stop and held his hands out, showing he was unarmed.

"Azami, I need to talk to you." Saburo puffed.

Bad timing. She lowered her weapon. "Go home, Saburo."

"Not until you listen."

"No. I lied to you about everything. I'm not an orphan. I ran away from Yamakage because I did not wish to marry a samurai. Now they have found me, I need to leave."

"Then I will come with you," he said, stepping closer.

"But I do not—"

"Wish to become a traditional wife. I understand. All I desire is your company."

She sheathed her kaiken and crossed her arms in suspicion. "Have you talked to Gilga-san?"

"Yes, he told me where to find you."

That explained it. "Did he give you a special drink?" Meddling again, Gilga-san was worse than the local matchmaker.

"No time. He urged me to hurry."

This threw her. "Why did you change your mind?"

He sucked in a deep breath. "I considered the reasons why I love you. You are independent, intelligent, and brave. If I had done this before asking for your hand, I would have realized my error. Rather than lose you, I wish to accompany you."

"What about your life and home here?"

"It is of little concern to me."

"I—"

He rested a cold finger on her lips, silencing her. "You are all that matters." He cupped her chin and drew her toward him for a kiss.

Heat spread from her lips and she pressed against Saburo, deepening the kiss and tangling her fingers in his long hair. Her heart beat its approval.

Shouts intruded. Azami spotted two samurai pointing in their direction and calling to others.

"Time to go." She grabbed Saburo's hand and they raced down the path to the lake.

With six dead and ten injured, she hoped the warriors wouldn't follow them right away. Hoped they'd assume the kappa wouldn't let them escape. A smart assumption.

Moonlight lit the trail, and, while glad to be able to see, Azami worried they would be visible to the samurai.

They ran until the sounds of pursuit died. When her breath no longer huffed so loud in her ears, the crash of the waves reached her. Arriving at the lake, they paused. Silver moonlight flashed and danced on the water. The surface undulated as if restless and irritated. Foaming curls of water rushed and pounded on the shore.

"All those windy days combined with a big moon have increased the tide," Saburo explained. "I hope the northern path is not underwater."

By his nervous glances toward the lake, Azami knew he didn't voice his true fear. Hand in hand they followed the road that ringed the vast lake, keeping away from the surf.

"Saburo, I've one more . . . confession," Azami said.

He squeezed her hand in encouragement.

"I'm not running away. It is a life full of fear."

Slowing his pace, he looked at her in confusion.

"I came here to challenge the kappa."

Jerking to a stop, he peered at her in utter astonishment. "But . . . you will . . . it. . . ." He drew in a deep breath. "You'll die. It's jisatsu!"

"It remains the only way I can *earn* my freedom."

He stared at her for so long Azami wondered if she'd lost him.

"And I cannot leave the people of Hokuga to the mercy of the kappa," she said, and meant it. "The samurai are unable to see past their code of honor. They will continue to die."

Saburo's shoulders relaxed. "And you won't?"

"All I know is I have to try."

The gradual infusion of color into the black sky announced the dawn's arrival. As sunlight swept across the lake, the pressure in Azami's chest relaxed a bit. Until she spotted a child playing in the rough surf.

Terrified for his safety, she waded into the chilly water, calling and gesturing for him to leave the water before he drowned. The young boy laughed, but he walked to the bank and sat on the edge, waving her over.

Saburo caught up to her as she neared the child. She stopped a few feet away and gaped. Not because delight shown on the boy's face, but because he had greenish-yellow scales instead of skin. And he had a dent on the top of his misshapen head that was filled with a white liquid. Fear's icy teeth bit into her.

"Oh, what a glorious morning! No longer boring." It splashed its webbed toes in the water. "I smell love in the blood. Yummy!"

Saburo grabbed her arm and tugged her back. "I cannot . . . let's run."

The kappa chortled. "Yes, yes! Run, run. Make it fun."

Azami sorted through the story Gilga-san had told months ago, when he had been entertaining guests. Her frantic pulse calmed. "No." She pulled her kaiken, wishing again for the longer reach of her naginata.

"Oh, what a delight. A fight." It jumped to its feet.

Saburo stepped in front of Azami, protecting her.

Huffing with annoyance, she pushed him aside. "Trust me."

To her relief, he nodded and backed away. Azami joined the kappa on the narrow bank. They faced each other. At five feet five inches in height, she never considered herself tall, but compared to the four foot kappa she towered over the creature. The height difference was all part of its game, luring its opponents into a false sense of security. It also waited for her to make the first move.

She bowed deeply to the kappa.

"Oh, a proper warrior." It returned the bow. As it dipped its head, the white liquid poured from the indentation and pooled onto the ground. When the kappa straightened, it didn't appear to be concerned about its loss.

Azami prayed Gilga-san's story had been accurate. Their lives depended on it. She lunged at the kappa, slicing at its neck with her kaiken. The blade narrowly missed as it jumped back. She advanced, thrusting the tip toward the kappa's chest.

It retreated a step, but then blocked the next jab. The blow was hard, but not strong enough to dislodge her grip on the kaiken. Confidence flowed through her veins, energizing her. Without the white liquid, the kappa's supernatural strength and speed were gone. For now. It would regain its powers in time. Already a small amount of fluid had returned.

She increased the intensity of her attack, striking and slicing without giving the kappa a chance to get close to her. It blocked and dodged. When she swung her dagger a little too wide, it darted in and latched onto her forearm—the one holding the kaiken.

It dug its claws deep into her flesh as it pressed close. A burning agony sizzled on her skin. A snap vibrated through her bones. Pain exploded in her arm. The kappa squealed with joy. With one hand, it raked its claws, slashing cuts. Then the kappa clamped its mouth over the bloody wounds. The level of white liquid inside its dent rose at a faster pace as it sucked her blood.

The horrifying noise spurred Azami into action. She stomped on its foot and slammed the edge of her free hand into its temple. It jerked with the blows, but hung on. She transferred her weapon to her left hand and jabbed the tip of the blade into the kappa's ribs. It let go, staggering back.

Hugging her injured arm to her stomach, Azami changed tactics and kicked it in the chest. It stumbled. She kept after it, using a variety of kicks. So used to being faster and stronger, the kappa couldn't adapt to this new attack. When its gaze slid to the water, she knew it considered escape.

Feinting left, she shuffled forward and to the right, hooking the kappa around the neck with her uninjured arm. Azami pressed the edge of the blade against its throat. The scales felt thick, but red blood welled under her knife.

"Oh, please, don't kill," it cried.

"Why not? You have killed many."

"Must eat."

"Not good enough."

"Do anything for you," it said.

"Always?"

"Yes, yes."

"Give me your word."

"Oh, my word is yours."

Satisfied, she released the kappa.

"Azami, no!" Saburo yelled, running over to her.

"It will be fine. He is an honorable opponent; his word will never be broken."

"How do you know?"

"Gilga-san. Despite his matchmaking tendencies, he's quite knowledgeable."

Gilga-san had also been correct about another one of the kappa's unique powers. The spirit was skilled in mending broken bones, and in reattaching severed limbs without leaving a scar.

When asked, it healed Azami's arm. Once she regained her energy, the three of them headed back to Hokuga. It didn't take long to encounter the samurai.

"Remember, do not kill anyone," Azami said to the kappa as fourteen warriors surrounded them with their weapons drawn.

"Must eat," it whined.

"Human blood? Or can you drink animal blood?"

"Oh, both. And like cucumbers. Yummy."

"You will be fed in exchange for protection."

It perked up. "Protect now? Fun? Make men run?" The white liquid completely filled the kappa's dent.

"Only if they attack us." She took the kappa's hand in hers. Then she turned in a slow circle and met each samurai's gaze, holding it until the warrior acknowledged her with a nod and sheathed his katana.

"What now?" Saburo asked.

"We go home."

THE HALLOWEEN MEN

WARNING! This next story is a horror story. *I don't write horror and avoid reading it. Even dark fantasy is too dark for me, but I was invited to write a Halloween story for* Halloween: Magic, Mystery and the Macabre. *And I couldn't pass up the challenge to try my hand at writing horror. The idea for this story sparked when I read an article about the annual Mardi Gras parade down in New Orleans, Louisiana. The article mentioned how once a person joined one of the parade krewes they were a member for life. Unless they broke one of the cardinal rules like removing their mask during a parade. This led to me thinking about wearing masks on Halloween. People put on masks once a year to celebrate the spooky. My thoughts then turned to a society that wore masks all year except on Halloween. Then the questions started: Why? Who? Where? Setting it in New Orleans seemed too—obvious, so I created my own city... sort of...just like water warps wood, my version is a warped view of Venice.*

THE HALLOWEEN MEN

T wo Halloween Men paused in front of our shop. Crouched inside the dark window display, I froze, hoping they wouldn't notice me among the merchandise. My navy blue merchant's robe blended in with the black velvet mannequin heads, my simple mask was unremarkable in the midst of the elegant and colorful masks on display.

Despite the *Closed* sign hanging on the door, the Halloween Man on the left twisted the knob. My heart crawled up my throat as metal rattled. I'd just locked it. His partner held a box in his gloved hands. They both wore wide-brimmed leather hats to keep the rain off their full-face Bauta masks. Drops of water beaded on their black robes, resembling little globs of molten glass as they reflected the weak yellow light from the street lanterns.

Go away. Please go away.

But he knocked. Each bang of his fist sent a spike of fear right through my chest.

I squeezed my eyes shut as I huddled in my dark corner. *Go away. Please go away.* But the knocking turned into a pounding that reverberated throughout the building.

They'll break the door down. Memories from childhood flashed—being jerked from a sound sleep by boots hammering up our staircase, voices shouting, my mother screaming as she disappeared in a sea of black hats.

Opening my eyes, I banished the nightmarish images. Only two stood outside. *How bad could it be?*

"Antonella, answer the door," my father roared from the back room unaware of the importance of our visitors. "Tell them to return tomorrow during business hours."

My body refused to obey even though the half-face, Columbina mask I wore met all the legal requirements.

My father shouted again as the thumping continued. The curtains parted and he stomped into the showroom, drew in a deep breath—to unleash a tirade on either the offending customer or me—and threw open the door.

The tirade failed to erupt. Not even my father would dare speak harshly to the Halloween Men.

"Master Salvatori, may we have a moment of your time?" the Halloween Man holding the box asked.

My father stepped back, allowing the men inside the showroom. Masks for every occasion hung from the walls and were stacked on the shelves. A few of the more expensive ones graced smooth-headed velvet mannequin heads to best display them. Beads and sequins sparkled even in the dim light.

The men dripped on the floor, making a puddle while Father lit a couple more lanterns on the counter. Trapped, uncertain, and still hidden in the shadows, I remained in my crouched position.

The Halloween Man placed the box on the counter and opened it. He removed a bright glittering heart-shaped

Columbina party mask cut from leather and decorated with red feathers. "Do you recognize this?"

Daggers of fear pumped through my body.

"No," my father said.

"How about this one?" He pulled another Columbina from the box. This one had been cut to resemble a butterfly.

"No."

"Are you sure?" the Halloween Man asked.

Father wore his usual navy Bauta with the small silver beads, but a hardness shone from his gaze. "Yes."

They stared at each other. My heart tapped a fast rhythm, drowning out the rain pelting the windows. I stifled the desire to bolt.

The Halloween Man looked away first. "What can you tell us about these masks?" he asked.

Father picked up the green and purple butterfly and examined it. Sequins outlined the wings and it had small peacock feathers for antennae. He measured the length and width and checked the back. He did the same for the red one.

I held my breath.

"Aside from their unconventional shapes and overly ornate embellishments, they are legal," Father said, setting it down.

The man huffed in disgust. "They make a mockery of the law! Proper masks are essential to societal order, not—"

His partner put a hand on his arm. "Tell us something we *don't* know."

"Have you checked—" my father said.

"Yes, we talked to the other *mascherari*. They believe the quality of the craftsmanship points to you."

Father waited. I bit my lip. Would they arrest him?

"And you, of all people know *this* is how it starts." The man stabbed a finger at the box. "We want to stop it before it begins. Before we have to teach another young *mascherari* a lesson."

"I'll keep an eye out," Father said.

His words seemed to satisfy them. They returned the masks to the box and left. Father re-locked the door.

"Antonella," he said, peering into the window display.

I jumped as Father focused his hard gaze on me. *Did he suspect?*

"What happens when the Halloween Men come for you?" he asked.

Yes, he did. "They arrest you?"

"Are you asking me or telling me?" he demanded.

"They take you into custody."

"And then what happens?"

Depending on the severity of the crime, punishment could be a public whipping, being locked in the stocks for a few hours or many days, being forced to wear a metal Bauta mask, and many more things I did not wish to think about. Getting caught in public without wearing a mask had the worst consequences. So horrible, no one spoke of them. My father never told me for fear of giving me nightmares.

Father saw the answer in my eyes. "Don't give the Halloween Men a reason to suspect you of wrong doing. Understand?"

I longed to ask what reason Mother had given them, but he never talked about her. Instead, I nodded.

"Good. The deliveries are ready, get moving or you'll be out after curfew."

"Curfew?" I hadn't had one since I turned eighteen.

"Yes, curfew. And tell Bianca that you will not be able to attend her Halloween party. You have work to do."

"But—" I clamped my mouth shut. There was no arguing with my father. Even the Halloween Men had backed down.

They appeared to be satisfied with his answer. *I'll keep an eye out.* Was he spying for them? That would confirm the rumors about him, which just increased my desire to move out.

And as long as I lived in his house, I had to follow his rules. My masks didn't sell as well as Father's, and my recent attempt to supplement my income had just brought the Halloween Men to our door. I shuddered. "Yes, sir."

I hurried to the back room to load the cart with the boxes.

Father followed me. "Mister Bellini gets two and Mistress Fiore ordered four party masks for her daughters." He handed me the list and their corresponding addresses.

I scanned the sheet, memorized it, and slid it into a pocket of my robe before pulling the two-wheeled cart behind me. Rain continued to pound the windows so I paused to draw my hood up, tucking my long black hair underneath. Then I strode out into the wet streets. Raindrops struck my chin and drummed on the waterproof boxes. Everything had to be sealed against the frequent rains. Even my robe resisted soaking in water. But in this downpour, it wouldn't last long.

The wheels of the cart splashed through puddles and sprayed against my boots. Tied up for the night, the boats in the canals bobbed in tune with the choppy water. No one else walked the streets, only the Halloween Men stood in their dark corners, watching for law-breakers. I yanked my hood lower even though my navy Columbina with the sedate silver trim met all government regulations. My back burned as I imagined their gazes piercing my skin and searching the depths of my soul for guilt.

Normally my forays into the city were a welcome break, but not tonight. I hustled through the city, delivering the special-ordered masks. On my return trip, I took a shortcut through the food district. At the bakery, a lantern glowed behind the closed curtains.

I pushed opened the door.

Bianca yelped in surprise and reached for her Columbina sitting on the counter. But then she relaxed her grip. "Don't scare me like that, Nella! I thought you were a Halloween Man. Your soaked robe looks black."

"You wouldn't have to worry if you wore your mask." I adverted my gaze from her exposed face. Eighteen like me, we'd been friends since I delivered a mask for her mother two years ago.

"I don't have to wear it, we're closed for the day." She leaned on her mop.

But this was a public area. And the image of the Halloween Men still burned in my mind.

"Besides," she said. "It was digging into my temple."

I crossed to the counter, leaving behind puddles that Bianca mopped up without comment. Her half-mask matched the color of her buttery yellow robes, marking her as a member of the confectionary class. Brown, orange, and red beads outlined the edges and around her eyes. I turned it over. The velvet had worn off along the one side, exposing the leather underneath. I dug into my pockets and found a patch, fixing the problem.

"Here." I held it out to her. "You can put it on."

She laughed and waved me off. "Put it back on the counter."

When I didn't move, she strode to the door, locked it, and drew the shades. "Better?"

A little. I set it down.

"Relax," she said. "Your stodgy father isn't here. Master-follow-the-rules-to-the-extreme Salvatori." She huffed with derision. "Not letting you take off your mask in your very own home is a form of abuse."

Not bothering to correct her for the hundredth time, I

settled on the stool behind the counter. I was allowed to remove my mask in the privacy of my bedroom, but she never remembered that detail. Plus I suspected I resembled my mother and seeing me was painful for my father. At least I hoped that was the real reason, otherwise Bianca might be correct.

Unaffected by my silence, she continued, "Once you have your own home, you can do whatever you want. Oh! I almost forgot." She handed me an envelope stuffed full with money. "They loved your masks, Nella. I sold every single one."

Fear mixed with pride—a strange combination. "You didn't!"

She waved away my concern. "No, I didn't tell anyone you made them. They bought them because they're fabulous, not because of your family name. I've orders for a dozen more!"

Overwhelmed, I said, "I can't..."

But she didn't hear me. She prattled on about our future shop—a place that would provide all your party needs: cakes, confections, food, decorations, and themed masks to match. Even though parties were held inside homes, the Halloween Men considered them public events and all guests had to wear masks. Wealthy hosts provided masks for their guests as a party favor.

Unless it was Halloween, of course. The only day the citizens could go out in public without their masks on. The day the Halloween Men retreated to...no one quite knew where. Rumors speculated they disappear back to hell where they'd come from. Who else but demons would conquer our city and force us to wear masks as a punishment? Others claimed they ascend to heaven. That they were angels sent to discipline us for our vanity and shallow nature. And a few people were certain the Halloween Men took off their masks and enjoyed the day among us.

It was the biggest day of the year with the grandest parties, parades, and entertainment on every street corner. Which reminded me...

I interrupted Bianca's dreaming to tell her about the Halloween Men's visit. "And since I have a curfew again, I can't stay and make more masks."

"They are *legal*, Nella. They can't arrest you because they don't like your designs."

Guess her father hadn't terrified her with stories about the Halloween Men since she was little. Mine did. All because of my mother. Had she broken the strictest law?

"Bianca do you know what happens if you're caught without a mask on?"

She plopped the mop into the bucket. "I've heard they drown you in the Grand Canal, but Mister Cavella says they lock you in the dungeons forever."

"You don't know?"

"No one does. No one has ever returned. Now stop fretting, Nella. *You* of all people will never be caught without a mask on, plus no one but me knows *you* made those masks. And they'll only be worn at private parties. Besides, I've already bought the material and supplies for you. They're in the icing room."

"My father knows." And that was more than enough.

"Oh, Nella don't let your father ruin your life."

"He's—"

"Lonely and doesn't want you to leave him like your mother."

I understood why she'd think that—the rumors claimed she left him. The truth was too hard to explain. And if I could just move out on my own, the pressure of those past sins would no longer haunt me.

"I'll find a way to make them." I promised.

"Yay." She ran to the back and returned with a box.

When I returned to the shop, my father was already upstairs in our apartment. I stashed the box of supplies in the workroom and then joined him for a late supper on the second story that housed our living area. Our bedrooms were on the third floor, and an attic occupied the entire fourth floor.

After Father retired for the evening, I snuck back downstairs and carried the box and a lantern to the attic. Careful not to make any noise, I cleared an area in the far corner—the one over my bedroom and as far away from my father's ceiling as possible. I set up a work area.

As sleet tapped on the roof, I cut leather into butterflies, snails, cat faces, and diamond shapes. I let my imagination run for hours.

Finished for the night, I considered. My father never came up here—the boxes were full of Mother's belongings, but just in case... I remembered putting a box of old sheets up here... somewhere. I dug around and opened one promising box.

Instead of sheets, I found clothes, then cookware, and then a box full of bright colorful masks. Odd. I examined one in the lantern light. Not my father's elegant conservative style, more brassy and bold. More like my true style. Mother's?

I sat back on my heels in shock. She had been a *mascherari*, too.

The glass bead rolled across the table. I bit back a curse and lunged for the escaping purple bauble before it fell. The sound of a bead hitting the floor would be enough to cause Father to look up from his work and with a single glance convey his extreme irritation over my clumsiness. The bead clung to my sticky fingers. I fumbled in an effort to glue a line of them along the edges of a basic black funerary Bauta. Most customers purchased the traditional somber color for their deceased loved ones.

Tired from working late the last three nights, I struggled to concentrate on the task at hand.

The bell jingled, signaling a customer. Father stood, smoothed the few wrinkles that dared to crease his midnight blue robe, and parted the curtains separating the back work-room with the rest of the shop.

No longer feeling as if under a microscope, I relaxed and concentrated on the pesky beads. I'd wanted to use the bigger size, but Father refused to let me add expensive materials to my masks. Very few customers purchased my creations when they sat beside a master craftsman's. Which was another reason why I decided to keep making those other designs. The Halloween Man's words, *before we have to teach another young* mascherari *a lesson* replayed in mind.

I banished those thoughts—they wouldn't find out—and held my newest creation at arm's length, examining it with a critical eye. Not nearly as edgy as my masks for Bianca, it met all the government requirements for a funeral mask, but it had my own personal...flair.

The curtains parted with a snap of fabric. "You have a customer," Father said from the threshold.

I stared at him. *Did he just make a joke?* No. Standing, I wiped my hands along my robes, earning a stern glare. I adjusted the Columbina on my face, checking to ensure it hadn't moved while I worked.

"Hurry up," Father said. "They're waiting."

I slipped pass him and entered the storefront.

Sleet pelted the big display windows and the wind howled outside. Two men wearing the gray robes of the manufacturing class stood in the center of our showroom. They wore charcoal-colored business Columbinas trimmed in gray and red. The man on the right examined one of my funeral masks.

Aware that Father remained in the doorway, I asked, "May I help you, sirs?"

The man holding the mask said, "Master Salvatori tells us you designed this?"

Was he a spy for the Halloween Men? "Yes, sir."

"We'd like to order one just like it except trimmed with our family's colors."

Shocked, it took me a moment to find the proper words. "I'm sorry for you loss, sir."

He nodded and although he kept his lips pressed in a thin line, amusement sparked in his deep blue eyes. Odd.

I retrieved the order sheet from the desk. "What colors, sir?"

"Red and gray, miss. And we'd like them on a white base."

White? I glanced up. While still within regulations, the color was...unconventional for a funeral mask. "When do you need this by?"

"Two days. Will that be a problem, miss?"

"No, sir." I'd finish it by tomorrow. "Where should it be delivered?"

"One forty-two Canal Street."

In the heart of the factory district—no surprise. I noted it on the sheet.

"How much?" the man asked.

"Oh, my father...er...Master Salvatori will assist you with the price."

The men glanced at each other as if I'd said something significant. My slip earned me another stern glare from Father before he turned cordial for the paying customers. Well as cordial as my father managed. He had a reputation of being gruff, but his masks were sought after by all the elite. Of course these men would get a discount since they chose one of my designs. Still, every bit helped.

Father shot me a look and I hurried to the back room. I abandoned my current project to work on the special order, pulling a piece of white velvet from the shelf.

When Father joined me, he said, "I expect that mask for Mister Cattaneo to be your very best."

I glanced at him. Did he purposely steer the customers to one of my masks? Was this his way to lessen the blow of trying to prevent me from making more masks for Bianca? Hard to tell.

The row of homes along Canal Street fronted a narrow waterway and even narrower sidewalk. Water sloshed over the edge. My cart's wheels barely fit as I navigated the broken pavement and dodged the waves.

The four-story-high houses appeared to have been squashed together by a giant. One forty-two was no exception. However its windows remained dark unlike its neighbors. I picked up the box and knocked on the door. Gray paint peeled off the thick wood and the bottom third was bloated and warped by the constant soaking from the canal.

After banging again, this time with more force, the door swung open, revealing a young man with short black hair and deep blue eyes. I started at him a moment, taken aback by his sharp nose, handsome features and welcoming smile. Realizing too late he wore neither mask nor robe over his clothes, I glanced down at the box in my hands. Heat spread down my back.

"Your order, sir," I said although he had to be only a few years older than me.

"Ah yes, Miss Salvatori. Do come in." He cupped my elbow and drew me inside, closing the door behind me with a thud.

Panicked, I raised my head. Lanterns blazed in a sitting room to my left. The scents of pine oil and wet muck dominated.

"This way." He headed down a hallway.

Clutching the box to my chest, I hesitated. This was unusual.

He returned. Amusement glinted in his eyes, but he remained polite. "My mother wishes to inspect the mask before we pay the balance. She's waiting in the back parlor."

Understandable. I didn't have my father's reputation for quality. *Not yet, but someday I will.*

As we walked down a tight corridor, the wood squeaked and flexed under our boots.

"The water is intent on reclaiming its territory," he said. "Most of the neighbors have moved all their furniture up to the higher levels because of the frequent flooding."

The reason they hadn't retreated to the upper floors sat in an oversized chair. The woman's large girth and misshapen legs were a bad combination for walking, let alone climbing stairs.

The young man handed the box to his mother. When she pulled out the mask to examine it, I glanced around the room. Two ladies who resembled the young man—probably his older sisters sat on a lumpy couch. His father sat in the wooden rocking chair. The runners had warped and it moved in fits and starts. Thump, thump, thud, bang.

None of the family wore masks. I stared at the floor feeling almost scandalized even though this was their home. Bang, thud, thump, thump.

"Excellent work, Miss Salvatori," Mistress Cattaneo said in a high-pitched musical voice.

"Thank you," I said, uncertain.

Thump, thump, thud, bang.

"She's the one, right?" her son asked.

"Yes, Enzo. You did well." She set the mask on a nearby table and reached for another box by her chair, setting it in her lap.

Enzo smirked at the ladies on the couch. They scowled back at him.

Bang, thud, thump, thump.

Unease swirled in my chest. Abandoning politeness, I said, "The balance is due on delivery, Mistress."

"Of course. Enzo, pay her."

He strode to a desk and yanked on a drawer. It squealed and then stuck tight.

Thump, thump, thud, bang.

"We'd like to place another order," she said.

"Certainly, just stop by the shop—"

"Not for *those* masks." She tsked. Opening the box, she held up one of my butterfly-shaped Columbinas. "I need two dozen more of these."

Expecting the Halloween Men to jump out of the shadows, I backed away. "I...they're not...I don't... Eep!"

Enzo blocked the doorway. Was he this muscular and tall before?

"Relax, we'll keep your secret," he said.

"I..."

Bang, thud, thump, thump.

"I didn't want to work through your agent, who refused to name you. We have a big New Year's party planned," Mistress Cattaneo said. "We'll pay you three times what your father charges."

"How did...?"

"Each *mascherari* has a distinctive style," Enzo said. "We

checked every shop in town, looking for yours. Imagine our surprise when you turned out to be Master Salvatori's daughter."

And imagine mine. If he found me so easily, so could... "The Halloween Men won't—"

"Let us worry about them," she said, waving away my concern. "We've invited all our clients, including the Medico Della Peste and once *he* sees your unique creations, the whole city will be clamoring for them. Your anonymity will only add to the allure."

Thump, thump, thud, bang.

I paused. The Medico Della Peste ruled over the city. If he was a client, it meant this family didn't work in the factories, but owned them. This meeting was a set up. Did they even live here?

Bang, thud, thump, thump.

Scanning their faces, I considered. They didn't appear apprehensive about the Halloween Men. Bianca's family was the same way. They followed the laws so they shouldn't have to be terrified. Neither should I.

And now was the perfect time to shed the fear. I gathered my courage. "I'm interested, but I can't make them in my father's shop."

"We have plenty of space you can use," Mistress Cattaneo said.

My thoughts raced. I'd still have to follow my father's rules and I couldn't keep up with the late nights. I drew in a breath —time to be bold. "I'd like a sponsorship to set up my own shop."

Thump, thump, thud, bang.

The details had been easy to work out. The Cattaneo family would become my patrons, setting me up in the house on Canal Street to start. They owned the entire row of homes and had used the currently empty one forty-two to make me feel more comfortable—apparently I had a reputation for being...skittish.

Once I'd made enough money to pay them back and be self-sufficient, I'd open my own shop. The deal seemed too good to be true, but Mistress Cattaneo assured me she didn't need interest on her investment, she wanted my masks.

The hard part would be telling my father.

I waited until after Enzo brought me the paperwork to sign a week after they'd agreed to sponsor me. His family had cleaned out the moldy furniture in one forty-two and converted the upper three stories to a workroom and living quarters for me. The speed of the renovations impressed me and confirmed the Cattaneo family was well connected. Surely, the Halloween Men would never arrest them.

Filling a box with my masks that had languished in my father's showroom—getting rid of the evidence, according to my conscience—I summoned my courage. As expected, he came out from the back room to see what I'd been doing. I blurted out my plans in a gush of words.

"You're a fool," he said. "The Cattaneo family will not be able to protect you."

"From what, Father? I've broken no laws. I'm of age and it's a legal agreement."

His gaze burned right through me, reminding me of the Halloween Men on the street corners. Sweat dripped under my mask. The desire to flee from his anger pulsed through my body, but I stayed, determined to see this through.

"Haven't you been listening to me all these years? They

don't need evidence to arrest you. Suspicion and rumors are all they need."

"Suspicion and rumors about what? Other than telling me of crimes and punishments, you never give me details. Maybe if you told me why Mother was taken, I'd understand."

He jerked back as if I had just slapped him.

"I saw them. What did she do?" I asked.

"You saw...?" He recovered a bit. "What did you see Antonella?"

"I saw enough." I yanked off my mask. Cool air caressed my hot skin. "You should be happy I'm leaving. Then there's no chance of seeing my face. Of seeing what you lost."

Open mouthed, he stared at me. I returned to packing.

A pounding on the door shattered my concentration. I jerked in surprise, knocking over a container of beads. My heart beat extra fast as I peeked out the window of my workroom. Bianca pressed against the door. Relief coursed through me. When would I be able to hear knocking without panicking?

Bianca banged again with her free hand. She held a white box in the other and she'd hitched her robe up to avoid soaking the hem in the ankle-deep water. I hurried down two flights of stairs to let her in.

She surged in with a wave of water, sputtering with exasperation. "You could have warned me to wear my waders."

I closed and locked the door behind her. "You said you'd be here this morning. That's low tide." Then when she continued to gaze at me, I added, "Sorry."

"It's worth the soggy socks to see your face, Nella."

I ducked my head. The desire to cover my cheeks and nose flared. It would take more than a week for me to get comfortable with being around people without my mask on. "You saw me last Halloween at your party."

"Barely. You arrived with your mask on, and then after an hour of hiding in a dark corner, you left."

"I wasn't hiding."

"So you say. This year you are to leave your mask at home and you *must* mingle. I invited Enzo Cattaneo and he accepted."

"Bianca!" My fingers itched to tie on my Columbina and hide the flush of heat in my face. Enzo had visited me every day since I'd moved here. Each time I had my mask firmly in place.

She held up two fingers. "You have two weeks to get used to the idea." Then she handed me the box. "Here are the pastries for Mistress Cattaneo to sample. They're all colored and shaped to match the butterfly masks, and the decorator will have examples of the complimentary decorations for her soon." Bianca twirled. "Our first client!"

In my head, my father's voice muttered, *if this party is a failure, she'll be your last.* I gritted my teeth. It had been easier to move out of his house than evict him from my thoughts.

After Bianca left, I settled my favorite Columbina on the bridge of my nose and tied the ribbon. The familiar pressure helped me concentrate on my work and kept Master-follow-the-rules-to-the-extreme Salvatori at bay.

The squeaky left wheel of my old rusted cart didn't quite cover the click-clack of boots following me. I tried hard all day to ignore the Halloween Men. Their interest in me was no different than the other masked citizens shopping in the crowded market plaza in the misty drizzle. Plus they all dressed the same, no way to confirm a certain two took particular notice of me. Pure fantasy.

But after I left the busy downtown and headed for the quiet rows of homes, it became difficult to discount my fears. In fact, they lingered and grew until sweat caused the cart to slip from my grip, spilling its contents onto the wet pavement.

I scooped up my packages in a panic, but it didn't matter. Mere steps away, the Halloween Men stopped to help.

"Good evening, Miss Salvatori," the shorter Halloween Man said as he righted my cart.

All moisture fled my mouth. I rasped. "Good evening, sirs."

"Returning home?" he asked.

"Yes."

"We noticed you moved from your father's house. I hope under pleasant circumstances?" He took the bundles from me and stacked them in the cart while his partner picked up the remaining mess on the ground.

My insides twisted. They'd been watching me. "Ah...yes. I'm starting my own mask shop." I touched my Columbina, ensuring it remained in place.

He aimed a soul-burning stare at me. "We haven't seen any paperwork..."

"Eventually. I've a patron right now." But they already knew all this. So why bother to ask?

"Ah, yes. The Cattaneo family. An interesting...choice for a patron. Their reputation is...well known. Perhaps you should resume your apprenticeship with your father. His reputation is...well regarded."

"I will think about it, sirs."

"You should do more than think. He'll keep you out of trouble, Miss Salvatori."

In a blur of motion, the Halloween Man pulled on the end of one of my ribbons holding my Columbina in place.

"No," I cried as the silky material slid then held tight, jerking my head to the side. I'd double knotted it, but I still pressed my hand to my mask in case he tried again.

"See? He has already taught you well. Most of the citizens are trusting fools. With one yank on their ribbons we have cause to arrest them. Understand?"

Fear swept through every part of my body. "Yes, sir."

They touched the brim of their black leather hats with tips of their right fingers in what might have been a salute before heading toward downtown.

My heart resumed beating in a sudden rush. If my mask had fallen off... Could they really arrest me if they were the ones who caused it? That would be cheating, even illegal. But I suspected they didn't care.

Once I calmed down, I analyzed the Halloween Men's comments and didn't like what they'd implied. After I dumped my supplies in my workroom, I rushed over to my father's shop. The showroom was empty, but he heard the bell and came out from the back room. We stared at each other in the semi-darkness for a moment.

"What happened?" he asked. Neither anger nor annoyance colored his tone.

I told him about my encounter with the Halloween Men. "Did you tell them about my masks?"

"Of course not. You are my daughter."

It took a moment for that simple sentence to sink in. The feelings behind it were more than just a statement of fact. They implied...affection. "Why are the Halloween Men so against my masks?"

"Because they will become popular. The other *mascherari*

will copy you and even our everyday masks will transform into exotic shapes and designs. The Halloween Men don't want that. When they invaded hundreds of years ago, they used the masks to remind us of our sins. Masks were once used to cover those who had been deemed ugly by our citizens. Beauty had been valued above all else and those considered unworthy had been forced to wear a mask in public. Due to our ancestors' vanity, the masks are a burden we must all bear, a punishment. They'll arrest all the *mascheraris* and those who survive will return to making stark utilitarian masks."

"How do you know all this?"

"You're not the first to embellish masks. Every generation has at least one *mascherari* who goes against convention. The Halloween Men have learned this and now stop the cycle before it can even begin."

And then it clicked, explaining that box in the attic. "Mother did it, too."

"No."

"But she—"

"The Halloween Men came for *me* that night, Antonella. You're mother left me after. She could not... I don't blame her. You were so young at the time, I thought you didn't remember."

Shocked, I stared at him. "Why didn't you tell me this before?"

"It is... difficult to talk about."

"What did the Halloween Men do to you?"

His lips pressed together and he held his arms straight down by his sides. The familiar posture meant I'd get no more information about that no matter how hard I tried.

I switched topics. "How did they find you?"

"I didn't hide. My masks filled the shelves."

The knot in my chest eased a bit. They didn't know about me.

Father watched me. "They suspect you, Antonella. That's enough. Come home."

"I can't. I have a patron. I signed a contract."

"I can fix that for you."

I crossed my arms. "Are you working for the Halloween Men?"

"I aid them on occasion."

Horrified, I stepped back.

"You've no idea what they're capable of, Antonella."

"Actually, I do. You've been telling me for years." I headed for the door. With my hand on the knob, I turned. "Just stay out of it. I can handle it on my own."

I strode out into the rain. My brave words fueled my steps. But as I passed more and more Halloween Men, my courage wavered.

"Do not worry, Nella," Enzo said after I told him about my visit with my father. He picked up one of my masks from the drying rack in my workroom and inspected it. "You're an employee of my family's business and under our protection. That's why they told you to return to your father. He can't protect you."

"Has your family ever...had trouble with them."

Enzo laughed. "All the time. We manufacture goods and sell them beyond the city's limits. My family gives the Halloween Men some extra...wine to look the other way." He returned the mask to the rack. "I have something important to ask you." Enzo took my hand in his. "Will you accompany me to Bianca's party?"

A strange and unfamiliar emotion pushed out my fear. I grinned. "Of course."

"Ah, you do know how to smile." He reached up and cupped my cheek. "Take off your mask, Nella. You don't need to hide from me."

True. With a sudden surge of courage, I untied the ribbons and placed it on the table. And even though I wanted to duck my head, I gazed at Enzo.

Enzo tucked a strand of my hair behind my ear. "It's a shame you have to hide such beauty under a mask. Even the Halloween Men would fall in love at the sight of you!"

My heart spun in my chest. "Don't be silly."

"I'm serious, Nella. Every man is going to envy me at the party."

And then he pulled me close and kissed me. New sensations surge through me, buoying me up like a boat at high tide.

Halloween festivities started at midnight. Most citizens gave up sleep for this once a year chance to be outside without a mask and robe. Enzo collected me and we walked through the plazas hand in hand. I'd worried my skittish nature wouldn't allow me to enjoy the day, but with the streets filled with people without masks, I just blended in. I relaxed.

Jugglers, comedians, and acrobats entertained the revelers. Young children collected candy from those who stayed inside. We sipped wine and ate linguini mixed with a white clam sauce. The sun peeked out from time to time.

By mid-afternoon, we collapsed onto a bench exhausted.

"You're so fun to watch," Enzo said. "It's like all this is new to you."

"It is," I confessed. "My father never let me go out on

Halloween until I was eighteen. And that first year..." Bianca had told the truth about me.

He laughed over my hiding in a dark corner. "This year is already better."

Yes. Much better. My life had started and I planned to embrace it.

"Come on." Enzo pulled me to my feet. "The Harlequins are putting on a show in Piccione Plaza. You don't want to miss that!"

He was right. I hadn't laughed so hard...ever. My sides hurt and tears rolled down my cheeks. Afterwards, we ate in a sidewalk café and then headed to Bianca's party.

Since the rain held off, her family set up in the street outside their bakery. A band played and pyramids of pastries filled the tables.

Bianca squealed when she spotted us. "You came!"

"Don't act so surprised," I said.

"I was talking to Enzo," she teased.

"Wouldn't miss it," he said.

After she introduced us to a few of her friends, Enzo asked me to dance. The evening flew by as we stuffed ourselves with creamy cannoli and burned off the sweets on the dance floor.

Despite the party, I couldn't completely shake my worries. During one break, I sought Bianca for a private chat, pulling her inside the bakery for a moment.

"Have the Halloween Men asked you about me?" I inquired.

"No. Since I stopped selling your masks no one has asked. Why?"

"Just checking." Relief raised my spirits. The Halloween Men hadn't taken any more notice of me since that time when I spilled my cart.

Enzo and I left the party with barely enough time to reach

my house. At midnight the Halloween Men would return to the streets. We ran through the city, laughing and jumping over puddles.

Slipping inside one forty-two, we gasped for breath. Mere minutes later, the bell tolled midnight.

"Looks like I'm stuck here," Enzo said with a sly smile. "I left my mask at home."

I opened my mouth to remind him I had a dozen of them upstairs, but clamped it shut as he closed the distance between us.

Enzo wrapped his arms around me and kissed me. Heat spiked, shooting to my core and igniting another new, but wonderful feeling. I desired more.

He broke away and gazed at me, questioning.

"Guess you'll just have to spend the night," I said.

"Rotten luck," he murmured, tangling his fingers in my hair.

"The worst." I slid my hands under his shirt.

After that we didn't talk.

It wasn't until late the next morning that we'd discovered someone had stolen all my butterfly masks for the Cattaneo's New Year's party. I blinked at the empty tables and drying racks in shock, thinking if I closed my eyes longer, all my weeks of hard work would reappear. They didn't.

Enzo checked the other rooms, looking for the culprits. He found nothing. Not even evidence of burglary. When he returned he asked, "Who knew about these?"

"Bianca, your family, my father, and according to him, the Halloween Men suspected."

"We can rule out my family and the Halloween Men. They wouldn't bother to steal the masks."

"Why not? You said your family has dealings with them. Perhaps they thought this was the best solution. We can't prove they took them."

Enzo shook his head. "It's not their style. They'd arrest you and then we'd bribe them to release you."

"You'd do that for me?"

The hard anger in his face softened. "Of course."

"Would it work?"

"It has in the past. How do you think the Halloween Men are able to afford new masks and robes every year?"

I'd never thought about it. Along with many other things.

"We can rule out Bianca, too," I said. "She would profit from the party's success."

"I'll talk to my mother," Enzo said. "We have a rivalry with the Farina family who is also having a big New Year's party." He swept his hand out. "If they knew about the masks, this might be a form of sabotage."

Which left my father. Which made the most sense to me especially if he wished to protect me. But I wouldn't tell Enzo my suspicions until after I visited him.

The rain faded the bright Halloween colors from yesterday, coating everything in dark gray. A few people hustled along the slick sidewalks, while the rest probably slept off their hangovers. Water sloshed and slapped. Empty bottles and confetti floated on the rough surface.

My boots tapped out a steady rhythm as I debated. Should I be angry that my father interfered or glad that he cared for me enough to go to such extremes? Both feelings swirled inside me.

I entered the shop without a plan. The bell jangled. Instead of my father, four Halloween Men stepped from the back room.

"I..." I inched toward the door.

"Miss Salvatori, we were just discussing you," the closest Halloween Man grabbed my arm, pulling me away from my escape route.

"I..." My thoughts buzzed into a jumble.

"We're not very happy with you or your father." His grip tightened.

"Master Salvatori lied to us," the second man said as he clamped a hand on my other arm.

"And you've been very busy creating things that offend us, Miss Salvatori," the third man said.

"But they're legal." My voice squeaked and fear liquefied my muscles.

"In size and coverage, yes. But offending us is the greater crime," the fourth man said.

"The Cattaneo family—"

"Not to worry," the fourth man said. "Your patrons will pay for your return. Once you've been punished." He jerked his thumb toward the back room.

The Halloween Men dragged me through the curtains because my legs had stopped working. They strapped me down on a table. Arms, legs, torso, and my head all immobilized. Then they stepped back, revealing my father. I pressed my lips together to keep from crying out.

"You're in luck," the second Halloween Men said. "Master Salvatori has agreed to do the punishment himself."

I yelled at my father. "You betrayed me."

"Not him. Miss Bianca Sommerso was most obliging this

morning and her hands should heal, for the most part, by the new year."

Oh no. Poor Bianca! I wanted to scream at the Halloween Men, but Father approached the table and met my gaze.

"I tried..." Father's shoulders slumped. "I failed." He reached behind his head and untied his mask.

I sucked in a breath. It was an awful time to finally show me his face. Except when he removed his Bauta, there was a plain navy Columbina underneath it. Confused, I stared until I noticed the mask wasn't tied on. Metal wire punctured his scarred skin around the edges of the mask.

The mask had been sewn onto his face.

Shock and horror and revulsion boiled up my throat, rendering me speechless.

"This is what the Halloween Men did to me fifteen years ago. What made your mother leave. I should have told you, shown you...the truth. I was trying to protect you," he whispered. "Instead, it is your fate as well." Father picked up a simple half-mask and placed it on my face.

I screamed and struggled against the straps until I puffed from exhaustion.

A Halloween Man leaned over me. "Keep still and it won't hurt as much. Besides, you should be grateful your father agreed to help us. He *is* a master with a needle and thread."

POSEIDON'S ISLAND

What is the opposite of horror? Comedy! I have touches of humor in all my novels and short stories, but those incidents are not planned. They arise as I'm writing and come naturally from the characters. When I was invited to submit a story to TV Gods, Summer Programming!, *the challenge for me was writing humor on purpose. The anthology's theme was to replace the cast of a popular TV show with mythical gods from any ancient culture. Right away, I knew* Gilligan's Island *would be my show. It was one of my favorites growing up. Plus the kids in my neighborhood used to act out the episodes in our backyards and I always wound up playing Gilligan. Research for this story was a hoot. I watched a dozen episodes of the show to prepare—after all this time it's still funny!. I also searched for names of minor Greek gods to be my castaways. I'm pleased with my version of* Gilligan's Island. *To me, it explains so much.*

POSEIDON'S ISLAND

"Just sit right back and you'll hear a tale..." Pilligan sang as he wound the anchor's rope into a neat coil on the ship's deck. The white wood shone in the warm tropical sunshine. He'd done a fabulous job of scrubbing it if he did say so himself. In fact, the S.S. Mini Cooper gleamed. It bobbed in the gentle waves like a seagull about to take wing.

When he finished with the rope, Pilligan set the sign out on the pier. Shaped like a ship's wheel the sign read: Island Charters. Exotic Trip. Free Lunches. Before they added free lunches, they hadn't had a customer in months. But now—

"Pilligan!" Captain's voice cut through his musings. "Clients at two o'clock."

"But Captain, you said they'd be here at eleven." Pilligan scratched his temple in confusion.

The Captain's big belly expanded as he sighed. The motion stretched his royal blue shirt almost to the ripping point. Taking off his captain's hat, he ran a big hand through his thick white hair. Pilligan flinched, expecting to be swatted by the hat, but Captain just pointed to the end of the dock.

Five passengers stood on land. They peered at the rows of sailboats, fishing trawlers, pleasure cruisers, and yachts docked at the Tropic Port.

"Go help them," Captain said.

"Aye, aye, Captain." Pilligan saluted.

"Oh, Pilligan?"

"Yes?"

Captain gestured to Pilligan's red shirt and white pants. "You're supposed to instill confidence as my first mate."

"Oh. Right." He raced below deck and looped a coil of rope around his right shoulder, tied on a flashlight and a fanny pack filled with...well, he wasn't sure, but it must be something important. When he returned, he held his arms out and asked Captain how he looked.

"Like a mighty sailing man," Captain said drily.

Pilligan preened. He hustled over the dock's wooden boards to greet their clients. As he neared the group of three women and two men, he slowed.

The red-haired lady was gorgeous. Her gold evening gown glittered in the sun and hugged her curves. And boy or boy, her figure put an hourglass to shame. The other girl had her brown hair pulled into pigtails and her complexion was farm fresh and milky pure. She wore a cotton half-shirt and short shorts. An older man and woman bickered good naturedly. The woman's copious amount of jewelry flashed sparks of sunfire and Pilligan was surprised the seagulls hadn't attacked her. And the older man wore a straw hat with his three piece suit. The last man stood a little bit away from the group. He clutched a stack of books to his chest, wrinkling his white button down shirt. His sandy brown hair matched his tan pants.

Pilligan introduced himself to the passengers.

"About time, my boy," the older gent said. "I'm Phorbas

Howl the three hundred and thirty third and this is my wife, Mrs. Lovey Howl." He pointed to a stack of luggage. "If you'd be so kind to carry them to your ship..." Mr. Howl pulled out a wad of cash. "I'll add an extra hundred if you avoid the puddles of rotten fish guts."

The red headed lady sidled up to him. "Pilligan," she said in a breathy whisper. "I'm going to need a big strong man to carry my suitcases."

"Uh, Miss..."

"Lampetia." She fluttered her long fake eyelashes at him.

"No. No," interrupted the sandy-haired man. "He needs to ferry my crates of books without getting them wet. I'm Aepytus." He shook Pilligan's hand.

"I can carry my own bags," the pigtail lady said. "I'm Euryte."

Pilligan looked at the mounds of luggage and bags. "Ummm. Do you know it's only a three hour tour?"

"A THREE HOUR TOUR." The words echoed all around them, but only Pilligan was startled by the booming voice. He peered at the passengers. They were a strange group of minor gods who now looked nervous.

"Then let's go, my boy," Mr. Howl said, waving cash in front of his face. "Time is money!"

They seemed anxious to leave. Pilligan shrugged and hefted a heavy suitcase, making the first of many trips to the S.S. Mini Cooper.

After stowing all the luggage—a miracle, considering there was a reason the ship was named after a tiny car—they set sail. An hour into the trip, the weather started getting rough. The tiny ship was tossed like lettuce in a salad. If not for the courage of—oh, who was Pilligan kidding? He blew chunks into the heaving ocean, curled into a fetal position, and cried for his mommy while the Captain was brave and sure and steered them straight into the rocks, causing them to shipwreck on an uncharted tropical isle.

With suitcases and luggage piled around them on the lagoon's beach, the storm weary group dried out on the sand. The passengers sat around a campfire eating their soggy free lunches when Captain told them the bad news.

"We were blown miles off course, our shipboard communications are dead, and there's no cell signal." The last comment caused a collective gasp of dismay. "All we have is a survival kit and this old radio, but it's busted." Captain held out a white box with a bent antenna.

Aepytus raised his hand. "I can fix it. I've a Masters degree in electrical engineering." He took radio, drained the water from it, straightened the antenna, and muttered something about using the salt in the ocean to build an alkaline battery.

Pilligan tuned him out. "What are our chances of being rescued Captain?"

"Well, Little Minnow, I'm sure the Coast Guard is out searching for us right now."

Panic boiled in his chest. They were marooned and doomed. Captain only called him Little Minnow when things were bad. Like getting a lollypop right before an injection bad.

"Of course they're coming," Mr. Howl said in a rich baritone. "I'm the Wolf of Olympus, a billionaire *after* taxes, and I've suitcases full of money."

"And I'm having tea with the mayor's second ex-wife tomorrow!" Mrs. Howl pressed her hands to her chest in dismay. Not a smudge of dirt sullied her white silk gloves.

"I've an audition," Lampetia said. Desperation laced her

voice. When she noticed everyone staring at her in pity, she fluffed her hair and purred, "It's a mere formality."

"My cows won't milk themselves," Euryte cried.

Static crackled through the air. Another storm! Pilligan hunched over and pulled his white floppy hat down over his ears, but the sound came from the radio. Aepytus fiddled with a nob as he tuned into an active frequency.

A whistle sounded then a male announcer said, "This just in... authorities have launched the search for the S.S. Mini Cooper. We received a passenger manifest..." The man continued, listing their names and their minor accomplishments. As each bio was read, the passengers brightened. "Ever effort is being made to find these lost gods, who no one knew existed until now."

"Do you know what this means?" Mr. Howl asked.

"That we're going to be rescued," Pilligan said.

"No," Lampetia said. "We're going to be famous!"

Cries of happiness echoed all around. Pilligan shook his head—minor gods were worse than demi-gods. Just then a faint whine of an airplane engine sounded.

Captain jumped to his feet. "It's the search plane. Quick, Pilligan! The flare gun."

Pilligan ran right into the Captain and bounced off. "Sorry, Captain." Then he stepped on Captain's foot as he rushed over to the survival kit.

"Hurry up." Captain urged him as the drone of the plane grew louder.

Fumbling with the flares, Pilligan dropped them on the beach. They rolled toward the waves lapping at the sand. He dove and grabbed one right before it reached the water. Whew.

The others waved their arms and yelled as the plane passed right over head. Pilligan loaded the flare into the gun, aimed it at the sky and pulled the trigger. A woomph sounded as a bright red spark streaked through the sky and...hit the airplane. Dead center. It exploded in mid-air.

Mouths agape, the others stared at Pilligan.

"Oops." He swallowed. Loudly.

Aepytus pointed to the sky. "Look."

A man dangled below a blue and yellow parachute that floated toward the island.

Pilligan's knees gave out and he plopped to the sand in relief.

"Let's hope he radioed in his position before ejecting," Mr. Howl said.

They watched as the pilot came closer, but then a strong wind gusted over the island. Palm trees shook and coconuts fell and the pilot was blown far out to sea.

After a moment of shocked silence, Aepytus said, "If my calculations are correct, he's going toward the shipping lanes. He's bound to be picked up."

They waited on the beach for another plane or ship to arrive. One day turned into two then into three. On the third day, the radio suddenly crackled to life.

The same announcer said, "This just in...the Coast Guard has found the pilot of a rescue plane that had disappeared while searching for the S.S. Mini Cooper. Other than a concussion and dehydration, the man is in good shape. When authorities asked him what happened to his aircraft, the man claimed he has no memory of the incident. The doctors confirmed the man has a classic case of amnesia. In other news, the search for the S.S. Mini Cooper has been called off."

Hostile glares focused on Pilligan. He made himself scarce.

Two weeks later, they were still stranded on the island, but they had built huts and chairs and hammocks and tables and dishes and beds and... It was amazing what they were able to construct from the island's natural resources. Plus the suitcases seemed to have an unlimited supply of clothing and accessories. It was almost mag—

"Pilligan! Stop daydreaming and help me put up the umbrella," Captain ordered.

"Aye, aye, Captain."

That night after Mr. Howl drank too much fermented coconut milk, he offered a million dollars to the person who discovered a way to get them off the island. They all brainstormed ideas, but Aepytus came up with the winning design. Actually it wasn't all that impressive. Even though they built huts and chairs and hammocks and tables and dishes and beds, no one, until now, thought to build a raft. Captain and Pilligan would sail it out to the shipping lanes and bring back help.

The girls sewed a sail, while Pilligan collected branches. He dropped his load onto the growing pile by the lagoon and checked in with Aepytus. The man worked at a complex apparatus that resembled a moonshine still. White smoke puffed and a sweet odor fogged the air.

"What are you doing?" Pilligan asked.

"Since I have a Masters degree in botany and chemistry, I'm making an adhesive for the raft from coconut sap, sugar, and—"

"What's an adhesive?"

"It's glue. We're going to glue the branches together."

"That's a good idea."

"I know. Now if you don't mind..."

Pilligan returned to his task and soon they had enough branches to construct the raft. With everyone assembled on the beach to help, Aepytus sent Pilligan back to his hut to fetch the glue. He ran the whole way and was hot and thirsty when he arrived. There was a coconut filled with milk and Pilligan downed that before grabbing the other coconut with the glue. He raced back to the lagoon. They built the raft and Captain and Pilligan launched it, jumping into the small craft before it could leave without them.

They sailed approximately ten feet before the branches floated apart, dumping them into the lagoon. They swam for shore. Standing on the beach, soaking wet, Captain growled at Aepytus.

But Aepytus was staring at Pilligan. "Did you get the adhesive from my hut?"

Pilligan opened his mouth to reply, but his lips were glued shut. Guess that wasn't coconut milk he drank. Oops. He made himself scarce.

Aepytus brewed another batch of glue and they launched the raft again.

"Good bye!" Lampetia waved a white handkerchief.

"Bye!" Pilligan called.

"Good luck," Euryte said.

"Thanks." Pilligan tipped his hat.

"Bon voyage!" Mr. Howl said.

"Uh...bon voyage back at you," Pilligan said.

"Watch out for sharks," Aepytus said.

"Sharks?" Pilligan tried to turn the raft around.

"Pilligan," Captain growled.

Twenty feet into the journey, the glue dissolved in the water and dumped Pilligan and Captain into the lagoon. This time Aepytus made himself scarce.

～

A few days later, Pilligan found a large rectangular crate that had washed up on the beach. He raced to get the Captain, but the entire population of the island followed Pilligan back to the lagoon.

Captain used a pry bar to open the crate. Inside was a robot. Constructed from a shiny silver metal, the automaton had a cone-shaped head with an antenna sticking out the top. Two square panels extended to each side of the robot's head, looking like ears. It had a rectangular body with lights and a control panel. It stood on metal legs, but its arms were made out of that flexible piping used in ducts.

"What do you think, Aepytus?" Captain asked.

"It's a robot."

Captain grabbed his hat, but didn't take it off. "Can you turn it on?"

"Well...I studied robotics when I was in school for—"

"For money's sake, my good man," Mr. Howl said in frustration. "Yes or no?"

"I was getting to that, Mr. Howl." Aepytus frowned, but he reached into the crate and pushed the fist-sized button labeled "power" on the robot's chest.

A rumble sounded from deep within the metal...er...man? Yes. Pilligan decided it was a man. Lights flashed and he sat up. They all jumped back a couple feet. But the robot didn't move.

"Now what?" Pilligan asked.

"Now what," the robot echoed.

"Hey, he can talk!" Pilligan inched closer.

"Hey he can talk," the monotone voice repeated.

"I might be able to program him to do some simple tasks," Aepytus said.

"Oooohh," Euryte said. "He can do the dishes and sweep the sand out of our huts."

"He can do the laundry and iron my gowns," Lampetia cooed.

"He can gather the coconuts and carry them back to camp." Pilligan rubbed his lower back, he was tired of fetching coconuts for everybody.

"Now see here, I'm a Howl and I'm used to certain luxuries. He can be *my* valet."

"*We're* used to living in luxury," Mrs. Howl corrected. "He can be *our* butler."

"That's a fine idea, Lovey." Mr. Howl kissed the back of her gloved hand.

"Now wait a minute," Captain said. "He can chop the fire wood."

An argument broke out as each person tried to shout over the others. The radio crackled to life, silencing them.

"This just in...," the announcer said. "A very expensive T.X. 14 robot has fallen off a container ship in the south Pacific. Massive search efforts along the shipping lanes are underway."

"Or we can program him to swim out to the shipping lanes and report our location," Aepytus said.

Cheers and back-slaps erupted.

Boy Aepytus is smart, thought Pilligan. *He's like a person that teaches stuff at one of those schools for smart kids.*

While Aepytus worked on the program, Pilligan was given the job of teaching the robot how to swim. All four men struggled to lay the robot on a narrow table belly down. Pilligan lay on another table right next to him.

"Move your arms and legs like this, Robot," he said, demonstrating how to swim the freestyle.

But Robot couldn't rotate his arms over his head, which also ruled out the butterfly stroke. And the breast stroke proved too difficult as well. So Pilligan taught him the only thing that worked. The doggie paddle. Or in this case, the robot paddle.

Once Aepytus uploaded the program, they directed the robot back to the beach. After a bon voyage party and a kiss from Lampetia, the robot started doing the robot paddle with his arms as he waded into the lagoon. The water rose up to his knees, then his waist, up to his chest and...over his head.

"It appears the robot cannot float," Aepytus said.

"You think?" Captain snapped.

At least no one blamed Pilligan. This time. They waited on the beach, but the robot never resurfaced. Disappointed, dejected, and depressed everyone shuffled back to their huts to drown their sorrows with coconut wine.

A week later as they ate lunch, the radio sizzled to life. "This just in...the missing T.X. 14 robot just walked onto a beach in Hawaii."

The castaways applauded. They were going to be rescued!

"...scientists examined the T.X. 14's data banks, but salt water corroded the files. We'll never know where the T.X. 14 was after if fell off the ship and before it walked onto shore."

Gloomy silence. Then. "Aepytus?"

"I'll brew up another batch of wine." Aepytus headed for his still.

"Better make that *two* batches, my good man," Mr. Howl said, staring into his empty mug.

A couple days later, Pilligan rested on the beach in a lounge chair. He'd fetched hot water for Mr. and Mrs. Howl, collected plants for Aepytus, helped the girls wash dishes, and fixed the holes in the grass walls of the huts. He was beat. The sun warmed him. The soft lapping of the water lulled him to—

Whap!

Wide awake, he jerked upright. A giant white net covered the island.

"Captain. Captain," Pilligan shouted, trying to stand, but something was hooked around his neck, prevented him from moving. He struggled to free himself.

"Be still," an unfamiliar voice hissed. "You'll scare off the *Pyrgus malvae tropicae regionibus*."

"The pyra-what?" Pilligan finally pulled the net off his head.

"Drat," the man said with a British accent. He hefted his net and stalked away.

Pilligan was annoyed at the stranger for interrupting his nap. He settled back on the chair. A second later he realized that a stranger was on the island. A stranger! Jumping up, he scrambled after the portly man wearing a pith helmet, khaki shirt, and khaki shorts. An orange belt, green knee socks and brown boots completed the outfit. The man appeared as if he were on a tropical safari.

"Mister, wait!" Pilligan cried. "What are you doing here? How did you get here? Do you have a boat?" The questions tumbled from his mouth in a rush.

"Do be quiet," the man said, peering through a pair of binoculars. He crept toward the bushes and swung his net. "Drat." Then he crouched down and crawled into the underbrush.

Unable to get the man's attention, Pilligan fetched Captain and the others. They finally managed to get a response from the stranger.

"My name is Lord Papillon. I'm hunting a very rare *Pyrgus malvae tropicae regionibus*." At their blank looks, the Lord sighed. "It's a Tropical Grizzled Skipper butterfly, recently only thought to live in the United Kingdom. Once I capture it, I will fire my flare gun and my ship will come and pick me up."

"Will you take us with you?" Captain asked.

"Of course."

They celebrated. Pilligan jumped up and down. They would be rescued. Finally!

"But not until I find that butterfly," Lord Papillon said.

"How long will that take?" Mrs. Howl asked.

"Days, weeks, months, years...I will stay on this island until I've captured it! Even if it takes forever."

They ceased celebrating. After a few days of frustrated waiting, they plotted how to speed things up. Aepytus made seven butterfly nets for the castaways. They spent an entire day hunting the Tropical Grizzled Skipper with Lord Papillon.

When they returned, they plopped onto the chairs in exhaustion.

"My blisters have blisters." Lampetia rubbed her feet.

"I'm probably two inches shorter," complained Euryte.

"That man is obsessed," Mr. Howl said. "We need a new plan and more coconut wine."

"That's it," Aepytus said.

"What's it?" Pilligan asked.

"I'll brew a stronger drink from berries and we'll get him drunk. While he's unconscious, we'll steal his flare gun and signal his ship."

The next day, the castaways invited Lord Papillon to a special tea in his honor. They poured cups of berry tea for everyone and toasted butterflies, the British Empire, and Pilligan's Aunt Beatrice, because by that time, they were all a bit drunk. They toasted to everything they could think of until they could think no more.

Pilligan woke...hours later? His head throbbed and

Lampetia had drooled on his red shirt. His only red shirt, which still looked brand new despite—

"Owww...my head," Captain groaned. "How long were we asleep?"

"According to my watch, only ten minutes," Mr. Howl said.

"According to my *calendar* watch, we'd been asleep for ten minutes and two days," Aepytus said.

"Where's Lord Papillon?" Pilligan asked.

They searched for him, but he was not on the island. Dejected, they sat around the table.

The radio buzzed to life. "Today we are interviewing the world famous butterfly collector Lord Papillon who has netted the rare Tropical Grizzled Skipper. Tell us how you found this unique beauty Lord Papillon."

The castaways leaned closer. Pilligan's heart tapped like the woodpecker that liked to peck on his head. Would Papillon mention them? Would they get rescued?

"I've no time for this nonsense," Lord Papillon said. "There's been reports of an extremely rare *Frigidum callophrys rubi* in the Artic and I must leave right away before the creature freezes to death."

"Good hunting, Lord Papillon," the radio announcer said.

A collective groan ringed the table. Mr. Howl picked up an empty cup. He shook it. "Perhaps more of that *tea?*"

Pilligan slumped in his chair. So close. Again. How many times has it been? A lot. He straightened. "Does it seem like one of those endless punishments to you?" he asked the others.

"What do you mean?" Euryte asked.

"You know, like that Sissy Pus guy who has to push the boulder up the mountain, but it keeps rolling back down."

"That's the dumbest thing I've ever heard, Pilligan," Captain said.

No one else said a word. They looked everywhere but at him and the Captain.

Standing, the Captain crossed his arms and peered at each of them. "All right, who pissed off Poseidon?"

Cheeks turning red, they stammered and fidgeted under his scrutiny.

"What did you do?" he demanded.

"I turned down a marriage proposal from his son," Lampetia said.

"He hired me to find a way to clean the contaminated water in the Bay of Olympus," Aepytus said.

"But that's a respectable thing to do," Mrs. Howl said.

Aepytus hunched his shoulders. "I turned to water into gelatin."

"Which flavor?" Pilligan asked.

Captain swatted him on the head with his cap. Pilligan rubbed his temple, he thought it was a good question.

"I was swimming and encountered a manatee. You know, one of those sea cows. It appeared to be in distress." Euryte wrung her hands. "When my cows are in pain it means they need to be milked. What I tugged on was not a teat."

"What was it?" Pilligan asked.

No one answered.

"I foreclosed on Atlantis," Mr. Howl said.

Groans all around.

"That's it. We're never getting off this island. He's going to keep torturing us with the possibility of rescue." Captain slammed his hat onto the table. "I knew I shouldn't have offered free lunches."

Pilligan didn't think it was fair of Poseidon to punish him and the Captain, but he was just a mortal—what did he know? Guess this would be his new home. He glanced around at their huts, the lounge chairs, the still, and—hey!

"This place isn't so bad," Pilligan said. "We have everything we need. It's warm. It's beautiful. No telemarketers. No taxes. No political debates."

They brightened.

"My dear boy, I think you may have something there," Mr. Howl said.

After that the mood on the island was downright jubilant. For the next few months, they sunned on the beach, surfed the waves, drank lots and lots of coconut wine and berry tea. With two beautiful single girls and three bachelors, there was quite a bit of hooking—

"Pilligan!" Captain called from the lagoon. "Pilligan!"

He raced to the beach with the others close behind. Captain pointed out to sea. Bobbing on the waves was a large Coast Guard cutter. A smaller boat jetted toward their lagoon.

"A rescue boat," Captain said.

"You all know what to do," Aepytus said.

"Hide!" Pilligan dove for cover.

BERSERKER EYES

Due to the mega success of The Hunger Games, *young adult (YA) dystopian novels were all the rage. YA dystopian is different from adult dystopian novels as they end with signs of hope. For the* Brave New Love *anthology, the theme centered on finding love in a hopeless world. The idea for my story grew from thinking about designer babies. My daughter was learning about genetics at the time and my thoughts turned to how the military might use that information to create a designer soldier. Once I had the basic plot, the challenge for me was keeping the story short. This one pushed for more words and could easily be turned into a novel. Too bad, the YA dystopian trend has waned.*

BERSERKER EYES

They watched us. And we watched each other. Searching for the telltale signs—a raised voice, clenched jaw, fisted hands, muscles as tight as security, and the serk gaze—we watched and waited. Anyone of us could be next. Every night before lights out, I stared at my own reflection, seeking the rage that might lurk behind my blue eyes. *Will I be next?*

Blue colored eyes and blond hair were recessive genes. Would my other recessive genes also manifest before my body stopped growing? The question plagued me as, I was sure, it did the others. I imagined a huge black question mark floated above my head.

Today, though was a rare day in the compound. Molly had been cleared. I walked with her to the administration building. Only security and teachers were allowed inside. And the cleared. There they rejoined their families and left the compound for good.

A small crowd of well-wishers had gathered to say good-bye, which was technically against the rules, but in this case security overlooked it. Although the guards eyed the new seventeen with suspicion. What was he doing here? He stood apart from the group and from the four guards waiting to escort Molly inside. Molly slowed, gnawing on her lower lip as she glanced at them and then around the compound.

I didn't need to turn my head to see what she saw—squat gray cinder block buildings interspersed with dirt-covered play fields and all surrounded by a tall chain linked fence topped with barbed wire. High security towers anchored the corners of the parameter.

"You're not going to miss this place," I said.

She pulled her brown-eyed gaze to mine. "No, but I'll miss you, Kate."

"For five seconds. Once you're reunited with your family, you'll forget all about me."

She grabbed my arm, stopping me. "Never. You're my best friend."

I smiled to ease the tension. "If I'm cleared, I'll make sure to find you out there." However my comment made her tighten her grip. "You better. Promise me that you will do everything you can to leave this place. *Everything.*"

"What—"

"Just promise me right now."

"Okay. I promise."

"And stay out of trouble."

Puzzled, I searched her expression. "I always do. Why—"

She glanced at the new seventeen. "He keeps staring at you. Stay away from him. Okay?"

"All right." That won't be hard to do. Security brought him in recently. Usually they arrived with zeros, ones, and twos, but he was placed with the seventeens when they escorted him into the compound a couple weeks ago. So far, he'd spent most of his time in detention for multiple escape attempts. Again I wondered why he was even here. The few days he'd been free, he'd avoided everyone.

We continued to the admin building. Molly handed me the too-delicate-for-her-backpack vase she had made from copper wires for her older sister. She'd been a four when she'd arrived. And unlike many of us who had been brought in much younger, Molly remembered her family. I held the statue while she hugged friends and said goodbye. Impatient to finish their day, security hustled her along and into the building before I could say farewell and return the gift for her sister.

Rushing forward without thought, I slipped inside before the door closed. I paused for a moment to let my eyes adjust from the bright sunshine outside. Then I looked around in disappointment. The hallway resembled all the hallways in the other buildings. We had elevated this building to super star status, I expected marble floors and extravagant paintings on the walls. Or at least rugs. But, no. The plain linoleum floors were as well worn as the one in our dorms and the walls as equally scuffed.

Voices to my left woke me from my musings. I turned in time to glimpse the end of the group turning down another corridor. Following the voices, I hurried to catch up but slowed as I drew nearer. Surely they wouldn't punish me for returning Molly's sculpture? And it seemed odd that we had gone down a number of steps. Perhaps I'd followed the wrong group.

I hung back, but when they entered a large room, I decided to approach them and get it over with. Stepping across the threshold, I paused. Everyone faced Molly who stood staring at them with a quizzical expression.

It happened so fast. A movement. A crack. Her forehead shattered. The surprise in her eyes as she flew back onto a plastic sheet.

The shock robbed me of breath and saved my life. Unable

to utter a sound, I watched in silence as they wrapped her body in the plastic. A surge of self preservation finally kicked in and I ducked out, running down one hallway after another. Eventually, I stumbled into a dead end and collapsed onto the floor.

The images of her murder replayed over and over in my mind. She'd been cleared! Why would they kill her? She was no longer a danger to society. Horror and fear boiled in my chest, churning into pure rage. Energy surged through my muscles as all my senses sharpened.

My body demanded action so I jumped to my feet. The desire to kill the guards who had murdered my friend pumped in my heart. My fingers curved into claws and I knew without a doubt I could rip those four men apart with my bare hands. The thought of blood and gore inflamed my need. Four men wouldn't be enough to satisfy me, I would kill them *all*.

Running fast down the halls, I hunted by scent. When I heard voices, I stopped as a memory tugged from deep within me. It had been very important to follow voices. I glanced at my hands. The vase Molly had painstakingly constructed from thin copper wire had been crushed beyond recognition in my fist.

But I grasped that one moment of lucidity and hung onto it, pushing the blood lust aside. My first clear thought was the realization that I'd serked. Witnessing Molly's murder had triggered the Berserker gene, which, until now, had lain dormant inside me. I was now a mindless killing machine and would be terminated.

Except, I had snapped out of it. Or had I? Fury surged through my veins, but I sucked in deep breaths, calming my ragged nerves. I clutched the vase. The wires dug into my palm and I concentrated on settling my emotions. Leaning against the wall, I closed my eyes and forced the need to destroy from my mind. My jumpsuit clung to me as sweat dampened the rough blue fabric.

"Kate, what are you doing in here?" a male voice demanded.

I startled and stared at the guard. His hand rested on the butt of his stun gun. Anger flared, but I kept a firm grip. Instead of lunging for his throat, I held out the ruined wire sculpture. "Molly forgot this," I said, proud my voice didn't shake. "I wanted to give it to her, but...got lost."

He peered at me, seeking guilt. I tried to appear scared and frightened about being caught in a forbidden area. It wasn't hard.

"Did you see Molly?" he asked.

"No, sir. I couldn't tell which way they went and then..." I gestured helplessly. "I'm sorry, sir." I hung my head. "Can I stop by my room before reporting for detention?" A shudder ripped through me. I'd only been in trouble once in my seventeen years here. Once was more than enough.

How could that new kid stand it? Although in light of what happened to Molly, it was better than being dead. But for how long? Anger and grief mixed dangerously. The need to see the guard's blood on my hands pulsed through my body.

The guard considered. "No need for detention, Kate. You're not one of the trouble makers."

The tightness in my throat eased. I followed the guard out into the compound. He gestured to the southeast corner. "Better hurry or you'll miss curfew and your dorm mother will give you detention for sure."

"Thanks," I said, meeting his gaze. Had he'd been one of the guards escorting Molly? Rage shot through me. I turned away and ran toward my dorm.

Thanks to the now active berserker gene, my super charged leg muscles would have carried me across the compound in a quarter of the time, alerting everyone. Slowing down required concentration and effort. By the time I reached my room, my jumpsuit was soaked with sweat.

We each had a single bed, dresser, and desk in our rooms along with a washroom. The washrooms were supposedly the only places in the entire compound that didn't have any cameras—hidden or otherwise. It made sense for us not to share a dorm. If one of us serked in the middle of the night, our roommate would be dead before security could arrive.

Keeping control of my conflicting emotions had been exhausting. I curled up on the tile floor of my washroom and let the boiling anger follow waves of grief for Molly. At one point, I was at the edge of giving in to the rage and becoming a mindless Berserker. The thought of killing as many security guards as I could before they terminated me was a satisfying daydream.

Did they really terminate the serkers? That was what they told us, but they also told us the cleared went home. Liars. Not to be trusted. Was anything they told us true?

According to the history teacher, genetic scientists played around with our genes to create designer babies. At first the changes were minor—hair color, eye color, height and weight, but then everyone wanted their children to have an edge over the others. To be smarter, and the military had been keen to produce super soldiers who were faster and stronger than our enemies.

In their haste, mistakes were made, mutations occurred, and evolution's survival of the fittest rule kicked in. The seventh generation born didn't appear to be any different than their ancestors until they reached maturity. Then they went berserk and killed everyone—family, friends, co-workers— everyone. Stronger, faster and out for blood, they banded together and decimated the population.

Finally the government's emergency agency, Domestic Security exterminated the Berserkers and the gene slicers, but couldn't eradicate the gene without killing fifty percent of the survivors. In response, DS tested every child born in a hospital for the Berserker gene. Those who have it were sent to compounds to be watched. Which was why a few soon-to-be mothers like Molly's avoided hospitals. Most of those kids were found within five years. However, the kids who didn't serk by age eighteen were allowed to go home—that was supposed to be the up side, the prize. But now...

Another round of all consuming rage left me gasping. I pressed my cheek to the cool floor as sweat dripped from my forehead.

A knock on the washroom's door pulled me back from a spell of blood lust.

"Kate, are you all right?" my dorm mother asked with concern. "Light's out was an hour ago."

"Stomach bug," I said.

"Oh dear. Can I come in?"

I scrambled to kneel in front of the toilet. "Sure." Flushing the water, I wiped my mouth on my sleeve as Mother Jean entered.

She fussed over me, taking my temperature, helping me change into my nightgown, fetching me a glass of ginger ale, and tucking me into bed. The whole time I fought the desire to rip her arms off and strangle her with my hands.

When she finally left, I was glad I didn't kill her. She was one of the sweetest dorm mothers if you didn't break any of the rules. Then she was one of the most feared. Or so I'd heard. After two days locked in a two-foot by four-foot dank cell without light, food, or water when I was a seven, I'd vowed never to get into trouble again.

I used the stomach bug excuse to stay in my room for the

next couple days. But I couldn't keep hiding. Eventually, Mother Jean would insist I go to the doctor, then they'd know about me for sure. Deep down I knew I was just delaying my termination. Being cleared or going berserk ended the same way so why fight it? Yet, I couldn't give in to the blood lust. I had promised Molly. Only now did I wonder why she hadn't promised me to get cleared. Did she know?

Perhaps I could escape. Except the new kid kept getting caught. But he didn't grow up in this compound and know every inch of it. A rough plan formed. But could I really break the rules? Just the thought made me queasy. In the end, only my promise to Molly kept me from chickening out.

The next morning I joined my dorm mates at breakfast. My hands shook as I filled my plate, but even though I was beyond starving, I didn't take too much. Eating mass quantities of food was another sign of someone on the edge of serking.

I kept tight control over my emotions, letting the conversation flow around me.

"...they brought zero twin girls in yesterday. Have you seen them? They're adorable!"

"Greg won the sixteen triathlon yesterday..."

"...Missy told me she heard Bethany tell Mother Jean..."

"This is the third day in a row that Jayden's been out of detention. Do you think he's stopped trying to escape?"

The last comment caught my full attention. I glanced around the dining room. Round tables were filled with noisy seventeens. All familiar to me. All wearing regulation blue jumpsuits. The girls had their hair tied in regulation knots and the boys wore their hair regulation short. To a new person, we probably looked identical.

But not to us. We had grown up together, starting out with close to a hundred, we were down to forty-three, mostly due to serking. I swallowed as rage pushed up my throat. Molly hadn't been the first of our class to be cleared. Had the other three been killed as well?

Suppressing murderous thoughts, I turned to Haylee who sat next to me. "Jayden?" I asked. "Is that the new seventeen's name?"

"Yep." She pointed a fork toward the far corner.

Jayden leaned back in his chair with his arms crossed, scowling at the few people who dared to sit at his table. They ignored him.

"I'm surprised he hasn't serked by now," Haylee said.

Emotional upheaval, like being arrested and sent to an internment camp was one of the triggers. Or watching your best friend's head shatter. I bit my lip to keep from losing control.

Pulling in a deep breath, I said, "I'm surprised he didn't get caught sooner. Seventeen years without visiting a doctor—"

Haylee leaned close. "His mother's a nurse or something like that, and his family lived in the woods away from civilization. Or so he claims." She stared at him. "He's been trying to convince us to band together and take control of the compound. Have you ever heard anything so ridiculous?" Haylee speared a sausage link on her fork. "At least he's entertaining. We've a bet going on how long he'll stay out of detention this time. Do you want in?"

"No. I lost a bet to Doreen and had to change disgusting diapers for two weeks."

Haylee wrinkled her petite nose. "She had me washing dirty dishes for her. Doreen always wins, I think she cheats."

Since we had no money, the bet winner won the right to exchange her most hated chores to the losers. I realized I would need money if I escaped. What else would I need? I glanced at Jayden. Perhaps I should talk to him.

The bell rang for our first class. It was the longest, most

exhausting day of my life. Each instructional class period was followed by a physical activity like dodgeball, capture the flag, kick the can, and various other sports. All of which I had to pretend to be normal at. My body wanted to show off my new quick reflexes and speed, but I kept firm control.

I never really questioned all the activities before. But after being knocked out of dodgeball, I stood to the side and contemplated why we would spend so much time playing these games aside from the physical exercise. Perhaps the teachers wanted to provoke us into serking. That happened quite a bit, but then again, kids serked in instructional classes, too.

Watching the two teams, I noticed the good teams worked together, feeding balls to the kids with accurate aim, using strategy to knock out the better opponents on the opposite team.

"Training," a voice said next to me.

I jerked in surprise and had to press my hands against my thighs to keep them from doing harm to the speaker before I could turn.

Jayden met my gaze. His eyes were a pale blue. "They're training you so you'll be better fighters when you serk."

Before Molly died, I would have scoffed at the notion. Instead, I asked. "So after spending a couple days here, you're suddenly an expert?"

"I've been here fifteen days." His tone was tight.

"The ones in detention don't count."

"I know—"

Furious in an instant, I said, "You know *nothing*. I've been here seventeen *years*."

He stared at me calmly. "You're right. I'm unfamiliar with everything in this prison. But I recognize training exercises when I see them."

His quick agreement and the word "prison" snapped me back to sanity. In all my life, I'd never considered this place a prison. We weren't criminals. We were here as a precaution. To keep our families and the remaining population safe. But I didn't know what to think anymore.

"A couple days ago you disappeared into the administration building and something happened while you were inside didn't it?" Jayden asked.

I said nothing as the memories of Molly threatened to send me over the edge. And that's how the rest of my day played out. Me finding a way to avoid participating in the games, and Jayden joining me, pointing out the obvious wrongness of my world. Obvious now that I viewed the compound with my berserker eyes.

"Have you noticed that not many of the seventeens have light colored eyes?" Jayden asked while we waited to be freed during capture the flag. "It's recessive—"

"I know it's recessive." I snapped at him. Was he purposely trying to provoke me into killing him? "So is blond hair. So what?" I glanced at his newly shorn blond hair.

"I'll bet Pete will be the next kid to serk. He has both. Plus he's twitchy."

"I don't bet anymore."

"Really? 'Cause you're betting with your life right now."

Before I could demand an explanation, Haylee ran over and freed us from jail. I took off for home base. If only getting out of here was that easy. And why didn't I ask Jayden about the outside?

During eighth period, I was running my best obstacle course time ever when David cut me off. I tripped and fell, landing hard on my right elbow. Pure rage flowed. Without thought I went after David with murderous intent.

Someone grabbed my left wrist, jerking me to a stop.

"Is your elbow all right, Kate?" a voice said.

I tried to shake the annoyance off, but it wouldn't let go.

"Elbow, Kate?" Louder this time. "Kate?"

Jayden's calm insistence cut through my haze. I blinked at him. Concerned, he peered back at me, but kept his tight grip on my wrist.

"Are you all right?" Mr. Telerico asked me. "Do you need to see the doctor?"

I realized everyone was staring at me. Probably wondering if I'd serked.

"No, sir. I just bumped it."

Mr. Telerico nodded and yelled for us to resume our exercise. "Take a minute Kate and we'll restart your time."

"Thank you, sir," I said.

He returned to his post.

"You can let go now," I said to Jayden.

He didn't. "If you can keep it together for another couple days, you'll make it."

"What are you talking about?" I yanked my arm with more force that I should have, but he held on. His strength quite a surprise.

"It's takes about five to seven days for the serker rage to settle. Once that happens you can control your emotions."

"That's ridiculous. How could you possibly know that?" I tried again to free my wrist. No luck.

"I've been through it."

I scoffed. "No way."

"Then why can't you break my hold?" he asked.

"Jayden, you're up," Mr. Telerico called.

He let go and ran to the starting line. I watched him as he navigated the obstacle course. Jayden's muscular physique matched the bigger boys. He didn't appear to be faster or stronger than them, but his graceful movements made the activity look effortless.

I realized I should have thanked him for stopping me from killing David.

Over the next two days, I struggled to contain my rage and blood lust. Jayden kept close to me. And I'd focus on him whenever my fury surged.

Of course my friends noticed my strange behavior and long silences.

"Stop moping, Kate," Haylee said the next morning—day six since I'd serked. "You've hardly said anything since Molly left. You'll see her on the outside."

"I've been sick—"

"Come on, it's me. Mother Jean might buy that lame excuse, but I know better."

"I miss her." I admitted.

She squeezed my shoulder. "We all do, but she made it. And you will too, if you stay away from Jayden."

"What do you mean?"

She gave me a "don't-be-stupid" look. Her light brown eyes matched her hair exactly. "No one buys his recent good boy routine. We all know he's plotting another escape attempt and I don't want you to be caught in the middle. You're going to be an eighteen soon. I know he's hot, but you can't serk now and ruin your chance to go home."

It was an impassioned speech. I opened my mouth to confide in her about the bitter truth when a realization hit me so hard I almost gasped aloud. So focused on myself, I hadn't considered my friends. Heck, the seventeens were my family. And they could all die within a year.

I gripped the edge of my seat to keep my expression neutral. Someone had to stop it. But how? They had hundreds of guards, fences, barbed wire, security cameras, and weapons.

Haylee didn't appear to notice my panic. She took my silence as agreement. "Besides, if Mother Jean or Father Bryan see you're spending too much time with him, you'll be transferred. And I don't want to lose you so soon after Molly."

The last thing Domestic Security wanted was for two people with a recessive berserker gene to become romantically involved. If any of the dorm parents suspected a couple, they disappeared—supposedly to different compounds far apart. Although, now I wondered if any of them made it out of here alive. My fingers punched through the vinyl cover of my seat.

Focus. Breath. Don't kill anyone.

Eight days after Molly's murder, I woke feeling as if a fever had broken. I could think clearly again. The rage had settled into a simmer under my heart. It waited for me instead of rushing through my body, demanding action at every little thing.

Since Haylee's comments, I'd been avoiding Jayden. However, today I sought him out. I managed to talk to him while waiting for our turn during a co-ed relay race.

"You made it," he said. "Not many who serk do."

Questions over his comment boiled up my throat, but I didn't have much time. "Does anyone leave these compounds alive?"

"Yes."

"Who?"

"The serkers. They're encouraged to give into the blood lust and then become DS soldiers for special army units."

"That's crazy. No one can control them."

Jayden gave me a tight smile. "They've learned a lot from these prisons. They don't want to waste mindless killing machines after all." The bitterness in his voice said more than his words.

"If that's the case, then we need to stop them."

Jayden laughed. "Good luck with that. I just want out of here."

"But you can't just stand by—"

He stepped close to me. His expression didn't change but he growled in a low voice. "Don't you dare presume what I can and can't do. Safe and secure here in your precious camp all these years, you've no idea what I've been through."

Stunned, I needed a moment to collect my thoughts. "But Haylee said you were trying to get everyone to revolt?"

"To provide me with a distraction. But you've all been brainwashed and are useless. No one will believe me about the truth of this place."

"What's the truth, Jayden?" I asked.

"This place is a serker factory. It's sole purpose is to produce serkers for the army."

Later, I couldn't recall what my response to Jayden had been. The next day passed in a blur as my mind replayed our conversation over and over. A few inconsistencies churned out. Like why was Jayden here? They would have tested him when they had found him and discovered he had serked. He could be working for DS.

I decided it would be best to avoid him altogether. Except he wouldn't get the hint and leave me alone.

"I helped you. Are you going to help me?" he asked after third period.

"No," I said.

"You're living on borrowed time. Sooner or later they'll find out about you," he said after fourth period. "You can come with me."

"I'm not leaving my friends," I said.

"Then you'll die." His confidence was unnerving.

"So will you." I shot back.

"All the more reason for us to leave."

"You act like it'll be so easy."

"I've a plan, but it needs both of us."

I waited.

"We'll need to get inside the administration building. It's the only way out."

"No." I walked away.

After seventh period, he intercepted me. "You can't do anything to help the others while you're in here, Kate. There are people on the outside who have been trying for years to overthrow Domestic Security and return us to our democratic roots."

"Years? Seriously?"

"Yes, why?"

"Will they succeed?" I asked.

His voice deepened. "Not without more serkers working for us." He glanced around. Most of the others headed toward the sports field. "You're the only one who's seen the truth of this place, Kate, and I need you."

His words *truth of this place* haunted me that night. The desire to help all the children living in the compound warred with my promise to Molly. In all the years I'd lived here, no one had tried to rescue us. If we didn't reunite with our families, then what were our families told when we were taken from them?

After a sleepless night, I decided that I needed more information. Unfortunately that meant spending time with Jayden, which would alert the guards or our dorm parents. I stared at the small red light shining from the ceiling of my room. When it was dark, they used heat sensors to make sure we remained in our rooms. But there had to be places in the compound not under surveillance beside our washrooms. And there was only one person I could ask. Doreen.

"So Miss Goody-Goody wants to know the sweet spots," Doreen said at breakfast the next morning.

Her mocking tone failed to provoke a reaction from me. If it had been a few days ago, I probably would have gone after her. And just knowing that I had the power to tear her to pieces gave me a boost of confidence. "What's it going to cost?"

"How do I know you won't run to Mother Jean and squeal?"

"Cut the act, Doreen. You know I won't tell."

She studied me as she chewed on her finger nail. "True, you're not a squealer, but then again you disappear as soon as there is a hint of trouble. This is new."

Doreen wanted an explanation for my interest. I glanced at Jayden sitting across the dining room.

She followed my gaze and snorted. "Wow, Kate. When you decide to break the rules you go all out. You know you'll eventually get caught. Right? Couples don't last long in here."

"I'm aware of the risks. How much?"

"Depends. Do you want a few trysting spots or all the locations?"

"All of them."

"It won't help him escape. He'll need more than that." That was the reason Doreen won the bets about people—she was scarily perceptive. She leaned forward. "What's really going on?"

Jayden's words, *you're the only one who's seen the truth of this place* echoed in my mind. The seventeens didn't trust him, but they trusted me. The bell rang and I made a quick and hopefully not fatal decision.

Surrounded by the clatter and scraps of chairs, I told Doreen about Molly.

She grabbed my arm. "You serious?"

"Yeah."

"Berserking nuts! I figured something wasn't right. If you start thinking about it, there are all kinds of clues. Like how we never get letters or anything from our families. But to murder us!"

"Easy, Doreen," I said, hoping to calm her. "Just breathe."

She drew in deep breaths as we walked together to our first class. Doreen didn't say another word until we reached the classroom. "Never thought serking would be the preferred choice."

"I'm going to stop it."

She laughed, but it had a shaky, almost hysterical edge. "How?"

"I'm working on it. How much for those locations?"

Doreen peered at me as if she'd never seen me before. "I'll have a map for you by the end of sixth period."

As promised, Doreen slipped me a paper with information and a diagram of the compound on it. The locations hidden from the cameras were marked in red. "Memorize it and flush it. You *don't* want to be caught with this."

"Thanks."

She paused. "Just don't leave without us. Okay?"

"That's the plan."

Half way through the eighth period races, I managed to get close to Jayden. He'd been ignoring me all day.

"If you want my help, then meet me during free time." I explained where.

His stance didn't change and his gaze remained fixed on the races. A nod was the only indication he'd heard me.

"Can you get there without alerting anyone?" I asked.

Annoyed, he looked at me. "Of course. Can you?"

"I think—"

"Don't over think it, Kate. Just act like you belong there. No nervous glances or any hesitation. Understand?"

"Yeah."

According to Doreen's information, no seventeens occupied the top floor of our dorm so the cameras have been turned off to save power. Producing energy had been the biggest hurdle after the Berserkers destroyed all the power plants.

The dorm's stairwells were watched, but during free time the activity inside them increased. Plus security concentrated on the common areas at that time. If Jayden and I could reach the third floor without alerting security, we should be safe. Key word, should.

I followed Jayden's advice and climbed the steps as if I did it every day. Sunlight filtered in through the windows located at the two ends of the hallway, but a murky semi-darkness filled the middle. At least no red lights shone from the ceiling.

No sign of Jayden. Worry and impatience mounted as I waited. Finally the door on the far end opened. He met me in the middle. After scanning the ceiling, he pointed to the dorm on the left. We entered the room, disturbing a layer of musty smelling dust. No red light greeted us, but Jayden led me into the washroom anyway.

He leaned on the sink and crossed his arm over his chest. "Does this mean you'll help me?"

"Sort of."

Jayden waited.

"I need some answers first," I said.

He motioned for me to continue.

"Why didn't they know you'd serked when they captured you?"

Pain flashed, but he closed his eyes for a moment, wiping away all expression. "Our unit had been betrayed and the force DS sent surprised and overpowered us. My mother ordered me to act normal so they wouldn't..." Every muscle in his body strained against the fabric of his jumpsuit. He swallowed. "... slaughter me with the others."

I pressed my hands tight together. "Everyone?"

"Except those carrying the berserker gene. They were sent to breeding compounds."

It took a moment for the words, *breeding compound* to sink in. "You mean—"

"Yep. Without the gene slicers, Domestic Security is forced to create more serkers the old fashioned way."

Horror threatened to overwhelm me. I focused on the one positive. "At least your mother wasn't killed."

Digging his fingers into his forearms, Jayden said, "She was past her childbearing years. My father lacked the gene and my two older brothers were killed trying to protect us. I'm the only one left. And I would have taken as many of those bastards out that I could have, except my mother made me promise to find a way to escape."

This wasn't going the way I had imagined at all. I scrambled to find a safer, or rather, kinder topic. "So the doctors didn't test you?"

"They scanned me for the gene, but since I wasn't serking

all over them, they figured I'd either serk in the compound or be cleared and go to the breeders."

Molly's shocked face filled my vision. "Then why did they kill Molly?"

"Is that what triggered you?"

I nodded.

He considered. "Either she was unable to have children, or they planned for you to witness the murder. Or both."

"But—"

"They need serkers more than breeders right now. Obviously you were a prime candidate for serking." He leaned forward. "What woke you from the blood lust?"

I explained about Molly's sculpture.

"That's amazing."

"Why? You made it through, too."

He huffed. "Because, after my brothers triggered me, they sat on me for five days." His rueful smile faded. "Are you going to help me?"

My mind swirled with everything he had told me. Could I even believe him? "One more question."

"Make it quick, free time is almost over."

"Why haven't any of your people tried to rescue us? Wouldn't they want to shut down these serker factories?"

"How do you know we haven't?" He shot back.

I waited.

He sighed. "They're too well defended. And large explosions tend to be indiscriminate. We didn't want to harm the kids."

A lame excuse. I might not know all about what's going on beyond the fence, but if I was rebelling against DS, neutralizing the serker armies would be my priority not freeing a bunch of kids. I let it go for now. "Okay, I'll help."

Jayden peered at me with suspicion. "Just like that?"

"I won't guarantee success. What's your plan?"

He quickly detailed his idea for us to get inside the administration building and fight our way out. "They don't have cameras in there and with two of us combined with the element of surprise, we'll be out of there before they can form ranks."

Voices kept me from telling him that his plan sucked. Jayden held a finger to his lips as he eased the washroom's door open a crack.

"...nowhere else."

"...his last confirmed location was in dorm seventeen, stairwell two."

"...check the right, we'll take left."

Oh no. The guards were searching for us.

Jayden pulled me away from the door. "They're looking for me. Stay here until it's quiet."

I grabbed his arm before he could leave. "What are you doing? You'll be caught and thrown into detention."

"Better me than you."

"But—"

"You need to maintain your..." A genuine smile sparked. "...innocence. Just don't do anything rash while I'm gone. Okay?"

I must have nodded because he headed out. After a couple seconds, the sounds of a scuffle and harsh shouts vibrated through me. Curling into a ball to keep from rushing to help him, I waited. In those awful minutes, I understood just a fraction of how it must have felt for Jayden to not fight while his family died around him. A deep respect for him nestled inside me.

While Jayden was in detention, I had entirely too much time to fret and to watch the compound and to *not* come up with a fantastic escape plan. Unfortunately, I had plenty of ones that sucked.

I also considered my other problem—the rest of the kids. Would the seventeens be willing to stage a revolt? Except some might serk from the stress alone. Then what would we do? Was there a way to determine who would serk and keep them out of the plans? Approximately fifty of my classmates had serked. I spent my free time writing down all the triggers I could remember. The list was impressive, basically anything at anytime could trigger someone. No help at all.

So back to Jayden. While there were places hidden from the cameras, there were still guards and teachers all around the compound. Jayden was right. In order to escape, we needed to get into the admin building, but security was always tight. My ability to get in unnoticed before seemed unlikely the more I studied the shift changes. Which made his comment about the guards wanting me to see Molly's murder sound less ridiculous each day.

And the thought that they'd killed her just to make me serk sent dangerous spikes of rage through me.

Focus. Breath. Don't kill anyone.

I needed to confirm if Molly could have children or not. That information would be in the doctor's office. Time to use my good girl charm, but first I needed to talk to Doreen.

"Breeders?" Doreen wrapped her muscular arms around her waist. "I think that's worse than dying."

"Maybe you'll serk instead," I said. It was sixth period and we were taking a break between games of dodge ball.

"Not funny." She studied me. "How's the plan coming?"

"Terrible."

"No surprise. This place is sealed tight."

"And I need more information. You up for a little deception?"

"Always. What do you want?"

I outlined my plan.

"You're going to have to be quick. There won't be a lot of time."

"I know."

"When?"

"Eighth period."

"Ah, the obstacle course. Good choice."

Nervous energy wasn't good for a serker. I fidgeted through seventh as my emotions rolled from calm to panicked and back again. Finally eighth period started. Keeping close to Doreen, I ran a few courses to burn off my anxiety.

Once my nerves settled, I started the ropes course. Half way through, I tripped and fell hard. I clutched my right ankle, yelling as if in pain and caused a scene until Mr. Telerico arrived.

"Twisted or broken?" he asked.

"Don't know," I panted.

"Can you put weight on it?"

I tried to stand, yowled, and flopped back on the ground.

Mr. Telerico spotted Doreen hovering nearby. "Doreen, help her to the infirmary."

"Yes, sir," she said. She hauled me to my good foot, wrapped my arm around her shoulders, and escorted me to the doctor's office.

As expected a couple guards trailed after us.

"Do you think they'll follow us inside?" Doreen whispered.

I let my "injured" foot touch the ground and shrieked, insuring they would. Pain was one of the serker triggers.

"Next time warn me about the noise, will ya?" Doreen grumbled.

We entered the infirmary. A nurse led us to an examination room. As she brought up my records on the computer, Doreen dumped me on the table and retreated to the hallway. One of the guards hovered in the doorway until the seventeen's doctor entered and shooed him back, shutting the door. No cameras were allowed in the exam rooms.

He smiled at me. "What happened?"

I recited my tale and he tsked over my ankle.

"It doesn't look—"

"...watching us all the time!" Doreen's aggravated tone grew louder. "She's injured not serking you idiot!" Ominous thumps sounded. "Stop it. Stop watching us!"

The doctor and nurse exchanged a worried glance. He pulled a syringe from his pocket and dashed for the door with the nurse on his heels.

As soon as they left, I slid off the table and raced to the computer. My fingers flew over the keyboard. Finally a good use of my serker skills. Pulling up Molly's chart, I scanned it, and then switched back to read through mine. I hopped onto the table just as the doctor returned.

"Is she all right?" I asked.

"Yes. Just a bit of heat exertion. She's resting. Now let's see about that ankle."

I played injured. The doctor concluded it was a bad sprain. He wrapped my ankle and gave me a couple pain pills. I limped to my dorm, hoping Doreen wouldn't get into too much trouble.

Only when I reached my washroom did I allow the information I found to sink in. Staring at my reflection, I focused on the blue in my eyes. Little flecks of gray dotted the irises. Funny how I hadn't noticed them before.

My chart claimed I was too even tempered to serk. Molly's reported she was in the peak of health. Mine said drastic measures would have to be used in order to trigger me. Molly's said she would become troublesome once she learned the truth.

In other words, they murdered her to trigger me. I closed my eyes as fury rushed. When I could think again, I had a plan. The only one with a slight chance of working. It all depended on if they would try to make me serk again. I hoped Jayden was right about the DS needing serkers more than breeders. He didn't know it yet, but he was about to risk his life on it.

Doreen returned after spending a couple days in detention for attacking a security guard.

"Almost lost it," she said, joining me between classes.

For the first time ever, Doreen looked scared.

"Yeah, I almost serked." But then she shook it off and smiled. "I can't be next. I've bets with five seventeens and four sixteens that Pete will be next. I can't ruin my winning streak."

Her comment about Pete stopped me. Jayden had said the same thing. "Why him?"

"Blond, attached earlobes, and he gets upset about cheaters."

"Attached earlobes? Seriously?"

"Yep. They're recessive, along with—"

"I know. Has anyone bet on me?" I asked.

She kept a straight face, but humor sparked in her hazel eyes. "No one."

"But I have—"

"You have the calmest temper in the entire compound. It's a losing bet."

Ha. I could prove her very wrong, except I'd be stunned and carted off to Berserker boot camp. Doreen's comments about Pete gave me a few things to think about. Did DS know people could "survive" serking?

Jayden was released from detention after ten days. The longest time for a detention. Ever. Healing bruises and cuts marked his face, he walked with stiff legs, heading straight for the dorm. Students stared after him with mouths open in amazement or nodding with respect.

I suppressed the desire to chase after him, planning to let a few days pass before I approached. But the next morning, he sat in the corner with elbows propped on the table and his head in his hands, appearing miserable. I hoped it was an act for the guards.

When the bell rang for first period, Jayden didn't move. As everyone filed out, I crouched next to him.

"Go away, Kate," he said without glancing at me.

"If you're late—"

"I won't go back to detention. They'll have to kill me first." Now he lifted his head and gazed at me in utter defeat. "I've thought about my plan. It sucks. There's no way out of this place. When they come for me this time, I'm not going to pretend to be weak."

"No, you're going to first period." I grabbed his wrist and jerked him to his feet. Towing him from the dining room, I headed toward the science building.

He stayed a step behind me not resisting, but not quite cooperating either.

I talked to him as we crossed the compound. "You can't give up, now. You made a promise to your mother, and I made a promise to my friend. If we break them, they'll haunt us forever, or so I've heard." I took his snort as a positive sign. "Besides, I have an idea on how to get us both into the administration building."

He jerked me to a halt. "How?"

"You might not like—"

"I'll do *anything* to get out of here."

But could I?

"Tell me."

I did.

He stared at me as the information sank in. When he drew breath to speak, I stopped him. "Think about it. You'll be in the most danger."

"When do we start?"

So much for thinking it through. As we continued to our class, I explained. "It has to be subtle. Little gestures at first, then more...reckless."

"Okay, I'll follow your lead."

I asked him if Domestic Security knew people could survive serking.

"Yes, but they don't want it to happen. Mindless soldiers don't argue or worry about things like morals and basic human decency."

Before we entered the building, Jayden paused. "Does this mean you've given up on rescuing everyone?"

"No."

He waited.

I sighed. "One problem at a time."

∼

And so Jayden and I started with sitting together at meals. Haylee didn't waste time warning me again.

"They'll send you away," she said.

"We'll be careful," I replied. A queasy feeling in the pit of my stomach roiled as I lied to her.

Doreen watched us with suspicion and challenged me during sixth period. "What are you doing? You're supposed to be working on a way out of here, not falling for the new guy."

And snap. The answer to my other problem popped into my head along with ten reasons why it wouldn't work. Plus Jayden wouldn't agree. Too bad.

I kept my expression neutral as I said in an even tone, "There's no way out. We're stuck here and might as well make the best of it."

"You're a lousy liar, Kate." She stormed off.

Jayden and I continued our...what to call it? Courtship sounded ancient. Our fake affair. Occasionally ducking into a hidden spot, we would emerge after a few minutes. My regulation knot would be askew and he'd have a goofy smile. Each time we took bigger and bigger risks.

One night during free time, Doreen surprised us soon after we slipped into the blind spot behind the math building.

Ready for a fight, she didn't hesitate in confronting us. "You're planning to escape without helping the rest of us. Aren't you?"

"Yes. It's impossible to save everyone, so we're saving ourselves."

Confused, Jayden glanced at me.

Doreen sucked in a breath.

"You're not worth saving, Doreen," I said. "You're just a big bully. All talk. No action. I mean, really. You were depending on *me* to be a savoir? I avoid trouble. You're as stupid as you are ugly."

Jayden hissed at me. "Are you insane—"

"You're dead!" Doreen wrapped her hands around my neck with amazing speed as she serked. Digging her fingers in to my throat, she snarled as the blood lust filled her eyes.

Pain and panic froze me for a moment. I needed air. Then my own serker instincts kicked in and, with Jayden's help, we pined Doreen to the wall.

He called her name over and over in that calm tone he'd used on me. She stopped fighting, but still hadn't come to her senses.

"I'll bet you can't control your emotions, Doreen," I said, matching his even tone. "I'll bet you'll let the blood lust rule you, Doreen. I'll bet you a month's worth of chores that you can't overpower your genetics like me, Doreen."

"You are insane," Jayden said.

With a visible effort Doreen focused on me. "You're going to lose, Kate."

"I hope so."

Jayden rounded on me. "You wanted her to serk! What if she didn't wake? You could have ruined everything."

"This is the only way I can help my friends and keep my promise."

"And I didn't merit being informed about this little diversion?" Anger spiked each word.

"I didn't know if it would work."

He bit off a furious reply as Doreen responded to the emotion, straining against our hold.

"Just keep it together," I soothed. "Ride it out like a muscle cramp. Eventually it will pass. You can do this."

When she stabilized, Jayden released her. "She's yours now, Kate. Good luck with your pet project. I'm done." He left.

I kept Doreen focused and centered over the next five days just like Jayden had done for me. He stayed away and everyone believed we had broken up. Funny, I felt as if we had. We hadn't done anything but talk during those pretend trysts, yet I missed them.

Once her serker rage settled, she didn't waste time targeting the next person. "I'm going to play cards with Pete and cheat. He'll serk."

She did, and I helped to wake him. But keeping close to him proved more difficult. During fourth period, Pete lost his temper playing basketball, drawing the guards close.

Doreen and I couldn't intervene without causing suspicion. If he gave in to the rage, I'd have to stay longer. But that was a problem since my eighteenth birthday was a week away. I couldn't leave Doreen alone. There had to be at least two serkers left behind or we had no chance of taking over the compound. Anxiety swirled.

Just when it appeared as if Pete wouldn't recover, Jayden stepped close to him and talked Pete through it. Relieved, I studied Jayden and wondered if he'd talk to me again.

"So that's your plan?" Jayden tilted his head toward Pete. Our group was running the obstacle course. "Trigger all the seven-teens so you have your own personal serker army." His voice held a hard edge.

"Yes, except it will be Doreen's. I've my cleared appointment with the doctor in five days." I noticed his alarm. "Don't worry, I plan to serk before then. Put on a show and take out a few of them before they stun me."

"Not a very good plan."

"No, but I screwed up the original one so..." I scuffed my shoe in the dirt, working up the nerve. "I'm sorry I didn't tell you about Doreen, but I knew you'd—"

"Refuse to help?"

"Yeah."

"You're right. I'd have refused, but how was I to know you could trigger her?"

"That's the other part. I didn't. I knew she had a couple close calls and I know her sensitive spots." I gave him a wry smile. "Being the good girl is hard work. In order to avoid getting into trouble, I kept on everyone's good side. Which means I know quite a bit about all my fellow seventeens. When I thought about all my classmates that serked—I mean really considered the causes, I eventually recognized a pattern."

"Why didn't you tell me all this?"

"It was just a theory."

"Well, it worked." He considered. "Let's hope your other plan goes as well."

"Are you sure? We only have a few days."

"Then let's not dawdle." He grabbed my hand for a second, squeezed, and let go. Jayden returned to his place in line with more energy than I'd seen from him.

It didn't take long to start the seventeens buzzing over our reconciliation.

Haylee blocked me in the stairway as we headed down to supper. "You are five days away from being cleared! Are you insane? What are you thinking?"

I leaned close and whispered, "Talk to Doreen. She'll explain everything to you."

"Are you ready?" Jayden asked me.

Yes. No. Yes. My stomach churned. Unable to trust my voice, I nodded. We sat close together in the dining room in plain view of all the seventeens.

Jayden stood and pitched his voice so it could be heard over the general din. "I don't care who sees us." He pulled me to my feet and kissed me, wrapping his arms around my back.

A collective gasp followed instant silence. No turning back now. Jayden deepen the kiss and I forgot to be worried as strange tingles flowed through me. It was a long kiss. Why not? No sense wasting what could be our last chance at...well, everything.

Rough hands yanked us apart. The four guards tsked and scolded as they marched us into the administration building. I kept a firm hold on my emotions. Would they try and make me serk again?

Yep. They led us down to the room decorated with plastic. The place where they had murdered Molly. Three guards pulled their stun guns, aiming toward me. But this time, when the remaining guard grabbed his revolver, Jayden moved to stop him.

My guys turned to the commotion, and then I moved. So lovely to use my full abilities without worry. I could have easily killed all three—their actions were so slow compared to mine. I dodged the stun gun prongs, knocked weapons from their hands, and rendered them senseless with strong kicks to their temples.

"Fun isn't it?" Jayden stood over the man who would have shattered his forehead with a bullet.

"Lots."

"Ready to get out of here?" He threw me a stun gun, keeping one.

"Oh, yes."

He grabbed my hand and we raced through the hallways. There really wasn't much more to the plan beyond getting inside. We encountered a few guards, knocked them out, and then kidnapped an office worker. Jayden forced him to lead us outside where we dashed into the woods.

I knew the ease of our escape was not the real battle. The real battle would entail convincing the rebels to return with us to help Doreen's serker army free the others.

But like I said before. One problem at a time.

For now, I let the pure joy of running full serker speed with Jayden take control.

CURSING THE WEATHER

When I was majoring in meteorology at Penn State University, some students thought I could actually control the weather and would blame me when it rained during home football games. My reply was always the same: "If I could control the weather, I wouldn't be here. I'd be watching the game in my mansion in Hawaii." Despite various technological advances, controlling the weather is still a fantasy. And it's not a stretch to link my background with the idea for this story, but the idea actually came from a documentary about the experts who produce firework shows. It featured a company from Japan. The first thing the workers did was fly a Teru Teru Bozu doll over their work site. The doll's purpose is to smile on the gods so they will grant them favorable weather. It seemed odd to me that these engineers and pyrotechnic professionals would still be superstitious in this modern day. That led me to contemplate superstitions and belief. Belief can be quite powerful. The challenge for this story was making my readers believe it's fantasy.

CURSING THE WEATHER

T he lash bit into Nysa's back. The force sent her sprawling onto the wooden floor of the empty inn as fire raced across her shoulders.

"Stop daydreaming," Gekiryo Lady ordered. "Back to work, you lazy urchin. If I catch you staring out that window again, you'll be cleaning out chamber pots."

Gekiryo Lady's threats were not idle. Nysa scrambled away from the stout woman, and bolted through the kitchen doors. Sweat and blood burned in the new cut on her back, but she didn't dare stop to bandage it. Instead she joined the servants, chopping beef for the stew and helped the cooks prepare for the mid-day crowd.

As she worked, her thoughts returned to what she had seen across the road. A Teru Teru Bozu doll had hung from the eaves of the roof of an abandoned cottage. The doll's body, made of long, white silk blew in the cold morning air. It looked as if a child had drawn the grin and uneven oval eyes of the doll's face. The construction was simple, resembling more a ball caught under a sheet than an actual doll. So why had her throat tightened when she spotted it dangling high in the air?

The doll's legend told that, when hung high, the Teru Teru Bozu smiled at the gods, attracting favorable weather. Now it symbolized the residence of a weather wizard.

In her experience, wizards equaled trouble. Nysa had overheard travelers discussing these new wizards, who controlled the weather. In the larger cities to the west, the weather wizards hung their dolls to let the citizens know they were open for business.

Here in Bunkiten, the small town was ideally located as a stop-over for pilgrims and merchants heading east. Most of the town's citizens were wealthy so a wizard could do very well.

But what would happen if someone infuriated this weather wizard? Floods? Droughts? Killing winds? More would be at stake than just one person's life.

The inn soon filled with the heady smell of spicy beef. The harsh sounds of many voices interrupted her thoughts. Nysa finished her kitchen chores and began collecting orders from customers.

With a food-laden tray balanced on her shoulder, she wove through the fog drifting from the paper lanterns. She avoided cushions and customers and headed toward a low table by the door.

Before she reached the table, she spotted the weather wizard. All strength drained from her body as sensation fled her limbs. The room spun. A horrendous crash cut through the conversation.

She came to her senses on the floor, lying in a puddle of saki. Fury bleached Gekiryo Lady's face, but she restrained herself in front of the customers.

"Clean up this mess." Gekiryo Lady's lips moved as she

spoke, but her teeth remained locked together. "Then clean yourself up." Gekiryo Lady turned to the tall man standing beside her and said, "Such a simpleton. I'm known for my kind heart, but I'm no push-over. She'll pay for the ruined food from her salary." She shot a fire-laced look at Nysa. "Get moving."

Nysa couldn't stop staring at the weather wizard next to Gekiryo Lady.

"Now," Gekiryo Lady said a little too loudly. Customers looked their way once more.

The word broke her paralysis. She scrambled to her knees to clean the mess. Gekiryo Lady seated the man at her best table, telling him all the while about Nysa's tragic circumstances and how she had taken the poor child in despite her deficiencies.

"Her mother was the finest Rakugoka in all the land," Gekiryo Lady said. "Her story telling was legendary until she got mixed up with a man. Then her stories turned sappy and love-sick. Bah. Who wants to hear that? I lost customers by the dozen."

Nysa suppressed the urge to slap Gekiryo Lady for her harsh words about her mother. Instead, she piled the wreckage of food and crockery onto her tray. She berated herself for the mishap. How foolish. Fainting at the sight of the wizard's red kimono. He wasn't after her. Didn't even know she existed until she had caught his attention with that scene.

When the mess was cleared, she retreated to the kitchen. The cook tsked at her appearance, and she hung her head. She was always doing something wrong. Had to be a dizzy spell from hunger, she consoled herself. She hadn't eaten in two days. And she knew that two days without food clouded the mind and caused lightheadedness. She recognized all the symptoms. She knew precisely how long she could function without food, how much she needed to get by for another day, which meals lasted longer in her stomach. After she bought the sustaining medicine for her mother each week, she shopped with great care.

When everything was done, she ran upstairs to her tiny room to change into a clean robe. She checked on her mother, smoothing Seibo's long black hair down around the pillow and pulling the sheets up to cover the gray skin and sharp angles of her bones. The devouring disease sucked a person's life sip by slow sip. Only the sustaining medicine that Gekiryo Lady brewed could hold death at bay. One missed dose meant the disease would advance another step.

When the dinner crowd filled the inn that evening, Nysa had no thoughts except to serve patrons and overhear gossip. The Yuki Inn was the most prosperous business in Bunkiten, and the ordered chaos of feeding customers, avoiding nasty hands, and dodging glances from Gekiryo Lady kept her busy. Talk of the weather wizard was at every table until the wizard himself arrived for dinner.

She tried to disappear into the kitchen, but Gekiryo Lady grabbed her arm and said, "Treat him like the Emperor. His presence will bring many coins to my fine establishment."

Approaching the wizard's table, she could feel Gekiryo Lady's eyes burning into her back. "Your order, Kenja?" She addressed him with the highest honorific she knew, but kept her gaze on his shoes. Scuffed black leather boots. Surprised, she glanced up. His young face held mild amusement.

"Why does everyone assume I'd be wearing dragon-skin boots?" he asked. His voice was soft and kind. When she failed to reply, he said, "I've never slain a dragon. In fact, I've never seen one." He leaned close and whispered. "I don't even think they exist."

She gaped at him. Wizards and dragons were like the Gekiryo Lady and her money. Inseparable. He was talking heresy. His eyes held a glint of mischief. Confused, she didn't know if he teased or confided.

"But Kenja, the dragon wizards make their living slaying dragons. The farmers swear by them." She stepped back, terrified by her own boldness.

"Yes, I know the stories," he replied with a smile. "The gallant, brave dragon wizard gallops off to the Fire and Smoke Mountains, is gone for days, but returns victorious. He's wearing dragon's teeth around his neck, and he has some scales. Maybe there's even a splash of dragon's blood across his cloak. But..." He glanced around the room. "No one witnesses the battle. No one sees the dragon. Dragons supposedly only attack late at night and are killed in the dark. How convenient."

Despite her wariness, she was drawn into the story. "But the burnt cows and half eaten sheep?"

"There are many ways to set fire to a cow, and wolves can be trained."

"The dragon skin, teeth, and scales?"

"Some lizards have the same patterned skin and long teeth. And the scales—"

"Could be chips from when the liquid fire crystallizes," she said, recalling the time when a miner had stayed at the inn and regaled everyone with his stories of fire and diamonds.

The weather wizard tapped a slender finger to his forehead. "Now I have you thinking."

She jumped, remembering where she was and to whom she was speaking. A glimpse over her shoulder at Gekiryo Lady sent darts of fear through her veins. "Y-your or-order, Kenja?"

He sighed. "Shabu-shabu stew and saki."

She hurried to fill his order and, after she served him, he stopped trying to engage her in conversation. Nysa returned to her chores in relief. But she kept an eye on him as visitors frequented his table, asking about the weather.

When she refilled his mug with saki, she overheard the wizard inviting a man to his cottage.

The next day the wizard came in for all his meals. Knowing she was uneasy around him, Gekiryo Lady probably took perverse delight in sending her to wait on him each time.

At breakfast he said, "Lady Akira agreed to marry Bunkiten's magistrate. Why would she do that?"

"Love potion," she replied. The gossips had been in a frenzy all morning.

"Really." He raised his black eyebrows.

Nysa studied his dubious expression in the weak light. Grey clouds sealed the sky, promising snow. His sharp features looked as if they had been carved out of stone. Despite an angry red scar healing on his long neck, he radiated the calmness and confidence of an older man.

"You don't think it has anything to do with the fact that her crops have failed three years in a row?" he asked.

She thought about Lady Akira's fierce independence and desire to gain land. Akira's farm hands had been complaining about missed wages and disappearing jobs. "Perhaps she realized that Takio is a very rich man."

He touched his forehead with a finger. She dashed away.

At lunch, he asked her, "Why would Lady Miya leave for her summer cottage when winter's coming?"

"She's been cursed by her ex-betrothed's mother for canceling the wedding—a disfigurement hex," she whispered.

"Then why did she take the midwife and falconer with her?"

She blinked at the wizard. "Perhaps there was another reason she canceled her engagement."

"And that would be?"

"She's with child and the falconer's the father." Nysa turned away before he could point to his head.

At dinner, he asked, "Why are you afraid of me?"

She paused. The weather wizard seemed so different from that *other* wizard. *That* wizard had worn dragon-skin boots and belt. He had glittered with dragon scales and jewelry made from dragon's teeth. His confidence and magical aurora had charmed everyone. They had all been under his spell, especially Nysa's mother.

She shook her head and asked for the weather wizard's order. No time for idle thoughts tonight, she needed to help clean up after dinner, and then she would be paid. If she hurried, she could still make it to the market before it closed.

Gekiryo Lady grumped and grumbled while she doled out the coins. "The high cost of running the best inn in the east is killing me." She shook her head in a mournful gesture. "I'll go broke, but my customers will sing my praises while I'm in the poor house."

Nysa ignored Gekiryo Lady's complaints. The woman could have two full cash boxes and still worry over every expense. When it was her turn to be paid, though, Gekiryo Lady smiled and Nysa froze in alarm.

"Let's see." Gekiryo Lady counted out six silvers. "One week's pay minus three spilled dinners." She dropped a coin back into the cash box. "Minus three broken mugs." Clink. "Minus three shattered plates." Clink. "Minus one week's rent." Clink. Gekiryo Lady handed her the remaining two coins.

"But that's not enough," Nysa said.

"That's your problem."

"Can't I pay for the mugs and plates over the next few weeks?" She pleaded.

Gekiryo Lady gave her a stony stare. "You'll have to choose, won't you?" She locked her cash box and cradled it to her chest. "I brewed a new batch of sustaining potion this morning. You know what the physician said, 'the fresher the better.'"

Nysa clutched her money and bolted through the door. Legs pumping, arms swinging, she tore through the streets at a dead run. She raced past the town limit and flew to the empty fields surrounding Bunkiten. Once there, she let a scream rip from her lungs with all her remaining breath.

She screamed until she'd spent her energy then collapsed onto the cold hard ground. Her breath made puffs of steam in the moonlight. Gazing into the dark sky, Nysa considered her options.

Buy food, I live and my mother dies. Buy medicine, Seibo lives, I die. And a week later, Seibo dies because no one is left to pay for the potion. Borrow money? From who? I've no one. Borrow money from Gekiryo Lady?

At first, she laughed aloud, but sobered when she remembered Gekiryo Lady's offer a few months ago to give her an advancement on her pay along with a contract binding her to Gekiryo Lady. In exchange for owning her, Gekiryo Lady would take care of her and Seibo. This meant she could not refuse certain customers who wanted more from her than a cup of saki.

Slavery and prostitution or death. Nice to have choices. Another alternative occurred to her. She could buy poison with her two silvers. A quick end for both her and Seibo. She shivered as the sweat on her skin froze. Winter's icy fingers caressed her cheeks. The long bleak winter would be harsh on her mother. Harsh enough to bring Fuujin, who would take Seibo's soul to the sky.

Hoping to flee the guilt, Nysa set a brisk pace back to town, but the weight of her decision clung to her back. The sustaining potion only held back the inevitable; her mother wouldn't last through the winter even with the medicine pumping through her body.

In town, she found an old man pushing his cart home. He had a loaf of bread and some cheese left. He took one silver for everything, glad to sell it so late.

She tore into the loaf with her teeth as she walked back to the inn. The bread tasted like ashes. Nysa could barely swallow.

Her steps faltered as she spotted white silk glowing in the moonlight. Another option occurred to her. The Teru Teru Bozu doll appeared to float above the dark cottage.

She pounded on the weather wizard's door, ignoring the lateness of the hour. Her body trembled. *Because I'm cold*, she chanted under her breath, hoping to convince herself.

The door opened an inch. "Who's there?" asked a voice from within.

"Nysa—one of the servers from the Yuki Inn," she stammered. "I need to talk to the wizard. It's important." She shivered on the step for five heartbeats before the door opened wider.

"Come."

The dark figure led her to a fireplace. Embers pulsed among the ashes. The figure bent, added wood to the fire and coaxed it into a blaze. In the firelight, she recognized the wizard. She was surprised he didn't have a servant or assistant.

His long black hair was unbound and wild from sleep. He pushed a strand from his eyes. "How can I help you?"

Her words poured out in a rush. "I would like to pay you to

lift a curse." She held out the silver coin. "If this isn't enough, I can pay you three more next week."

The wizard took her cold hand and pressed her fingers over the coin. "You're freezing, child. Come sit closer to the fire." He eased her into an armchair by the hearth. Kneeling beside her he asked, "A curse?"

His closeness unnerved her. For a moment she wished she hadn't come. She gathered her strength and said, "My mother refused to prostitute herself for a wizard." Nysa swallowed as the memory of the dragon wizard lumped in her throat. Her mother had given him her heart and soul, but had balked when Danniko wanted to sell her body to others. "He cursed her with a devouring spell, then demanded all our savings as payment to lift the hex. Except..." She stopped unwilling to tell this wizard how foolish she had been.

"He left with all your money." The wizard stared into the fire. He stroked the scar on his neck. "I've heard about this...this man. How is your mother now?"

"Near death. If it weren't for Gekiryo Lady's sustaining potion, Seibo would be dead."

His gaze snapped to her. "When did you start the potion?"

"Right after Danniko left." She remembered how fast Gekiryo Lady had been, brewing up the physician's recipe for Seibo.

"Your mother started taking the potion after being cursed?"

"Yes."

"Now think about this." The weather wizard touched her sleeve. "What would be best for your mother?"

She pulled her arm away from the man. There was nothing to think about. "Lift the curse."

"What if there was no curse? What then?"

She suppressed the urge to shake the wizard. *Stop playing games and help me,* she wanted to yell.

"Think," he urged, pointing to this forehead.

"If there's no curse then..." Nysa paused. Her mind re-examined the whole horrible incident. "It's the potion, but—"

"Right!" He clapped his hands together, looking pleased. "Quit giving your mother the potion."

She stared at him. Had she heard him right? "She'll die."

"No, she won't."

Suspicion leapt into her mind. Fooled by a wizard once, she wouldn't repeat her folly. "What do you know? You're a weather wizard."

"Elemental reader, more exactly, but I still know. Besides, *you* figured it out."

She stood. "You should have just taken my silver and waved your hands in the air," she said. "It would have been kinder and more profitable than trying to trick me with your nonsense."

Fleeing his house, she was a fool for believing he could help her mother. She returned to her room and fidgeted on the hard floor next to Seibo, trying to sleep. When the weak light of dawn brightened the window, she rose and ate a small meal of bread and cheese. Soaking some bread in water, she pushed soggy pea-sized lumps into her mother's mouth. She reached to massage Seibo's jaw and neck to aid her swallow when her mother gulped the food, parting her lips for more. After feeding her mother more bread than she had eaten in a long time, she descended the stairs and joined in the kitchen's swarm of activity.

"Looking well-fed this morning, Nysa," Gekiryo Lady's rough voice cut across the room. The buzz of conversation diminished as the kitchen staff strained to overhear.

"Seems the ungrateful urchin chose to feed herself and let her mother die."

The other servants shot Nysa reproachful and disgusted glances during the course of the day. She did her best to ignore them. At dinner that night, she served a table full of merchants in high spirits. While they ate shabu-shabu stew they discussed the details of preparing their caravan for the morning.

"We'll be the only ones in Chainbara," one man said, raising his mug in a toast. "To high prices and high demand. This'll be our best haul yet." The merchants clanked cups.

"You'll be the only ones frozen to death in the mountain pass when the snows come," a man from another table called. But the merchants just smiled.

At the end of their meal, the merchants gave Nysa a silver coin for a tip. "Aren't you worried?" she asked them, amazed by the generous gift.

"Paid the weather wizard three golds to hold the snows off for one week," one man said. He slurred his words and reeked of saki.

His companions shushed him, pulling him with them as they left the inn.

Later, as the servants and Nysa scrubbed the kitchen, Gekiryo Lady made an elaborate entrance, holding a vial of potion high in the air. "Seems the selfish runt has no sense of decency. But I can't let a poor woman die, even if she isn't *my* mother," Gekiryo Lady said. Then she thrust the glass bottle into Nysa's hands. "Here urchin. I'll take the cost out of your pay over the next three weeks."

Gekiryo Lady left the kitchen, leaving her to suffer the hostility of her fellow servants.

That night, she sat on the edge of her mother's bed. In the faint candlelight, she was unable to see any color in Seibo's pale face. She held the potion in her hands. What a strange day. First a tip, then a kindness from Gekiryo Lady. Peculiar thoughts swirled in her mind as she fed her mother some bread.

Had the wizard been right about the potion? He hadn't come to the inn all day. Was he ashamed that she'd caught him trying to trick her?

"Mother, what should I do?" she whispered. An ache chewed at her heart. She missed her mother's sweet voice, sudden embraces, and joyful spirit. Before the curse, people had traveled to Bunkiten from all over just to hear Seibo's stories.

What sort of life does she have now? None. She decided to let her mother go; it had been selfish to keep her barely alive, preventing her from telling stories in the sky.

Nysa kissed her mother's cheek, and lay with her on the bed. With her mother's frail body wrapped in her arms, she slept at last.

The next morning, determined to stick with her decision, she poured the medicine out the window. Before leaving for her duties, she reached to fix her mother's hair. Nysa's hand froze in mid-air as her mother opened her green eyes. Her breath locked.

Seibo gazed at Nysa and smiled, then closed her eyes once again. Her chest barely rose. Nysa knew her mother wouldn't last the day.

"Good bye," she whispered. "Save me a story for when I join you in the sky." Her vision blurred with tears. She wiped them away with a corner of her sleeve.

The weather wizard didn't show again that day, and there were empty tables during meal times.

Gekiryo Lady fretted and scowled at everyone. "This place should be full," she mumbled to herself.

She had reason to worry. With the winter approaching, most of the merchant caravans stayed in Bunkiten until the spring.

Gekiryo Lady grabbed Nysa by the shoulder. Her sharp fingernails bit deep into Nysa's skin as she asked, "What were you saying to the wizard? Did you anger him? Has he cursed us?"

Nysa shook her head. "I just served him."

Gekiryo Lady slammed Nysa against a wall. "If I find out you're lying, I'll feed you to the vultures."

Nysa hurried from sight. What if she had caused the wizard to cast a spell on the Yuki Inn? She shrugged. It wouldn't matter once her mother passed to the blue world. Nysa would then be free to find other employment. Maybe even become a Rakugoka like her mother? *No. Ridiculous. Who would want to listen to me?*

Dread pulled at her legs when Nysa returned to her room that evening. She fumbled in the darkness to find and light the lantern. The weak yellow glow cast a mournful shadow over Seibo. By the way her mother's sunken skin clung to her skeletal face, Nysa knew only a few breaths remained before the sky would claim Seibo.

A sudden desire to find Gekiryo Lady and beg for more potion boiled in her heart. Who was she to decide if her mother should live or die? They had both made so many mistakes. What if this was yet another?

She strode to the door, reached for the handle, and stopped. Returning to her mother's side, Nysa held her hand and waited for death to release them both.

"Nysa?" her mother's voice rasped.

She jolted awake. She blinked in the quiet darkness. A dream? A ghost?

"Nysa, are you there? I can't see," her mother said.

"Mother?" She hurried to re-light the lantern and, once lit, Nysa threw herself at her, hugging her tight.

"Did Danniko lift the curse?" Seibo asked, hope shining in her face.

"No. Danniko left months ago." When her mother's face blanched with fear, Nysa added, "The curse is gone."

"How?"

"I'm not sure." Nysa had thought the wizard had done nothing, but perhaps he had felt some remorse and lifted the spell after all?

As if sensing her confusion, Seibo didn't push for answers. "I'm hungry," she said simply.

Nysa fed her bread and cheese. When she finished, Nysa could see the effort of talking and eating had worn her out. Nysa tucked her mother back into bed. She sat holding Seibo's hand, marveling at its warmth. When her mother fell asleep, Nysa left the inn, seeking information.

The Teru Teru Bozu doll blew sideways in the strong damp wind. Nysa knocked on the wizard's door.

"How did you know?" she demanded as soon as the door opened. A hand reached out and pulled Nysa inside. The door slammed behind her.

"Don't want to lose all my warmth," the wizard said. He led her to the fire. Instead of an armchair near the hearth, the wizard had pulled a table close. On it was a large map of the country. Strange symbols had been written on the map near the cities and towns.

"Is your mother doing better?" he asked.

"Yes. Did you lift the curse? Have you hexed the inn? What—"

He hushed her. "One question at a time."

She drew a deep breath. "The curse?"

"You know there was no curse." The wizard raised a hand

to stop Nysa from speaking. "Gekiryo Lady's potion was poisoning your mother."

"Why?"

"She was probably well-paid by Danniko."

Nysa found this difficult to believe. "Why would he spend his money when he could just use his magic?"

"Because there is no magic. Only superstitions, rumors, and fear."

"You must think I'm a simpleton." Nysa rose to leave. "You call yourself a weather wizard and then try and tell me there's no magic." A thought struck her. "What about the merchant caravan? Why did you take their money, if you're not holding back the snows?"

"They paid for a service. I determined the first snow storm won't arrive until next week. Plenty of time for them to reach Chainbara."

"How?" Nysa asked, confident that she had finally caught him in a lie.

"Messengers, maps, mercury, horse hair, and my Teru Teru Bozu doll." He smiled at her confusion. "*You* call me a weather wizard. But *I* call myself an elemental reader. My real name is Jiro. You're not a simpleton." He put a finger to his forehead. "Think about it. And when you're ready, come back and I'll teach you more."

"What about my mother?"

"Bring her with you. I have extra room."

Suspicion crawled along Nysa's spine. The wizard had probably heard of her mother's beauty. "I don't—"

"You're no longer afraid of me. Now you need to trust me."

He was right about the fear, but to trust him was entirely different.

Over the next few days, Nysa's mother grew stronger and Gekiryo Lady grew meaner.

"Must have been that fresh potion," Nysa explained. Although, she worried when her mother began to come down to the common room. The few customers would sit near her mother to listen to her stories, and business increased slightly, but not enough to appease Gekiryo Lady.

With time to think, Nysa's mind filled with the weather wizard's claims. He had never answered her question about hexing the inn. Finally, she asked one of the loyal customers what was going on.

"Rumors," he said. "Ugly ones saying Gekiryo Lady uses horse meat in her shabu-shabu stew, and horse piss in her saki. That she makes poison."

"Then why are you here?" Nysa asked him.

He slurped his stew, chewing thoughtfully. "People believe in rumors because it's easier than figuring it out for themselves. I don't abide by hearsay. Especially not when my mouth and stomach tell me otherwise." He took a gulp of saki.

Making her own decisions based on facts was what it came down to, Nysa realized. Had she ever seen a wizard perform real magic? Had she ever seen a real dragon? She had decided to let her mother go. Good choice. Not all her choices would turn out so well, but they would be hers.

After the dinner crowd left and with her mother shivering under a heavy cloak, Nysa knocked on the wizard's—Jiro's door. Their tiny bag of possessions was slung over Nysa's shoulder. Fat flakes of snow drifted down, covering the street with a thin layer. The snows had waited a week just like Jiro had predicted.

Jiro's smile widened when he saw them. He stepped aside and helped Nysa guide her mother inside.

After a few days, Jiro began to teach Nysa about the network of elemental readers and how they sent weather information to one another by messenger. Taught her how to map and track the storms, how to read the mercury and the curling horse hair. And how to interpret the wind dances of the Teru Teru Bozu doll.

During Nysa's lessons, Seibo told stories at the inn.

"How could you go there after what Gekiryo Lady did to you?" Nysa asked.

Her mother smiled. "I'd rather know where the vipers are than be surprised. And she's paying me more."

"Why?"

"I threatened to weave a few stories about her behavior."

A mischievous glint flashed in Seibo's eyes as she hugged Nysa tight. Nysa was thrilled to have her mother back.

Nysa stood at the window of Jiro's cottage and watched her mother walk to the inn for her evening performance. A few customers trickled in for dinner.

Jiro joined her. "They say some wizard hexed her establishment." He tsked.

Nysa thought this was another lesson. "There's no magic," she said, "rumors were to blame." She contemplated the fate of the Yuki Inn. "Could you reverse the damage?" she asked.

He pointed to his temple. "Think."

If rumors caused the damage, then they should undo the damage. "A few well timed comments to the right people would bring her customers back," she said.

"Gekiryo Lady's a ruthless, horrible person who doesn't deserve good fortune. Tell me why you would want to help her?" he asked.

"I want to help my mother. She's worthy of a large audience for her stories." Nysa thought about her time working at the inn. "But I would like Gekiryo Lady to suffer for what she did to me and my mother."

A feather of fear brushed her skin when Nysa thought of confronting Gekiryo Lady. Over the last six months, the woman had made Nysa pay her five golds to poison her own mother. *What would make Gekiryo Lady suffer?*

As if reading her mind, Jiro wizard said, "Go to the inn." He shooed her out.

Nysa stood in the street, debating. Dread welled up her throat. She turned to go back, but spotted Jiro in the window, watching. *Maybe I'll go have a bowl of shabu-shabu stew and listen to my mother.*

A warm blast of hurtful memories hit Nysa in the face as she opened the inn's doors. The pungent smell of saki and wet wood transported her back to a place she'd thought never to be again.

She had barely taken a single step inside before she was noticed.

"What do you want?" Gekiryo Lady demanded.

Nysa mentally flinched from the women, but then she met her mother's gaze from across the room. Seibo gave Nysa a nod of encouragement.

Now or never. She was no longer this woman's servant. She was apprenticed to an elemental reader. Nysa repeated the word apprentice to herself, and looked Gekiryo Lady right in her hard little eyes. Magic might not exist, but the threat of it was still a powerful weapon.

"Your inn has been cursed," she said.

Gekiryo Lady took a threatening step toward her. "Witch. I knew you had some—"

"I didn't curse you," Nysa interrupted, "but I can have the hex lifted."

"What can you do? You're just an urchin. Penniless and powerless."

"I'm an apprentice to a very powerful wizard. But if you don't want my help..." She glanced casually around the room. "I'm sure once my mother fully recovers from her *illness*, she won't have any trouble finding another job. After you go bankrupt, that is." Nysa moved to leave.

"Wait." The word tore from Gekiryo Lady's mouth, sounding as if she had swallowed a piece of jagged glass. "Lift the curse," she ordered.

"It'll cost you." Nysa fought to keep her voice steady.

Red splotches appeared along Gekiryo Lady's forehead and the tops of her ears. A warning signal that in the past would have sent Nysa scurrying for cover. She stood her ground.

"How much?" Her lips moved, but her teeth remained clamped.

"Ten golds."

Gekiryo Lady clamped her hands together. Her arms shook. "Five."

"Nine."

Sweat beaded on Gekiryo Lady's forehead, she bit her lip. "Six."

"Eight or I leave."

Gekiryo Lady winced. Nysa enjoyed every moment of Gekiryo Lady's discomfort.

"Fine." She stormed off to her cash box.

Nysa followed.

Gekiryo Lady thrust the gold into Nysa's hands. "If the inn's not packed by tomorrow, I'll find you, and no wizard will be able to save you."

Nysa looked at the woman hunched over her cash box. "You don't scare me," she said. "I think you're pathetic. All you care about is your money. But money can't love you. And money won't welcome you into the sky."

She turned her back on the woman, found a good table, ordered a bowl of shabu-shabu stew, and listened to her mother. The stew was fantastic.

Returning to the cottage, Nysa tried to give Jiro the gold coins. "For teaching me."

He refused to take them. "You're going to need them when you set up your own business."

"Business?"

"To continue to spread the weather network. When you're ready, you'll make your own Teru Teru Bozu doll and go east. Find a place, set up shop, and find an apprentice."

"An apprentice?"

His gaze softened. He fingered the scar on his neck. "Yes. Someone who's in need. Someone to train and send on their way."

BRAND SPANKING NEW

If it's not obvious from reading Godzilla Warfare, Lieutenant Leo *is one of my favorite characters. He was just supposed to be the bullet pilot, a flat two-dimensional character. However, he became a fun, quirky, and endearing character. So when I was invited to submit another military SF short story to* Best Laid Plans, *I knew Leo would be involved. The challenge for the anthology was to write about a mission that goes sideways despite the best laid plans. I thought it would be fun to write about a rookie on a "routine" mission for Mother Earth.*

BRAND SPANKING NEW

"Get dressed," the medic said.

Eunice pushed up on her right elbow. She covered her breasts with her left arm. The medic huffed in amusement either from her delayed modesty—she had to strip prior to lying on the procedure table or from her question. Or possibly from both.

"Where is it?" she asked him.

"That's classified, Private Daniels." His brisk manner softened for a moment. "It's for your protection."

"Do you know where I'm going?" she asked.

"No. Your pilot will know. Report to deck twelve, barrel two. Relax, Daniels, this is a routine delivery."

She sat up and swung her legs off the side of the cold table. He could be casual and relaxed. He didn't have a DSU inserted somewhere underneath his skin. As Eunice dressed in her uniform, she scanned her arms and legs, searching for a cut or mark or anything to indicate the skin had been cut, but she found nothing. She ran her fingers through her short brown hair, feeling for a lump on her scalp. Again nothing.

A strange creepy crawly sensation skittered over her. She stifled the desire to shake like a wet dog. The crushing disappointment she'd felt when she learned her first assignment for Mother Earth would be as a courier, had turned into trepidation. Transporting information had seemed so innocuous and dull. Yet...

Eunice hurried through the corridors of the military base on Mercury Three. As she navigated the mind-numbingly drab base, she mentally cursed her recruiter. *See the universe,* he'd promised, but so far all she'd seen were the interiors of two military bases, which had identical layouts. Granted, the only way to get off planet was to join the military or pay billions. Mother had stopped building colonies over a hundred years ago.

While she'd been growing up and dreaming of traveling, the United Federation of Planets (UFoP) had gained more and more member planets, stealing them from Mother Earth. Sure they'd agreed to pay back Mother's huge investment in setting up the colonies. But what would happen when they decided to stop payments? By that time, Mother's empire would have shrunk to a handful of planets and she'd have no resources left to enforce the treaties.

Perhaps that was why Mother had switched tactics. Instead of fighting the colonies that wished to become independent, she was working with them. But UFoP had sliced into the Kasner-space communications collective (although they claimed innocence) so Mother had to send messages the old fashioned way. Hence the couriers.

At least, I'll finally be able to visit other planets. Excitement built and Eunice reported to deck twelve, barrel two to meet her pilot. First impression—his gray skin exactly matched the color of his unruly hair. *He's ancient for a lieutenant.*

Remembering her basic training, she snapped to attention. "Private Daniels, reporting for—"

"Relax, Private. I don't do the whole salute and shout routine. Name's Leo." He eyed her. "Where's your stuff?"

She patted her pockets. "It's only an overnight trip."

"Ah a woman who knows how to pack." He thumped his chest. "Love at first sight."

She stared at him. *Was this guy for real?*

"Hop into the bullet, I'm just finishing pre-flight." He returned to the collective's screen built into the side wall.

Eunice scanned the area. A long thin tunnel disappeared to the left and a round black metal container rested on the tunnel's track. One end was cone shaped, while the other looked like it had been chopped off. Probably a probe. "Uh...Leo, where's the bullet?"

He spun, mouth agape. "You're the courier, right?"

"Yes."

"You've never flown in a bullet?" The question was more a groan.

"I've never couriered before. I'm just out of training."

"Holy shit with a crown and scepter. You're a spanking newbie!" He gestured at her fatigues. "I should have noticed your shiny newness and fresh from the factory smell. Shit." Leo tromped over to the probe, muttering under his breath.

The top of it just reached his shoulder. "This is the bullet. Fastest conveyance known to man." He smacked the side. It clanked. Then he opened the hatch and swept his hand out, pointing. "Navigational and life support equipment in the nose, pilot's seat, passenger's seat, cargo area, and the Kasner-Phillips engine behind that panel."

"Oh." A feather of fear twirled in her chest. Eunice had learned about the KP engine in basic training. But they were mostly used for emergencies because of the dangers. Her sergeant had said this was a routine delivery.

"What do you think?" Leo asked.

"It's...ugly."

He laughed, flashing big yellow teeth. "That it is. No frills for sure. But it'll get us to Venus Five in no time."

So that was where they were going. Eunice hoped she'd have some time to look around before they returned. All she had to do was show up, let them remove the DSU and head back to Mercury Three for her next assignment. Routine.

Eunice strapped into the passenger's seat. Leo handed her a stack of self-sealing bags.

"What are these for?" she asked.

"Just in case you get Kasner-speed sick. Make sure you press the bag to your face and seal it tight when done. Floating vomit is the nastiest of the nasty. If it happens, you can find another way home."

She searched his expression. *Was he kidding?* His bright gaze was a little too bright. A crazy gleam swirled. How many trips had he made at Kasner-speed? Too many too close together would scramble his brain and turn his insides to goo. *My first mission may be my last. Wonderful.*

Leo settled into his seat, sealed the hatch tight, and fired the engine. Eunice's pulse jumped in her throat.

She leaned forward. "How long have you been flying bullets?"

"Dozens of years. I started with cargo ships and flew anything with an engine, but after my first trip in a bullet, there was no turning back."

Great. She'd heard some pilots became addicted. Just her luck to be assigned one of them.

"Don't worry, my shiny new recruit. I've turned down promotions so I could fly. I'm the best of the best."

The tightness in her stomach eased. Feeling better she relaxed, and asked him how many couriers missions he'd flown.

"This is my first."

Before she could react, Leo said, "Barrel two ready to launch." He glanced back at her. "I'd warn you what to expect, but you won't believe me."

"That bad?"

"Worse." He faced forward. "Fire!"

An invisible wall slammed into her, driving her into the seat. Squashed flat, she struggled to breath, to think, to exist in three dimensions.

"Engaging Kasner-speed!" Leo shouted.

Her insides exploded. Bones shattered and ripped through her skin. All in silence and without pain. Then the pieces of her physical body fogged around her, fragments of bone, drops of blood, shredded bits of muscles, clumps of brain matter. And in the center a thread of consciousness remained. Just enough for Eunice to understand the horror and freak out.

A sense of the physical returned with a pushing, sticking, pressing, and tingling feeling. Once she was whole, she didn't even had time to marvel over the solidity of her body before her stomach rebelled. Grabbing for a vomit bag, she heaved, fearing the action would cause her to shatter again. But she remained solid.

"You'll get used to it." Leo assured her.

Oh no she won't. As soon as they landed on Venus Five, she'd find another way back, another career if she had to. *Just notch one successful mission and go home.*

"We have bigger problems," he said.

Before her trip through Kasner-space, she would've been worried about his comment. Now—not so much. "And?"

"We were followed by a Phillips-class cruiser, X-military."

"How do you know?"

"For us experienced travelers, we know that the cloud of body parts around our consciousness is really the universe. When you're at Kasner-speed you are everywhere and nowhere at once."

"And in all that...stuff, you saw an XP?" She didn't hide her disbelief.

"Yes I did, and I changed direction, Ms. Raw Recruit so they don't learn our destination. Do you know how many bullet pilots can change course like that?"

"A dozen?"

"One."

Impressive. "Is UFoP chasing us?"

"Not sure who." Leo seemed distracted.

"Where are we now?"

"I've no idea."

She closed her eyes. Lost in space was such a...cliché.

"Not to worry. I've pinged the universe and should have a response... Holy shit with a harp and wings."

"Now what?"

"They're still on our tail."

"How is that possible?"

"Must of installed a KP engine. But with that sized ship, it'd have to be...humongous!"

Eunice considered and she didn't like the direction of her thoughts. "And they'd have to put a tracer on us." Once a ship reached Kasner-speed there were an infinite number of vectors of travel.

"Right. Just what are you transporting anyway?"

"Data."

"Ah Data Pirates. They've been selling stolen info to UFoP so it appears as if UFoP is playing by the rules. What kind of data?"

"I've no idea. This was supposed to be a routine delivery. My sergeant said so, and the medic said so."

"And you believed them?"

"Of course."

He groaned. "Spanking newbie. Never ever trust a superior officer when they say, 'it's routine.' The military is all about routine. There's no need to *say* it's routine. That would be redundant."

"Oh."

"You've a lot to learn. If..."

"If what?"

"Never mind. I've just received a demand from the pirates to hold my position so those bastards can pull us in. Not bloody likely. I've got enough juice for one more K-stretch. Where shall we go?" he mused to himself.

"Why don't we just go to Venus Five? What's the big deal if they know our destination? Once there, won't our forces protect us?"

"Where's the fun in that?"

Eunice clamped down on her reply. His comment just confirmed it. Leo's brain had Kasner-rot.

"Think about it, Recruit. They put a tracer in my bullet."

She connected the dots. "They have someone working on the inside."

"Right. Do you know who?"

"No. Do you?"

"No. So wouldn't it be in all our best interests to find out who they are and who their pals are?"

"Yes. But, Leo there're only two of us and an XP has—"

"Fourteen crew members and enough space to carry a company of soldiers," Leo said. "What's your point?"

She thought it was obvious. "We're outnumbered. It might be...difficult to learn anything about who is chasing us."

"Nonsense. Oooohhh...I know where we are. Perfect. There's a moon not far... Try to pay attention this time, Private."

"To what?"

"Engaging K-speed."

Ugh. She blew apart. This time as the bits of her body expanded, she wondered if this was what it would be like if she had been ejected into outer space without a protective suit. An odd thought. She doubted her consciousness would survive for long in real space.

After she coalesced, she dry heaved into another vomit bag. If she survived this mission, she was transferring to a desk job.

The bullet jumped. The straps bit into her shoulders, keeping her in place.

"Holy shit with wine and a chalice! These guys are serious."

Eunice was afraid to ask. She couldn't believe she fell for the load of crap the recruiter fed her.

"We're hit, but don't worry," Leo said.

Yep. K-rot. No doubt. At this point being captured by the enemy didn't sound so bad.

"The moon I'm heading for is basically a giant rock, but it has an atmosphere that can support us. I'm gonna aim for the sunny side, but the landing's gonna be rough." Leo turned in his seat and met her gaze.

The crazy goofiness was gone. And that scared her more than anything else.

"Just don't let them peel you, Private. Trust me to do the rest." Leo returned to the controls.

Peel me? She tried to wrap her head around that and failed.

Then they hit the atmosphere.

Hard.

Then the ground.

Harder.

Pain sliced through her temple, waking her. Blurry dark gray shapes formed mountains around her. Sharp rocks jabbed through her torn uniform. Her entire body ached. Eunice pushed into a sitting position. The fuzzy landscape faded behind black and white dots. She drew in deep breaths to keep from passing out. The air smelled of rust and tasted gritty. After a couple minutes her surroundings sharpened.

It wasn't pretty. All jagged rocks, rubble, and one crumpled bullet. She must have been ejected during the crash. By the amount of damage, she knew she was lucky to be alive. Staggering to her feet, Eunice limped over to the ship. Relief that Leo's body hadn't been crunched into pulp was replace with worry. A fair bit of blood stained what remained of the control panel.

She scanned the area. Where was he? Perhaps he searched for help or water or...something. Her brain refused to cooperate with this guessing game. It wanted to scream, "He left us!"

Determined to stay optimistic, she walked a loop, seeking footprints or perhaps a note for her scratched into the hard dirt. Nothing.

"We're going to die!" her brain yelled.

She ignored it until the distinct whine of a transport's engine cut through the air. A black speck in the gray sky grew as it dropped toward her.

"Told you." Her brain was smug.

After another sweep of the area, Eunice knew she had some time. There was no place nearby for the transport to land. They'd have to send a patrol out to fetch her. She could run and hide unless they had heat sensors. And if they didn't, then what? They'd leave and she'd die of thirst. Maybe Leo signaled for help before they crashed. Maybe he was hiding and wondering why the brand spanking newbie was standing like an idiot out in plain sight.

The engines roared above her. Shit. Her orders hadn't included this contingency. *And why not, Private Daniels?* Because everyone was too damn busy telling her this was routine.

Leo's last bit of advice came unbidden. *Just don't let them peel you. Trust me to do the rest.*

Nothing about avoiding capture or keeping quiet. The hard part...no the impossible part was trusting him. Eunice had trusted the recruiter; a mistake; had trusted her sergeant, bigger mistake; and had trusted the medic, huge mistake. Why trust Lieutenant Leo? She glanced at the bullet. So far, Leo hadn't lied to her. Plus she was determined to finish the mission.

All right Leo, I'll trust you. She sat on the ground and rested her back against the still-warm metal of the bullet. Crossing her arms over her knees, she leaned her aching forehead on her forearms.

The crunch-scrape of boots over the rocky soil warned of their approach. Eunice listened and counted about a half dozen of them. When they spotted her, they fanned out, pointing their Watson-921s at her. It had enough fire power to blow a hole in her chest. A laugh caught in her throat. Did she look dangerous? She hadn't even been issued the standard JS-97. Another red flag she'd missed.

The four men and two women wore civilian clothes, but even Eunice with her limited experience knew they were ex-military. They checked the cockpit of the bullet.

"Where's the pilot?" one man with buzzed black hair asked. He holstered his weapon, and pulled a metal cylinder that was as long as his hand from his belt.

Irrationally more afraid of the new weapon, she stood. "I don't know," she said.

He searched her for weapons, then pressed the cylinder to her neck, shooting an icy liquid into her. She stumbled back as cold spread throughout her body.

"Where's the pilot?" he asked again.

"I don't know."

He exchanged a glance with the woman standing on his left. "Why don't you know?"

"I woke and he was gone, gone, gone. Left me all alone. Poor poor me, the brand spanking newbie." The words bubbled from her mouth. She couldn't stop them.

"What a coward," he said. Then he studied her. His blue eyes creased in concern. "Christ these recruits are getting younger and younger."

The ground under her feet swayed. Eunice clutched the man's arm to keep from doing a face plant. "I'm twenty, and you're really, really cute." Mortified, she clamped her mouth shut, but he ignored her.

"We don't need the pilot," the woman said. She gestured to another man. "Sid, attach the hook to the wreck, we'll snag the bullet on our way out. The KP engine will fetch a nice profit."

Eunice's man put his hand on hers. "Where's the DSU?"

"I don't know," she sang, feeling giddy. "It's for my protection. A safety harness for my brain." She giggled.

"They didn't do you any favors, sweetheart. The DSU is manufactured from skin cells so I can't find it with my medical scanner. I'll have to search underneath all your skin."

And finally the true significance of Leo's words hit her. Terror sliced right through the drug's effects, sobering her in an instant. *Just don't let them peel you.* Surrounded by six armed guards, how the hell was she going to stop them?

∾

No plans formed as they escorted her to the transport ship. The medic kept a firm, almost protective grip on her. Nothing popped up when he secured her into a seat, or when they lifted off, and swept down to snag the bullet. Not a single idea crossed her mind as they flew into the XP's cargo bay. Panic burned in her guts.

"Do you even know what you're carrying?" the medic asked her as he escorted her through the hallways. Two armed guards followed them.

"Just data. Routine data."

He barked a laugh. "Oh my, they screwed you big time, sweetheart. You're carrying the schematics for Mother's newest, deadliest weapon. One that can blast through a planet's shield. It's a game changer."

She stopped. "Are you sure? I'm just a new recruit."

He smiled, but there was genuine regret in his gaze. "Yes. They sent out an experienced and well known courier on a heavily armed Phillips-cruiser with a full escort a few days ago —an obvious decoy."

"Oh." Eunice froze in place as the information sunk in.

The ship rocked to the left then to the right. She stumbled, and grabbed his arm. "What was that?"

"We're leaving orbit. There's nothing to worry about."

He could be calm. But from the depths of her fear, a plan formed. "What's your name?"

He hesitated. "Devon Marshall."

"I'm Eunice. Are you guys looking for recruits? I don't have much experience, but I'm willing to learn."

Devon laughed a full throaty chuckle as they continued. "Thinking about betraying Mother Earth?"

"She started it."

He agreed, then sobered and wouldn't meet her gaze.

Oh no. "I'm not going to live through the procedure. Right?"

"If we had more time..." He took a deep breath. "No."

When they entered the infirmary, panic boiled in her stomach. The guards assumed positions outside the doors and Devon took her firmly in hand.

Instead of struggling, she pressed against him, looking up. "Please, don't."

His arms tightened around her, and his expression showed his conflict. "Game changer, Eunice. I'm really sorry."

She buried her head in his chest and sobbed, letting all her fear and anger flow.

"Uh...look...maybe I'll find it right away and I'm good with skin grafts..."

She stepped back. "I'm sorry." She sniffed. "Some soldier I turned out to be. I just need a minute. Is there a washroom?"

"Of course." He strode to a cabinet and removed a robe. "Here." Devon gestured to a washroom. "When you're done, take off all your clothing and put this on."

She gave him a watery smile. "Okay." Keeping her shoulders hunched, she shuffled into the washroom and closed the door. There wasn't a way to lock it on this side.

Leaning against the door, she gathered her courage. Now what? She spotted a call button and speaker. Perhaps she could use the wires...

Ah, who the hell was she kidding, she was a brand spanking newbie. The first time she'd been in a spaceship was two months ago. All she had was her basic training. She considered. There had to be something she learned during those eight weeks of hell that she could use now. Eunice sorted through the massive amount of information she'd learned, including proper military procedures, spaceship stats, weapons, warfare tactics, and military strategy.

Devon knocked on the door. "Is everything all right?"

No, you asshole. You're going to flay me.

"Just a minute, please." she squeaked, sounding as pathetic as possible.

Her thoughts continued to race, then they snagged on one lesson. *Okay Leo, I trust you, so all I need to do is hold up my end.* Eunice stripped, threw on the robe, kicked off her boots and socks, and opened the door.

As Devon led her to the procedure table, she concentrated on being a raw recruit, fresh from the factory. She shook with fear. Tears streaked down her face and she huddled on the table while Devon programmed the med-unit for surgery.

He instructed her to remove the robe. She stood and untied the belt with fumbling fingers, pulling it through the loops. Devon picked up the anesthetic and approached. Eunice shrugged off the robe, it plopped to the floor. He skidded to a stop, staring at her. *Brand spanking new body, too. Score one for the recruit.*

Eunice's training kicked in. She wrapped the robe's belt around his hand holding the medicine. Pulling his arm straight up, she spun behind him then yanked his wrist down. Devon shouted in surprise. Before he could fight back, she pushed the button, sending the anesthetic into his neck. He collapsed.

Eunice had about two seconds to celebrate before the door flew opened. She dashed for the latrine and shut the door, but knew she couldn't hold it. She prayed her memory wasn't faulty. The moon they had crashed on was small and an XP cruiser of this size should have enough power to leave orbit smoothly. That bump when they left orbit might have been a signal. In other words, she was betting her life on a should-have and a might-have.

She pressed the big red call button. *Okay, Leo, your turn.*

"How can I assist you?" a mechanical voice asked.

"Lock the washroom's door!"

The bolt popped into place. Holy shit with a halo and a robe!

The guards banged on the door, shouting at her to unlock it.

"Do you require anymore assistance?" Leo's voice replaced the mechanical one. He sounded very smug.

"Can you take me to Venus Five?"

"Already enroute. Sit tight."

"Leo, you *are* the best of the best."

"I know."

After they landed, Leo collected her from the washroom. As they walked through the empty corridors of the XP, he explained that once she was out of harm's way, he flew the XP to Venus Five and delivered the group of pirates to the military police.

"MP's already fumigated this nest of nasties," Leo said.

"How did you get onto the ship, let alone gain control of it?" she asked.

"While you were believing I'd abandoned you, I was hidden in the engine compartment of the bullet. It threw off enough heat to mask my presence."

"And when they took it to the cargo bay—"

"No one thought to search it because they were so focused on your Shiny Highness. Nice blubbering baby act by the way."

"Thanks. How did you get into the bridge?"

He huffed as if insulted. "I don't need a bridge to fly. I just cozied up to that beautiful huge Kasner-Philips engine and she sang for me." Leo's expression took on an avid glow of someone in a state of pure bliss.

"I sang for you, too, Leo. On my knees and bent over the latrine."

He laughed. "You'll get used to K-speed, Recruit."

"Not bloody likely."

They reported to the commander of the base. He congratulated Leo on his quick thinking and Eunice for keeping her skin on. Well, not those words exactly.

"Should I report to the medic, sir?" she asked. She couldn't wait to deliver the DSU and be finished with this mission.

"No need, Private Daniels. We didn't implant the data in you. You were our decoy this time. And an excellent one at that." The commander left in good spirits.

Eunice stared after him as fury burned in her chest.

Leo laughed and slapped her on the back. "Welcome to the military, Private Daniels." When she didn't respond, he added, "Look on the bright side."

She sputtered. "What bright side?" she demanded.

"You're no longer brand spanking new."

DR. TIME

I've always been fascinated with the concept of time. Time travel is one of science fiction's well loved tropes. Because who wouldn't want to go back in time and change one bad decision? When I was asked to contribute to The Stories (in) Between *to celebrate the thirtieth anniversary of Between Books—an independent book store in Delaware that had stayed in business despite the arrival of big chain bookstores and online giants—I returned to the concept of time. Dr. Time is also about sending a message and a bit...more through time. The challenge of this piece was getting the timing worked out for the climax. I was happy with the results and glad to be a part of the anthology. A decision I've no desire to change.*

DR. TIME

"Dr. Clemmer?" Ian Kain called over the rattle of the dehumidifier. "I see you're still toiling away down here in your dungeon."

Gaye Clemmer eyed Dr. Kain's clean white lab coat and slicked-back brown hair with suspicion. Kain never came down to visit her unless he wanted to brag or to harass her.

"I've just finished talking with the head of our department. You remember Dr. Myers?" He paused, giving her a self-satisfied smile. "Since I've proven Young's Generational Theory, I have secured another multi-million dollar grant from Trellanix Corp."

When she failed to respond he said, "Since you don't bother to show up for department meetings, I'm sure you'll read about it in *Time*."

She was right, gloating was on his agenda, yet a hint of malice lurked behind his glib words.

Dr. Kain scanned her basement lab with a proprietary look. Gaye followed his glance. Who would want this dank, under-lit room that reeked of mold? Her ancient desk, tables, and equipment had been wedged in the various open spaces between the water heater, furnace, and her dehumidifier.

"With all that money, I have to expand my operation." He bared his teeth in what he must have thought was a smile. "I need a place to store my files and supplies."

She refused to comment; to give that bastard any satisfaction.

Undaunted, he went on. "Dr. Myers said your funding will expire by month's end. Unless you prove your theories." He smirked. "I'm still amazed that you managed to secure funding for this ridiculous project in the first place."

He walked over to the large, vault-shaped Relocater Device, opening the door. He poked his head inside. "I can use the computer and keyboard in there. Plus, this will be a great place to store my back-up drives. Sealed to keep the humidity out, right?"

"Why don't you step all the way in and see?" Gaye touched a switch at her desk and a bright red glow appeared in the device.

Ian Kain danced back as if threatened with a knife. He shot her a venom-filled glare.

"Funny, Dr. Clemmer, but let's see who's laughing when the janitors are hauling this junk to the dump." He wiped his hands on his coat, and strode from the room without uttering another word.

Relieved, Gaye waited until his footsteps on the gritty cement stairs faded before she accessed her locater program.

As she worked on getting the glitches out of the code, her mind returned to Ian's comments. Department meetings, Gaye thought in disgust, were a waste of time. Why bother to show up when her colleagues used every opportunity to mock her and her research à la Kain?

They had assigned her a lab in the basement of McMullen

Hall. Dating back to the nineteenth century, it was one of the oldest buildings on the University's campus. The obvious slight was a mere inconvenience. Gaye had funding and a brilliant idea; all she needed was time.

One month left. The hardest part would be getting the locater program perfected by the deadline. The Global Positioning System had been a boon to her research for coordinates on the ground, but she still needed complex calculations to position the planet Earth in the universe. Determining the Earth's exact position, or locating it at a certain point in time was critical. A miscalculation would be disastrous.

Spending the month working late nights and weekends would be worth the astonished look on Kain's face. To Gaye, that would be better than getting a multi-million dollar grant.

Gaye hunted. She followed the creature's tiny scrambling as she crawled along the cold cement floor, scanning the corners. Catching a slight movement by the waste can, she pounced.

"Got you!" she cried. Grabbing the rat's tail, she yanked it up. The black rodent swung and twisted in the air.

"If you're the critter that's been chewing my papers," Gaye said, "I'll take you over to Runkel Hall where they use poisoned bait."

"Uh, excuse me," said a voice.

Startled, she nearly dropped the rat. A young man with a mess of bright yellow hair and long sideburns stood in the lab's doorway. Piercings glittered in both his ears and hung from his nostrils. He clutched his backpack to his stomach.

"Can I help you?" Gaye asked.

"Um, I was sent to help *you*." He glanced at the steps as if gauging the distance to freedom.

"In my research?" She was the kiss of death to any graduate student who wanted a career, so they avoided her.

"No. Dr. Kain sent me to help you pack."

"You can tell Kain that I still have three weeks. I'm not packing. In fact . . ." Gaye walked toward the student. He shrank back.

"Here." She thrust the rat at the boy.

He pressed against the wall, dodging the creature.

"Take this to Kain. If he's determined to move into my lab, he might as well get to know his roommates. They have a lot in common."

It was too much for the yellow-haired boy. He bolted up the steps, taking them three at a time.

Gaye laughed despite knowing she had just added fuel to the rumors about her. Shrugging, she placed the rat into an old cat-sized crate with the intent of dropping him off at the park on her way home. He'd probably run right back here. She pictured a tiny, well-beaten rat trail from the lake to her lab. They probably had maps, and compared stories of their capture in group therapy.

She placed the crate next to the steps so she would remember to take it with her. When she turned her back to her desk, an icy touch brushed her spine.

She spun. Nobody was there, but something had changed. For a mouth-drying minute, Gaye stood still, unable to pinpoint the difference. Then she spotted a champagne bottle sitting on the portion of her desk that she always kept clear. The section that had a black X taped onto it.

The bright silver ribbon wrapped around the neck held a note. Gaye moved toward her desk while a marching band played in her chest. Was it real?

Her fingers slid along the smooth glass of the bottle and

fumbled to untie the note. Familiar handwriting declared: *We did it!*

She dropped to her knees in stunned amazement. Pure stubborn determination had sustained her through years of research, but to have actual proof that her Relocater Device worked overwhelmed her.

Standing on gelatin legs, she stared at the bottle. The champagne was the most expensive brand at the liquor store. She had planned to buy the bubbly and relocate it back in time to celebrate her breakthrough.

A fluted glass waited within her desk drawer. Gaye considered sharing the alcohol with her new rat friend for a toast as she retrieved the glass. But when she reached for the bottle, it had moved to the edge. Impossible.

The room felt excessively quiet. The dehumidifier had shut off, but Gaye couldn't remember when. The water pan must be full. She applied logic to calm her thundering heartbeat.

An unmistakable feeling of being watched hovered in the room. It seemed as if the airborne moisture had condensed into a being, changing the flow and thickness of the air in the lab. She licked her lips, tasting the sudden dryness.

Ridiculous, she chided. Paranoid. One minute you're overjoyed and the next worried that someone will steal the technology. And not just a regular someone, but a water-droplet being.

Gaye shook off her apprehension. But when she headed to the dehumidifier, she caught movement at the edge of her vision.

The champagne tipped over the lip of the desk. Unable to catch it, Gaye watched the bottle fall. Glass exploded as it hit the floor, splashing champagne onto her pants, and soaking her shoes.

When the dehumidifier kicked on with a roar, Gaye moved

so fast she left puddles on the ground. Grabbing her briefcase and the rat's cage, she raced up the stairs.

Out in the fresh air, Gaye calmed. She chalked up her over-reaction to stress combined with the excitement of success. After purchasing a new bottle of champagne, she headed home to celebrate.

Bypassing the lake, she carried the rat to her apartment. Celebrating alone didn't appeal to her, and, once home, she fed the rat cheese and milk, and went to bed instead of toasting her accomplishment.

When she entered her lab the next morning, the stench of alcohol greeted her. Glass shards and droppings from her other furry roommates peppered the champagne-sticky floor. Gaye set the rat's crate next to her computer, and swept up the mess.

She sighed. When Dr. Myers had seen the grant check for her research project, he had offered her lab space next to Kain's on the sixth floor. That offer had been rescinded as fast as a cockroach evading a foot when that lousy bastard Kain complained that Gaye had stolen his grant money.

Wempor Technology had already awarded her their Futurist Endowment before she finished her Ph.D. She had applied for the endowment along with a thousand other scientists. If Gaye had known Kain would revert to infantile behavior when he failed to win it again, she would have moved to another university.

Opening the one high window, she let the cold March air replace the fermented mildew smell. She kept busy to avoid dwelling on the unsettled feeling in her chest. Gaye worked on her locater program, commenting out loud to her rat.

Little things distracted her from time to time. Like the fact that her storage box had been moved to the right side of her computer, her calculator had been flipped over, and her phone had been turned toward the wall. It was as if her mother had visited and rearranged everything.

Unable to concentrate on her program any longer, Gaye moved everything back into its correct position. Then the dehumidifier kicked off. Gaye fidgeted for a while until the silence drove her to her feet.

Halfway across the room, she paused. Footsteps scraped on the cement steps, warning her of a visitor. Or an intruder? Gaye scanned the room for a weapon until she saw the familiar nest of lemon-yellow hair.

"Hello?" the boy called, startling when he spotted her standing in the middle of the lab, staring at him. "I'm here to—"

"I'm not packing."

His Adam's apple bobbed as he swallowed. "Er . . . help . . . help you with your research."

His wide-eyed gaze locked onto the Relocater Device. Perhaps he thought she would relocate *him*. Although, if she sent him back to his barber, she would be doing him a favor.

"Sorry, but my grant money doesn't include a stipend for a grad student," Gaye said. She expected him to sigh with relief and bolt up the stairs.

Instead, with a dread-filled voice, he said, "Dr. Kain is paying my stipend." He swallowed. "I'm on loan. He said it was only fair to help you prove your theories since you have so little time."

She clamped her mouth shut before a sarcastic comment about Kain and fairness could escape. Studying the boy, she considered the offer. Definitely a spy for Kain. But why would he bother? He thought her project was a joke. Maybe he wanted to keep an eye on her so she didn't set any booby traps in the basement before she left.

If she sent the boy back, Kain might be down here more often—rather unappealing. She preferred her rats.

She could agree to the boy's help, but only when she could keep an eye on him. After all, it was free labor. If he proved too meddlesome, she would act out a few of the crazy professor rumors circulating around the department about her, and scare him away. Shouldn't be too hard to do; he looked a little shaky.

"Okay. Can you start now?" she asked.

He nodded, gnawing on his bottom lip.

"First thing." She pointed to the dehumidifier. "Empty the water pan outside. Water that new cherry tree by the front door. Do you know the one? Someone taped an American flag to its trunk."

He stared at her.

"I don't want to waste water; we've had a dry winter." She didn't know what else to say, and the boy still wasn't moving.

"Go ahead." Gaye shooed.

He finally rushed over to the corner. In his haste, he tripped over the power cord, bumped into the dehumidifier, and sloshed water onto his coat.

She suppressed a sigh, and returned to her desk. Her fingers froze over the keyboard. The storage box was once again on the wrong side. Glancing at the crate, she asked the rat, "Did one of your friends move my box?"

"What?" the grad student asked. His foot was on the first step, and he wobbled under the weight of the water pan.

"I'm not talking to you."

"Okay," he said, drawing the word out as if he humored a mental patient. Despite his heavy load, the boy shot up the stairs, splashing water in his haste.

Without him, the air in the lab smothered and pressed on Gaye's face. She noticed additional items that were not in their original place. The overpowering knowledge that someone was in her lab scratched at her skin. The water-droplet being? Gaye tasted the air, seeking answers.

Overworked, she thought. Stressed out. Drawing in a few deep breaths, Gaye rationalized. It could be a rat, scurrying around on her desk when she wasn't looking. And moving the storage box up and over the keyboard? No. Maybe it had to do with the Relocater Device. When the champagne bottle arrived, it had displaced the air. Perhaps the gust of wind blew the items askew. But the storage box hadn't been knocked out of place, it had been moved. Relocated.

Maybe the water-droplet guy was bored, playing poltergeist for a laugh. A feather of fear brushed her stomach. Focus on the science, Gaye chanted in her mind.

When the boy came back, she showed him how to pull coordinates from a Universal Positions Graphic map, a time-consuming but relatively easy task. She set him up at the table.

There were no more "incidents" that day. She only jumped once when the boy stumbled over his metal folding chair. He had class.

He handed her the coordinates and started for the stairs.

"Hey, bo . . ."

"Bradlee, with two e's, Shepherd," he said.

"Are you coming back tomorrow?" The sudden reluctance to work alone pulled at her chest. Ridiculous, she knew, especially since she had been the sole occupant of her basement lab for the last five years. However, the fear remained.

"I can."

Relief puddled. "Same time?"

"Okay."

Getting back to work in the empty lab proved difficult. She stared at the storage box, daring it to move.

An icy hand touched her neck.

She shot to her feet. Her chair slammed into the wall.

Where the champagne bottle had once been, there was now a white envelope. A message from the future. Gaye's fear evaporated as she dove for the letter, and missed. The envelope slid away from her hand. Had her dive blown it? No. The envelope continued to sail across the desk and into the air.

Determined, Gaye chased the message. Defying gravity, the letter headed straight for the water heater. A pilot light burned underneath. The envelope dipped toward the flame.

A suicidal note. She sprinted and snatched the envelope before it could catch fire.

Panting, Gaye held her prize tight. It was too risky to open it in the lab. She picked up the rat's crate and backed out of the basement.

Gaye checked the lock on her apartment door twice. She loaded the dishwasher and tidied her small one-bedroom apartment. She kept glancing at the letter, but couldn't bring herself to read it.

The envelope rested on her scratched kitchen table. All her furniture had been bought at a consignment shop. There were no decorations or pictures hanging on her walls. Her textbooks and old files had been piled in a corner of the dining room to save them from the lab's moisture.

She opened her letter only when her TV was on loud, the rat's crate cleaned out, and Little Devil fed. Yes, she had named the rat. Yes, it was yet another lonely, pathetic gesture.

The note read: *I thought you might enjoy knowing that Kain's new grant money falls through when his research methods are examined. Seems his science doesn't match his results. This wonderful event happens on March 27. Perhaps you would like to do some gloating of your own before he receives word? Oh, and watch Bradlee with two e's. His klutziness ruined some of Kain's research and Brad's trying to get back into his favor. By the way, Wempor Technology is thrilled with our success and promises tons of money, but asks that we keep it quiet for now.*

The letter was signed in her own handwriting. A queasiness rolled in her stomach. Important events were happening in the future beyond her control, and a strange feeling of wrongness simmered in her chest as if she had committed a crime.

When Gaye arrived at her lab the next morning, Bradlee stood in the middle of the room, looking as pale as drywall dust. In her mad sprint up the stairs the day before, Gaye had forgotten to lock the door.

Scanning the room, she couldn't tell if he had been snooping. Things on her desk had been moved out of place, but that had become the status quo. Her computer was on. She couldn't recall if she had turned it off. A slightly crumpled piece of paper rested on her desk. Another note?

Gaye glanced at Bradlee to see if he had read it. The boy's gaze jumped from corner to corner as if he followed the erratic path of a fly. He turned in a slow circle, yet remained oblivious to her presence despite the fact she stood in full view at the bottom of the steps. The dehumidifier rattled and hummed.

"Bradlee," she said. When he didn't react, she called louder, "Bradlee with two e's."

He spun around, but his feet didn't keep pace and he ended

up tripping over them. "Jeez Louise, don't sneak up on me like that," he said.

"What are you doing here?" she asked.

"You told me to come."

"Oh. Okay." Gaye hadn't realized the time. She placed Little Devil's crate next to her desk. Ignoring the wrinkled paper, she rummaged around for the file of calculation sheets. She wanted to give Bradlee something to do before she read the note.

"Do you know this place is haunted?" Bradlee asked. Again he peered into the corners as if searching for something.

Gaye paused. A heavy presence filled the room. "What gave you that idea?"

He shrugged.

"Well, this is a scientific laboratory. Ghosts and goblins don't exist. Science and cold hard facts belong here. Do you understand?"

He nodded and she set him to work on the calculations. It was bad enough being the crazy professor; she didn't need another rumor to start circulating that she worked in a haunted lab.

When she finally picked up the paper, her hand shook. Bradlee had felt a presence, too, so she wasn't imagining it, but she couldn't decide if that was a good thing or not.

To make matters worse, the paper had one word on it. *Stop.* The printed letters looked like a kid had written them. Gaye copied the word below it to compare. Not her handwriting, yet it reminded her of childhood. Maybe a prank sent by Kain via Bradlee.

Instead of working on her locater program, Gaye sat at her desk, trying to figure out why the note evoked images of her youth. At this rate she wouldn't get the Relocater Device working before the university kicked her out.

And that was another problem. She had been so determined to prove to Kain and to the department that she was right, that she hadn't fully thought about all the consequences.

Future Gaye was having fun, sending champagne and notes back to herself, telling Wempor Technology about the discovery. It seemed rash. It seemed dangerous. It seemed irresponsible to mess with her own past and future.

It seemed wrong. And what about the . . . presence? Why would Future Gaye send it? Perhaps it came from the far, far future where humans had turned into condensed water-vapor beings to adapt to extreme greenhouse warming. The being had traveled back to see the great Dr. Clemmer for itself.

Perhaps the department wasn't too far off, calling her the crazy professor.

Like a puppy, logic chased its tail in her mind. She heard a snap. Unfortunately, it wasn't sudden understanding.

"Damn," Bradlee said.

She swiveled her chair.

"Broke my pencil." He sighed. "You know," he said, scratching at a yellow sideburn with the eraser, "I can bring my laptop tomorrow. It would be quicker, and you wouldn't have to input all these numbers into your computer. Just transfer the file."

His comment made her wonder if he had searched through her computer files while waiting for her this morning. "If you want," she said in a neutral tone.

She found another pencil and handed it to him. Bradlee switched the pencil from his right to left hand, and began working.

Must be left-handed, Gaye thought. Then chomp, the puppy caught its tail. She pulled the one-word note closer. Taking a pen in her left hand, she wrote "Stop." The same shaky letters. An exact duplicate. Like when she was a kid, having fun trying to write with her left hand. So much for the prank theory.

Bradlee left for class, and Gaye was alone with her swirling thoughts. The note would make more sense if it had been from Kain. Determined to ignore the strange events, Gaye concentrated on her locater program.

She succeeded in debugging the program, but couldn't get it to link up with the Relocater Device's computer. Gaye planned for a late night until the furnace hissed, disturbing her. The ancient contraption broke every year. The last thing she needed right now was to have the repairmen tramping in here, getting in the way, asking her questions instead of doing their work.

Upon inspection, the furnace seemed fine. Another hiss sounded behind her.

She braced. Reluctant to turn around, she summoned the courage. Just like pulling off a Band-Aid, it was best to do it fast. She spun. A cloud hovered four feet away. It hissed again and transformed into a human shape.

Horrified, yet fascinated, Gaye froze. The cloud woman's face contorted with effort as she tried to speak.

"Kain." A whispery fizz. "Watch."

For a second the woman came into sharp focus. Gaye gasped, recognizing herself sculpted in cloud. The woman pressed her white vapor lips together in frustration as she faded.

Unfortunately, Kain chose that moment to appear at the base of the stairs. Gaye gaped at him, her thoughts as messy as Bradlee's yellow hair. Was Kain made of cloud too? At first, she failed to understand his words.

". . . see how Bradlee was working out," he said.

"Bradlee with two e's?" she asked.

"My grad student," he snapped.

"Oh, fine. Thank you. Did you . . ." She had wanted to ask him about Cloud Gaye, but reconsidered.

"Any results yet?"

Blunt as ever. Gaye was surprised he hadn't brought a measuring tape and interior decorator along.

"Soon."

He laughed. "You still believe you can travel through time in a time machine made of an old bank vault and some junk-yard parts?"

"A Relocater Device."

"Relocater, time machine, doesn't matter what you call it, it's still fantasy."

Unchecked, the words burst from Gaye's mouth. "It *does* matter. It makes all the difference between success and fail-ure." She stepped toward him. "I could even relocate your multi-million dollar grant check right into my office. No time travel involved. But I forgot . . ." She smacked her forehead in a mocking gesture. "Your grant money disappears before you even get it. You'll be reading your go-to-hell letter from the government in two days. Fantasy results never work in obtaining research money, *Doctor* Kain."

Regret followed Gaye's outburst. When Kain's face emptied of color, she knew she should have kept her mouth shut.

In a tight voice, Kain said, "I should have known better than to try and help a psychopath. Thank God you'll be gone, or should I say *relocated*, from this university in two weeks."

He strode to the stairs. Gaye could have sworn she saw a damp handprint on his back.

With Kain gone, Gaye had to deal with rationalizing the presence of the Cloud Gaye. A message from the future? A warning? Perhaps Future Gaye had tried to relocate herself back in time, and, because she already existed in this time period, she arrived as an intangible being, unable to interact. Although she had interacted, in a ghost-like way.

Gaye's head throbbed with the complications. She sank to the floor. It had been much simpler before. Prove her theory. Have a party. The end.

As she stood, Gaye spotted an exposed wire lying under her desk. She inspected it and discovered that the wire had been gnawed almost in half. Those rats must feed off the electricity. No wonder they were so bold. Then she realized the broken wire connected the computer to the Relocater Device. She replaced the damaged wire and fixed the communication problem.

Jubilant, she raced back to the computer. It acknowledged the device. Fingers flying over the keyboard, Gaye initiated her first test. She placed a pencil in the device and sealed it tight. Dancing with energy, Gaye started the program.

The Relocater Device hummed, cracked, and pinged. Just when she thought it was either going to explode or melt, she heard a loud pop. The pencil rested directly on the black X on her desk.

Not bad for a bank vault with junkyard parts. Now she had a reason to celebrate. She took the champagne bottle from Little Devil's crate. Should she send it back in time? Done that. Gaye popped the top.

Letting Little Devil free in a surge of happiness, Gaye poured him a bowl of champagne. He sniffed the air, and waddled over to the treat. When he was done, he waddled back into the crate and fell asleep.

Over the next two days, Gaye tested her device on real-time transfers, avoiding the time vector for now. The bigger the object she relocated, the louder the pop. Bradlee never returned, which was fine with her. Busy and excited, Gaye also ignored the hissing efforts of Cloud Gaye. As for the warning, what could she do? She'd been avoiding Kain as always. As long as she kept her mouth shut about the device, she should be all right.

Gaye calculated the coordinates for the night when the champagne bottle arrived. She programmed them into the computer to test if the device would shut down with an error message because of the time vector. Even though future Gaye had made it work, present Gaye needed to check.

A bang vibrated through the floor. She glanced up. Ian Kain stood at the base of the stairs, trembling like a revved up engine in neutral. With a paper crushed in his fist, he advanced on Gaye.

"You knew!" He snarled. "You crazy, deluded bitch. How did you know?"

She opened her mouth, but he grabbed her arm and dragged her over to the Relocater Device.

"Are you going to tell me that this piece of junk works?"

"Yes," she said, hoping the answer would defuse his anger.

He stood still for a heart-slamming moment. "Show me."

Gaye heard a hiss. Cloud Gaye gestured madly behind Kain. Too late now. "No. I'm sorry about your grant, Dr. Kain. But I have a lot of work to do." She pried his hand off.

"Show me," he said.

He was not going to bully her. "No."

He pulled a gun from his lab coat. "Show me, now."

The hard metal lines of the gun's barrel pointed toward Gaye. Reason drained from her body, leaving behind a numbing jumble of thoughts. An image of Kain winning awards and accolades flashed through her mind. He was not going to steal her invention. "Go to hell."

A loud roar echoed in the lab as Kain shot her in the chest. She flew back, hitting the Relocater Device's door.

Surprise preceded pain as Gaye stared at Kain. He gaped back in horror as her body slid to the floor.

She couldn't breathe, there was no time left. "Doctor Time," the students had called her. Gaye laughed, but choked on the hot blood pouring from her mouth. Her lab blurred. Kain disappeared. She melted into the blackness.

Later, Gaye's spirit rose from her dead body. The desire to warn herself about Kain was overpowering. The Relocater Device had been programmed for the night the champagne bottle appeared. The computer and keyboard inside the device accessed the controls.

Could she do it? Why not? She had done it before. And this time, she would do it right.

LOST & FOUND, INC.

In the not so distant past, stories about the fairy world and the Fae were all the rage. The invites went out, asking for Fae stories for an anthology. The theme was to focus on the Fae who are living and hiding in our world. Even though I wasn't a big fan of stories about fairies, I decided to accept the challenge. After a bit of research about the various fairy courts, I sparked on the idea of writing about an exiled Fae Princess. However, the plot took the main character back into the world of Fae and that was a different direction than the editor of the anthology wanted so it was rejected. I found another anthology with a similar theme, but it was geared more toward paranormal romance readers, so I re-wrote the ending and submitted it. This time it was accepted until the publisher decided not to publish it. Instead of hunting for another home, I decided to save the story for this collection. And I included the original ending! Which one do you like best?

LOST & FOUND, INC

Exile doesn't suck as much as I thought it would. Sure, there were a few problems at first. Since I was stripped of my full magic, I only have enough to disguise myself as a human. But I've learned how to blend in by growing my curly black hair long to cover my pointy ears, wearing colored contacts, and mimicking the local accent.

I use my tiny bit of remaining glamour to help pay my rent, buy food, and do all those mundane human tasks in order to stay comfortably alive. Yep. I have a nice little business going. And the humans in Lancaster County, Pennsylvania are grateful for my services. Well, the honest ones are. The others, I'm not too concerned about.

In fact, I'm on my way to make a delivery. Driving along the idyllic back roads in my bright red VW bug, I crank the driver side window down to breath in the fresh country air. Ugh. Too bad it's the first nice day of spring, and every farmer is spreading manure on their fields. I close the window tight.

I pull up to a respectable suburban house. The door opens before I even turn off the engine. A mother and her two kids rush out while the dad waits in the threshold. This is the best part of my job. Well, getting paid is the best, but this comes in a close second. Hey, a girl's gotta eat.

I open the door and the cocker spaniel, who's been slobbering all over my back windows, leaps over the driver seat and into the waiting arms of his family. I give them time to fawn over the dog.

"Thank God! We were so worried," the mother says. "Gwen, where did you find Boston?"

"He was chasing ducks at Overlook Park," I lie, then ask, "About my fee?"

"Oh yes. Of course. Come inside." She ushers me into the house.

Dad and the kids feed the dog treats and lavish him with attention. Up until a couple days ago Boston had been curled up in a ditch, soaking wet and starving. But that's not something I tell my clients. They usually feel bad enough for losing their dog or cat in the first place, no need to add more grief.

"Should I make the check out to you, or—"

"Make it out to Lost & Found, Inc," I say.

As Mom writes the check, she babbles with happiness. "Susan said you were the best, but Boston has been gone so long, and with the highway so close, and with the train tracks down the hill...we thought the worst." She rips off the check and hands it to me. "It's worth every penny."

And I earned every penny. Took me four days to track him through the fields with my limited magic. I wave good-bye to the...I glance at the check...Horst family and drive to downtown Lancaster. I snag a spot on Prince Street right in front of my other client's row home. As I park, I notice a group of teens staring at my car. I knock on her door, but keep an eye on them.

An elderly lady peeks through the barred window. She

smiles, showing off her remaining two coffee-stained teeth. After a series of clicks, she opens the door a foot. I slip inside. She slams it shut and relocks it. The woman has been a wreck since her house was burglarized last month. Holding up a piece of her stolen jewelry, I dangle it from a long finger.

She squeals like a twelve-year-old getting her first cell phone. "My great-grandmother's necklace! I thought I'd never see it again."

Then I give her the rest.

"You're amazing! Where did you—"

"It's better if you don't know."

The wrinkles on her face deepen.

I rush to assure her. "Don't worry, the kids who swiped your money and jewelry won't return. They don't know you have it back." And with a bit of magic, Caleb, who'd planned to fence the goods, no longer remembers being in possession of the jewelry. Too bad, I can't recover her money. Bills and coins disappear without leaving an energy trail for me to track.

"How much do I owe you?" she asks.

"Nothing. Your insurance company offered a finder's fee." Yes, I lie again. But she's a neighbor and on a fixed income. Plus it pisses me off when criminals prey on the weak.

"Why don't you stay and have a cup of tea?" she asks. "It gets so quiet around here at night."

"Sorry, I can't. I have another delivery," I say. Exile is bad enough. I don't want to spend my free time socializing with humans.

She won't let me leave empty handed. As I balance a home-made shoo-fly pie in one hand, I walk to my apartment three blocks away. It's not the best of neighborhoods—the teens are gone, but four young men have taken their place. They're more interested in me than my car. They follow me after I pass them.

My pointy ears are good for funneling sound, and they

mention my name along with Caleb's. Damn, my magic on him wasn't strong enough. I hurry to my building and take the stairs two at a time.

When I enter my apartment on the fourth floor, I'm huffing. I lock the door, but I'm far from safe. I already have company. The scent of lilacs and clover fills the air, sending a sharp stab of fear deep into my chest. Not a human visitor, but a Fae. Which means one thing.

Trouble.

I stare at the gorgeous man lounging on my couch. Thick black hair, blue-blue eyes, perfect white teeth, long eyelashes, he has chiseled features to match his chiseled body. All the Fae are gorgeous, so it's no surprise, but I haven't seen my kind in over two years so it's a shock to my system. He's wearing black jeans, cowboy boots, and a form-fitting T-shirt.

Sliding my pie onto the counter, I lean my hip on the edge, trying to produce a casual stance. "What are you doing here?"

He laughs. The deep sound rolls right through me, triggering memories of my childhood. I squash them back down in my mind where they had been living in relative obscurity.

"No, hello? Or happy to see you?" he asks.

"Do you want me to lie?"

"Ah, Gwendolyn. You're still the same."

Voices yell as feet pound on the building's stairs. The four thugs have gotten inside my building. Oh joy.

"Either tell me why you're here, Quinlin or leave," I say.

Quinlin surges to his feet in one liquid motion. Then he saunters around my small, one-bedroom apartment, examining the few possessions I've collected over the last two years. He tsks at the used furniture. "You could have gone anywhere in the human world—Paris, London, Rome, New York. Yet you chose Lancaster, Pennsylvania."

He's in no hurry to leave. The men bang on my door, rattling my locks. They shout obscenities, calling me uncomplimentary names and telling me they're going to teach me not to steal from their boss. I need to call the police. Now.

Quinlin is amused by the threats. "Still causing trouble, too. Why am I not surprised?"

"As much as I'm *not* enjoying our little tête-à-tête, you need to leave. I've other more pressing...business to attend to."

Turning his gaze to me, I rock back on my heels as the full force of his magic slams into me, reminding me that you don't want to piss off a Fae. And especially not a prince of the Irish Court, either. Sudden silence fills the room.

"The men will not bother us," he says.

"You didn't—"

"No. I've relocated them to Paris."

My relief mixes with apprehension. At least I'll have a few days to find another apartment. Unless Prince Quinlin has other plans.

"Why are you here?" I demand.

A twitch of annoyance creases his perfect face. "Your growing lost and found business has attracted some interest among the Fae."

That alarms me. "How much interest?"

"A few Fae have noticed. Your father has kept track of your whereabouts and activities. He's the one who informed me."

The thought of my father keeping track of me sends needles of fear into my heart. I'm supposed to be safe from him. According to Fae law, he is forbidden all contact with an exile of his Court. Of course, with my father, King Alun of the Welsh Court those laws are debatable and often ignored. But with Quinlin...

"Wait. Why was my father telling *you* about me?" The Fae Courts don't play well together. Lies, double crosses, betrayals, and secret alliances plague relations between Courts. At the time of my exile, the Irish and Welch Courts were close to war, which was my fault, hence the exile.

"If he came to see you, there would be...problems. King Alun sent me instead."

"Why?"

"We'd like to hire you to find something that is lost."

"Sorry, but I don't work with Fae." And I doubt I possessed enough magic to track anything beyond the gloom.

"We believe it can be found in the human world."

Interesting. "Still no."

"What if I told you it was important to your father?"

"Hell no."

He clenches a fist and taps it on his thigh—a sign I'm trying his patience. Probably not a good idea.

Quinlin glances around my apartment again. "Do you like living here?"

"It's okay."

"Do you wish to return to Fae?"

A brief flare of longing warms my chest. I've missed a few... Fae, but the thought of returning to be a pawn for my father makes me sick. "Not if I have to live with my father."

"Then it's in your best interest to work with us."

"What convoluted piece of logic did you pull that from?"

He stares at me as if he's won. "If we don't find your sister, then King Alun will revoke your exile."

"He can't do that."

"He can if you're his only remaining heir."

I curse.

"Your concern for your sister is...heartwarming." His voice drips with sarcasm.

"Morwenna probably ran away. I don't blame her. Was my father trying to create another alliance by offering her to the highest bidder?"

A brief flash of shock crosses Quinlin's face before he smooths his expression. "Is that what you believe your father was doing with you?"

"Hell yes. All he wanted was an alliance with another Court and he was willing to auction me off. King Declan must have offered the most since I was to be given to one of your brothers." Like a captured chess piece.

Quinlin's body stiffens. Icy rage tainted with magic focuses on me. I stay on my feet by pure will power alone.

"You were betrothed to me," he says.

Oh crap. At least, it explains why my father sent him. And here I thought it was because we had been childhood friends.

I clear my throat. "So if I find my sister, then my father will leave me alone?"

With a sharp tone, he says, "Yes. No *Fae* will bother you."

Until she sneaks away again. I suppress a sigh. He could have told me about my sister right away, but the Fae love to dance about, testing for weakness and holes in the armor before they strike.

"All right, I'll try." I gesture to the tattered brown couch. It may be ugly, but it's comfortable. "Have a seat. Do you want a drink?"

"No."

He's still pissed. I brew a pot of tea, pour a cup, and sit down on the far end of the couch. Quinlin perches on the edge of the worn, maroon-colored plaid armchair across from me.

"Tell me what happened to Morwenna."

"She left your father's castle four days ago with a retinue of guards and servants as per her station. Morwenna was bound for the Scottish Court, but she never arrived. Her carriage was found at the border between Courts. Her servants and guards had been...killed and she was gone."

I mull over the implications. "Why was she traveling to the Scottish Court?"

"To meet her intended."

That's a surprise. "Prince Seumas?"

He nods.

"Has my father given up on an alliance with your court?" I ask him.

"No. The four United Kingdom Courts have agreed to work together. Morwenna and Seumas weren't part of the terms. We've all been spending so much time together while our fathers negotiated, they declared their plans to wed after the four Kings reached an agreement. But her disappearance may cause a rupture."

The four Courts have been fighting for centuries. "Why join together now?"

"Survival. The Eastern European Courts have combined. If they attack us..."

Bad news. "Any suspects?"

He smiles, but it doesn't reach his eyes. "Take your pick. We've searched all of Fae. No life sign of Morwenna. And no one has sent a ransom demand."

I consider. "Did you bring something of hers?"

He pulls a thin white baby's blanket from his pocket. It's stained and torn. I take Morwenna's most cherished possession from his hands. Underneath the Fae taint of lilac and cloves, is her scent of cinnamon and vanilla.

Memories flood my senses, drowning out the world around me. I close my eyes as images from the past swell. Playing in our favorite park, talking about everything and nothing at the same time, giggling over the various visiting princes, and making plans for our futures. Neither included exile and kidnapping.

Regret touches my heart. I've missed my sister the most these last two years.

Opening my eyes, I meet Quinlin's gaze. "I need to start at the place where she disappeared. I'm going to need..."

"Help?"

"My full magic back."

"Not possible."

"Then, I need help."

At least he doesn't gloat. "That's why I'm here."

With a strange unease swirling in the pit of my stomach, I glance around my apartment as if it is my last look. Quinlin holds his hand out. Clutching Morwenna's blanket to my chest, I grasp his hand. His magic surrounds us and the human world blurs as we cross the gloom.

The gloom is a dead zone caught in perpetual twilight. It's a barrier between the Fae world and the human world. Only Fae with strong magic can traverse it quickly, and a few, like Quinlin, can control with pinpoint accuracy where they will arrive on each side. Those with weaker magic can get trapped inside and have to be rescued. A few humans have been known to stumble into the gloom. None of them have escaped.

All Fae are born with magic, but the amount varies. The strongest become kings and queens, who marry and produce powerful off-spring. The rest seem content to live their long lives in Fae. Unless they are killed. A rare occurrence despite all the political nonsense between Courts. No one wants all-out war.

We stop at the edge of Fae. I sway as a temperate breeze

laced with the scents and sounds of Fae fills the void in my soul. Funny how I didn't realize the emptiness until it was filled.

Traveling inside Fae requires more mundane methods than magic. Quinlin's soldiers wait nearby with horses. They hail him with warm welcome, but stare at me with cold censure. I'm not here to make friends, so I ignore them. Although I wonder why the six of them are armed with swords, knives, and a few crossbows.

Dropping the human disguise, Quinlin has returned to wearing more traditional Fae clothing of black pants tucked into riding boots and a long tunic cinched tight with his sword belt. I'm still wearing my jeans, calf-high leather riding boots, a red tank top and matching cardigan.

The men mount their horses. Quinlin turns to me. "Do you remember how to ride?"

Instead of answering, I grab the mane of the extra horse. He's a handsome thoroughbred with a glossy chestnut-colored hide. I swing onto his bare back—the Fae eschew saddles and tack.

"How far is it?" I ask.

"Half a day's ride."

"Lead on."

We ride in silence, which suits me. The Fae countryside is similar to Lancaster County. Farms, fields, and livestock are interspersed with houses, barns, and small towns. Each Fae Court has an area that equals its home region. The weather and season match as well. The Welsh Court's lands are as small as Wales, but the Welsh Fae are powerful because of the robust beliefs of the Welsh people.

Quinlin explains we are in the English Court's lands. With the recent accord, Fae from the four Courts are free to travel within all of them.

After a few hours, I sense we're getting close. The foul smell of death taints the air and my unease grows. We crest a rise. A carriage lays on its side. Grooves in the dirt mark where the carriage tipped over. There are no bodies, but the ground is stained with blood and offal.

Worry for my sister gnaws on my stomach. I halt my horse and dismount. The door to the carriage was ripped from its hinges. Dried blood coats the splinted wood around the lock. Morwenna's? I run my finger along it. I feel a tug of connection. It's hers. Inspecting the interior, I fail to discover anymore blood or anything else for that matter. My sister never traveled light.

"Where are her belongings?" I ask Quinlin. "Did you return them to my father?"

He scans the area. "The kidnappers must have taken them."

Relief eases the sharpness of my fear. "If they bothered to drag along her suitcases, then they plan to keep her alive." For now.

"Then why haven't they contacted King Alun?"

"That's for you to figure out." Holding Morwenna's blanket close, I turn in a slow circle. A slight pull stops me. "This way." I mount and head back the way we arrived, keeping my horse at a walk.

Quinlin and his men follow. Stopping at each intersection, I make a circle, seeking that tug.

By nightfall we haven't gotten very far, and I'm having trouble focusing.

Quinlin suspends the search until morning. "You're exhausted," he says.

We make camp. Quinlin's soldiers have packed an extra bed roll and blanket for me. As we relax around the campfire, the guards who aren't on watch ignore me as they talk quietly among themselves, but Quinlin sits next to me.

"If you had your full power, how long would it take you to find your sister?" he asks.

"As fast as the horse could run," I say.

"You were always good at finding things."

"I thought it was a natural ability." I huffed. "I didn't realize it was a part of my magic." Until it was gone.

"Yet you make a living from that ability." Quinlin pokes the fire with a stick, sending sparks into the darkness.

"It's but an echo of what I once had. Frustrating to no end, but, as you said, useful for survival."

He stares at the fire in silence. I'm drained, but I'm reluctant to lie down. By tomorrow afternoon, I'll probably be back in the human world. And I don't want to waste my time in Fae asleep.

"You didn't know?" he asks in a quiet voice.

"About the betrothal?" I guess.

A nod.

I consider how much I should tell him and decide I owe him an explanation. "My father ordered me to pack my clothes. He said I was to marry an Irish Prince." My father's stern face fills my mind.

"And that caused you to—"

"No. What caused me to lash out, was, when I asked him which prince of the five of you, he didn't know nor care. All that concerned him was King Declan honoring the terms they had agreed on." Fresh anger swells. "And this was from a man who spent days picking the best male foxhound to breed with his favorite bitch. You'd think he'd extend the same courtesy to his oldest daughter."

"I can see why you were upset, but to almost start a war..."

"Seems extreme," I finish for him. "And you're right. It was over the top, but this wasn't the first time my father used me for his political schemes. In fact, he quite enjoyed putting me in the middle, convincing me of one thing or another and then yanking the curtain back, revealing the truth or part of the truth."

My father's voice rings in my ears. *Lighten up, Gwendolyn, it's just a prank. It's just good fun. It's what Fae do.* Except I was the only one getting hurt.

"I ran away dozens of times, but he always found me. Then I tried to beat him at his own game," I say.

"What happened?"

"I won. He was...furious, livid, incensed...take your pick. All those words seem too mild to me. I spent...months locked in a cell below our castle." Actually, the time I spent in the cell was rather peaceful. "When he announced my betrothal, I lost it."

"Yes, you did." Quinlin gives me a wry smile. "Did you intend for the assassin to miss?"

"Of course. Your father did nothing wrong. I was desperate."

"And you wanted to be caught?"

"Yes. That way my father would be forced to either exile or execute me to appease yours, preventing a war."

"You could have been executed."

"Another reason to miss."

"Still, it was a risk."

I shrug. Execution or exile. At the time, it felt the same.

"Why didn't you say something about King Alun then?" he asks.

"And who would have believed me?"

Quinlin says nothing, conceding the point. I notice the others have grown quiet, but they advert their gazes when I glance up. Exhaustion finally pulls me down to my bed roll. The air has cooled and I snuggle under the soft blanket.

"Would you have *lost it* if King Alun told you I was your intended?" Quinlin asks in a low voice.

Probably not. "In that case, I would have told the assassin to aim at you."

"Hey." But he is smiling. His good humor transforms his face, making him look years younger.

I hold onto his image as I fall asleep, dreaming of staying in Fae and being far far away from my father's reach.

I wake, feeling refreshed. The pull toward Morwenna is stronger. We cover twice the distance in only a few hours, heading toward the gloom. I wonder if being in Fae has caused my powers to grow.

We stop to rest the horses around mid-day. Quinlin's guards aren't as cold to me. Either they're getting use to me, or they overheard our conversation last night.

As we're preparing to continue, Quinlin and his soldiers pull their swords and face the opposite direction. Three seconds later, the drum of many hooves shakes the air. The noise grows louder as they come toward us. Fast.

In a heartbeat, they've surrounded us. Now I know why Quinlin travels with six guards. Unfortunately, he needs about a dozen.

At first, I don't recognize any of them.

But Quinlin relaxes, allowing the tip of his sword to drop toward the ground. "What are you doing here?" he asks his brothers.

Blane and Arlen don't answer. Instead, Arlen turns to Blane and says, "I told you he'd break the law for her. Didn't I?"

"You said within a year. It's been two," Blane says with a petulant tone.

Quinlin tries again. "What are—"

"Move aside, brother," Arlen orders Quinlin. "We're here to finish what should have been done two years ago." He pulls his sword from it scabbard. "Kill the traitor."

Uh oh. My heart jumps in my chest.

"She's not—"

"Don't defend her. *She* hired an assassin to kill father," Blane says. "Besides her presence in Fae is in direct violation of the conditions of her exile. Unlike you, *we're* following the law."

Quinlin steps between me and his brothers. His sword is, once again, held in the ready position. "She's here to help find Morwenna."

"You're an idiot to trust her," Blane says. "Stand down and let us finish this."

I touch Quinlin's arm. Magic rips through me and I wonder for a moment if he's stronger than both his brothers. Doesn't matter, I won't let him use his sword or magic against them. I move out into the open.

"Gwen—"

"No." I cut him off, then turn to the men. "Would you consider a temporary cease fire?" I ask. "Let me find Morwenna first, and then you can..." I swallow. "You can exact your justice."

"Gwen, no," Quinlin says.

"We can't trust you to return," Arlen says.

"Then come along with us."

The brothers exchange a surprised glance.

"No. This ends now," Arlen spurs his horse toward me.

The point of his sword aims at my heart, which is trying to climb up my throat. Quinlin tackles me. We land in a heap as the horse gallops past.

"You're just dragging this out," Blane says as he dismounts. In his hands are two long daggers.

He advances. Quinlin's on his feet and between me and his brothers. Again.

"Stop," I order.

And everyone freezes for a second. I'm amazed—have my full powers returned? No. Vibrations pulse through the soles of my feet. As one, the soldiers around us band together to face the new threat.

A small army arrives, led by a well-dressed royal.

I glance at Quinlin. "Another brother?"

He shakes his head. "Prince Seumas."

Ah. Morwenna's intended.

"Stand down," Seumas bellows from atop his huge black stallion. "By the order of the four Kings, you are not to harm Gwendolyn Elwina Alun."

"Elwina?" Quinlin asks.

"My mother's name."

"Oh."

There is a heated discussion between Arlen, Blane and Seumas. In the end, Seumas prevails and I live. For now.

As we resume the search for my sister, we're a bloated posse, consisting of four princes, twenty-four soldiers, and one exile. The tug of connection to Morwenna is strong. Within a few hours, we arrive at the edge of the gloom. Where the connection dies.

Quinlin touches my shoulder. "Can you track her through the gloom?"

At his touch, that pull toward my sister strenghtens. "I think so, but I'm going to need your...help. We need to walk slowly into the gloom. Not zip through with your magic. And all the others have to remain here."

"They're not going to like it."

"Too bad. Their magic will confuse the connection."

Quinlin's right. Arlen and Blane bicker and accuse me of trying to trick them. Seumas stops them with a snarl. I notice dark smudges lines his eyes and a furrow is etched in his brow. He is truly upset and grieving over my sister's disappearance. Lucky her.

I take Quinlin's hand. We step into the gloom. The light fades to gray as all colors drain from the world. Despair wells. I'll never find my sister. She's dead by now.

Quinlin squeezes my hand. "Ignore the bad feelings. It's part of the gloom's defenses."

I slog through the gloom, each step an effort as I follow the tug toward Morwenna. Guilt rises. How could I bring two Courts so close to war? Why couldn't I have just obeyed my father? I would be married to Quinlin and not in exile. I never should have charged that family so much money to find their dog. I took advantage of them. I should help that nice elderly lady who's scared of being robbed again. Offer to do her shopping, sit and have tea with her at night.

The gloom draws out all my faults, transgressions, and spitefulness, dangling them in front of me. I'm a horrible person. I suck. All I want to do is curl up in a ball and cry. But Quinlin pulls me along.

We finally reach the end. Drained and heart-sick, I stumble a few feet away from the edge, and plop down onto the ground. Quinlin drops next to me.

"Now we know why it's called the gloom," he says.

"No kidding. Do I kill myself now, or wait until after we find Morwenna?"

"Wait until after. I'm sure Seumas would appreciate it."

"Gee, thanks."

Quinlin waves a hand. "Happy to be of service."

Once the harsh effects of the gloom fade—not completely,

but enough to function, we glance around. We've arrived at a location that resembles the one we had left. Lancaster? Hard to believe the kidnappers would hide my sister in my backyard.

Quinlin gains his feet. All his good humor is gone. "What game are you playing now?"

"Excuse me?"

"You know what I mean."

"No, I don't. Morwenna is in that direction." I point.

"That's deeper into Fae."

Fae? I pull in a breath. Lilacs and clover. We didn't pass through the gloom. Instead we were transported to another location in Fae. "Where are we?"

He crosses his arms.

"Humor me," I say.

"Irish territory."

Oh crap. "How close to your castle?"

"Gwen—"

"Please answer."

He inclines his head in the direction I'd just pointed. "A few hours by horse. Are you going to tell me what's going on?"

"In a minute. Can I?" I reach for his hand.

His angry grip is painful, but I ignore the discomfort as I tap into his magic. The tug to Morwenna sends me to my knees. I concentrate, following the line of her energy. It's official. I suck.

"When you searched Fae for my sister, did you look in any of the United Kingdoms?" I ask.

"Of course not, why would..." His face pales as he puts the clues together.

"She was kidnapped because of me. Your brothers want their revenge. They knew you and my father would bring me back to find Morwenna, giving them the perfect excuse to kill me."

"This is going to break the alliance." His shoulders sag.

I can't ruin another coalition. My mind races. How do we solve this without causing any more trouble?

He releases my hand. "Let's go confront—"

"No. I've another idea."

"I can't believe I'm sneaking into my own home," Quinlin whispers to me.

We're crouched behind the wall around his mother's rose garden, waiting for the sun to set. This is the only location where the ivy has grown over the wall.

"You don't want your other brothers or parents to see you. It'll ruin—"

"I know. It's just...odd."

"Pretend you're fourteen again and we're playing capture the flag. Me and you against all your brothers. Except, this time, Morwenna is the flag."

He grins. "We were unbeatable. Of course, now they say we cheated."

"We didn't. A flag has no...energy. I follow the energy trail to a lost dog or cat. Jewelry and other treasured possessions are different as they're seeped in their owner's energy."

When the sun sets, we climb over the stone wall and drop into Queen Finella's garden. Quinlin has a key to the little-used side entrance. We slip inside.

"Guest rooms?" Quinlin asks.

I give him the don't-be-stupid look.

"Right. The dungeon it is."

He leads the way. As I follow him through the back hallways and little-used stairways, memories of playing hide and seek run through my mind. When our Courts had been allies, my family would frequently visit. When they weren't, we didn't see them for years. Long years as far as my young self was concerned. Like the last two.

Quinlin stops. He peeks around a corner then backs away. "Guards," he whispers.

"She's down there, I feel it."

"Me, too. Frontal assault?"

"No." I consider. "Can you put a glamour on me and make me look like Morwenna?"

"Why?"

"For a distraction. I'll waltz by the guards, they'll chase me, and you free my sister."

"They're trained not to leave their post."

"But if they see Morwenna, who's supposed to be on the other side of that door..."

"But what if they don't know she's down there?"

"Then they won't chase me and we'll do it your way."

"Okay." He concentrates.

Magical energy surrounds me like a bubble then tightens. I feel it clinging to my face, pressing against my body, and hanging from my waist.

"You're wearing her purple satin gown. It's puffy and it swishes when she moves."

I reach down and touch the layers of magic. Gathering a fistful, I lift. "Am I lifting the gown?"

"Yes."

I walk toward the guards.

"Wait," Quinlin says. "What if you're caught?"

Good point. "How do I release the magic?"

"Say your full name."

"If I'm caught, I'll break the spell. The important thing is for you to free Morwenna. You can do that, right?"

"Yes. I know where the keys are kept. Where are we going to meet up afterwards?" he asks.

"Just head toward the gloom. Give me something of yours and I'll find you." I hold out a hand.

Without hesitation, he pulls his ring off and drops it into my palm.

I suppress a gasp. The only time a royal Fae takes off their ring is when they exchanges it with their intended's. Mine was confiscated upon exile. I shake my head. "Not something valuable. Just a handkerchief or something like that."

He closes my hand around the ring. "If you're caught, you can use that to explain what you're doing here."

"Oh." Either relief or disappointment, possibly both, flows over me. "Good idea."

I tuck his ring into my pocket, and continue down the hallway. Before I turn the corner, I draw in a breath to settle my nerves. Then I concentrate on what Morwenna would be doing and thinking if she escaped. I run my fingers through my now long copper curls and yank a few out of place. Or, at least, I hope they appear to be mussed.

Rounding the corner as if in a hurry, I skid to a stop as I spot the two guards. I cover my open mouth with a hand, and let out a yip of surprise. We stare at each for a heartbeat. Then one guard yells, "Hey!"

I spin on my heels and run. More shouting follows, then the pounding of boots sound behind me as they give chase. Fear and adrenaline spur me on. I fly around corners and down corridors without a plan except to keep ahead of the guards.

Where is everyone? The place is deserted. Then it registers. This level is used mostly for storage. Apples!

Paying more attention to my location, I head for the north wing and increase my pace despite the need to suck major air. Inside a large store room are barrels and barrels of apples stacked on top of each other in pyramid shapes. The one in the far corner appears to be filled with apples, but Quinlin and his brothers have hollowed the inside out, creating the perfect hiding spot if I can remember how to find the door.

I half whisper, half gasp my full name to drop the glamour. Out in the hallway, the guards argue over which way to go. Tugging at anything and everything, my heart does flips. Doors bang as they check the other rooms. Nothing works.

Out of ideas, I duck behind the pyramid even though I know they'll find me. I grab Quinlin's ring to show them. The metal warms against my fingers and I feel a tug. The location of the hidden entrance pops to mind. I kneel, lift the panel, and dive inside two seconds before they enter the room.

Biting my lip, I ease the panel into place as they rush around, searching. Would it be too much to hope they don't possess enough magic to discover me? Probably.

They knock over a few barrels. I slide Quinlin's ring onto my thumb. He's outside the castle and moving away. The tightness around my throat eases. At least I managed to do one thing right.

When the guards leave, I stay put, remembering the trick we used to play when we were the seekers. We would hide and wait. Sure enough, one of the others would creep from their hiding spot and get caught.

I gauge the time based on how far away Quinlin feels. When he reaches a safe distance, I open the panel. Encouraged by the silence, I crawl from the barrels. That's half the battle. Now I need to find a way out. Deciding to leave by the Queen's garden, I stick to the little-known passageways and am outside in no time.

A brief thrill of victory surges through me as I slip between the long rows of rose bushes. I'm smart enough to avoid the thorns, but not Quinlin's other two brothers.

They ambush me by the wall, jumping from the shadows with weapons in hand. Being capture by the guards would have been bad, but nothing compared with being caught by these two. Icy fingers of fear sweep across my skin.

"She smells like apples, Torin. I told you she'd hide in the barrels." Padraic, the youngest brother gloats.

"Yes, you did," Torin, the oldest of King Declan's sons, agrees. "And I was right to guess Arlen and Blane would botch a simple task. No matter. Padraic, you have the privilege of killing the intruder before she makes another assassination attempt on Father."

Padraic advances. The sharp blade of his dagger gleams in the moonlight.

I back away. "I told the assassin to miss. I would never hurt your father."

"Doesn't matter," Torin says.

"Quinlin believes me. Talk to him first." My voice squeaks with panic.

"Of course he believes you. He's been in love with you since you were both five." Torin huffs. "He begged father to offer such outrageous terms for your betrothal. And then you pulled that stunt."

I keep moving back, but I'm losing precious maneuvering room. Stopping, I say, "You're right. It was a terrible thing to do. Here, give this back to your brother." I hold out my thumb, showing them Quinlin's ring.

"Did you steal that?" Padraic demands.

"No. He gave it to me."

"You're lying. Quinlin would never be that stupid," Torin says.

Gee, thanks. "Take it before…" My throat hitches.

Padraic reaches with his left hand. I move. I grab his wrist and step back, pulling him off balance. Then I shuffle closer and kick his right wrist. The dagger drops to the ground.

Torin rushes me with his sword. I turn so Padraic's in his path. Torin slows. I shove Padraic into him. They collide. I run to the wall, scramble up the vines, but a hand seizes my ankle and yanks. Hitting the ground hard, I lay gasping.

Torin stands over me with his sword aimed at my throat. I close my eyes and press Quinlin's ring to my chest.

"That's enough, boys," a deep voice booms out.

I open my eyes. Torin remains in place.

"Stand down, Torin."

"But she tried to kill you."

"Torin move away. Now." King Declan's tone clearly warns that he will not be disobeyed.

"Next time, traitor." Flicking his wrist, Torin swipes the tip of his sword along my neck.

Pain burns, but I don't move until Torin sheaths his sword and stalks away. Padraic follows. I'm left alone with King Declan. Perhaps he wishes to kill me himself. I struggle to my feet and curtsey.

"Relax, Gwendolyn. I'd ask you what you're doing here, but I've a sneaking suspicion I don't want to know."

"Your sons love you," I say.

"Yes, and the attempt on my life scared them."

"I'm sorry to have caused you so much trouble."

He waves a hand. "A minor skirmish, but I will accept your apology. Consider us..." King Declan glances at the ring on my thumb. "Friends."

I curtsey again. "Thank you."

"Don't let me keep you." He shoos me toward the wall. "I'm sure you have things to do."

Smiling, I hurry to the vines.

When I reach the top, King Declan calls, "Gwen?"

I pause and look at him.

"Don't break his heart again."

"Yes, your highness."

Quinlin and Morwenna wait for me at the edge of the gloom. She squeals and throws her arms around me in a rib-cracking hug.

"Are you all right?" I ask, holding her out at arm's length so I can examine her. She's wearing a purple satin gown. It's torn and filthy, but no wounds mark her skin.

"I've missed you so much!" she says.

"I'm sorry I was such a brat," I say to her.

"Don't apologize. Father was truly awful to you."

"At least you'll soon be safe from him as well," I say. "But I left you to deal with him. Did he use you as a patsy for his schemes?"

"He tried."

"And?"

She laughs. "I played dumb. Drove him crazy when I acted clueless and oblivious to his elaborate conspiracies. He was so happy when Seumas asked for my hand. Downright gleeful to get rid of me."

"Smart girl." Which reminds me. "Did Quinlin tell you the plan?"

"Oh, yes. And not to worry, I won't say a word."

The plan involved telling everyone in Fae I'd found Morwenna hidden in the human world. She'd been kidnapped by a rogue Russian Fae that Quinlin dispatched. Quinlin's brother's can't tell the truth or they'd risk starting a war with the Scottish and Welsh Courts.

Before Quinlin takes Morwenna back, he returns me to my

apartment. No sense for me to tempt Blane and Arlen by remaining in Fae any longer.

We arrive in my living room, but Quinlin keeps my hand. He stands close. "Once I talk to my father and the other Kings about King Alun, your exile will be revoked. You can live in Fae again."

I glance around. Even though it's shabby and sparse, it's home. I meet his gaze. "I don't want to live in Fae. I like... helping the people here. They need me." Before he could jump to the wrong conclusion, I hurry on. "But I'm not averse to visiting often. I'd like to attend my sister's wedding. And I'm not averse to having visitors either. I get lonely."

He smiles. "Then I better return so I can ensure you'll be allowed to attend."

Before he disappears, I remember his ring. I tug it off my thumb, but he won't take it.

"Keep it." He slides it back on my thumb. Then he pulls me toward him and kisses me deeply. It ends way too soon. "When you're lonely, hold the ring up to your lips and say my name."

"What will happen then?"

"You won't be lonely anymore."

ORIGINAL ENDING:

Quinlin and Morwenna wait for me at the edge of the gloom. She squeals and throws her arms around me in a rib-cracking hug.

"Are you all right?" I ask, holding her out at arm's length so I can examine her. She's wearing a purple satin gown. It's torn and filthy, but no wounds mark her skin.

"I've missed you so much!" she says.

"I'm sorry I was such a brat," I say to her.

"Don't apologize. Father was truly awful to you."

"At least you'll soon be safe from him as well," I say. "But I left you to deal with him. Did he use you as a patsy for his schemes?"

"He tried."

"And?"

She laughs. "I played dumb. Drove him crazy when I acted clueless and oblivious to his elaborate conspiracies. He was so happy when Seumas asked for my hand. Downright gleeful to get rid of me." Morwenna does a victory dance.

Quinlin was right. Even ruined, the purple gown swishes when she moves. My body numbs with shock. How did he know it swished? It's one thing to be told she was wearing a purple gown, but that detail seemed...

"Oh, dear," Morwenna says, studying my face. She tries to hide a smirk. "I think Gwen finally caught on."

"Took her long enough. I was beginning to get bored," Quinlin says.

"All...this." I swallow as my stomach boils with nausea. "All...a ruse?"

"More like a game with lots of players," Quinlin says. "Although the ending was uncertain. I thought for sure Torin would kill you. Consider it payback."

I'd fallen for their tricks. The clues were so obvious with hindsight. Morwenna's blanket. The timing of Seumas' and King Declan's arrival. Only two guards by the dungeon. The years in the human world and my desire to return have dulled my edge. My father's voice, *It's what Fae do*, echoes in my mind over and over.

"I'll take my ring back." Morwenna yanks it off my thumb. She slides it onto her index finger.

Quinlin wraps an arm around her shoulders. "We've been married for a year." He pauses. "Aren't you going to congratulate us?"

I summon my strength. "Good luck, you'll need it because, really, how can you ever trust each other? At least you deserve each other." As I say the words, I believe them. I know I'll be hurting for a long long time, but I've learned another important lesson. "Take me home."

Quinlin returns me to my living room. With a mock salute, he disappears. I scan the room. All is in order. Caleb's thugs haven't come back. Not yet. I've only been gone for a few days, and I'm exhausted.

I'm cutting a huge slice of shoo-fly pie, when a harsh knock sounds. Peering through the peephole, I relax. I open the door, inviting the old...Mrs. Miller inside.

She beams at me. "I'm sorry to bother you, but I was worried when I noticed your car hasn't moved for three days."

"I've been sick with a cold. But I'm feeling much better now." Which was true. In Fae it was all an endless game, but here, I could make an honest living. "Will you stay and have some tea with me?" I ask.

SWORD POINT

Back in 2008, vampires were all the rage due to the overwhelming popularity of Twilight. *Invited to submit to an anthology of vampire tales titled,* The Eternal Kiss: 13 Vampire Tales of Love and Desire, *I had mixed feelings. I didn't want to jump on the vampire "band wagon." Also, it would be challenging to write about love-sick vampires. However, the editor assured me the vampires didn't have to sparkle. Well, then. My interest rose and I did some research on vampires. Based on all accounts, vampires are strong and fast. From my sparring experience, I know you don't want to let your opponent get too close, and, unless you're super strong, once a vampire is close enough for you to drive a stake through its heart, it's too late for you. At the time, I'd been watching the 2008 Summer Olympics* every night—I'm still a big fan—*and I was so impressed by a US fencer named Mariel Zagunis. She won a gold medal with a saber. I'd dabbled with fencing, taking a class on how to fight with a foil. Combine those two things, and I sparked on the idea of using a wooden sword to keep a vampire from getting too close. This story ended up being a ton of fun to write and is another one of my favorites.*

SWORD POINT

Ava glanced at the grimy alley. *This can't be right,* she thought. Crushed newspapers, bags of garbage, and pools of muck lined the narrow street. But a faded sign with *Accademia della Spada* hung above the door.

Odd. A famous establishment located in the armpit of Iron City.

She hitched her equipment bag higher on her aching shoulder and headed toward the building. Since she lived in the suburbs across town, it had taken her over an hour to reach this place by bus. Ava pulled her coat's hood over her head as cold rain drops dripped from the night sky.

An unsettled feeling rolled in her stomach. She should be ecstatic and thrilled. This was a dream come true. Perhaps the combination of the location and the rainy Monday had doused her excitement.

A prickle of unease raised the hairs on her arms. She paused, certain someone watched her, but the teenager lounging on a stoop across the street had his hoodie pulled down over his face as if asleep.

When she spotted two large blue eyes staring at her, she

smiled in relief. A young boy peered at her through the dirty window of the building next to the Academy. He hid behind his mother when Ava drew closer.

Through the window, Ava recognized a karate dojo. Parents sat in folding chairs as their children, clad in oversized uniforms with bright colored belts, kicked in unison. A young man with a black belt wove between them, correcting postures or giving praise. His shoulder-length hair had been pulled back into a ponytail, revealing a tattoo on his neck. The two black marks resembled Chinese calligraphy.

Ava lingered by the window, observing the lesson. *I'm not procrastinating. I'm learning. That shuffle-kick is very similar to fencing footwork.*

The teacher paired the children, and they practiced kicking into a pad. Ava caught the teacher's attention and he scowled at her. She jerked away as if she'd been slapped and continued to the Academy.

The elaborate stone entrance was marred with graffiti. She wrinkled her nose at the smell of urine and pressed the buzzer.

"Name?" The intercom squawked.

"Ava Vaughn."

The ornate door clicked open. The depressed inner-city exterior hid a modern fencing studio. Amazed, Ava stared. In the wide open space, students in white fencing gear sparred on long thin red strips. Others practiced lunges and attacks in front of mirrors. The ring of metal, the hum of voices, and the mechanical chug of fitness equipment filled the air.

An instructor carrying a clipboard approached. "Ms. Vaughn?"

She nodded.

He eyed her, clearly not impressed. "Change and warm up. Then we'll evaluate you."

Before he could shoo her away, she said, "But Bossemi—"

"Invited you, I know. Doesn't mean you'll train with him. You have to impress us first." He poked his pencil toward the locker rooms in the back.

As Ava changed clothes, she thought about the Three Rivers Regional Competition. She had fought well and won all her bouts, gaining the notice of Sandro Bossemi, a three-time Olympic Champion from Italy.

Fencers from around the world re-located just to train at the Accademia della Spada, which translated to the Academy of the Sword. Admittance to the school was by invitation only. Ava dreamed about training here.

However, reality proved to be another matter. Even though she had out-fenced all her opponents at the competition, the students at the Academy countered her efforts to spar them with ease. She couldn't even claim her youth as an excuse. A few fourteen and fifteen year olds trained here, making her feel old at seventeen. After her first night of practice, Ava doubted she would be asked back.

A moment of panic engulfed her. *What will I do?* She steadied her hyperactive heart. *I'll train even harder and Bossemi will invite me again.*

When she lost her last bout, Mr. Clipboard joined her. He had been evaluating her all evening. She braced for the dismissal.

"Tomorrow you'll work with Signore Salvatori," he said. He flipped a paper. "We'll arrange a practice time with your tutor. I'll need contact information."

It took her a moment to recover from her surprise. "I go to James Edward High."

"Oh." Scanning the page, he marked it. "Then you can have Salvatori's seven to ten p.m. slot. Do you speak Italian?"

"No, but I'm fluent in French." Since fencing bouts were officiated in French, she had been determined to learn it.

"Salvatori only teaches in Italian so you may want to learn a few words for your lessons each evening."

"Each?" Ava tried to keep up with the information.

"If we are to teach you anything, you're to be here every night, and from two to five on Saturday. You have Sunday off; Sandro Bossemi is a devout Catholic."

Dazed, Ava walked to the locker room. Conflicting emotions warred in her. She was thrilled to not be dismissed, but daunted by the training schedule.

By the time she changed, the room was empty. She would have loved to leave her heavy gear bag here, but she had school practice tomorrow afternoon. *Guess I'll be doing my homework on the bus.* When she calculated her travel time, she realized she would also be eating her dinner on the bus. *Peanut butter and jelly sandwiches with a side order of diesel fumes. Wonderful.*

Pulling out her cell phone, she called her mother.

"Donny's 24-Hour Diner, how can I help you?"

"I'd like an extra large banana split to go please," Ava said.

Mom laughed. "Ava, sweetie! How was practice?"

"Like a *Pirates of the Caribbean* movie, Mom. I pillaged and burned."

"Showing off on the first night isn't a good way to make friends." Her mother kept her tone light, but Ava knew the little dig was aimed at her.

For Ava, fencing had always come first. She didn't have time for friends she didn't need. Her mother disagreed.

Ava drew in a calming breath. "How soon can you pick me up?"

Silence. Her mother worked full-time and attended college classes at night, but to pay for Ava's training at the Academy, she scaled back her course load to one class so she could take another job as the night manager of Donny's.

You don't reach the Olympics without sacrifice.

"You can come during your dinner break," Ava prompted.

"Ava, I can't. I only get thirty minutes to eat. Can you get a ride? It could be a good ice breaker for making a friend."

Her fingers tightened on the phone. Her mother just wouldn't quit. Perhaps if she had an imaginary friend her mother would get off her back.

"I already made a friend," Ava said.

"Already?" Doubt laced her mom's voice.

"Yeah. Her name's Tammy, she lives in Copperstown. Her parents own the Copper Tea Kettle."

"Oh! The place with all those fancy teas?"

"Yeah. They're big tea drinkers. Look, Mom, I've gotta go. I'll get a ride with her. Bye." Ava closed her phone, and checked the time. Ten minutes until the next bus.

She left the locker room and almost ran into a group of fencing coaches, including Mr. Clipboard talking with the karate instructor. They all jumped back when they spotted her, and conversation ceased.

"Sorry. Didn't mean to surprise you," she said into the silence. No response. As she passed them, her back burned with their stares.

That was creepy. If the Karate Dude doesn't want people to watch through his window, he should buy curtains.

When she reached the bus stop, she dropped her heavy equipment bag on the sidewalk in relief.

"You lied to your mother," a man said behind her.

She spun. The Karate Dude stood five feet away, peering at her with loathing. "Tammy isn't one of the Academy students."

Anger flared. "You perv. You shouldn't be hanging around the girls' locker room."

"And you shouldn't have come here alone." His intent gaze pierced her body like the point of a sword. "Your kind is always overconfident," he said.

"My kind? Fencers?" Fear brushed her stomach. Perhaps this was one of those situations her mother warned her about.

"You can quit with the charade. I know what you are."

And he was a dangerous wacko. Should she scream or call the police? He put his hand in the pocket of his black leather jacket. Ava grabbed her phone, searching the street for help. No one.

The Karate Dude yanked out a bottle. In one fluid motion, he flipped the lid off and flung the contents into her face.

She yelped and swiped at her cheeks. *Acid?* Wiping her eyes in panic, she steeled herself for the pain. Nothing. A few drops of the liquid dripped into her mouth. Water?

Karate Dude's satisfied smirk faded.

"What the hell was that for?" she demanded. Ava dried her face on the sleeve of her coat, and smoothed her—now wet—blond hair from her eyes.

"You're not...I thought..." He sputtered and seemed shocked. "But you're so pale..."

Ava spotted the bus. "Stay away from me, you sicko freak, or the next time I'll call the police."

The bus squealed to a stop and the door hissed open. She grabbed her bag, sprinted up the steps, and dropped into the seat behind the driver. Glaring at the freak, she didn't relax until the doors shut and the bus drove away.

Ava dreaded returning to the Academy. All because of that Karate Freak. But it wouldn't stop her from going. Oh no. She loved fencing, and hoped to join gold medalist Mariel Zagunis in the record books. Mariel was a goddess! She was the first American woman in a century to win fencing gold with a saber. *A century!* Ava dreamed of doing the same with the foil.

She had competed with all three weapons, but a foil's bout with its feints, ducks and sudden attacks appealed to Ava more than the epee or saber. The sport fed her competitive streak, while the rhythm and cadence of the moves made her feel elegant and graceful. She even enjoyed researching the long history of the sport, which surprised her mother since anything not involving a foil in her hand tended to be done under protest and as quickly as possible.

Holding her cell phone—with 911 already dialed—in one hand, and her bag in the other, Ava stepped from the bus. With her thumb ready to push the send button, she scanned the street. A few parents hustled their kids to karate class, and two Academy students walked toward school.

Ava sprinted to catch up with the fencers. She trailed behind them despite their annoyed looks. When she spotted the Karate Freak teaching his class, she remembered to breathe. Once inside the Academy, she should be safe.

Mr. Clipboard seemed surprised to see her. Ava debated. Should she ask him about last night or not? He had been in the group talking to Karate Freak. He tapped his watch when she approached. She didn't have time. *I'll ask him later.*

By the time the session ended, Ava no longer cared about the Karate Freak. All she wanted to do was crawl inside a locker and hide. Salvatori hadn't spoken any of the Italian words she learned. Eventually, he stopped talking and used gestures for most of the session, adjusting her stance by touch.

He corrected everything she had learned from Coach Phillips. When she thought she had mastered a move, he proved her wrong. Frustrated and humiliated, Ava felt like a beginner again. Coach Phillips treated her like a professional, while Salvatori acted like he worked with an amateur. Perhaps she should ask for another coach.

At the end of the lesson, Salvatori dismissed her with a curt wave. Exhausted, she aimed for the locker room and stopped.

Karate Freak leaned against a side wall, watching her. No one seemed bothered by his presence, and Ava didn't have the energy to care. She changed in a hurry, wanting to leave before the Academy emptied.

Once again she armed herself with her pre-dialed phone. She was half way to the door before Karate Freak caught up to her. At least this time a few people milled nearby.

"Go away," she said, brandishing the phone.

"Look, Ava, I'm sorry about last night," he said.

He knew her name. She stepped back. *Wait a minute. Did he just apologize?* According to her mother, the male species was incapable of apologizing.

"I thought you were someone else." He pulled his hair away from his face, attempting to look sincere.

If he wasn't a freak, he'd be hot—grayish blue eyes, hawk nose and he appeared as if one of his parents was of Asian descent. But he overdid the whole karate warrior look with his tight black T-shirt and black jeans. Maybe she should call him the Ninja Freak. Either way, his explanation was lame. She remained unconvinced.

"I know it sounds weird. We've been having trouble with... another school. And I thought you were one of them, spying on us."

"So you threw water on me? That's weak. Get lost." She walked around him. But he trailed her.

"It's a long story, and you wouldn't believe it if I told you."

"Fine. Whatever. Apology accepted, now go away." She pushed through the door, hoping to leave him behind.

He kept pace with her. "At least let me make it up to you. How about a free lesson?"

"On how to be a jerk? No, thanks."

Unfazed, he gestured toward the school. "No. Isshinryu karate. You know, martial arts? All fencers should cross train. Karate is great for improving your reflexes and footwork."

"No." She didn't trust him.

"If this is about last—"

"Look, I don't even know you, and frankly, I don't have any interest." She continued to the bus stop.

He walked with her. "I can rectify one of those." He held out his hand. "I'm Jarett White, owner of the White Hawks Isshinryu Club."

Owner? He didn't look old enough, but she shook his warm hand. He held hers a moment past awkward.

"Your hand is ice cold." He studied her face as if that was a bad thing.

She pulled away. "It's November."

"How about a free session on self defense? It could help you around here."

"I really don't have time." Except Sunday, but that was her day to get everything else done. And her "to do" list spanned pages.

He considered. "Yeah. I guess Salvatori has you on the novice training schedule. That's brutal."

Despite her irritation, she was intrigued. "How do you know?"

"I trained with Sal for two years before Sandro took me on." His gaze grew distant. "Sandro helped me qualify for the Junior Olympic Fencing Championships."

Impressive. He must have been recruited by the best universities. "Where did you go to college?"

"I'm taking business classes at the community college."

She gaped at him in pure astonishment. With a fencing scholarship, he could have gone anywhere.

Jarett noticed. "I earned my black belt at age twelve, and I enjoy teaching karate. Plus I'm my own boss. How many twenty-year-olds can say that?"

Weak excuses. Ava felt sorry for him. Teaching a bunch of snot-nosed kids instead of competing at the Cadet level. He must have burnt out. Before she could remark, the familiar roar of the bus signaled its approach.

"You really shouldn't be taking the bus this late," Jarett said. "Or lying to your mother about getting a ride home, there's dangerous people downtown."

She hefted her bag. "I didn't lie to my mother." The bus's door opened, revealing the smiling red-haired driver. "Jarett, meet my friend Tammy." Ava gestured to the bus driver.

He gave her a wry grin. "Let me guess, her parents own the Copper Tea Kettle."

"Yep. And the most dangerous person I've met so far...is you." She stepped onto the bus.

Jarett saluted her with an imaginary sword. "Touché."

Much to Ava's annoyance, Jarett insisted on walking her to the bus stop every night. He'd talk about karate and fencing, but he always kept watch, scanning the area as if expecting an ambush.

After a few nights she actually looked forward to his company. And he agreed with her about Mariel being a goddess.

"She was added to the 2004 Olympic team as a replacement, then goes on to win the gold. How sweet is that?" He stabbed a hand in the air.

"Pretty sweet. To be at the Olympics has to be..." Ava searched for the word, but couldn't find the perfect one.

"Awesome."

She thought about Jarett's many talents. "Does your community college have a fencing program?"

"No. But I went to Penn State University for a year. Their coaches are excellent."

"Why didn't you stay?" The question just popped from her mouth. She wished she could erase it as his smile faded.

"I needed to be home. Some things are more important than fencing."

Ava found that hard to believe. *Nothing* was more important than fencing. *Nothing.*

Jarett was extra jumpy. He spooked at any noise, and stared at everyone who walked by them as they waited for the bus. There were more people out tonight than Ava had seen before. *Friday night.*

When he glanced around for the fourth time in a minute, she asked, "Why do you do that?"

"Habit. You should always know who is around you so you're not surprised."

"Sounds paranoid."

"Consider the first night I met you. You were completely oblivious to the fact I was right behind you all the way to the bus stop. I could have grabbed your bag and been gone before you even reacted."

"I have fast reflexes," she said.

"Consider how much faster you'd be if you knew a second sooner?"

She conceded the point. All too soon, the bus arrived. Ava mounted the steps with reluctance. She almost laughed out loud. Five days ago, she ran up these steps to get away from Jarett. Now she didn't want to leave. The door hissed shut behind her. Tammy gave her a distracted hello as Ava sat in her usual seat.

"Full bus tonight," she said to Tammy.

"Yeah. All the college kids from the 'burbs are headed downtown." She tilted her head to look into the big mirror above her and checked out the passengers.

Ava looked back. Groups of friends hung together, laughing and talking loudly. A few high school kids tried to look cool in front of the college kids. One kid sat alone, staring out the window. He wore a black hoodie with a grinning skull on it. When the bus pulled away from the curb, he waved to someone outside.

Settling in for a long ride, she pulled out her history book to study. It remained unopened in her lap. She was distracted by thoughts of Jarett and by Tammy glancing in her mirror every few seconds. Ava finally asked her why.

"There's a punk in a black hoodie. I think he's on drugs so I'm keeping an eye on him." Tammy said.

As Tammy slowed for the next stop, Ava turned around. The punk stared at her. Pale skin clung to his skeletal face. He grinned, displaying crooked teeth and black gums. Yikes.

"Got a runner," Tammy said with delight. Her hand hovered over the door switch. As soon as a runner reached the point that they might actually catch the bus, Tammy would shut the door and pull away.

"You're evil," Ava said.

"Everyone needs a hobby. He's getting closer...Wait for it... Wait for it...Ah, hell." She slumped back in her seat. "It's your friend."

Jarett bounded up the steps and dropped a token into the fare collector. "Thanks," he said, not even out of breath. He didn't acknowledge Ava, but she recognized his hard expression—the sword point. The same cold fury had burned in his eyes when he had thrown the water on her. But this time, he focused it on the grinning skull punk.

As the bus accelerated, Jarett knelt on the seat next to her, facing backward. "I thought I should make sure the bus was safe," he said. He kept his right hand inside his jacket pocket and his gaze never left Grinning Skull.

Ava suspected he knew the kid. When the bus reached the trendy downtown area, it emptied of students, leaving her, Jarett and the punk. They rode for a while in silence. Tension radiated, filling the air. Ava startled when the kid dinged the stop signal. Jarett jumped to his feet. Grinning Skull stood in the aisle, facing him.

Tammy opened the exit door in the middle of the bus.

"Next time," Grinning Skull said, waggling boney fingers at Jarett. In a blink, he was gone.

"I told you that guy was on drugs," Tammy said. "Did you see how fast he moved?"

Jarett relaxed into his seat as the bus drove away.

"A friend of yours?" Ava asked.

"No. He's a troublemaker in my neighborhood. When I saw him on your bus, I just wanted to make sure he didn't bother you."

Conflicting emotions fought in her chest. She was pleased at his concern but annoyed he thought she couldn't defend herself. "Don't you have other things to do? It's Friday night. Won't your girlfriend be mad?" *So lame!*

By his sly smile, Ava knew he saw right through her.

"No worries, my harem will wait for me," he teased. Then he sobered. "I wish. Between training, classes and work, there's no time for fun. I'm guessing it's the same with you. Although I'm sure the guys at your school must be lined up three-deep trying to get your attention."

"Of course." She flicked her long ponytail dramatically. "There's a daily fight over me in the hallways."

He laughed. The rich sound buzzed through her. She decided it didn't matter why he was here, she would just enjoy his company. For Ava, the ride home flew by.

Ava used the access code Mr. Clipboard had given her to enter the now-empty Academy. Her mother followed, exclaiming over the equipment. Ava had two hours until her lesson with Salvatori, but a ride downtown from her mother was worth the wait. Plus her mother wanted a tour of the school.

"I'll pick you up after my economics class." Her mom left.

The silent studio gave Ava the creeps. She should warm up and practice before the others arrived, but she hesitated outside the dark locker rooms. Instead of changing, she explored the Academy. A few of the coaches' offices lined the far left wall. Bulletin boards with flyers decorated the space between them.

Ava discovered a hallway in the far left corner of the building. Here the modern renovations ended and the original wood floor and arched windows remained. Half-moon-shaped stained glass transoms sat atop thick ornate doors. Curious to see what lurked behind this double wide entrance, Ava found Sandro Bossemi's private studio and office.

She entered. The office held the typical furniture and clutter. Foils, epees and sabers rested in the corners. A large, almost life-sized crucifix hung on the far wall with a realistic Jesus nailed to it. The poor guy was frozen with his face creased in agony and wounds bleeding. Yikes.

None of Bossemi's gold medals were on display. Disappointed, she returned to the corridor. Two other doors remained. One connected to Jarrett's office, which explained how he'd magically appeared in the studio. The room led to his dojo.

Through the open office door, she watched him teach a few adults. They failed to look as impressive in their white uniforms as Jarett did. His flexibility and speed was striking compared to their awkward attempts. How could she have thought he was a perverted jerk?

She returned to the Academy. The last door had *Vietato L'ingresso* written on it. *More Italian words I don't know. Probably an equipment room.* Ava turned the knob. Despite the strong smell of garlic, her guess seemed right, but the row of swords didn't glint in the weak light. She picked one up. The heavy weapon was made of wood and the tip had been sharpened to a nasty point. *I could stab someone with this.*

Bottles of water lined the shelves, matching the one Jarett had used when he threw water on her. Crossbows with wooden bolts hung on the wall. Even the points of the arrows were made of wood. Her queasiness turned into apprehension when she found crosses and wooden stakes. *This is beyond weird. It's bordering on serious mental illness. Did Bossemi believe in—*

"What are you doing in here?" Jarrett demanded.

Ava's heart lunged in her chest.

Before she could reply, he gestured to the door, "Can't you read?"

"Not Italian."

He tapped the words with his index finger. "*Vietato L'ingresso.* No admittance."

Ignoring her heart's antics, she shrugged. "If you really wanted to keep people out, you should lock the door."

He motioned her from the room, then shut the door when

she joined him in the hallway. "We need to be able to get in there quickly."

"Why? What're all those weapons for?"

He shook his head. "Not yet. Sandro decides who is ready or not."

She wanted to protest, but he changed the subject.

"I'm done with my class and you still have time before training. How about that self-defense lesson?"

Ava considered the incident last night. Perhaps he wouldn't be so protective if she agreed. Odd. The thought of walking to the bus alone didn't produce the relief she expected.

"Okay, but you have to answer one question."

Wariness touched his eyes. "What's the question?"

She had a million to ask, but knew he'd probably dodge most of them. Ava pointed to the left side of his neck. "What do your tattoos mean?"

He relaxed. "It's Okinawan for hawk. Isshinryu is an Okinawan marital art." Jarett guided her through the door and into his office. Framed pictures decorated the walls. He pointed to a photo of a red-tailed hawk. "Hawks are a symbol of victory. My sensei tattooed the characters onto his neck when he earned his black belt, starting a tradition."

"Your sensei?"

"Okinawan for teacher." He huffed in amusement. "Hang around here long enough and you'll learn Okinawan and Italian." He stopped before the mats and gestured to her feet. "No shoes."

She kicked off her street shoes and stepped onto the thin black foam. The mats interlocked like a jigsaw puzzle. Next to the main entrance, the window spanned the whole front of the dojo.

Jarett faced Ava and grabbed her wrist. His thumb overlapped his fingers. "Holy chicken wings, Batman. Don't you eat?"

She tried to jerk her arm free, but he held on.

"When we work on self-defense techniques, I'm not going to let you go unless you force me. Now, to break my grip, pull through my thumb. It's the weakest part of the hold." Jarett demonstrated.

Ava tried again and managed to free herself. They practiced a variety of wrist and arm holds for a while.

"You're stronger than you look," he said. "And quick to learn. Some of my students just don't get it."

He taught her how to break a bear hold and other body locks. Ava liked being held by him. He smelled of Polo Sport. When she managed to roll him off of her, she paused as a brief surge of pride followed an "ah ha" moment.

Jarett met her gaze and beamed. "If you know what to do, you can escape from anyone, no matter how big."

"What if they have a knife or a gun?"

"That's a whole other lesson. I'll show you next week."

The prospect thrilled her. When it was time for her fencing lesson, she cut through Jarett's office and noticed a framed photo propped on his desk. In the picture, Jarett stood next to an older Asian man. Both wore karate uniforms with black belts. Both had matching tattoos and the same shaped face.

"Is that your sensei or your father?" she asked.

Jarett plopped into his chair. "He was both." Sadness tainted his voice.

She frowned and tried to think of something appropriate to say.

"Looking for the perfect Hallmark words of comfort?" He gave her a wry grin. "They don't exist in this case. My father was murdered."

She thought she felt bad before. "That's horrible. Did the police arrest anyone?"

Jarett's expression hardened. "The killer was taken care of. We made sure of that."

A thousand questions lodged in her throat. Afraid of the answers, she swallowed them and retreated to the Academy.

The Saturday afternoon practice included a welcome change in routine. During the last hour, the coaches staged a mock tournament. Ava endured being embarrassed, but not because of her fencing skills. With just a week of training, her attacks and parries had vastly improved, surprising her. Signore Salvatori even gave her a "buono." High praise indeed.

No. The embarrassment came from her mother. She arrived in time to watch the bouts. Bad enough to have her mother there, but then the woman compounded Ava's mortification by cheering and hooting for her. Good thing the fencing mask hid her red face.

When Ava finally slinked from the locker room, she stopped in horror. Jarett was talking to her mother. *Just kill me now.*

She rushed over, intent on hustling her mother out the door.

"...did you see her feint-disengage attack? It was perfect," her mother exclaimed.

Ava jumped into the conversation. "It wasn't perfect, Mom. I didn't win any bouts."

Her mother swept her hand as if waving away a fly. "It's just a matter of practice, persistence, and experience."

Ava rolled her eyes. *Mom's such a dork.*

"I like that. Can I tell it to my students?" Jarett asked. He even managed to appear sincere.

Bonus points.

Her mother blinked at him for a few seconds. "Ah...sure." She cleared her throat. "I'm sorry, I thought you trained here."

"I do, but I teach karate, too."

"Oh."

"Did you have trouble parking?" Ava asked her mother, hoping the change in topic would get her moving away from him.

"Not at all, but, Ava... Do you think you can get a ride home with Tammy?"

"Why?"

"A few of my classmates invited me to dinner nearby." Her mother practically bounced on the balls of her feet in excitement.

Ava was tired, hungry, and had been looking forward to a quick ride home. She opened her mouth to complain, but stopped. Her mother had already read Ava's disappointed expression. She no longer bounced.

If Ava said she couldn't get a ride, her mother would skip dinner to take her home. She couldn't even recall the last time her mother did something for herself. She had given up her social life for Ava, and her daughter had been too focused on fencing to notice.

So why did I realize this now? Jarett. Perhaps the water thrown in her face had woken her up. A good thing. Now the only other things she had to worry about were punks on the bus, and strange wooden stakes in Bossemi's closet.

"Sure, Mom. I'll get a ride."

Delight flashed in her eyes. "Thanks sweetie. See you at home!" She kissed Ava's forehead and swept out the door.

"Sweetie?" Jarett smirked.

"Don't start."

"That was pretty clever. You told her you'd get a ride home, but didn't say how, so technically you didn't lie to her. Does Tammy work Saturdays?"

"No." She dug in her bag for the bus schedule. She'd missed the five fifteen bus by ten minutes, and the next one wasn't due until six thirty. Her stomach grumbled. She hunted for money, finding only a few bucks. "Is there a hot dog cart around here?"

He winced. "Hot dogs? No wonder you're so thin. You should be eating healthy foods."

She clamped down on a laugh. He'd probably have a fit over her daily diet of junk food.

Despite his protest over her food choices, he led her to a local food stand. The shoppers had gone home, and it was too early for the theater crowd, so the area was empty. Jarett set a quick pace, and Ava hustled to keep up.

On the way back to the bus stop, Jarett entertained her with stories about his karate students.

"...little guy was so proud of his new move, he ran over to his father and kicked him right in the... Damn." Jarett grabbed her upper arm. "Listen," he said in a tight voice. "If I tell you to run, you run to the Academy. Understand?" He talked to her, but he watched three figures walking toward them.

"Yes, but—"

"Not now." He squeezed once and let go. Reaching inside his jacket, he pulled out a mini crossbow, loaded a small bolt and aimed it at them. "Don't come any closer," he said.

They stopped. A street light illuminated their pale and gaunt faces. Resembling half-starved street punks, they wore ripped baggy jeans that sagged around thin waists, exposing colorful boxers. A ton of bling hung from their necks on thick gold chains. Hoods had been pulled up.

Ava recognized Grinning Skull from the bus. His friend's shirt had skeletons playing in a band on it, and a cobra design wrapped around the punk on the right's sleeve.

"You can only shoot one of us before we move," Grinning Skull said. "That leaves two and I doubt your girlfriend is armed."

Ava's stomach twisted as the small bit of confidence she had gained by learning a few self-defense moves fled.

"She knows nothing about this," Jarett said. "Her bus will be here soon. Once she goes, we can...talk."

Skeleton Band cackled. The sound scraped like glass against stone. "You didn't tell her about us? What a naughty boy you've been Jarett White Hawk. Tsk, tsk."

"Irresponsible," Cobra agreed. "Jarett'll pay with his life. Like father like son."

"And the girl?" Skeleton Band asked.

"Ours." Grinning Skull looked at Ava with hunger.

Ice pumped through her veins yet she felt hot and sweaty.

The three advanced.

"Run," Jarett ordered. He shot the crossbow, hitting Cobra in the stomach.

Before she even moved, the punks flickered. One second they stood fifteen feet away, the next they surrounded Jarett and Ava. *Like a cartoon. Except this is like a badly-drawn horror cartoon.*

Jarett dropped the crossbow, pulled a bottle from his pocket, and tossed water into Skeleton Band's face. The punk shrieked as his skin melted and steamed.

Another flicker and Grinning Skull grabbed Ava in a steel grip. She couldn't move. Panicked, she yelled for Jarett, but he was caught tight by Cobra who appeared fine despite the bolt still in his stomach. Grinning Skull opened his mouth. The putrid stench of decay gagged her. He bent close to her face. She cringed as his ice-cold cheek brushed hers.

When he bit her neck, she screamed. She never thought she'd be the kind of girl to scream, but terror and pure revulsion had built inside her to such a degree that screaming was the only way to release it.

Grinning Skull pushed against her as if slammed from behind. He grunted and went slack, knocking Ava to the ground. He landed on top of her. A dead weight. She stared at his face and nausea boiled up in her throat. The skin disintegrated before her eyes, peeling off the bone, which crumbled into powder.

Ava kicked the dusty clothes off of her. She wanted to puke, to scream, to faint, but she held it together and focused on Jarett and Bossemi. The master fencer held a wooden sword. Two piles of clothes lay at his feet—the remains of Cobra and Skeleton Band.

Bossemi gestured to the clothes and shoes. Jarett swept them up.

"Al'interno. Rapidamente!" He barked before running to the Academy.

Ava scrambled upright and followed him with Jarett fast on her heels. When the door shut behind them, they sagged with relief.

"Sandro, I'm—" Jarett started.

"Idiota." Bossemi turned to Ava. "Andiamo… Come. We must clean your wound."

In all the excitement, she had forgotten about the bite. Pain throbbed when she touched her neck. Blood coated her fingers. Her vision blurred, but a sharp order from Bossemi snapped her out of it. She didn't even realize Jarett supported her until they reached his office.

She met Jarett's gaze. He looked miserable. But she didn't have time to question him. Bossemi instructed her to lie down flat on his couch. He put a towel under her neck.

"This will hurt," he said.

When he brandished a spray bottle and metal hook-shaped

tool, she closed her eyes. He might not have much of a couch-side manner, but he was honest. It hurt. By the time he had cleaned the bite and bandaged it, tears had puddled in her ears.

Jarett sat on the edge of the couch, holding her hand. Bossemi dumped the blood-soaked towel into a hamper.

"Tell her what she needs to know," Bossemi said. "I'll organize a watch." He handed Jarett his wooden sword, then left.

Jarett stared at the weapon with resignation.

Ava pulled her hand away from his and struggled to a sitting position. She wanted answers. "Talk. Now."

He sighed. "At least I don't have to convince you they're real."

"The punks?"

His gaze focused on the life-sized crucifix. "Not punks. Vampiros."

Vampiros. Italian for 'vampire'. Instinctively, she wanted to protest—vampires populated horror novels and movies, not real life. But she couldn't explain how the punks disintegrated into powder. "Go on," she said.

"They've been around since biblical times," Jarett said.

Ava remembered the attack. "But they flickered and were so strong." She shuddered.

"That's why we use swords and crossbows. If they grab you, you're almost as good as dead."

"What about the stakes I saw in the closet?"

"We use those during the day. We hunt them while they sleep. Safer that way."

"We?"

"The Hawks. Sandro taught us how to find and fight the vampiros. He recruits candidates from the fencers he invites to his school. Some join us. Others leave. And some won't get recruited at all."

"Would I have been recruited?"

He considered. "If I hadn't messed it up, probably not."

"How did you... Oh."

"'Oh' is right. I thought you were a vampiro. You're pale and thin. I wasn't the only one." He sounded defensive. "The other coaches suspected you too. Plus we had just attacked one of their nests, and thought you were trying to get revenge."

"A nest of them? How many vampiros are there?" she asked.

"There are nests in most of the major cities of the world. The Hawks are there too. It's an on-going battle. Sometimes we manage to wipe out an entire cluster, and sometimes they get to us first."

Ava remembered his sad story. "Did they kill your father?"

Jarett's body tensed and his grip tightened on the sword. "Yes. They drained his blood, starving his brain of oxygen. Once the brain dies, a demon takes possession of the body. It's not like in the movies. Police don't find a bloodless corpse. There is no burial and no dramatic rising from the dead. The victim just changes. They lose weight, becoming pale, nocturnal creatures."

She followed the logic. "Then your father is a..." She couldn't say the word.

"Not anymore." Anguish strained his voice. He closed his eyes. "He came to visit me at school. They go after their relatives and friends first. I knew as soon as I saw him."

Ava waited. Despite the obvious outcome, Jarett needed to tell the story.

"My father had been a Hawk all my life. We moved from city to city, hunting vampiros. But I didn't want to join the Hawks. I wanted to fence. I was selfish and my father died."

"You can't blame—"

"Yes I can. I'm the one who flung the holy water on him. He dissolved before my eyes."

She searched for the appropriate words. What did Jarett call them? Hallmark words. She didn't think she would find a sorry-your-father-was-a-vampire sympathy card. Instead she asked him why the vampiros disintegrated.

"The demon keeps the body alive. Once the demon is killed, the body is destroyed. The older they are, the faster they go. If they're very new, we use extra holy water to help them along."

They sat for a while in silence. Ava's wound burned and pulsed. She touched the bandage.

"You better call your mom and tell her you won't be home tonight," Jarett said.

"Why?"

He braced as if about to deliver bad news. "You need to stay here until the venom runs its course. Sandro cleaned your wound, but the vampiro's saliva mixed with your blood."

Her insides twisted. "Will I—"

"No. You're not going to turn into a vampire. But they know you've been bitten, and they'll come for you."

That was truly horrifying. "Aren't we protected?" Ava gestured toward the crucifix.

"No. The wood has to touch them."

Bossemi burst into the room, panting and brandishing another wooden sword. "The Accademia...surrounded."

Jarett shot to his feet. "The Hawks?"

"On the way." He inclined his head toward Ava.

"She believes."

"Buono." Bossemi tossed Ava his sword. She caught it in mid-air. He thumped a finger on his chest. "Aim for...il Cuore."

Her own heart increased its tempo, signaling its desire to retreat.

"She doesn't know how—" Jarett began.

"Vampiros will break-in before Hawks arrive. Andiamo!" Bossemi raced across the hall, stopping at the equipment room. Leaving the door unlocked now made horrifying sense. Jarett armed himself with holy water and Bossemi grabbed another sword.

The loud crackle of breaking glass cut through Ava. She clutched her weapon to her stomach, which threatened to expel her dinner.

Bossemi and Jarett exchanged a surprised glance. They positioned themselves by the door to the dojo. Ava stayed behind them to protect their backs.

"They're bold. What did you do?" Bossemi asked Jarett.

"I killed Vincent."

"Idiota! I told you to wait. You can't kill the leader without taking out the entire nest."

"He murdered my father. I—" His argument was cut short by the arrival of the vampires.

Ava marveled at Bossemi's lethal speed. Between him and Jarett, the doorway filled with dusty clothes. A splitting noise sounded behind Ava, she turned in time to see the boarded up windows of the Academy open and dark figures climb inside.

She yelled, "Vampiros!"

Jarett joined her at the end of the hallway as the two vampiros flickered. Bossemi remained by the dojo's door. Ava held her weapon with the point down, backing up as a vampire stalked her.

"En garde, Ava. Attack!"

Jarett's order broke through her fear. She raised the tip and lunged, stabbing the point into the vampire's heart. But there was no time to reflect on her action, as another vampire sprinted toward her.

Time blurred. Her arms ached from wielding the heavy

sword and her breath puffed. But she kept the sword's point moving. If a vampiro grabbed her weapon, she would be done.

The three of them had found a good defensive position. The studio filled with other vampires. The Hawks had arrived, but even more vampiros poured into the room. The sheer number of vampires soon overpowered and disarmed the Hawks. The ones attacking Jarett and Ava stepped out of range. Bossemi stood behind her.

"We have seven of your members, Sandro. All we want is Jarett White Hawk and Ava. Two for seven. You can't beat that."

Ava glanced at the captured Hawks. She recognized Signore Salvatori and Mr. Clipboard. They both shook their heads 'no' when she met their gaze. They were willing to give up their lives for her. *Why?*

"Leave Ava alone and I'll come," Jarett said. He dropped his sword.

"No." The word burst from Ava's mouth. She didn't want to lose him. He was right, some things were more important than fencing. His life and the lives of all the Hawks.

"Tirer le signal d'incendie," Bossemi whispered in a language Ava understood—French.

She tossed her weapon to the floor.

"Ava, you are *not* going with them," Jarett said.

"Shut up! I'm tired of taking orders from you." She pushed him, giving him a pointed look. "First you assume I'm one of them." *Push.*

He caught on, and backed up.

"Then you nag me about taking the bus." *Push.*

The vampiros watched them with amusement.

"And you don't even warn me about these things!" She shoved him hard. He fell to the floor with a solid thump as she reached the fire alarm. She yanked the handle down.

Ear splitting bells pierced the air. Everyone hunched against the noise, but the vampires remained unharmed. Ava appealed to Bossemi. He held up a finger as if to say wait.

The sprinkler system switched on. Water sprayed and the vampires began to melt.

"I never thought they'd dare attack me in my Accademia," Bossemi said. "But having a priest bless the water in my fire system, just in case, seemed like a good idea."

Jarett whooped and hugged Ava.

"You will now train with me," Bossemi said to Ava.

"To be a Hawk?"

"Do you want to be one?"

Ava didn't hesitate. "Yes."

"Maybe. Maybe Olympics first, then a Hawk. We'll see." He moved away, shouting orders in Italian.

Surprised by his comment, Ava pulled away from Jarett so she could see his face. "But you—"

"Would never have qualified for the Olympic team. Once I realized the truth, I decided to stay here and be a Hawk."

"Does that mean Bossemi believes I might qualify?"

He smirked. "It's just a matter of practice, persistence, and experience, Sweetie."

She groaned and punched him in the gut.

MONGRELS

When I finished writing Mongrel, I asked my daughter to read it because I was worried the story was too..."out there." She handed it back to me and said, "Where's the rest?" She enjoyed it, but thought there should be more. I had a word count limit and a deadline and was happy with where the story ended. However, over the years, many of my readers have also asked, "Where's the rest?" And now I can finally respond, "Here it is!" A brand new short story for my loyal readers. For this story, the challenge was to stop myself from going into "novel writing mode."

MONGRELS

Fire blooms under my skin right where Logan's teeth sink into my wrist. He pulls away. Blood stains his lips. My blood. I meet his gray-eyed gaze as needles of torment climb my arm. My pups whine and press against my legs.

"What's happening?" I whisper—all I can manage.

"Transformation."

The agony inside my flesh sizzles toward my neck.

Logan grabs my shoulders. "I've got you."

I open my mouth but snap it closed when my boiling blood aims for my heart.

"I've got you." Logan repeats.

Sharp claws dig into my heart. A level of pain well beyond ten takes my breath and all rational thoughts away. I collapse as my heart is torn into pieces, sending scalding hot pokers to my extremities.

My world shrinks to a ball of anguish. I'm burning alive, being devoured from the inside out. I cling desperately to the ashes of my soul, but even they are consumed.

~

I don't even get a chance to tie on my apron before Vinny is bellowing at me from the kitchen. Weaving through the piles of take-out boxes, barrels of pickles, and crates of vegetables, I walk into the acrid fog of hot grease, sizzling beef, and Vinny's Aqua Velvet aftershave. Having an enhanced sense of smell isn't always a good thing.

"What's the problem?" I ask. "I've tables to prep."

The owner and top chef of Vinny's Burger Joint flips a burger without looking at the grill because he's too busy scowling at me. At fifty-years old, round, bald, and with muscular forearms covered in tattoos, he's a living cliché.

"Someone broke into the bakery down the street. That's the fifth break-in this month." He peers at me as if I'm the culprit. "I don't want you feeding my leftovers to the homeless anymore."

His two statements don't connect in my mind. "Why not?"

"I don't want them breaking into my joint, stealing my stuff."

He's a typical human, making unsubstantiated leaps of logic. Unsubstantiated means not supported or proven by evidence.

"Vinny, you ever think that the reason your business *hasn't* been targeted is because of the homeless people?"

He pauses. "Well, I don't like them hanging around all the time."

If I strangle him, could I claim I saved the world from more stupidity? "They don't *hang* around. They come after we close. And they keep an eye on your place at night."

"How do you know?" he demands.

I give him a flat stare.

His expression softens. "Sorry, Mongrel, I forgot."

He could, but I'll never forget those two years I spent living on the streets.

"All right, you can keep feeding them. Go on, now. The lunch crowd'll be here soon."

I touch his arm in thanks. He grunts, but his heart isn't in it. Despite his bluster, Vinny is good people. He gave me a job when I had no experience. I hurry to set up the tables. Already a few customers have arrived. As I take orders and deliver the best damn burgers and fries in town, I think about the break-ins. Is that something I need to tell the pack? If so, that means I have to interact with them and not ignore them like I've been doing.

I trust Logan, the pack's alpha. He was the one who bit me and turned me into a werewolf eight months ago. The others... Well, here's a sampling of the comments I heard when I met them for the first time in my wolf form:

"She reeks. I think she might be white underneath all that grime."

"Too light to be of any use for night ops."

"She's adorable!" (This one rankled. I've seen werewolves and fought them. Adorable wouldn't be the word I'd use.)

"Look at those smelly dogs with her. I hope they don't yap all night long."

"She's so tiny. Is she even a werewolf?"

"Size doesn't matter. Sharp teeth and claws are all you need. As long as you have the gumption to use them."

"Did you see the way she cowered behind Logan? No gumption."

They had to know I could hear them, but they didn't care as they pressed close to gawk at me. Why did I expect werewolves to be better behaved than a bunch of high school kids? And I wasn't cowering. I was just overwhelmed. First time in wolf form isn't fun. There's no colors—everything is in shades of gray, the smells are strong enough to singe the hairs in your nose, and the sounds are deafening. Good thing I've learned how to tune most of it out.

I head to table four to get their drink order and stop in my tracks. A familiar, sickening odor hits me full force. My ex-foster father and a young teen are sitting at the table. He's studying the menu and hasn't seen me. I make a U-turn and duck behind the counter.

Flagging down Geena, the other waitress, I ask her to take table four.

"Is something wrong? Do I need to call Louie?" she asks.

Vinny's son, Louie is six foot five inches tall and enjoys tossing rude customers out on their asses.

"No. He's just someone I'd like to avoid." And tear into tiny pieces with my sharp teeth and claws. How's *that* for gumption?

"All right."

I cover table one for her. There's no danger of the beast, a.k.a. my ex-foster father noticing me. Waitresses are translucent. Translucent means allowing light, but not detailed images to shine through. Customers interact with us, but they don't really see us. (And, yes, translucent is one of the Graduate Equivalent Degree's vocabulary words. Also, yes, I passed the test.)

I keep an eye on the beast. He should be in jail, but the police and social workers and even the fancy lawyer the pack hired all said there was no proof of sexual assault. My claims were unsubstantiated. It was his word against mine. I shouldn't have waited two years to report him.

Live and learn, they say. Whoever *they* are. Learn, I did. And I'm still learning. Here he sits with another foster girl. Even after my report. Oh no. This won't do. This time I'm not waiting two years.

When he goes to the restroom, I slide into his seat. The young teen squeaks in surprise. She's thirteen, maybe fourteen. His scent is mixed with hers and I have to clamp down hard on my wolf.

"You need to report him to your social worker," I say.

Her expression changes in an instant. She knows exactly what I mean.

"I...can't." Her gaze drops.

"You can. Your social worker will take you out of the house right away and he won't hurt you or anyone else anymore."

She glances up. "My younger brother loves him. He promised to adopt him and send us to college if I...cooperate."

"He's a pedophile and a liar. You need to report him for both you and your brother's sake. Be brave."

Now she meets my gaze. "Were you brave?"

"No. I ran away."

"Then how can you expect me to be brave?"

The door to the men's room squeals. My time is up. But I'm not done. Not at all.

The rest of the day passes by in a blur. My thoughts swirl with possible ways to help that girl and her brother. Is it considered kidnapping if I rescue them? I'm so distracted that I don't notice that my usual group of homeless people are not waiting for me by the dumpster in the back alley that evening.

Instead, three men step from the shadows. I drop the bag of burgers. My wolf is poised to take over.

"Easy there, Mongrel. We only want to talk." The man in the middle spreads his hands to show he's unarmed.

I know better. He's a wolf and so are the other two. I'm outnumbered and trapped and we all know it. "So talk."

He gives me a slimy smile. "You've been bitten by two alpha werewolves, do you know what a rare creature you are?"

"My mother always said I was special." I can't remember

my mother, but I like to think she would say that.

"Cute. But I think you've no idea. Otherwise, you wouldn't be working for minimum wage at this greasy spoon." He pauses.

"Well, go on, enlighten me."

"She certainly has the attitude," mutters the guy on his left.

Middleman shoots him a sour look, but turns his pleasant I-just-want-to-talk face back to me. "You're beyond dominant. An alpha of the alphas. You should be in charge. Not just of *your* pack, but *all* the packs."

I laugh. Obviously he missed the intel where I'm half the size of Logan. This is not the expected response. He shifts his weight and clears his throat. I wait.

"We're here to invite you to be the alpha of our pack."

I've no desire to be an alpha, but I am curious. "What about your current alpha?" I ask.

"Logan killed him."

Ah, *that* pack. The one who attacked me and Logan when he was injured. "No thanks."

"Our pack has plenty of money. You won't have to live in a small ground level apartment—"

"No, thanks." My words are strong, but inside my heart thumps out a warning. They know where I live. And for the record, I like being on the ground level. There's a big sliding glass door for my pups to go outside to the enclosed courtyard.

"But this job—"

"I like it. Honest work is good for the soul."

"This is a waste of time," the guy on the right says.

Middleman sighs. "Will you at least think about it?"

I should have said yes. But I'm a stubborn idiot. "No. Go away."

In one quick motion, the guy on the left pulls out a tranquilizer gun and shoots. At the pfft sound, my wolf dodges the dart. She calls me to shift, but, by the time I do, I'll be a pincushion. The other two men rush me, pinning me against the wall.

I struggle as the gun's nozzle swings toward me. No. Not gonna be helpless ever again. I drop my weight, surprising them enough that they let go. I roll away, hop to my feet, and run. They give chase. There's nothing wolves love better than a game of chase.

Even in my human form, I'm faster and stronger. Not at superhero levels, but I could out run the world's fastest person. Except I can't outrun fellow werewolves. Which is why I only run to the front entrance of Vinny's. Diving through the door, I close it and throw the bolt, locking it just in time.

Geena stares at me. Her broom hovers in mid-sweep. "Mongrel, what—"

"Locked myself out," I say.

"Uh huh." She eyes the men right outside.

I wait. Are they going to break through the glass door? Make a scene? Middleman meets my gaze. There's a promise in his eyes as he backs away. They continue down the street. But it's not a win. Oh no. There's another ambush in my future. At least the next time I'll be ready.

Cutting through the kitchen, I open the back door to the alley and take a deep sniff. Ugh. The greasy fermented tang from the dumpster fogs the air. No werewolves. And no homeless. Those wolves must have scared them off. I pick up the bag of burgers and go inside.

"Vinny," I say.

"Yeah?" He doesn't look up from cleaning the grill.

"I need to take the next couple days off."

"What?" Now he glances at me. "Why?"

"Family emergency."

"You don't..."

I don't have a family. I don't ask for days off, except for one day a month. I work opening to close seven days a week, all to save money for college. I wait for Vinny to put it together.

"Yeah, sure." A pause. "Let me know if you need my help."

Warmth spreads in my chest. "Thanks, Vinny."

"Yeah, yeah. Get on outta here. I'm not paying you to stand there and jaw all day."

Jaw means to talk. No, not a GED vocabulary word, but Vinny slang. I finish helping Geena and say good night.

After checking that I'm not being followed, I head to my old squat. I had a sweet spot underneath the railroad bridge, but I'm more focused on the scattering of burn barrels and homeless people warming their hands. Nights in October can get pretty cold.

Handing out the burgers, I ask about the break-ins. Do they know who's behind them?

"It's one of those protection schemes," an older woman says between puffs of her cigarette. "They break in, ransack the place, and steal the petty cash. Then they send in their goons-in-suits the next day to offer protection from future break-ins."

"Yeah, for a monthly fee," says another in disgust. "They rake in the money 'cause the business owners are too scared to stand up to them. A bunch of sheep."

"I'd be scared too," chimes a gaunt man. "They can run you outta business, man. And guess where you end up next?" He spreads his hands wide, indicating our surroundings.

"Has this been going on for a while?" I ask.

"Naw. This is new," cigarette lady says. "But it's a cancer. Soon every place in downtown will be under their control."

"Yeah, and no more burgers from Vinny's." Gaunt man licks the grease from his fingers.

As I leave the abandoned parking lot, the instinct to protect my town races through my blood like fire. It never seems to end. There's always someone trying to take what isn't theirs. Like those werewolf goons and a certain ex-foster father.

I find a dark secluded spot, remove my clothes, and hide them. Shivering in the cold air, I call my wolf. She arrives as if she'd been waiting backstage for her time on center stage. She's always ready. It's strange. A shifting of souls, but both mine. It's painful—a seven out of ten. But Logan promised each time it will hurt less.

Once the shift is complete, I stretch like a dog. Now that I have my full wolf senses, I sniff the air, seeking dangers. No way I'm gonna show up at my apartment in my human form and be caught off guard again. I set off at a quick trot, keeping to the shadows even though my coat is silver. Not as bright as being white. And *not* adorable. I prefer handsome.

None of the other wolves in the pack are my color. Most are dark grey. The others are dark brown, black, and one is a deep russet. The other alpha who bit me was a tawny color. I wonder if being bitten by two alphas is the reason I'm different. And that makes me think about the other pack and their claims that I'm an alpha of the alphas. No way that's possible. The last thing I want is to be in charge.

I slow as I approach the apartment building, seeking the werewolf goons. I do a wide loop around it. A tightness in my chest eases when I'm unable to find any ambushers.

The five-story red brick shoe factory has been renovated into apartments and is owned by the pack. All the residents are werewolves. And there's lots of extra perks. Like the doorman who opens the main locked door into the lobby when you don't have the fingers to type in the code.

"Good evening, Miss Mongrel," he says.

His tone is neutral, but curiosity swirls in his gaze. Probably because I'm late and I'm in wolf form. He escorts me to unit 101 and unlocks my door. I woof a thanks and go inside.

401

My five pups rush me, yipping and sniffing and dancing around my paws so I almost trip on them. I'm not in wolf form very often...well, except the full moon of every month, and they think it's *so very* exciting. I head to my bedroom to shift back to my human form. Company will be arriving soon.

I yank a sweater over my head and I'm pulling on a pair of jeans when the knock sounds right on time. Padding to the door with bare feet, I don't need to peer through the spyglass to know Logan waits on the other side. The doorman dutifully reported my unexpected late arrival to the pack's alpha, who lives in the penthouse.

"What happened?" he demands as he enters, ignoring the pup's over enthusiastic welcome.

At six feet tall, he's half a foot taller than me. Lean and muscular, he's wearing a pair of black sweat pants and a gray T-shirt. He's older than he looks. Much older, but you'd think he was in his mid-twenties. Another werewolf perk—eternal youth. His scent is a mixture of leather, pine, and sandalwood. Nice. I draw in a lungful before answering.

"There's been a series of break-ins downtown." I explain what I learned from my friends.

"We know about them. I've a few wolves looking into it. Why are you concerned? They haven't hit Vinny's."

"Yet. I should have been told about this." I'm outraged.

"If you attended the pack meetings, you would have been," he shoots back.

I deflate. The thought of all those people, staring, judging, murmuring their nasty comments... I shudder.

Logan's harsh expression softens. "I get it, Mongrel, I do. We've given you some space and time to adjust. But it's been eight months." He runs a hand through his black hair. "Perhaps you need to talk to a professional."

"I can't afford a shrink."

He growls. "We have plenty of money."

"And you paid for the lawyer, and you pay for this place. I don't want to owe the pack anymore."

"There's the problem right there," he says. "It's *our* pack, Mongrel. Not *the* pack. We're in this together. Remember? We're a bunch of mongrels."

I remember. But it's one thing to *say* it, another to *be* it.

He sighs. "Maybe you need to find another pack. One that you might connect with better."

Connect with strangers? That thought is horrifying. "I'd rather be alone." Then I laugh, taking Logan by surprise. "The cliché," I say. "You know...a lone wolf."

He smiles, but it doesn't last. Too bad. His smile warms me like my own personal burn barrel.

"Is that what you really want?" he asks.

Is it? I glance at my pups. They kept me company on the streets and I was fine. Well...not quite. Even when I thought Logan was just a giant Wolfhound, I enjoyed his company and it hurt like hell when he left.

"No."

"What do you want, Mongrel?"

"I want to be able to trust people again."

"Well, you'll never be able to trust everyone, but you can trust me and your pack mates."

"Are they my pack mates?"

"Of course. Why do you ask?"

A rare creature, Middleman said.

"Am I different because I've been bitten by two alphas?"

He hesitates. "Where did you hear that?"

A classic dodge. "When were you going to tell me?"

"Once you adapted to being a werewolf. Once you started asking more questions."

"I'm asking questions now."

"Why—" He stills. "You came home in wolf form. What scared you?" There's power in that question. My pups whine and hunker down in submission.

I'd like to tell him I wasn't scared, but... I all but had my tail between my legs. So I relay my back alley encounter with the goons. He keeps his expression neutral, but his fingers curl into fists and the veins in his neck pop.

When I finish, he erupts, "Christ, Mongrel. Why didn't you tell me this right way?"

"I'm here. Safe. And I'm more concerned about Vinny's."

"You shouldn't be." Agitated, Logan paces. "Yes, you are special because you've had two alpha sires. And I've no idea if that has any effect on you because there hasn't been anyone else with two alpha sires before. What the Mason wolves said is just speculation, Mongrel." He stops. "I've been waiting for you to..." He spreads his arms wide. "Become part of the pack before I told you. Before asking if you'd want to...see if you have any extra abilities."

That made sense. "But why did that other pack...Oh."

"Yeah, oh. They didn't want you as their alpha. They thought that would entice you." He huffs a laugh. "When that failed, they turned to plan B, grabbing you. Probably so they could experiment on you and take advantage of any special skills you might have."

A weird weakness flows through me and I sink onto the couch. My encounter with them was a near miss. Logan sits next to me. Without thinking, I lean against him and he tucks me close. I draw strength from him. Every single time he's visited me, he freely shared his special alpha waves.

"We won't let them get you, Mongrel. Can you call in sick the next couple of days?" he asks.

"I'm not going to hide."

"I know. But, by then, I'll have a few wolves available to

protect you."

"That doesn't solve the problem."

"You're right. We need to scare the Mason pack out of our territory. This town and the state park and game lands surrounding it are ours. Long claimed. However alphas are compelled to expand their packs by adding new members, claiming more territory. Well, most alphas. I'm not as driven and there are a few others like me—the new breed. Too bad, the Mason pack is determined to take me out."

"You or the pack?"

"Me. That's how alphas get new members. They kill another alpha and take their members."

"But that means the Mason pack should now be yours since you killed their alpha."

"Should be, but I was too weak when I killed him. Another alpha took hold of the pack bonds."

"Bonds?" A scary word. Am I bonded to Logan?

"A connection, a sharing of energy, the deep relationship like being part of a family...it's hard to explain. It's like...you with your pups. You'd do anything to protect them." He smiles. "Even fight five werewolves."

"But you said I could join another pack."

"You haven't bonded to the rest of our pack so you could go anywhere."

Not happening. "Scaring off that Mason pack won't solve the problem. They'll just keep coming back. You need to claim them."

"I can't."

"Why not?"

"I'm not strong enough. You saw what happened when I fought their last alpha. He would have killed me, except you interfered and saved my life."

I stabbed that alpha with a silver knife. Werewolves are

generally hard to kill. But silver is our kryptonite. We weaken immediately, and, if it's in us longer than a couple hours, it's good bye wolfie.

"What about their new alpha?" I ask, "You're back to full strength."

"He's stronger. And I...don't..."

"Want to kill someone?"

"Yeah." He gives me a self-deprecating smile. "I'm not a typical alpha. I'll defend myself, but I don't seek out other alphas. It's really just a matter of time before—"

"Don't say it!" The force of my words surprises us both. "There's another solution, we just haven't found it yet."

"We?"

"Shut up."

He laughs.

I promise Logan I won't go downtown for the next couple days. He wants me to stay at the apartment, but I've another problem to solve. And it's on the other side of town—a safe distance away from downtown burglars and Mason wolves.

As I gather what I think I'll need for my...op, I consider how best to stop my ex-foster father. It's similar to Logan's problem with the other alpha. I can't scare him off. Well... I could for a few days, but he'd claimed the temptation was too hard to resist. I can't kill him. Well... I could, but that'd be murder. Justified, in my opinion, but the courts wouldn't see it that way.

By the time I reach the nice suburban neighborhood, I've a rudimentary plan. I stash my bag in the woods behind the house. No one is home. Not yet. I know their routine. This is familiar ground.

My emotions cycle from bored to scared to anxious and around again, like I'm chasing my tail. Memories threaten to overwhelm me. I get flashes—my clueless ex-foster mother, sweet and stupid and so hurt when I accused her husband of rape—learning how to hunt—laughing by the campfire—the creak of the bedroom door. I shudder and focus on my plan.

There's a nice creek in the patch of woods behind the house. Before shifting, I stuff my clothes into my pack. Then I call to Mongrel the Wolf, letting her step into the spotlight. Your turn.

After the shift, I play in the creek, splashing and rolling in the mud until I'm a wet muddy mess—just in time for dinner.

The kitchen table is next to the double wide sliding glass doors, allowing a nice view of the yard surrounded by hickory trees. I whine and paw at the doors. Pressing my nose to the glass, I give the occupants a pleading look. The ex-foster parents have a soft spot for dogs.

The door opens. I whine again and shiver. "Oh, the poor thing," ex-foster mother says.

Gotcha.

After being hosed off and dried with a towel, I'm allowed to join the family (just until my owners are found). It's so... normal, yet my stomach is twisting into a thousand knots. The teen does her homework on the kitchen table and her brother plays video games with the beast. The house is just as I remember it—clean and neat. Nothing to indicate that a predator lives within.

I pad over to the teen and nudge her arm with my nose. She gives me a pat on the head as if not quite sure what to do. I meet her gaze and hold it. Uncertainty turns to recognition. I rest my head in her lap while leaning against her legs, trying to communicate that she doesn't need to be brave on her own.

My plan hits its first hurdle when the ex-foster father refuses to let me into the teen's bedroom that night. He puts me in the laundry room with a bowl of water and a bowl of stale kibble and closes the door, which has a doorknob and not a handle. Well, shoot.

I wait until one a.m. before I try turning the knob with my teeth. No luck. And my paws just slip off. Argh. Shifting doesn't take long, but it takes energy and it's painful. And I'd have to do it twice. I glare at my paw. All I need is a thumb and some fingers. Can I change just one body part? It won't hurt to try, right? Concentrating on my paw, I call a hand.

Pinpricks of pain dance over my paw as fingers grow from my claws. It feels just as weird as it looks. Trust me. My bones elongate and the fur recedes, turning into skin. I think I'm gonna be sick. No wonder I keep my eyes closed when I shift. I quickly open the door. And I'm not gonna try to explain how it is to walk with three paws and a hand. Ugh. Just...ugh.

But I'm glad I kept my hand as the door to the teen's room is closed, but not locked. There's no lock on this door and how I wished there were. Lying in that bed, I wished for dead bolts, chains, and a steel door. I imagined booby traps with poisoned darts, toxic gas, and knives shooting out of the sides. All to keep him from entering my room.

The teen whimpers when the door opens. A hot bolt of pure rage slices through me. Every muscle, every fiber of my soul longs to tear that man's throat out. I fight the desire, focusing instead on calling a paw to replace my hand. No need to freak her out.

Her back is to the door and she's huddled under the covers. Once again I consider murdering the beast. Would it really be murder? I think not.

I woof just loud enough for her to hear. She jerks up in surprise and turns on the lamp by her bed. We blink at each other for a moment.

"What... How..." she tries.

I jump on her bed and she skootches back. Nudging her cell phone on the night stand, I give her a *significant* look.

She glances at it and then back to me. "The phone?"

Go on, I urge silently. *Pick it up.*

It takes another nudge for her to pick it up. Then I glance at the bookcase before beaming another *important* gaze. When she fails to understand, I do it again, except after the bookcase, I nose her phone, and then make eye contact. After two more rounds, her expression finally clears.

Understanding is followed by fear. "I...can't."

Yes, you can. And you better hurry because it's getting close to 3 a.m. and the beast will be waking soon.

I sidle up to her. When she doesn't back away, I lean against her. The same way I leaned on Logan. But this time, I give strength instead of take it. And you know what? I've lots and lots to give. *Be brave. You're not alone.*

After a few minutes, she draws in a deep breath and releases it. "Will you stay?" she whispers.

I nod.

"Will you let me know when..." she swallows "he's coming?"

Another nod.

She scrambles off the bed and works to position her phone on the bookcase, hiding it so only the camera lens is visible if you know where to look. I stand by the door, listening. When the floor boards creak in his room, I do a low woof. She freezes for a second, then starts the video on her phone.

Back in bed, she takes a book off the nightstand and I hide under the bed. It doesn't take long for the beast to enter.

"I couldn't sleep," she says to his question. Smart.

I'm not gonna detail what happens next. I fight with my wolf for what feels like hours, but is only minutes. She asks him the same questions I had. She is so very brave.

And before you yell at me, I don't let things go too far. As soon as he damns himself for the hidden camera, I shoot out from my hiding place, barking loudly. He almost hits the ceiling. Then he's yelling at me to shut up and tries to kick me.

I dodge and bark and bark and dodge. It's fun. Of course his wife and the boy are woken by the commotion. They discover him stark naked in the middle of the teen's room.

He's smooth. He blames me instantly. Heard the dog in her room, came to investigate, he was too hot for pajamas. An excuse for everything. And the wife nods her head, already believing his lies. That's okay. The teen has the video she can email to her social worker. It has enough evidence to send him to jail. The case won't be thrown out because it's her word against his.

I exchange a glance with her. *Keep being brave, I'll be with you*, I promise before I'm dragged to the front door and kicked out.

Yes! Mission accomplished! I howl with joy at the waxing moon. It'll be full in three days and the desire to call my wolf will be irresistible. As far as I'm concerned, there are worse things in life than one night a month as a wolf.

My thoughts churn as I consider how best to help the teen when she has to deal with the lawyers and social workers and the unbelievers. It's only when I'm back to where I stashed my pack that I realize my mistake. Well, I smell my mistake. The familiar scent of the Mason werewolves are all around me. I failed to learn my lesson from Vinny's alley and allowed my plans to distract me. Let's hope it isn't one of those fatal mistakes.

∼

Werewolves the size of Logan slink from the shadows, surrounding me. I count eight.

Middleman steps into sight. He's still in human form. "You're lucky that you haven't established a strong pack bond because this will be easier for you, Mongrel." He gestures.

Downwind, the rustle of leaves sounds as a group of men step into view. Logan is dragged between two of them. My heart turns to ice. His shirt is soaked with blood. The handle of a silver knife juts from near his clavicle. He's weak and dying. Cold fury rises within me.

Middleman tsks with mock concern. "The break-ins and protection scheme we ran downtown was the perfect distraction. He failed to watch his back."

I stare at him. Does he have a point? Or am I supposed to swoon over his evil genius?

He continues, "I'm offering a simple exchange. Join my pack and I promise I won't kill Logan. I'll even back away from his territory. No more break-ins." His tone is reasonable.

But I'm far from reasonable. He hurt Logan and, therefore, I *need* to hurt him. *Bad.*

"Don't join their pack, Mongrel," Logan says.

"Don't be ridiculous," Middleman says. "If I kill you, I'll claim your pack, which includes Mongrel. I'm offering her a chance to save your worthless life."

Logan laughs...well, he tries, poor guy coughs blood. "Like you said, Mason, she hasn't established a strong pack bond. Good luck trying to claim her."

"Ignore him," Mason says. "You will not be harmed, Mongrel. You'll be an honored member of our pack."

Our pack. Those two words turn the ice inside me into a snowstorm. I meet Logan's gaze. *My* alpha. *Our* pack of mongrels. And *I* protect what's *ours*. The storm triggers an avalanche. It roars and builds and pounds, pushing me to reach beyond myself. To reach for the source of our strength. The moon. I howl, asking the moon for help. She responds and energy surges through me.

My teeth and claws elongate. Muscles bulk and expand. Bones grow. I rise above the other werewolves until I'm eye level with Mason. He gapes at me. Not so adorable now, am I?

His wolves attack. But I'm so much stronger, quicker, and bigger. I'm the big bad wolf and I swat them away, sending them flying. The men holding Logan drop him and run. I go to him. He's also staring at me, but it's with a surprised delight. Carefully grabbing the handle of the knife with my teeth, I pull it out. Logan grunts in pain.

Then I track down Mason. He's running fast, but I'm faster and catch him easily, knocking him down. I chomp on his left leg and drag him back to Logan.

Logan's sitting up. A good sign.

He takes one look at my captive and laughs. "There's your answer, Mason." But he sobers and says to me, "I'm not strong enough to take his pack. And I shouldn't be alpha. You should."

That's not happening. Annoyed I drop Mason's leg, but keep a paw on him to prevent him from running away. I press against Logan, giving him my strength. His injury heals and I deflate back to my original size.

Logan stands. He rubs his shoulder, but he's looking at me. I point my nose at Mason, who hasn't realized he can now muscle me off with ease. We still have a problem to solve.

"Call your wolf, Mason. Let's do this properly," Logan says.

"Properly? And when I kill you, what's *she* going to do?"

I bare my teeth at him.

"If you succeed, Mongrel can challenge you if she wants."

"I can't fight that...*monstrosity*."

Oooh. Monstrosity. I like! Too bad, I don't know if I can connect to the moon and become a monster again.

"That's *your* problem." Logan takes off his bloody shirt. There's a new scar on his muscular torso, but it appears to be long healed.

I glance away when Logan unzips his jeans. Mason clambers to his feet and also starts to strip. I turn my back, giving the two alphas some privacy. Plus I've no desire to watch them shift. At least alphas shift faster and without pain.

Soon two werewolves face each other. Mason's almost black—a shadow among shadows. Logan's also black, but the tips of his coat shine with reflected moonlight. Mason lunges first and then it's all teeth, claws, and the smell of blood.

The desire to help Logan burns up my throat. He's not a strong fighter. Well, not compared to Mason. My fear for him builds along with my energy and I sense I have enough strength to howl for help again. But I can't. This is Logan's fight. If I step in, I'll be claiming alpha status.

I'm not an alpha. I know that. Then what am I? Mongrel the Monstrosity. A protector. A sentinel. Not a leader. Logan's a different type of alpha. One who isn't driven to expand his territory or to kill. He was right. He's not going to last long against the aggressive alphas. But that's what I'm here for.

Once I make the decision, calling the moon is easy. I pluck Mason off Logan and throw him against a tree trunk. Logan's on Mason before he can regain his senses. A second later, Logan tears his throat out.

When the light in Mason's eyes dies, Logan looks at me. Blood coats his muzzle and there's a question in his gaze. I lean against him, sharing the moon.

Claim Mason's pack bonds, I urge.

He studies me a moment more, then closes his eyes, tilts his head back, and howls. The sound sends a shiver through me. The air thickens and my heart swells. For a brief moment, I sense over a hundred werewolves. It's as if they'd been standing in the dark and have all turned on a flashlight so I can pinpoint their locations. The awareness of my pack mates eventually fades, but the pack bonds remain tangled in my heart.

~

After we shift back to our human form, Logan shakes his head sadly. "We cheated."

"No, we didn't," I say. "You're the alpha. I'm the protector. We're working together to stop the endless violence between alphas." I explain my epiphany.

Logan is quiet for a few moments. "No, you're not a monstrosity, Mongrel. You're our guardian."

"That does sound better, but it's not as scary."

"Do you want to be feared?"

Do I? I must admit it has a certain appeal. No need to worry about who to trust because no one would cross me. Ever. Yet... That's not a healthy way to live. Neither is being in survival mode all these years. I want to start living again.

"No," I answer. "I'd rather be loved and respected."

"You already have my love and respect. Once you get to know the others, you'll quickly earn theirs as well." He takes my hand.

I glance at our intertwined hands. "Pack love? Or something more?"

"I would like to explore the...more."

Explore the more. I'm equal parts thrilled and terrified.

"*When* you're ready," he adds. "Let's go home."

Home. And for the first time in three years, I have a home.

THANK YOU

Thank you for choosing *Up to the Challenge*. I hope you enjoyed my collection. If you'd like to stay updated on my books and news, please sign up for my free email newsletter here:

http://www.mariavsnyder.com/news.php

(go all the way down to the bottom of the page). I send my newsletter out to subscribers three to four times a year. It contains info about the books, my schedule and always something fun (like deleted scenes or a new short story or exclusive excerpts). No spam—ever!

You're also welcome to come join your fellow MVS fans on my Facebook reading group called Snyder's Soulfinders. Why Soulfinders? Because according to Plato, "Books give a soul to the universe, wings to the mind, flight to the imagination, and life to everything." The Soulfinders are all about books, especially mine, but also others as well! It's a great place to find fellow readers and make friends from all over the world. There are perks, too, like exclusive give aways, getting all the news first, and an insight into my writing process. Please answer at least 2 of the 3 questions as we don't want any trolls in our group, just Soulfinders. Here's a link:

https://www.facebook.com/groups/SnydersSoulfinders/

Please feel free to spread the word about this book! Honest reviews are always welcome and word of mouth is the best way you can help an author keep writing the books you enjoy!

Please don't be a stranger, stop on by and say hello. You can find me on:

- Facebook: https://www.facebook.com/mvsfans
- Goodreads: https://www.goodreads.com/maria_v_snyder
- Instagram: https://www.instagram.com/mariavsnyderwrites/

ACKNOWLEDGMENTS

I'd like to thank all the anthology editors who I worked with over the last fourteen years: Jeanne B. Benzel, Patricia Bray, Paula Guran, Lee C. Hillman, W. H. Horner, Danielle Ackley-McPhail, Mike McPhail, John O'Neill, Kat O'Shea, Joshua Palmatier, Greg Schauer, Ekaterina Sedia, Trisha Telep, and Jeff Young. It was a pleasure and an honor to work with you!

A big thank you to my intern Daniel Sellers, who helped arrange the stories in this collection. You gave me a wonderful starting point and insightful feedback. I wish you all the best with your writing career.

To my beta readers, Nat Bejin, Reema Crooks, and Michelle Haring, thanks so very much for helping me with this collection! Your comments, edits, and encouragement have meant the world to me.

Special thanks to Joy Kenney, my talented cover artist. I love this cover. The colors are perfect and I love the grid of "windows" to another world. You created what I couldn't quite articulate. Thanks for putting up with all my emails.

And to my family, a huge thanks for all your love, support, and lemon pies.

EXTENDED COPYRIGHT INFORMATION

ABOUT THE AUTHOR

When Maria V. Snyder was younger, she aspired to be a storm chaser in the American Midwest so she attended Pennsylvania State University and earned a Bachelor of Science degree in Meteorology. Much to her chagrin, forecasting the weather wasn't in her skill set so she spent a number of years as an environmental meteorologist, which is not exciting ... at all. Bored at work and needing a creative outlet, she started writing fantasy and science fiction stories. Over twenty novels and numerous short stories later, Maria's learned a thing or three about writing. She's been on the *New York Times* bestseller list, won a dozen awards, and has earned her Masters of Arts degree in Writing from Seton Hill University, where she is now a faculty member.

When she's not writing she's either playing volleyball, traveling, or taking pictures. Being a writer, though, is a ton of fun. When else can you take fencing lessons, learn how to ride a horse, study martial arts, learn how to pick a lock, take glass blowing classes and attend Astronomy Camp and call it research? Maria will be the first one to tell you it's not working as a meteorologist. Readers are welcome to check out her website for book excerpts, free short stories, maps, blog, and her schedule at MariaVSnyder.com.